Traci Douglass is a *USA TODAY* bestselling author of contemporary and paranormal romance. Her stories feature sizzling heroes full of dark humour, quick wit and major attitude, and heroines who are smart, tenacious, and always give as good as they get. She holds an MFA in Writing Popular Fiction from Seton Hill University, and she loves animals, chocolate, coffee, hot British actors and sarcasm—not necessarily in that order.

Juliette Hyland began crafting heroes and heroines in high school. She lives in Ohio, USA, with her Prince Charming, who has patiently listened to many rants regarding characters failing to follow their outline. When not working on fun and flirty happily-ever-afters, Juliette can be found spending time with her beautiful daughters, giant dogs, or sewing uneven stitches with her sewing machine.

Also by Traci Douglass

One Night with the Army Doc
Finding Her Forever Family
A Mistletoe Kiss for the Single Dad
A Weekend with Her Fake Fiancé

Unlocking the Ex-Army Doc's Heart
is **Juliette Hyland**'s debut title

Look out for more books from Juliette Hyland
Coming soon

Discover more at millsandboon.co.uk.

THEIR HOT HAWAIIAN FLING

TRACI DOUGLASS

UNLOCKING THE EX-ARMY DOC'S HEART

JULIETTE HYLAND

MILLS & BOON

First Published in Great Britain 2020
by Mills & Boon, an imprint of HarperCollins*Publishers*
1 London Bridge Street, London, SE1 9GF

Their Hot Hawaiian Fling © 2020 by Traci Douglass

Unlocking the Ex-Army Doc's Heart © 2020 by Juliette Hyland

ISBN: 978-0-263-27970-2

MIX
Paper from
responsible sources
FSC® C007454

This book is produced from independently certified FSC™ paper
to ensure responsible forest management.
For more information visit www.harpercollins.co.uk/green.

Printed and bound in Spain
by CPI, Barcelona

THEIR HOT
HAWAIIAN FLING

TRACI DOUGLASS

MILLS & BOON

May there always be warmth in your Hale,
fish in your net,
and Aloha in your heart.

Traditional Hawaiian Blessing

CHAPTER ONE

"SIR, CAN YOU tell me your name?" Dr. Leilani Kim asked as she shone a penlight to check her newest patient's eyes. "Pupils equal and reactive. Sir, do you remember what happened? Can you tell me where you are?"

"Get that thing outta my face," the man said, squinting, his words slightly slurred from whatever substance currently flooded his system. "I ain't telling you my name. I know my rights."

"How many fingers am I holding up?" she asked.

"Four." He scowled. "How many am I holding up?"

She ignored his rude gesture and grabbed the stethoscope around her neck to check his vitals. "Pulse 110. Breathing normal. Blood pressure?"

"One-thirty over 96, Doc," one of the nurses said from the other side of the bed.

"Find any ID at the accident scene?" Leilani asked over her shoulder to the EMTs standing near the door of the trauma bay. "Any idea what he's on?"

"Cops got his license," one of the EMTs said, a young woman name Janet. "His name's Greg Chambers. According to the officer who ran his plates, he has a history of DUIs and a couple arrests for meth too."

"Great." It wasn't, in fact, great. It was exhausting and brought up a lot of memories Leilani would just as soon forget, but that wouldn't be professional, and she couldn't afford to seem anything but perfect these days with the Emergency Medicine directorship up for grabs.

A quick check for signs of distress on the guy—airway, breathing, circulation—all seemed intact and normal. Next, she moved to palpate the patient's torso and extremities. "Do you have pain anywhere other than your head, Mr. Chambers? Can you feel your arms and legs?"

"I feel you poking and prodding me, if that's what you mean." The guy groaned and raised a hand to the bandages covering his scalp. "My head hurts."

"Smashing it into a windshield will do that," Leilani said, finding no evidence of broken bones or internal bleeding on exam. She returned to his head wound. He was lucky. If only the people Leilani had loved most in the world had been so fortunate.

She blinked hard against the unwanted prickle of tears. Must be the exhaustion. Had to be. She never let her personal feelings interfere with her duties.

"Everything okay, Doc?" Pam, the nurse, asked while adjusting the patient's heart monitor.

"Fine. Thanks." Leilani gave her a curt nod, then turned to the paramedics again. "Any other casualties from the accident?"

"Other than the palm tree he hit at forty miles per hour?" Peter, the other EMT, said. "No. No other passengers or vehicles involved, thank goodness. When we arrived, the patient was standing outside his vehicle, texting on his phone. He took one look at us and complained of neck pain before collapsing on the ground claiming he couldn't stand."

"Where's my truck?" Mr. Chambers grumbled.

"Your vehicle is a total loss, sir," Leilani said, hackles

rising. People died because idiots like this guy drove under the influence. She checked the laceration on his head.

"No!" He wrenched his arm away from the phlebotomist who'd arrived to take his blood. "You can't take it without my consent. I know my rights."

Energy and patience running low, Leilani fixed the man with a pointed stare. "You keep complaining about your rights, Mr. Chambers, but what about the rights of the other people on the road who just wanted to get home to their family and friends? You put innocent lives at risk driving while intoxicated. What about *their* rights?"

His chin jutted out. "Not my problem."

It will be, if your test results come back positive, she thought, but didn't say it out loud.

Leilani had dealt with her share of belligerent patients during her ten years working at Honolulu's Ohana Medical Center, but this guy took the cake. She turned to Pam. "Call radiology and see if they can get him in for a stat skull X-ray, please. Also, we need a Chem Seven, tox screen and blood alcohol level." Then, to the phlebotomist, "Strap his arm down if needed."

"I'm no addict," the guy yelled, trying to get up and setting off the alarms on the monitors. "Let me out of here."

Several orderlies stepped forward to hold the guy down as Leilani recorded her findings in the patient's file on her tablet.

"How much have you had to drink tonight, sir?" she asked, glancing up.

"Few beers," the patient said, shrugging.

The scent of booze had been heavy on his breath, and Leilani raised a skeptical brow. Based on his delayed reaction times during her exam and his uncoordinated movements, he'd had way more than he was letting on. "And?"

"A couple shots of whiskey."

"And?"

His lips went thin.

Right. Her simmering anger notched higher. The fact someone could be so reckless as to get behind the wheel when they were obviously impaired sent a fresh wave of furious adrenaline through her.

Movements stiff with tension, she set her tablet aside and returned to the bandages on the guy's forehead, peeling them back to reveal a large bruise and several small cuts. She dictated her findings as she went. "On exam there are no obvious skull fractures. Several small lacerations to the forehead and a golf-ball-sized hematoma over the left eye. No obvious foreign bodies seen in the wounds, though we'll need the X-rays to confirm. Sutures aren't necessary, but Pam, can you please clean and dress this again." She glanced over at the EMTs once more. "You said he hit the windshield?"

"Glass starred from the impact."

"Okay. Let's examine your spine next, Mr. Chambers."

"No." He attempted to climb off the bed again. "I want to go home."

"You're not going anywhere until I sign the discharge papers and the police release you from custody," Leilani said, leveraging her weight to hold her uncooperative patient down. People always assumed because she was petite she couldn't handle it if things got rough. What those same folks didn't know was that she was an excellent kickboxer and had already survived way more hardship than most people faced in a lifetime. She was more than capable of fighting her own battles.

"Cops? Aw. Hell. No." The patient gave Leilani a quick once-over. "What are you, ten?"

"Thirty-four, actually." She opened his brace with one hand and carefully palpated his neck with the other, moving her fingers along his spine before cupping his head and turning it slowly from side to side. "No step-offs. Pam please order a stat spinal series as well, since he complained of difficulty walking at the accident scene. Mr. Chambers, were you wearing a seat belt at the time of the accident?"

"Nah. Don't like them. Too confining."

That was kind of the point. Seat belts saved lives. She was proof.

The phlebotomist finished drawing her last vial of blood, then placed a bandage on the patient's arm. "I'll get this right up to the lab, Dr. Kim."

"Thanks." Leilani picked up her tablet once more. "Patient has a possible concussion and will need observation for the next twenty-four hours. Pam, make sure the jail can accommodate that order."

"Will do, Doc," Pam said.

"I ain't going to jail," Mr. Chambers snarled.

"The police might think differently. You caused quite a bit of property damage, from what I've been told, and this isn't your first offense." Leilani rubbed the nape of her neck, her fingers brushing over the scar there. Twenty years since the accident that had changed her life forever, but the memories still brought a fresh wave of pain.

"Police are ready to question the patient whenever you're finished, Dr. Kim," Pam said, hiking her head toward the two uniformed officers standing just outside the door.

"Okay." Leilani turned back to the patient. "Almost done, Mr. Chambers. Just a few more questions."

"Not saying another word," the man said, his scowl dark. "Told you I know my rights."

"Anything I can help with, Dr. Kim?" a new voice said, deep and distracting as hell.

Leilani turned to see Dr. Holden Ross wedging his way between the cops and into the room as Pam was leaving to call in her orders. Ugh. Just what she didn't need. The ER's new locum tenens trauma surgeon barging into her case uninvited. He'd only been here a month, so perhaps he didn't know any better, but it still irked her. She didn't do well with people overstepping her boundaries. She'd worked hard to put up those walls over the years, both professionally and personally. Letting people too close only meant a world of hurt and trouble when they left. And in Leilani's experience, everyone left eventually. Sometimes with no warning at all.

The fact his gorgeous smile filled her stomach with anxious butterflies had nothing to do with it.

She straightened and smoothed her hand down the front of her white lab coat, giving him a polite smile to cover her annoyance. "No. I've got it, thank you, Dr. Ross. Just finishing up."

"Got something you can finish up right here, darlin'." The patient shot her a lewd look and grabbed his crotch.

How charming. Not.

Holden's expression quickly sharpened as he moved to the patient's bedside, his limp drawing her attention once more. She wondered what had caused it before she could stop herself, though it was none of her business. His metal cane clinked against the bedside rails as he glared down into the drunken man's face, his stern frown brimming with warning. "Show Dr. Kim some respect. She's here to save your life."

"I appreciate your concern, Dr. Ross," Leilani said,

clearing her throat. "But I've got this. I'm sure there are other patients for you to deal with."

"Actually, I'm just coming on shift." He leaned back, his gaze still locked on the patient. "Fill me in on this guy, so I can take over after you leave."

Darn. He was right. Her shift was over soon, and she needed to get home and rest. Leilani looked over at her colleague again. Holden looked as fresh and bright as a new penny, while she probably looked as ragged as she felt. Add in the fact she seemed irrationally aware of his presence today—not just as a colleague, but as a man— and her stress levels skyrocketed.

The last thing she needed right now was an ill-advised attraction to her coworker.

Distracted, Leilani turned away to futz with her tablet. "What time is it now?"

"Quarter past six," Holden said, moving around the bed to stand next to her. He propped a hip against the edge of the counter, using his cane to take the weight off his right leg. "Your shift ended fifteen minutes ago."

The low hum of the automatic blood pressure cuff inflating on the patient's arm filled the silence. Gossip was already flying amongst the staff about how handsome, intriguing Dr. Ross had ended up at Ohana. Everything from a bad breakup to a good recommendation from some powerful donors. There was one rumor, however, that concerned Leilani the most—that he'd come to their facility at the request of the hospital's chief administrator, Dr. Helen King, and that he was in line for the same directorship she wanted.

Ugh. She shook off the thoughts. None of that mattered at present. She had a patient to deal with. Plus, it was silly to operate off rumor and conjecture. She was a woman of science; she dealt with facts and figures, concrete ideas.

Nothing silly or scary like gossip or emotions. Acting on "what-if's" and messy feelings could bring a person to their knees if they weren't careful. Leilani should know.

Pam poked her head into the room again. "Sorry to interrupt, but Dr. Ross, there's a new arrival for you. Female with abdominal pain for the last six hours."

"Duty calls." Holden held Leilani's gaze a moment longer before pushing away from the counter to scan the tablet computer Pam handed him. Leilani found herself unable to stop watching him, darn it. Her curiosity about him was a mystery. Sure, he was charming and would've been just her type, with those dark good looks and soulful hazel eyes. Not to mention he was more than competent at his job, according to the residents on staff. Neither of those reasons was good enough to go poking around into things that were better left unexplored though. Besides, Dr. Ross would hopefully be gone once a suitable replacement for his position was found. Leilani's life was here, in her native Hawaii, and right now her attention was on her career.

There'd be plenty of time for a personal life later.

Maybe.

Shaking off the odd pang of loneliness pinching her chest, she continued to complete her documentation while Holden rattled off his orders for Pam.

"Okay. Let's start by running an HCG to make sure the new patient's not pregnant, since she's not had a hysterectomy," Holden said, tapping his tablet screen several more times. "I've added a couple of additional tests as well to get things rolling."

"Thanks, Dr. Ross." Pam took the tablet and disappeared around the corner once more, leaving just the two of them and the patient in the trauma bay again.

Leilani stayed determined to power on through because that's what she did. She was a survivor, in more ways than one. She swallowed hard and rubbed her neck again. The scars reminded her how life could change in a second. There was no time to waste.

Her patient's snores filled the air and she shook the man gently awake. "Mr. Chambers? Can you tell me where you are?"

He squinted his eyes open and scrunched his nose. "Why are you asking me this crap?"

"Because you could have a concussion." She glanced over at Holden and gave a resigned sigh. He obviously wasn't going to leave until she shared the case details with him. Seemed he was as stubborn as she was. Not a good sign. After another resigned sigh, she ran through the details for him. "Single car MVA. Male, twenty-six years old, drove his pickup truck into a tree. Head struck windshield. Denies lack of consciousness. He's alert and—"

"Let me go, dammit!" The patient flailed on the bed and clawed at the neck brace. "Get this thing off me!"

"Combative," Leilani finished, giving Holden a look before returning her attention to Mr. Chambers. "Sir, tell me where you are, and I'll get you something for the pain."

He rattled off the hospital's name, then held out his hand. "Where's my OxyContin?"

"Acetaminophen on the way," she countered, typing the order into her tablet and hitting Send.

"Hell no." The patient struggled to sit up again. "Opioids. That's what I want."

Holden stepped nearer to the patient's bedside again, his face pale. "Calm down, sir."

"Go to hell!" The patient kicked hard, his foot making hard contact with Holden's right thigh.

Holden cursed under his breath and grabbed his leg, "What's he on?"

"Not sure yet. Definitely alcohol, but probably drugs too. Waiting on the tox screen results," Leilani said, scanning her chart notes for an update and finding none yet. "Patient has a hematoma on his forehead and a few lacerations, as you can see. No palpable fractures to the neck or spine, no internal bleeding or injuries upon exam, though I've ordered X-rays to confirm. According to the EMTs, his head starred the windshield, so no air bags either. I'd guess the vehicle was too old."

"Before 1999, then," Holden murmured as he rubbed his thigh and winced.

"Before 1998," Leilani corrected him. "Air bags were required in 1998."

"Sorry to disagree, Dr. Kim, but I researched this during my time in Chicago. Air bags became mandatory in 1999 in the United States."

"Then your research was wrong." Leilani battled a rising tide of annoyance as her grip on her tablet tightened. She of all people should know when air bags became mandatory. The date was seared in her mind for eternity. "It was 1998. Trust me."

"Why are we even arguing about this?" he asked, the irritation in his voice matching her own.

"I'm not arguing. I'm correcting you."

"That would be fine if I was mistaken. Which I'm not."

"I beg to differ. The date was September 1, 1998, to be exact."

She squared her shoulders and held her ground, feeling a strange rush of both energy and attraction. No. Not attraction. She didn't want to be attracted to this bullheaded man. Period. Still, her heart raced and her stomach fluttered despite her wishes. Must be the exhaustion. Had to be. She turned away, incensed, both at herself and Dr. Ross.

"The Intermodal Surface Transportation Efficiency Act of 1991 went into effect on September 1, 1998."

Her words emerged in staccato fashion. Rude? Maybe, but then he'd been the one to insinuate himself into her case without asking. She did a quick internet search to prove her point, then held the evidence on screen before his face.

"See? Every truck and car sold in the US had to have air bags for the driver and front seat passenger."

Holden scanned the information, then crossed his arms, the movement causing his toned biceps to bunch. Not that she was looking. Nope. He narrowed his gaze and studied her, far too perceptively for her comfort. "And you know all that verbatim why?"

Because they would've saved the lives of my family.

She swallowed hard and turned away, not about to share the most painful secrets of her past with a virtual stranger, even though some odd little niggle inside of her wanted to.

Gah! She must be way more tired than she'd originally thought. Sleep. That was what she needed. Sleep and food, because perhaps her blood sugar was low. That could explain her stumbling heart rate. Perhaps could even explain how she seemed hypersensitive to the heat and nearness of him now as they faced off over the span of a few feet. Might also explain her weird sensory hallucinations, like how the scent of his skin—soap and musk—seemed to surround her. Or the way her fingertips itched to touch the shadow of dark stubble just beneath the surface of his taut jaw.

Ugh. Leilani clenched her fists on the countertop, the weight of his stare still heavy behind her. He was waiting on her reply and didn't appear to want to leave until he got it. Fine. No way would she tell him the truth, so she went with a half lie instead. "I watch a lot of documentaries."

"Hmm." He sounded thoroughly unconvinced. "I like those shows too, but that's a lot of random facts to remember for no rea—"

"Radiology's ready for your patient, Dr. Kim," Pam said from the doorway, giving Leilani a much-needed reprieve.

"Thank you," Leilani said as two techs wheeled Mr. Chambers out the door.

Holden still stood there though, watching her closely. "I'll handle him when he's done, Dr. Kim. Go home."

"I'm fine, Dr. Ross." Keeping her gaze averted, Leilani headed for the hallway, thankful to escape. "I've got plenty of paperwork to catch up on before I leave, so I'll still be here to wrap up his case."

Holden couldn't understand the enigma that was Dr. Leilani Kim and it bothered him.

Figuring people out was kind of his thing these days. Or at least attempting to understand what made them work, before they did something completely unexpected, like shoot up a room full of innocent people.

Frustrated, he ran a hand through his hair before heading down the hall to check on his abdominal pain patient. Each step sent a fresh jolt of pain through his nerve endings, thanks to that kick from Dr. Kim's patient.

He stopped at the nurses' station to grab his tablet and give his right leg a rest. Honestly, he shouldn't complain about the pain, since he was lucky to still be breathing, let alone walking, after an attacker's bullet had shattered his right femur and nicked his femoral artery. He could have just as easily bled out on the floor of that Chicago ER, same as David…

No.

Thinking about that now would only take away his edge and he needed to stay sharp, with a twenty-four-hour shift looming ahead of him. Bad enough he still had that argument with Dr. Kim looping through his head. There was something about her excuse for knowing all those obscure facts about air bags that didn't ring true. And sure, he loved documentaries as much as the next person—in fact, those things were like crack to an analytical nerd like himself—but even he couldn't recite back all the information he'd learned in those films word for word like she had. It was odd. And intriguing. He'd had a good reason for discovering all that information, namely for an article he'd written for a medical journal. But her?

Not that he should care why she knew. And yet, he did. Way more than he should.

Irritated as much with himself as with her, he shook his head and pulled up his new patient's file. The last thing he needed in his life was more puzzles. He already had more than enough to figure out. Like where he planned to live after his stint here in Hawaii was done. Like if he'd ever walk without a cane again. Like when the next attack might occur and if he'd be ready this time or if he'd become just another statistic on the news.

The area around the nurses' station grew more crowded and Holden moved down the hall toward his patient's room and open space. He didn't do well with crowds these days. Preferred to keep to himself mostly, do his work, handle his cases, stay safe, stay out of the way and out of trouble. That was what he focused on most of the time. Which is what made his choice to charge into

Dr. Kim's trauma bay so strange. Usually, he wouldn't intrude in another colleague's case unless he'd been called for a consult, but then he'd overheard her arguing with her obviously intoxicated patient and something had smacked him hard in the chest, spurring him into that room before he'd even realized what he was doing.

Holden exhaled slowly and dug the tip of his cane into the shiny linoleum floor. His therapist back in Chicago probably would've said it was related to his anxiety from the shooting. After all, the gunman back in Chicago had been intoxicated too. He'd wanted opioids, just like Dr. Kim's patient was demanding. There was a major difference this time though. No firearm.

He took another deep breath. Yes. That had to be it. Had to explain his weird fascination with finding out more about Dr. Leilani Kim too. The fact she was beautiful, all dark hair and dark eyes and curves for days on end—exactly his type, if he'd been looking—had nothing to do with it.

He definitely wasn't looking.

It was simply the stress of being in a new place, and his posttrauma hypersensitivity to his surroundings. He'd only been here a month, after all. Yep. That was it. Never mind his instincts told him otherwise. Holden didn't trust his instincts. Hadn't for a year now.

Twelve months had passed since the attack on his ER in Chicago. Twelve months since he'd lost his best friend in a senseless act of violence. Twelve months since he'd failed to keep the people closest to him safe.

And why risk getting closer to anyone again when they could be lost so easily?

The tablet pinged with his patient's results and he pulled them up, scrolling through the data. Pregnancy test negative. White blood cell count normal, though that didn't necessarily rule out appendicitis. Amylase and lipase measurements within normal limits. Next steps—an ultrasound and manual exam.

"Hey, Pam?" he called down the hall. "Can you join me in Trauma Three for a pelvic?"

"Yep, just give me a sec to finish up calling the lab for Dr. Kim," she said, holding her hand over the phone receiver.

He nodded, then leaned a shoulder against the wall to wait. Ohana Medical Center was relatively quiet, compared to the busy downtown ER he'd come from in Chicago. Back then he'd loved the constant hustle, but after the shooting, going back to work there had been too painful. So, he'd chosen the locum tenens route instead. And it was that choice that had eventually reunited him with his old friend, Dr. Helen King. In fact, she was the reason he'd ended up at Ohana. He owed her a debt he could never repay, but he'd wanted to try.

Which explained why he was here, in the middle of paradise, wondering how soon he could leave. Staying in one place too long didn't suit him anymore. Staying put meant risking entanglements. Staying put too long made you vulnerable.

And if there was one thing Holden never wanted to be again, it was vulnerable.

A loud metal clang sounded down the hall and his senses immediately went on high alert, his mind throwing up reminders of a different ER, a different, dangerous situation. His best friend lying on the floor, bleeding out and Holden unable to stop it because of his own injuries. His chest squeezed tight and darkness crept into his peripheral vision as the anxiety took over.

No. Not here. Not now. Can't do this. Won't do this.

Pulse jackhammering and skin prickling, Holden

turned toward the corner, trying to look busy so no one questioned why he was just standing there alone in the hall. He'd spent weeks after the attack learning how to cope with the flashbacks, the PTSD. Sometimes the shadows still won though, usually when he was tired or anxious. Considering he'd slept like crap the night before, he was both at the moment.

"Sorry for the holdup," Pam said, near his side and breaking through his jumbled thoughts. "Things are a bit crazy right now, with tourist season and all."

He nodded and hazarded a glance in her direction.

Her smile quickly dissolved into a frown at whatever she saw in his face. "You okay, Doc?"

It took him a moment to recover his voice, his response emerging more like a croak past his dry vocal cords. "Fine." He cleared his throat and tried again, forcing a smile he didn't quite feel. "Isn't it always tourist season in Hawaii?"

"It is," said another voice from the staff break room across the hall. Leilani. Crap. He'd been so distracted he'd not even seen her go in there. Adrenaline pounded through his blood. Had she seen his panic attack?

When she came out of the room though, she thankfully gave no indication she'd seen him acting strangely. She just walked past him and headed for the elevators as radiology wheeled out her inebriated patient.

The lingering tension inside Holden ratcheted higher as the patient continued to shout at the staff while they wheeled him back toward the trauma bay. "Pain meds! Now!"

Leilani headed behind the desk at the nurses' station once more. "Let me check the images."

Holden followed behind her, the pain in his leg taking a back seat to his need to prevent a possible calamity if her patient got out of hand again. He reached the nurses' station just as Dr. Kim pulled up the patient's images on the computer. "No embedded glass in his scalp, cervical vertebra appear normal. No damage to the spinal cord or—"

"I'm getting the hell out of here!" A jarring rip of Velcro sounded, followed by a resounding crack of plastic hitting the floor. "And I will take everyone down if I don't get my meds!"

The cops still waiting near the doorway tensed and Holden's heart lodged in his throat.

Oh God. Not again.

Undeterred, Leilani took off for the patient's room. "Time to get this guy discharged."

"Wait!" Holden grabbed her arm. "Don't go in there."

"That's my patient, Dr. Ross." She frowned, shaking off his hold. "Don't tell me how to do my work. We need that bed and he's cleared for discharge. He's the cops' problem now. Excuse me."

She continued on down the hall, signaling to the officers to follow her into the room.

"I want my OxyContin!" Mr. Chambers yelled, followed by a string of curses.

Holden breathed deeply, forcing himself to stay calm, stay present, stay in control.

This isn't Chicago. This patient doesn't have a gun. There are police officers present. No one will get hurt.

From his vantage point, Holden saw the patient sitting up on the side of the bed, his neck brace on the floor. Leilani approached slowly, her voice low and calm.

"Your X-rays were all negative. We're going to release you into police custody."

"Already told you," the patient said, teetering to his feet. "I ain't talking to no cops."

Time seemed to slow as Holden moved forward, his vision blurring with memories of the shooting. So much blood, so much chaos, so much wasted time and energy and life.

Breathe, man. Breathe.

The patient straightened, heading straight for Dr. Kim. The cops moved closer.

Her tone hardened. "I'd advise you to stay where you are for your own safety, sir."

"My safety?" The patient sneered. "You threatening me?"

"Not a threat." Leilani squared her shoulders. "Touching me would not be wise."

"Wise?" The guy snorted, his expression lascivious. "C'mon and gimme some sugar."

The cops placed their hands on their Tasers, saying in unison, "Stand down, sir."

Holden rushed toward the room, his cane creaking under the strain. He couldn't let this happen again, not on his watch. He couldn't fail, wouldn't fail.

Just as Holden shoved between the officers, the patient turned at the sudden commotion and swung. His fist collided hard with Holden's jaw and pain surged through his teeth. He stumbled backward. The cops pulled their Tasers as the patient grabbed Dr. Kim's ponytail. Fast as lightning, she swiveled to face Mr. Chambers, slamming her heel down on his instep until his grip on her hair loosened. Then, as he bent over and cursed, she kneed him twice in the groin. The guy crumbled to the ground and the cops took him into custody.

Over. It's over.

Holden slumped against the wall as time sped back to normal.

While the cops handcuffed Mr. Chambers and read

him his rights, Leilani rushed to Holden's side. "You're bleeding."

Confused, he glanced down at his scrub shirt and saw a large splotch of scarlet. Then the ache in his jaw and teeth intensified, along with the taste of copper and salt in his mouth.

Damn.

"Here." Leilani snatched a few gauze pads from a canister on the counter and handed them to him. "Looks like there's a pretty deep gash on your lip and chin." She leaned past him to call out into the hall. "Pam, can you set up an open room for suturing, please?"

"No, no." He attempted to bat her hands away and straightened. "I can stitch myself up."

He was a board-certified trauma surgeon, for God's sake. Though as the adrenaline in his system burned away, it left him feeling a tad shaky. His lip pulsated with pain. At least it was a welcome distraction from the cramp in his thigh. "Seriously, I've got it."

"Don't be silly. It will be easier for someone else to stitch you up." She tugged him out the door and down the hall to the nurses' station once more. "Just let me sign off on Mr. Chambers first so they can get him out of here."

While he waited, he blotted his throbbing mouth with the gauze pads and admitted she was right, much as he hated to do so. He was in no fit state to treat anyone at the moment, including himself. Which brought another problem to mind. "What about the abdominal patient?"

"Let the residents take it. That's why they're here." Leilani finished her signing off on her discharge paperwork, then nudged Holden toward an empty exam room. Behind him, the cops hauled Mr. Chambers, still cursing and yelling, out to their waiting squad car.

Leilani led him into the room Pam had set up, then

shut the door behind them. "Take a seat on the exam table and let me take a look at your lip."

He did as she asked, allowing her to brush his hand aside and peek beneath the gauze pad. This close, her warmth surrounded him, as did her scent—jasmine and lily. A strange tingle in his blood intensified. It was far more unsettling and dangerous than any punch to the face. She moved closer still to examine his cut lip and he jerked away, alarmed.

"Don't!" he said, then tried to backpedal at her concerned look. "I mean, *ow*."

He turned away and she walked over to the suture kit set out along with a small vial of one percent lidocaine and a syringe on a wheeled metal tray. "The split is through the vermillion border, so no Dermabond or Steri-Strips. Sutures will give you the best result—otherwise it could pop open again."

Holden stared at his reflection in the mirror nearby to distract himself, frustration and embarrassment curdling within him. He already felt like an idiot after getting punched by her patient. Having her sew him up too added insult to injury. Pain surged through his leg and he gripped the edge of the table.

"Any dizziness?" Leilani asked. "He hit you pretty hard."

"No," Holden lied. He still felt a bit light-headed, but that was more from anxiety than the blow to his face. Needing to burn off some excess energy, he slid off the table and moved to the nearby sink to splash cold water on his face. The chill helped clear his head and after drying off his face with paper towels, he plucked at his soiled scrub shirt. "I should change."

"Hang on." Leilani ran back out into the hall and returned with a clean scrub shirt a few moments later. "Here."

"Thanks." He limped behind the screen in the corner and stripped, tossing the bloodstained shirt on the floor before slipping on the clean one. It was too big and the V-neck kept slipping to the side, revealing the scar from his second bullet wound through his left shoulder. He fiddled with the stupid thing, glancing up to find Leilani watching him in the mirror on the wall.

He attempted to play off the awkwardness of the situation with a joke. "Checking me out?"

"No." She looked away fast, but not before he spotted a flush of pink across her cheeks. His interest in her spiked again, despite his wishes to the contrary. She was his work colleague. Theirs was a professional relationship, pure and simple. Anything more was definitely off-limits. He made his way back to the exam table as she pulled on a pair of gloves, then filled a syringe with lidocaine.

"People can be unpredictable, can't they?" Leilani said, jarring him back to reality. "Like Mr. Chambers. You think they're going to do one thing, then they do something completely different. Lie down, please." Reluctantly, he did as she asked. The sooner they got this over with, the better.

Leilani moved in beside him again and he did his best to ignore the heat of her penetrating through his cotton scrub shirt, the soft brush of her bare wrist against his skin as she stabilized his jaw for the injection. "Hold still and try to relax. This may burn a bit."

"I know." He did his best to relax and met her intent stare. "Hard being on the receiving end of treatment."

She smiled and his pulse stumbled. "I understand, Dr. Ross. Doctors usually make the worst patients." She leaned back, her gaze darting from his eyes to his left shoulder, then back again. "But you've obviously had treatment before."

He swallowed hard and looked away, anxiety still shimmering like hot oil through his bloodstream. "Obviously."

"Sorry. I didn't mean to bring up a sore subject." Her hand slipped from his jaw to rest on his sternum, her smile falling. "You're tachycardic."

"I'm fine," he repeated, grasping her hand, intending to remove it from his person, but once her fingers were in his, he found himself unable to let go. Which was nuts. He didn't want entanglements, didn't want connections, and yet, here it was—in the last place he wanted to find one. Which only made his heart beat harder against his rib cage.

Get it together, man.

"Dr. Ross?" she asked, concern lighting her gaze. "Holden? Are you with me?"

The unfamiliar sound of his first name on her lips returned a modicum of his sanity. "Sorry. No, I'd rather not talk about my injuries. Bad memories."

"Okay. No problem. I understand completely. I have a few of those memories myself." Her calm tone, along with the understanding in her eyes, slowly brought his inner angst down to tolerable levels. She pulled her hand from his, then walked over to her tablet on the counter and tapped the screen. "How about some music? What kind do you like? Rock? Country? R & B?"

The change of subjects provided a welcome escape and he grabbed on to it with both hands. He stared up at the ceiling and couldn't care less what she played, as long as it distracted him from the past and her weird effect on him. "Uh…whatever you like is fine."

"Okay." Ukulele music filled the air as she moved in beside him again, a twinkle in her dark gaze as she raised the syringe once more. "I know this situation is uncomfortable for you, Dr. Ross, but the sooner you let me get started, the faster it will be over. I'll even make you a deal. Let me suture you up and I'll take you to a real luau."

"What?" He frowned up at her.

"A luau. You know, poi, Kalua pig, poke, *lomi* salmon, *opihi, haupia* and beer. The works. Plus, you might even get to see a genuine Don Ho impersonator."

"Um…a genuine impersonator?" He gave her a confused look.

She laughed. "Yep. He's the best on the island. Be a shame for you not to get the full Hawaiian experience while you're here. Unless you've already been?"

No. He hadn't been to a luau yet. Hadn't really been anywhere on the island, other than the resort where he was staying and the hospital, to be honest. And sure, he'd planned to take in some sights while he was here, of course, including a luau, but he'd not really made any firm decisions. The fact she'd asked him now, both piqued his interest and set off all the warning bells in his head. "Are you asking me out on a date, Dr. Kim?"

"What?" She stepped back, looking nearly as alarmed as he felt. "No. I just felt bad because my patient punched you and wanted to make you more comfortable, that's all." That pretty pink color was back in her cheeks again, and damn if that unwanted interest in her didn't flare higher.

This was bad. So, so bad.

Luckily, she shrugged and turned away, her tone chilly now. "But I certainly don't want to give you the wrong impression. And I can see now that my asking was a mistake. Forget I mentioned it."

Holden wanted nothing more than to do that, but it

seemed he couldn't. In fact, her invitation now buzzed inside his head like a bothersome fruit fly. He propped himself up on his elbows, feeling completely discombobulated. "I didn't mean to make you uncomfortable."

"Same." She glanced back at him over her shoulder. "I'm not even sure why I mentioned it, to be honest."

The sincerity in her tone helped ease the tension slithering inside him and he lay down flat again, blinking at the ceiling. Seemed they were both rusty at this whole social interaction thing. "I haven't really seen anything since I've been on the island."

"I can give you some suggestions, if you like, since Honolulu's my hometown. My parents own a hotel here," she said, returning to his side, her gaze narrowed as she took his chin again and lifted the syringe. "Okay, here comes the burn."

While the numbing medication took effect, Holden found himself reconsidering her offer. His therapist had told him during their last session back in Chicago that he needed to get out more. She could show him around, perhaps introduce him to some people, broaden his horizons. On a strictly professional basis, of course. Plus, spending more time with her should help lessen the strange heightened awareness he felt around her. Desensitization 101. Taken in those terms, accepting Leilani's invitation made good sense. He blurted out his response before he could second-guess himself. "Okay."

"Okay what?" She frowned down at him.

"Okay, we can go to a luau." His words started to slur as the medication took effect, making his bottom lip ineffective. "Show me some sights too, if you have the time."

Dr. Kim blinked down at him, looking as stunned as he felt. She seemed to consider it for a long moment before nodding. "Fine. But only as colleagues. Understood?"

He nodded, then exhaled slowly as he tapped his lip to make sure it was numb.

"Good." Her quick smile brightened the room far more than he wished. "Now, no more talking until I get this done. Otherwise, I can't guarantee this will heal symmetrical."

She got to work and he closed his eyes, the better to block her out. He still couldn't quite believe he'd said yes to her invitation. Part of him still wanted to get up and get the heck out of there, but the other part of him knew she was right. It was easier for someone else to stitch him up.

CHAPTER TWO

LEILANI STILL COULDN'T quite believe what had happened with Holden Ross. What had she been thinking, offering to take him sightseeing, let alone to a luau? Ugh. She didn't date coworkers. Didn't date anyone really these days, truth be told. Sure, she'd had relationships in the past, but nothing that had worked out long term. And the past six months or so, socializing had taken a back seat with the directorship position on the line.

But this wasn't really socializing, was it? He was new in town and she was being hospitable, that's all.

Like a good neighbor.

A neighbor you'd like to get to know a whole lot better.

Flustered, Leilani turned to face the counter.

This was so not like her to get all giddy over a man. Especially a potential rival for the job she wanted. Never mind there was something wildly compelling about him. Like the flash of panic in his eyes when she'd asked about his previous injuries.

Unfortunately, his reaction was all too relatable—the gut-wrenching terror, the uncertainty of being bruised and battered and broken and alone. If it hadn't been for the kindness and patience and fast thinking of the medical staff the night of the accident, she wouldn't be here today.

The old injury at the base of her neck ached again, reminding her of those who'd saved her, after the rest of her family had been lost. And that was probably exactly why she should be avoiding Holden Ross like the proverbial plague, instead of escorting him around her island as his tour guide. Maybe she could find some way out of it. Work usually gave ample excuses. There was bound to be a case or two requiring her assistance, right? Leilani ripped open the suture kit and pulled out a hemostat.

The music streaming from her tablet on the counter switched to a different song, this one slow and sweet and filled with yearning. Her own chest pinched slightly before she shoved the feeling away. She had nothing to yearn for. She had a great life. A good career. Adoptive parents who loved her and supported her decisions. A new house. A pet who adored her—U'i, her African gray parrot.

And sure, maybe sometimes she wished for someone special to share it all with. She'd get there when she was ready.

If you're ever ready...

She was taking her time, that was all. Being cautious. Never mind she still woke up with nightmares from the accident sometimes. She'd get over it. All of it.

Someday.

"No one told me you're a ninja," Holden said, his words wonky due to his numb lip.

"Those skills come in handy more often than you know." She opened a 6–0 suture and grabbed the curved needle with the hemostat to align the vermillion border with one stitch. Once that was done, she switched to a 5–0 absorbable suture for the rest. "Just four or five more then we're done."

"Internal?" he asked, though the word came out more like "ee-turtle."

"No damage to the orbicularis oris muscle that I can see, so all external." She tied off another stitch, then grabbed a couple more gauze strips off the tray, soaking them in saline before carefully pulling down his bottom lip. "Let me just check the inside to make sure there aren't more lacerations hidden in there."

The salt water dripped down his chin to the V-neck of his scrub shirt.

"Oops. Sorry." Leilani grabbed a tissue from the tray and dabbed at the wet spot, doing her best not to notice his tanned skin and well-defined muscles. Sudden, unwanted images of her kissing from his neck to collarbone, then down his chest, lower still, made her mouth go dry…

"Dr. Kim?" Holden said, yanking her back to reality.

Oh God.

Mortified, she tossed the tissue back on the tray then gave him a too-bright smile. "Almost finished."

He frowned, then looked away, the movement giving her another glimpse of the scar on his left shoulder. She gave herself a mental shake. His body and his wounds were none of her business. That was the exhaustion talking, making her nerves hum and her curiosity about him soar. She continued with the sutures, berating herself.

Focus, girl. Focus.

The song on her tablet switched again, this time to a sweeping, sexy guitar concerto.

Holden blinked up at the ceiling, looking anywhere but at her. "That's pretty."

"One of my favorites." Leilani tied off another stitch then started on the next.

He waited until she was finished before asking, "Where'd you learn to fight?"

It took her a minute to figure out his slurred question. "Oh. You mean with Mr. Chambers? I kickbox. I've taken classes since I was fifteen."

"Wow." Then, out of the blue, he reached up and cupped her face. Her pulse stumbled.

"What are you doing, Dr. Ross?" she managed to squeak out.

"That guy pulled your hair hard," Holden said, gently tilting her head to the side.

"I'm fine. Really." Her breath hitched at the intensity of his gaze.

Oh goodness.

The romantic music washed around them, and unexpected heat gathered in her core. Not good. Not good at all.

Holden Ross was the last man she should get involved with. He was her colleague. He was strictly off-limits. He was far too tempting for her own good. Any connection she felt to him needed to be severed, any awareness currently scorching her blood needed to be doused. End of story. She couldn't risk allowing him closer.

Can I?

Blood pounded in her ears and forbidden awareness zinged over her skin. She ignored the first and tamped down the last before forcing words past her suddenly dry throat. "Thank you, Dr. Ross. Now, let's finish these stitches and get you on your way."

"Holden," he said.

"I'm sorry?" She held the needle poised over his lip for the last stitch.

"Call me Holden."

"Okay." Leilani placed her thumb on his chin to pull slight tension and her finger along his chiseled jawline to steady her hand.

"So, you're native Hawaiian then?"

"Please try not to speak." She sat back. "And yes. Born and raised. My parents own a resort in town."

She could hear the sadness in her own voice and as perceptive as he was, she had no doubt he'd hear it too. Despite all the love and joy her adopted family had given her, part of her would always miss the ones who'd gone. The pain of the accident had never truly faded. Nor had the fear of losing someone else she cared for. She tied off the last stitch, then sat back with relief. "All done."

He sat up and looked in the mirror on the wall again. "Nice job, Dr. Kim."

"Thanks." She began cleaning up from the procedure. "There are more clean scrub shirts on the rack in the hall, if you want to grab a different size."

"Will do." He grabbed his cane and limped toward the door, then turned back to her once more. "Thanks again."

"No problem." Leilani watched him walk away, feeling that riptide of interest tugging at her again and knowing that if she gave in, it could pull her right under. And drowning in the mysteries of Dr. Holden Ross was not part of her plans.

The following morning, after his shift, Holden drove his rental car through the streets of Honolulu toward the Malu Huna Resort and Spa, the steady, hypnotic beat of the windshield wipers almost putting him to sleep. His current residence was only fifteen minutes outside of downtown but driving in the rain after work wasn't exactly his favorite thing.

He pulled into a handicapped parking spot near the entrance to the hotel then stared in through the front windows at the breakfast crowd filling the lobby of the resort. The unusual, crappy weather actually suited his mood far better than the cheerful tropical decor inside the place, but if he wanted to get to his room, he had to traverse the maze of tourists and guests filling the tables in the lobby.

After a deep breath, he cut the engine and grabbed his cane, before glancing at himself one last time in the mirror. The numbing medication in his lip had long since worn off and his lower jaw and into his teeth ached. Eating would be a joy for a while. Not that it mattered. He ate his meals alone in his room most of the time anyway, avoiding the other guests. No sense ruining everyone else's time in paradise with his gloomy attitude.

With a sigh, he got out of the car, then hobbled toward the entrance, his head down to keep the rain off his face. The automatic doors swished open and a gust of warm air swept around him, scented with maple and bacon from the food-laden coffers of the all-you-can-eat buffet in the dining room. His traitorous stomach growled, but Holden didn't stop to fill a plate. Just kept his eyes focused on the elevators ahead as he made a beeline through the lobby. Since the shooting, he had a hard time spending long periods with large groups of strangers. He found himself too distracted, always scanning the room for danger.

His therapist back in Chicago had urged him to build up his tolerance slowly. So far, Holden hadn't tried that suggestion out, preferring his own company to constantly being on guard for the next attack.

Weaving through groups of tourists dressed in shorts and T-shirts and sandals, he felt more out of place than ever in his wrinkled scrubs, his name tag from work still pinned crookedly on the front pocket. He excused himself as he sidled by a quartet of women bedecked with leis and sun hats and nearly collided with a potted palm tree for his trouble.

The lobby of the Malu Huna looked like a cross between a *Fantasy Island* fever dream and a Disney movie in Holden's estimation—with its rattan furniture, gauzy white curtains and golden pineapple design inlaid in the shiny tile floor. There was even a parrot behind the front desk, squawking at the people passing by. Holden glanced over at the bird as he waited for his elevator. An African gray, if he wasn't mistaken. One of his roommates back in college had had one. Smart as a whip and quick learners. They'd had to be careful what they said around the bird because it picked up words like crazy, especially the bad ones.

Holden punched the up button again.

"Dr. Ross?" a voice called from across the lobby and his heart sank. The owner.

The elevator dinged and the doors whooshed open.

So close and yet so far.

He considered making a run for it but didn't want to be rude.

Forcing a weary smile, he turned to face the Asian man who bustled over to him from the dining room. The shorter guy beamed up at him now, his brightly colored Hawaiian shirt all but glowing beneath the recessed overhead lighting. "Won't you join us for breakfast?"

Holden glanced at the roomful of people and his stomach twisted hard. "Oh, I'm not really hungry."

Once more, his stomach growled loud, proving him a liar.

The hotel owner raised a skeptical brow, his grin widening. "Your body says otherwise. Please, Dr. Ross? We'd love to show you our hospitality during your stay." He gave Holden a quick once-over. "You look as if you could use a good meal. Come on."

Before he could protest, the man took his arm and

guided him across the lobby. Familiar panic vibrated through his bloodstream and he looked over the man's head out the rain-streaked windows toward his car. It was only breakfast. He could do breakfast.

Sit. Eat. Talk.

Except the idea of making conversation with strangers made his spine kink.

Sure, he talked to patients all day long, but that was different. At the hospital, he had a plan, a specific purpose. Those things made it easier to shove his anxiety to the back of his mind. Small talk, however, required interest and energy, both of which Holden was running critically low on at the moment.

A year ago I could talk with anyone, party with the best of them.

But now, postattack, his social skills had vanished, leaving him feeling awkward and weak. He hated feeling weak. Weak meant vulnerable. And vulnerable was something Holden never wanted to be again.

He made one final valiant attempt at escape as the hotel owner dragged him thorough the dining room and a maze of packed tables. "Honestly, I can just order room service. I'm tired and grubby and probably won't make good company anyway, Mr....?"

"Kim," the man said, stopping before a table where two women sat. "Mr. Kim. But you can call me Joe. Please, sit down, Dr. Ross."

"Holden," he mumbled, staring at the woman across the table from him. Dr. Kim stared back, looking about as happy to see him as he was to see her. "Please, call me Holden."

She'd mentioned her parents owned a hotel in town while she'd stitched him up, but he'd been so focused on ignoring her and all the uncomfortable things she made him feel, that he'd let it go in one ear and out the other.

Now he felt like an even bigger idiot than before. "Uh, hello again."

"Hello," she said, fiddling with the napkin in her lap. "Are you going to sit down?"

Sit. Yes. That sounded like a marvelous idea, especially since his thigh was cramping again. With less grace than usual, he pulled out the empty chair and slid into it, stretching out his aching leg as he hooked his cane over the back of his seat.

Mr. Kim, Joe, was still smiling at him, as was the woman beside him, presumably Mrs. Kim.

Trying his best to not flub up again, Holden extended his hand to the older woman. "Dr. Holden Ross. Pleasure to meet you."

"Same." Mrs. Kim's dark gaze darted between Leilani and Holden. "You work with my daughter?"

"Yes. I'm filling in temporarily at Ohana Medical Center." He sat back as a waitress set a glass of water in front of him. "Trauma surgery."

"Excellent," Mrs. Kim said. "You and Leilani must work together a lot then. Funny she's never mentioned you."

Leilani, who was quieter than he'd ever seen her before, stared down at her plate of food. "I'm sure I mentioned him, Mom."

"He'll have the buffet," Joe said to the waitress, ordering for Holden. "And it's on the house."

"Sure thing, Mr. Kim," the waitress said, walking away.

"No, no," Holden protested. "I can get this. My locum tenens position comes with a food allowance, so…"

"Locum tenens?" Mrs. Kim said, leaning closer to him. "Tell me more about that, Dr. Ross. Sounds fascinating."

"Holden, please," he said, eyeing the crowded buffet table nearby and longing for the peace and quiet of his hotel room. "I…uh…"

"Hey, guys." Leilani's calm voice sliced through his panic. "Leave the poor man alone. He's just worked a long shift. He needs coffee and a nap, not the third degree. Right, Dr. Ross?"

He swallowed hard and managed a nod.

Leilani poured him a cup of coffee from the carafe on the table and pushed it toward him. "Busy at the ER?"

"Yeah." Talking about work helped relax him and as he stirred cream and sugar into his cup, he told them about the cases he'd seen and the funny stories he'd heard from the staff and soon he'd even answered the questions the Kim's had asked him without locking up once. The whole time, he found himself meeting Leilani's gaze across the table and marveling at the sense of peace he found there.

Whoa. Don't get carried away there, cowboy.

His peace had nothing to do with Leilani Kim. That was absurd. They barely knew each other. It was the routine—talking about work—that calmed his nerves. Nothing else. Nope.

"Well, this has been fun," Mrs. Kim said once he'd finished, pushing to her feet. "But my husband and I need to get back to work at the front desk."

Joe looked confused for a minute before his wife gave him a pointed look. "Oh right. Yeah. We need to get to work. You kids stay and have fun. Lani, be sure to invite him to the luau next Friday." He shook Holden's hand again. "See you around the resort."

Holden watched them walk away, then turned back to Leilani. "So, this is the resort your family owns?"

"Yes." She gave him a flat look, then cocked her head toward the buffet. "Better get your food before they start tearing the buffet down."

CHAPTER THREE

LEILANI EXHALED SLOWLY as Holden hobbled away toward the food line. If she'd left five minutes earlier, she would've missed her parents trying to play matchmaker again, this time with the last man on earth she should be interested in.

They were colleagues, for goodness' sake. She didn't date people from work.

No matter how intrigued she might be by Holden's tall, dark and damaged persona.

Part of her wanted to get up and leave right then, but manners dictated she stay at least until he returned with his plate. They did have to work together, after all. She didn't want things to be awkward—or more awkward than they already were—between them.

So, she'd wait until he got back to the table, then make her polite excuses and skedaddle. For once, Leilani was grateful for the long shift ahead of her at work. Twenty-four hours to keep her busy and away from dwelling more on her encounter the day before with Holden. But first, she planned to hit the gym for a good martial arts workout.

She rolled her stiff neck, then sipped her water. Even tired as she'd been, her sleep had been restless, her dreams filled with images of dealing with combative, intoxicated Mark Chambers again. Those moments then had quickly blurred into memories of the long-ago accident that had taken the lives of her parents and brother. Mixed in were flashes of Holden, changing his scrub shirt, the scar on his shoulder, the wary look in his warm hazel eyes as she'd stitched up his lip. The rough scrap of stubble on his jaw that she'd felt even through her gloves as she'd held his chin, the clean smell of shampoo from his hair, the throb of his heart beneath her palm as she'd dabbed the saline solution from his chest...

"So," he said, shaking her from her thoughts as he straddled the chair across from her and set a plate of scrambled eggs, toast and bacon on the table in front of him. "You honestly don't have to stay if you don't want to. I can tell you'd like to leave."

Leilani did her best to play it off. "Don't be silly. I just have a busy day ahead."

He sat back as the waitress returned to fill a cup of coffee for him. The server gave Holden a slow smile filled with promise and a strange jab of something stabbed Leilani's chest. Not jealousy, because that would be insane. She had no reason to care if another woman flirted with Holden. He was a coworker, an acquaintance. That was it.

Holden continued to watch her as he stirred cream and sugar into his coffee, his gaze narrowed. His skeptical tone said he saw right through her flimsy excuse. "Well, don't let me keep you. I wouldn't be here either if your dad hadn't dragged me in."

She frowned at him. It was true she'd planned to leave soon enough, but that didn't mean he shouldn't want her to stay. A niggle of stubbornness bored into her gut, and she accepted a refill on her coffee from the waitress. At Holden's raised brow she said, "I've got a few minutes."

He took a huge bite of eggs and lowered his gaze. "Don't stay on my account."

"Are you always this jovial, Dr. Ross?" she snorted.

"No. Most of the time I eat alone in my room," he said, devouring half a piece of bacon before glancing at her again. This time, his stoic expression cracked slightly into the hint of a smile. "Sorry. Out of practice with socializing."

A pang of sympathy went through her before she could tamp it down. Seemed they were in the same boat there. She sipped her coffee while he finished off his plate, then sat back in his seat. ER doctors learned to eat fast, at least in Leilani's experience, since you never knew when you'd be called out for the next emergency. Leilani wasn't sure where he put all that food, since there didn't appear to be an inch of spare flesh on him. A sudden, unwanted flash of him with his shirt off in the exam room flickered through her mind before she shook it off.

Nope. Not going there. Not at all.

With a sigh, she finished the rest of her coffee in one long swallow, then stood. "Right. Well, I really do need to go now. Have a nice rest of your day, Dr. Ross."

Holden wiped his mouth with a napkin, then gave a small nod. "Your shift at the hospital doesn't start until two. It's only 9:00 a.m. now."

"What?" Heat prickled her cheeks as he caught her in a lie. Outrage mixed with embarrassment inside her and came out in her blunt response. "I wasn't aware my schedule was your concern, Dr. Ross."

He downed another swig of coffee. "It's not. Helen mentioned it earlier."

At the reminder of Ohana's head administrator, Leilani's breath caught. Reason number one billion why she shouldn't be spending any more time than was necessary with this man. Not with Holden potentially vying for the same job she wanted. "Dr. King told you my schedule? That seems odd."

"Not really. She mentioned it in relation to some project she wants us both to work on." Leilani opened her mouth to respond, but he held up a hand. "Before you ask, she didn't give me any details yet. Said she wanted to discuss it with you first, as the acting director." He exhaled slowly, his broad shoulders slumping a bit, and he gestured toward her empty chair. "Look, I'm sorry if I was grumpy before. Please, don't rush off on my account. It's actually kind of nice to have someone to talk to besides myself."

Much as she hated to admit it, Leilani felt the same. Sure, she had friends and her parents, but they weren't physicians. She couldn't talk shop with them like she could another doctor. Not that she really planned to discuss cases with Holden Ross, unless a trauma surgeon's skills were needed, but still. Torn between making her escape and being more enticed by his offer than she cared to admit, Leilani slowly took her seat again. "You don't get out much?"

"No. Not since…" Holden's voice trailed off, and that haunted expression ghosted over his face once more before he hid it behind his usual wall of stoicism. He cleared his throat. "Working locum tenens has a lot of advantages, but creating bonds and connections isn't one of them. Maybe that's why I like it so much."

"Wow. That sounds a bit standoffish."

"Not really." He shook his head and frowned down into his cup. "Just smart."

Huh. Leilani sat back and crossed her arms, studying him. Having been through a nightmare herself with the accident, she recognized the signs of past trauma all too well. Something horrible had definitely happened in his past—she just wasn't sure what. Given his limp and the wound she'd spied on his left shoulder, she'd bet money a bullet had been involved. That was certainly enough to ruin anyone's outlook on their fellow humans and relationships.

Before she could ask more though, he shifted his attention to the windows nearby and the gray, overcast day outside. "Does it rain a lot here?"

"Not really," she said, the change in subject throwing her for a second. "But it's March."

"And March means rain?"

"In Honolulu, yes. It's our rainiest month." Leilani held up her hand when a server came around with a coffeepot again. Too much caffeine would upset her stomach. "Why?"

"Just interested in the island." The same waitress from earlier stopped back to remove Holden's dishes and slid a small piece of paper onto the table beside his mug. From what Leilani could see, it had the woman's phone number on it. Holden seemed unfazed, taking the slip and tucking it into the pocket of his scrubs before reaching for the creamer again. The thought of him having a booty call with the server later made Leilani's gut tighten. Which was stupid. He was free to see anyone he liked, as was she. She wasn't a workaholic spinster, no matter what her parents might say to the contrary. Leilani had options when it came to men and dating. She was just picky, that's all. She had standards.

Holden must've caught her watching him because he said, "I promised to check on the waitress's son later. The kid's got what sounds like strep throat."

Uh-huh. Sure.

She managed not to roll her eyes through superhuman

strength. His social life was of no concern to her. She flashed him a bland smile. "Nice of you."

He shrugged. "So, what are you rushing off to this morning? If you don't mind me asking."

Her first response was a snarky one that yeah, she did mind. But then she caught a hint of that lonely sadness and wariness in his eyes again and she bit back those words. She didn't want to get friendlier with Holden Ross, but darn if there wasn't something about him that kept her in her seat and coming back for more. She could lie and make up a story, but what was the point? So she went with the truth instead. "I was going to do my daily workout."

"Oh?" Holden perked up a little at that. "I've been meaning to try the hotel gym, but with my crazy schedule at work, haven't made it there yet. Mind if I tag along, just to see where it is? Then I'll leave you alone, I promise."

Alarm bells went off in Leilani's head. She already felt way more interested in this guy than was wise. Spending more time with him would only put her at risk of that interest boiling over into actually liking him and the last thing Leilani wanted was to open herself up to getting hurt again. Even the possibility of letting someone close to her heart, to be that vulnerable again, honestly filled her with abject terror.

"Let the man go with you, *keiki*," her father said from where he was helping clean up a nearby table, and Leilani tensed. Jeez, they were really on snooping patrol today. "Show our guest the gym."

She glanced over at her father and gave him a look. Her dad just shook his head and moved on to another section of tables to clean. They thought she was being ridiculous and maybe she was, but she needed to do things on her terms. Stay in control. Control was everything these days.

Holden chuckled and gulped more coffee. "Kiki?"

"Keiki," she corrected him. "It means child in Ha-waiian."

Ever since they'd adopted her, the Kims had always called her that. First, because that's what she'd been. A scared fourteen-year-old kid with an uncertain future. Now it was more of a pet name than anything.

Leilani exhaled slowly before pushing to her feet again, her good manners too ingrained to refuse. "Fine. If you want to come with me, you can. Get changed and meet me in the lobby in fifteen minutes. Don't be late, Dr. Ross."

Holden's smile widened, his grateful tone chasing her from the restaurant. "Wouldn't dream of it, Dr. Kim."

The workout facilities at Malu Huna were much like the rest of the resort—clean, spacious and well-appointed—even if the decor was a bit much for his Midwestern sensibilities. More golden palm trees decorated the tile floor here and large murals of the famous Hawaiian sunsets bedecked the walls. There were neat rows of treadmills and stair-climbers, weight machines, stationary bikes and even a boxing area, complete with punching bags and thick mats on the floor.

Holden followed Leilani as she headed for those work-out mats, her snug workout clothes clinging to her curves in all the right places. Not that he noticed. He was here to release some tension, not to ogle his colleague. No mat-ter how pretty she was. It had been too long since he'd been with a woman, that was all. The slip of paper with the phone number the waitress had given him flashed in his mind. He hadn't lied to Leilani earlier, but he hadn't been entirely truthful either. He had spoken to the wait-ress a few days prior about her sick kid and offered to see him, but then the waitress had also asked him out. At the time, he'd declined because he'd been tired and busy and not up for company. But now, with loneliness gnawing at his gut again, maybe he should give the server's invitation second thoughts.

Leilani strapped on a pair of boxing gloves, then turned to face him once more.

Holden stopped short. "Are you going to hit me?"

"Not unless you provoke me." She raised a dark brow at him.

He snorted. "Remind me not to get on your bad side."

"Don't worry. I will." She grinned, then turned to face the heavy bag. "Well, this is the gym. Enjoy your workout."

Looking around, he considered his options. Treadmill was out, with his leg. So were the stair-climbers as they put too much pressure on his still-healing muscles. Stationary bike it was then. He hobbled over and climbed onto one, setting his course to the most difficult one, and began to pedal. Soon his heart was pumping fast, and sweat slicked his face and chest, and he felt the glorious rush of endorphins that always came with a hard workout. Near the end of his course, Holden glanced over to where he'd left Leilani on the mats and found her working through what looked like kickboxing moves with the punching bag.

Her long hair was piled up in a messy bun atop her head now and her face was flushed from exertion. Her toned arms and back glistened with perspiration beneath the overhead lights as she walloped the heavy bag over and over again. Jab, hook, cross, uppercut. Sweep, cross, kick. Jab, cross, slip. Front kick, back kick. Roundhouse kick. Repeat. Holden found himself entranced.

Once his bike program was done, he moved back over

to where she was still dancing around the bag, her movements as coordinated and graceful as any prima ballerina. Even the hot pink boxing gloves didn't detract from Leilani's powerful stance. She looked ready to kick butt and take names. On second thought, just forget the names.

His gaze followed her fists driving hard into the bag. Then he couldn't help continuing to track down her torso to her waist and hips landing finally on her taut butt in those black leggings.

Whoa, boy.

Yep. Dr. Leilani Kim wasn't just pretty. She was gorgeous, no doubt about that. He glanced back up to find her staring at him, her expression flat.

Oops. Busted.

"You know how to fight," he said, for lack of anything better.

She steadied the swinging bag, then punched one glove into the other, blinking at him. "I do. Very well. Years of training, remember? I'm not afraid to use those skills either."

"I remember you taking down that patient. Don't worry. Point taken." Holden stepped back and chuckled. Back before the shooting he'd been into boxing himself, but he hadn't tried since his injury. He turned to head back to his bike but stopped at the sound of her voice.

"You box?"

"I used to," Holden said, looking back at her over his shoulder. He gestured to his right leg. "Haven't since this though."

"Want to give it a try now?" she asked, tapping the tips of her gloves together. "Be my sparring partner?" Her gaze dipped to his cane then back to his eyes. "I'll take it easy on you."

Whether or not she'd meant that as a challenge didn't matter. He took it as one. The pair of black boxing gloves she tossed in his direction helped too. He caught them one-handed, then narrowed his gaze on her. For the first time in a long time, he wanted to take a chance and burn off a little steam. "Fine."

He strapped on the gloves, then moved back over, setting his cane aside before climbing atop the mat to stand beside Leilani.

"We can stick to bag work, if it's easier on your leg."

"Sparring's fine." He finished closing the Velcro straps around his wrists, then punched his fists together. "Unless you're scared to face off against me?" His tone was teasing. It felt easy to tease her. He didn't want to think about why.

Leilani snorted. "Right. You think you can take me?"

"I think you talk big, but you look pretty small."

"Them's fighting words, mister." She moved several feet away and faced him before bending her knees and holding her gloves up in front of her face. "All right, Dr. Ross. Show me what you got."

Holden smiled, a genuine one this time, enjoying himself more than he had in a long, long time. "My pleasure, Dr. Kim."

They moved in a small circle on the mat, dodging each other and assessing their opponent. Then, fast as lightning, Leilani struck, landing a solid punch to his chest. He gave her a stunned look and she laughed. "Figured you already had a split lip. Didn't want to damage that handsome face of yours any further."

That stopped him in his tracks.

She thinks I'm handsome?

The reality of her words must've struck Leilani too because the flush in her cheeks grew and she looked away from him. "I mean, I'm taking pity on you. That's all."

Pity. If there was one word sure to set Holden off, it was that one.

All thought of keeping away from Leilani Kim went out the window as he went in for the attack. Apparently still distracted by what she'd said, she didn't react fast enough when he charged toward her and swept his good leg out to knock her feet from under her. Of course, the movement unbalanced him as well, and before Holden knew it, they were both flat on the mat, panting as they tried to catch their breaths in a tangle of limbs.

He managed to recover first, rising on one arm to lean over her. "I don't need your pity, Dr. Kim."

She blinked up at him a moment, then gave a curt nod. "Understood."

"Good." He pushed away to remove one of his gloves and rake a hand through his sweat-damp hair. "Are you all right?"

"Other than my pride, yes." She sat up next to him and removed her gloves too, several strands of her long, dark hair loose now and curling around her flushed face. "I didn't mean to insult you with what I said, by the way. It was just trash-talking."

"I know." He released a pent-up breath, then wiped off his forehead with the edge of his gray Ohana Medical T-shirt. "The whole pity thing is still a touchy subject for me though, with my leg and all."

"Sorry. I should've realized." She got up and walked over to a small fridge against the wall to pull out two bottles of water, then returned to hand him one. Leilani sat back down on the mat and cracked open her water. "What exactly happened, if you don't mind me asking?"

He gulped down half his bottle of water before answering, hoping to wash away the lump of anxiety that still rose every time someone asked about his injury. He did mind, usually, but today felt different. Maybe because they were the only ones in the gym, and that lent a certain air of intimacy. Through the windows across the room, he could see a bit of the gloom outside had lifted and weak rays of sunshine beamed in. Maybe it was time to let some of his past out of the bag, at least a little. He shrugged and fiddled with his gloves once more. "I got shot. Shattered my femur."

"Yikes. That's awful." Leilani grabbed the white towel she'd tossed on the floor nearby when they'd first arrived and wiped off her face. He glanced sideways at her and did his best not to notice the small bead of sweat tickling down the side of her throat. Tried to stop the sudden thought of how salty that might taste, how warm her skin might be against his tongue.

Wait. What?

He looked away fast as she wrapped the towel around her neck, then faced him once more.

"So," she said, her clear tone cutting through the roar of blood pounding in his ears, not from anxiety this time, but from unexpected, unwanted lust. "Is that when you took the bullet to your shoulder as well?"

Holden nodded, not trusting his voice at present, then drank more water. He didn't want Leilani Kim. Not that way. She was his coworker. She was just being nice. She was drinking her water too, drawing his attention to the sleek muscles of her throat as they worked, the pound of the pulse point at the base of her neck, the curve of her breasts in that tight sports bra.

Oh God.

Move. He needed to move. He started to get to his feet, but Leilani stopped him with a hand on his arm. "I'm sorry that happened to you. I know what it's like to be in a situation where you feel helpless and alone."

The hint of pain in her tone stunned him into staying put. From what he could see, she'd had a fairy-tale life here in paradise, raised in this wedding cake of a hotel.

"How's that? And please, call me Holden," he said, more curious than ever about this enigmatic, beautiful woman. To try to lighten the mood, he cracked a joke. "You get hit by a pineapple on the way to surf the waves?"

Her small smile fell and it felt like the brightening room darkened. She shook her head and looked away. "No. More like hit by a truck and spent six months in the hospital."

"Oh." For a second, Holden just took that in, unsure what else to say. Of course, his analytical mind wanted to know more, demanded details, but he didn't feel comfortable enough to do so. Finally, he managed, "I had no idea."

"No. Most people don't." She sighed and rolled her neck, reaching back to rub her nape again, same as she had the other day in the ER with that combative patient. Then she stood and started gathering her things. "Well, I should go get ready for work."

Of all people, Holden knew a retreat when he saw one. He got up as well, reaching for his cane to take the weight off his now-aching leg. Doing that foot sweep on Leilani hadn't been the most genius move ever, even if his whole side now tingled from the feel of her body briefly pressed to his.

He grabbed his water bottle and limped after her toward the exit, pausing to hold the door for her. Before walking out himself, he looked over toward the windows across the gym one last time. "Hey, the sun's out again."

Leilani glanced in the same direction, then gave him a

tiny grin. "Funny how that works, huh? Wait long enough and it always comes back out. See you around, Holden."

"Bye, Dr. Kim," he said, watching her walk away, then stop at the end of the hall and turn back to him.

"Leilani," she called. "Anyone who leg-sweeps me gets to be on a first-name basis."

CHAPTER FOUR

THE ER AT Ohana Medical Center was hopping the following Wednesday and Leilani was in her element. She was halfway through a twelve-hour shift, and so far she'd dealt with four broken limbs, one case of appendicitis that she'd passed on to a gastro surgeon for removal, and two box jellyfish stings that had required treatment beyond the normal vinegar rinse and ice. The full moon was Friday and that's when the jellyfish population tended to increase near the beaches to mate. There weren't any official warnings posted yet, according to the patient's husband, but that didn't mean there weren't jellyfish present. They were a year-round hazard in Hawaii.

So yeah, a typical day in the neighborhood.

Leilani liked being busy though. That's what made emergency medicine such a good fit for her. Kept her out of trouble, as her parents always said.

Trouble like thinking about that gym encounter with Holden Ross the week prior.

She suppressed a shiver that ran through her at the memory of his hard body pressed against hers on that mat, the heat of him going through her like a bolt of lightning, making her imagine things that were completely off-limits as far as her colleague was concerned.

Since that day, they'd passed each other a few times

in the halls, both at the hospital and at the hotel, but
hadn't really said more than a friendly greeting. Just as
well, since time hadn't seemed to lessen the tingling that
passed through her nerve endings whenever he was near.
In fact, if anything, the fact they'd taken a tumble on that
mat together only seemed to intensify her awareness of
him. Which probably explained why she was still hung
up on the whole thing. Leilani tried never to let her guard
down but Holden had somehow managed to get around
her usual barriers.

Boundaries were key to her maintaining control. And
control required no distractions.

Distractions led to accidents and accidents led to…

Shaking off the unwanted stab of sorrow in her heart,
she concentrated on the notes she was currently typing
into her tablet computer at the nurses' station. The EMTs
had just radioed in with another patient headed their way
and she wanted to get caught up as much as possible before taking on another case.

As she documented her treatment for the latest jellyfish sting patient—visible tentacles removed from sting
site, antihistamine for mild allergic reaction, hydro-
cortisone cream for itching and swelling, ice packs as
needed—she half listened to the commotion around her
for news of the EMTs arrival with her next patient. She'd
just closed out the file she'd been working on when the
voice of the sister of one of her earlier patients, a guy
who'd broken his arm while hiking near the Diamond
Head Crater, broke through her thoughts.

"Doctor?" the woman said, coming down the hall. "I
need to ask you something."

Leilani glanced over, ready to answer whatever questions the woman had, then stopped short as the woman

headed straight past her and made a beeline for Holden, who'd just come out of an exam room.

He glanced up at the buxom blonde and blinked several times. "How can I help you, ma'am?"

"My brother was in here earlier and I'm concerned he won't take the prescription they gave him correctly, even after the other doctor explained it to him. She was Hawaiian, I think, and—"

"Dr. Kim is the head of Emergency Medicine. I'm sure the instructions she gave him were clear." Holden searched the area and locked eyes with Leilani. "But if you still have concerns, let's go see if she has a few moments to talk to you again, Mrs....?"

"Darla," the woman said, batting her eyelashes and grinning wide.

Leilani bit back a snicker at her flagrant flirting.

"And it's Miss. I'm single. Besides, I'm old-fashioned and prefer a male doctor."

Holden's expression shifted from confused to cornered in about two seconds flat. Darla didn't want medical advice. She wanted a date. Leilani would've laughed out loud at his obvious discomfort if there wasn't a strange niggle eating into her core. Not jealousy because that would be stupid. She had no reason to care if anybody flirted with Holden. It was none of her business. And it wasn't like men hadn't tried to flirt with Leilani in the ER either. It was another occupational hazard. No, what should have bothered her more was the woman doubting her medical expertise. Shoulders squared, she raised a brow and waited for their approach.

Holden cleared his throat and stepped around Darla to head to the nurses' station and Leilani. "Dr. Kim is one of the best physicians I've worked with. She's the person to advise you and your brother on his medications, as she's familiar with his case." He stopped beside Leilani at the desk, tiny dots of crimson staining his high cheek-bones. "Dr. Kim, this lady has more questions about her brother's prescription."

Leilani gave him a curt nod, then proceeded to go over the same information she'd given to Darla's brother an hour prior. Steroids weren't exactly rocket science, and from the way the woman continued to focus on Holden's backside and not Leilani, it seemed Darla could have cared less anyway. Finally, Darla went on her way and Leilani exhaled slowly as the EMTs radioed in their ETA of one minute.

Showtime.

Refocusing quickly, she grabbed a fresh gown and mask from the rack nearby and suited up, aware of Holden's gaze on her as she did so. Her skin prickled under the weight of his stare, but she shook it off. The incoming patient needed her undivided attention, not Dr. Ross.

"What's the new case?" Holden asked, handing his tablet back to the nurse behind the desk. "Need help?"

"Maybe," Leilani said, tying the mask around her neck. "Stick close by just in case."

"Will do." He took a gown and mask for himself, then followed her down the hall to the automatic doors leading in from the ambulance bay. His presence beside her felt oddly reassuring, which only rattled her more. She was used to handling things on her own. Safe, secure, solo. That's how she liked it.

Isn't it?

Too late to stew about it now. The doors swished open and the EMTs rushed in with a young man on a gurney. Leilani raced down the hall next to the patient as the EMT in charge gave her a rundown.

"Eighteen-year-old male surfer struck in the neck by

his surfboard," the paramedic said. "Difficulty breathing that's worsened over time."

They raced into trauma bay two and Leilani moved in to examine the patient, who was gasping like a fish out of water. "Sir, can you speak? Does it feel like your throat is closing?"

The kid nodded, his eyes wide with panic.

"Okay," Leilani said, keeping her voice calm. "Is it hard to breathe right now?"

The patient nodded again.

"Are you nodding because it hurts to talk or because you can't?" Holden asked, moving in on the other side of the bed once the EMTs got the patient moved from the gurney.

"I…" the kid rasped. "C-can't."

"No intubation, then," Holden said, holding up a hand to stop the nurse with the tracheal tube. "Dr. Kim, would you like me to consult?"

Nice. The other trauma surgeons on staff usually just commandeered a case, rarely asking for Leilani's permission to intercede. Having Holden do so now was refreshing, especially since she'd asked him to stick close by earlier. It showed a level of professional respect that she liked a lot. Plus, it would give her a chance to see first-hand how he handled himself with patients. For weeks now, the nurses had been praising his bedside manner and coolness under pressure. About time Leilani got to see what she was up against if they were both vying for the directorship.

"Yes, please, Dr. Ross." She grabbed an oxygen tube to insert into the kid's nose to help his respiration. "Okay, sir. Breathe in through your nose. Good. One more time."

The kid gasped again. "I c-can't."

Leilani placed her hand on his shoulder. "You're doing fine. I know it hurts."

Holden finished his exam then stepped back to speak to relay orders to the nurse taking the patient's vitals. "We need a CTA of his neck and X-rays, please. Depending on what those show, I may need to do a fiber-optic thoracoscopy. Call ENT for a consult as well, please."

"Where's my son?" a man's voice shouted from out in the hall. "Please let me see him!"

After signing off on the orders, Holden moved aside to let the techs roll the patient out of the trauma room, then grabbed Leilani to go speak to the father. "Sir, your son was injured while surfing," Holden said, after pulling down his mask. "He's getting the best care possible between myself and Dr. Kim. Can you tell me your son's name?"

"Tommy," the man said. "Tommy Schrader. I'm his father, Bill Schrader."

"Thank you, Mr. Schrader." Leilani led the man down the hall to a private waiting room while Holden headed off with the team to complete the tests on the patient. "Let's have a seat in here."

"Will my boy be all right?" Mr. Schrader asked. "What's happened to him?"

"From what the EMTs said when they brought your son in, Tommy was surfing and was struck in the throat by his surfboard. He's got some swelling in his neck and is having trouble breathing." It was obvious the man cared deeply for his ENT and it was always hard to give difficult news to loved ones. In her case, they'd had to sedate her after delivering the news about her family's deaths. At least Tommy was still alive and getting the treatment he needed.

"When I got the call from the police, I panicked. I told

Tommy the surf was too rough today, but he didn't listen." Mr. Schrader scrubbed his hand over his haggard face. "All kinds of crazy things went through my mind. I've never been so scared in all my life."

"Completely understandable, Mr. Schrader. But please know we're doing all we can, and we'll keep you updated on his progress as soon as we know more. They're doing X-rays and a CT scan on him now to determine the extent of damage and the next steps for treatment." She patted the man's shoulder, then stood. "Can I get you anything to drink?"

"No, no. I'm good. I just want to know my son will be okay."

"He's in the best hands possible," Leilani said. "Let me go check on his status again and I'll be right back."

"Thank you," Mr. Schrader said. "I'm sorry I don't know your name."

"Dr. Kim." She gave him a kind smile. "Just sit tight and I'll be back in as soon as we know more."

"Thank you, Dr. Kim," Mr. Schrader said.

Leilani left him and headed up to radiology to check in with Holden. She'd no more than stepped off the elevators when he waved her over to look at the films.

"See how narrow this is?" Holden asked her, pointing at the films of the kid's trachea. "There's definite swelling in his airway. In fact, given that there's maybe only one or two millimeters open at most, it's starting to close off completely. There should be a finger's width all the way up."

Definitely not good, especially since the airway normally narrowed at that point anyway, right before the vocal cords. Which brought up the next issues.

"What about his voice box?" she asked.

"That's my concern," Holden said, the grayish light

from the X-ray viewer casting deep shadows on the hollows of his cheeks and under his eyes. "Looks like the surfboard made a direct hit on that area. The voice box could've been broken from the impact. It's a high-risk injury in a high-risk area of the body." He shook his head and leaned in closer to the films. "At least this explains his trouble breathing."

"Are you going to operate?" Leilani asked.

Holden exhaled slowly. "No, not yet. Hate to do that to a kid so young. My advice would be to treat him with steroids first and see if the swelling goes down. Watch him like a hawk though. If conservative treatment doesn't work, then I'll go in with the thoracoscopy."

"Agreed." Leilani stepped back and smiled. Working with Holden felt natural, comfortable. Like they were a team. "Best to keep him in the ER then for the time being. That way if he needs emergency assistance, we're there."

"Yep. Let's do it."

She and Holden rode back down to the trauma bay with the medical team and Tommy, then called his father into the room.

Holden and Leilani exchanged looks, then she nodded. He stepped forward to take the lead. "Mr. Schrader, I'm sorry to tell you this is a very, very serious situation. Your son's airway is currently compromised due to swelling from the surfboard strike. It's possible his voice box had been damaged. If that's the case, it could have long-term effects on his speech."

"Oh God." Mr. Schrader moved in beside his son and took the kid's hand. "I told you not to go surfing today. I was so worried."

"I know," Tommy managed to croak out, clinging to his dad's hand. "Sorry."

"Our biggest concern though, at this point," Holden

continued, "is that if his larynx—his voice box—is too badly damaged, your son runs the risk of losing his ability to breathe. We need to keep him here at the hospital, in the ER, for at least the next twelve hours for observation. That way if his condition worsens, we can rush him into surgery immediately, if needed. I'd also like to get a consult from one of the throat specialists on staff to get their opinion."

"Whatever you need to do," Mr. Schrader said. "I just want my son to be okay."

"Great. Thank you." Holden stepped back and glanced at Leilani again. "Both Dr. Kim and I will check on Tommy periodically through the night to keep an eye on him then."

"Yes, we will. You won't be alone." Leilani leaned in to place the call button in the kid's hand and give him a reassuring smile. Once upon a time, that had been her in a hospital bed—scared and unsure about the future. "And if you feel your breathing gets worse at any point, you just press that button and we'll rush back in right away, okay?"

Tommy gave a hesitant nod.

"Someone will always be here for you, Tommy," Holden said, meeting Leilani's gaze. "I promise. We're not going to let anything else happen to you."

The kid swallowed, then winced.

"Don't worry. We'll be in here checking on you so often you'll get sick of seeing us." Leilani winked, then headed toward the door with Holden. "Promise."

"And I'll be here too, son," his dad said, pulling up a chair to the beside.

She and Holden walked back to the nurses' station, discarding their masks and gowns in the biohazard bin and stopping to wash their hands at the sink nearby. His limp seemed less pronounced today, though he still used his cane to take the weight off his right leg.

She glanced over at him and smiled as she soaped up, then rinsed off. "You handled that case well."

"Thanks." He smiled, then winced, tossing his used paper towels in the trash and reaching up to touch the sutures in his lower lip.

"Stitches bothering you?" she asked, leaning a bit closer to inspect his wound. "Looks like it's healing well."

"I'm fine. It just stings a bit when I forget it's there," he said, holding up a tube of lip balm. "This helps though."

"Glad to hear it." Leilani turned away from the cherry flavored lip balm he held up. That was her favorite flavor. And now, for some reason, her mind kept wondering what his kisses would taste like with cherries in the mix. Ugh. Not good. Not good at all. She stepped back and looked anywhere but at him. "So, I should probably get back to work on another case then."

"Yeah, me too." He fiddled with the head of his cane, frowning slightly. "Hey, um, I meant to ask you about the luau."

"Luau?" she repeated, like she was channeling her pet parrot. Her pulse kicked up a notch. Damn. She'd been hoping he'd forget about all that. Apparently not. She forced a smile she didn't quite feel and flexed her fingers to relax them. Considering she'd just been having inappropriate thoughts about this man—her coworker—if she was wise, she'd get the heck out of there as soon as possible. Unfortunately, her feet seemed to have other ideas, because they stayed firmly planted where she was.

At least he seemed as awkward as she felt about it all, shuffling his feet and fumbling over his words. It was actually quite endearing… Leilani's heart pinched a little at the sweetness, before she stopped herself.

Keep it professional, girl.

"The other day, last week, uh," he said, keeping his gaze lowered like he was a nervous schoolkid and not a highly successful surgeon. "Anyway, I think your dad mentioned the luau at the hotel and I'd seen some flyers on it too, and I wondered if you still wanted to take me." He hazarded a glance up and caught her eye. "Not that I'll hold you to that. I just…" He exhaled slowly and ran his free hand through his hair, leaving the dark curls in adorable disarray.

No. Not adorable. No, no, no.

But even as she thought that, the simmering awareness bubbling inside her boiled over into blatant interest without her consent. Damn. This was beyond inconvenient. Of all the men for her to be interested in now, it had to be Holden Ross.

He huffed out a breath, then cursed quietly before straightening and meeting her gaze head-on as his words tumbled out in a rush. "Look. I don't get out much and I'd like to see some sights while I'm here, and since you offered the other day, I thought I'd take you up on that, if the offer…if it still stands. Not a date, because I don't do that. Just as two people, colleagues…" He hung his head. "I'm off tomorrow and Friday."

Leilani blinked at him a moment, stunned. Blood thundered in her ears and she turned away to grab her tablet from behind the desk, needing something, anything, to keep herself busy, to keep herself from agreeing to his invitation and more. Because for some crazy reason that's exactly what she wanted to do.

Think, girl. Think.

Saying yes could lead to a friendship between them

beyond work, could lead to those uncomfortable tingles of like for this guy going a whole lot further into other *l* words. Not *love*, because that was off the table, but another one with a capital *L*. Lust. Because yeah, Holden really was just her type. Tall, dark, gorgeous. Smart, funny, sexy as all get out.

So, she should definitely say no. He was her coworker, her potential rival.

Except that would be rude. And she just couldn't bring herself to be rude to him. Maybe it was that haunted look in his eyes she spied sometimes. Maybe it was his obvious awkwardness around commitment.

I don't date.

Well, neither did she at present. Or maybe it was the air of brokenness about him that called to the same old wounded parts in her.

Whatever it was, she didn't want to turn him down, even though she should.

There was one problem though.

She looked back at him over her shoulder as she brought up the next patient's information on her screen. "Malu Huna's luaus are only on Friday nights. And I have to work tomorrow. If you wanted to see the sights on Friday," she said, taking a deep breath to calm her racing nerves, "then I guess we could. It will make for a long day though. Are you sure you're up to that?"

"I am if you are," he said, his cane clinking against the desk as he moved closer. "I'll double up on my pain pills so I'm ready for anything."

Ready for anything.

Damn if those words, spoken in that deep velvet voice of his, didn't conjure a whole new batch of inappropriate thoughts. The two of them on the beach, holding hands and running into the waves together, lying in the sand afterward, making out like two horny teens, the feel of that dark stubble on his jaw scraping her cheeks, her neck, her chest, lower still…

Oh boy. I'm in trouble here.

Heat stormed her cheeks and she swiveled to face him, not realizing how close they were until it was too late. Her hand brushed his solid, warm chest before she snatched it away. Holden's hazel eyes flared with the same awareness jolting through her, before he quickly hid it behind a frown.

"Look, if you don't want to—"

"No, it's fine. I promised you and I always keep my word." She focused on the file on her screen again, trying in vain to calm her whirling thoughts. This was so not like her. She never went gaga over men. Yet here she was, blushing and stammering and acting like an idiot over the last man on Earth she should be attracted to. And yet, she was. Much as she hated to admit it.

Gah! Images of them lying together on that mat in the hotel gym zoomed back fast and furious to her mind. No. If she was going to get through this with her sanity and her heart intact, she needed to think logically about it. She'd show him her island home, not just the tourist sights, but her favorite spots too. Besides, it might give her a chance to find out more about his relationship with Dr. King and his real motives for being here in Hawaii. Taken in that light, she'd be a fool not to take him up on his offer, right? She took a deep breath, then set her tablet aside. "Fine. We'll tour the town, then end with the luau. Meet me in the lobby at the hotel at 8:00 a.m. the day after tomorrow and don't be late."

Holden opened his mouth, closed it, then he smiled— the slow little one that made her toes curl in her comfy white running shoes. Ugh. No more of that. She turned away to head into her next exam room as his surprised tone revealed an equal amount of shock on his part. "Uh…okay. Eight o'clock on Friday it is."

Four hours later, Holden was finishing up his shift by checking for the last time with Tommy Schrader. The kid was lucky. The steroids had helped reduce the swelling in his larynx and it didn't look like the thoracoscopy would be necessary after all.

When Holden arrived upstairs to Tommy's room, several of the kid's surfer friends were there, along with Tommy's father. Tommy was holding court like a king on his throne from his hospital bed, sun-streaked shaggy blond hair hanging in his face and his voice like gravel in a blender. But the fact the kid was speaking at all was a minor miracle. His injury could've been so much worse, and Holden was glad such a young guy wouldn't carry lifelong scars from his accident.

Unlike Holden himself.

He cleared his throat at the door to the hospital room to announce his presence. "Sorry if this is a bad time. Just wanted to check in on my patient one more time before my shift is over." He limped into the room with his cane and smiled at Mr. Schrader and the new guests. "Tommy's very lucky."

"Dudes, you have no idea," Tommy rasped out, smiling at Holden, then his friends. "They were gonna stick a camera up my nose and down my throat and everything."

"Whoa," his friends said, both as shaggy and sunburned as Tommy. "Man, that's gnarly. You were gonna be awake for that?"

"Patients are usually awake for thoracoscopy, yes," Holden confirmed as he reached Tommy's beside and leaned closer to examine the kid's throat. The swelling was greatly reduced, even from the last time Holden had checked him about an hour prior. He'd be fine to discharge.

He straightened and turned to Mr. Schrader, who was sitting on a chair near the window. "Your son appears to be healing just fine now, though Dr. Kim will continue to check on him for the remainder of his stay. I don't imagine there'll be any lingering effects, but I'll leave orders to discharge him with another round of steroids and some anti-inflammatory meds too. Then have him check in with your family physician in two weeks."

"Sounds good." The father shook Holden's hand. "Thanks so much, Doc. Now that I know my son's gonna be all right, once I get him home I'll make sure his older brothers keep an eye on him too. And try to talk him out of surfing so close to a full moon again."

Holden grinned and turned back to Tommy. "Listen to your dad. Take care, Tommy."

"Thanks, Doc. *Mahalo*," the kid said, shaking Holden's hand too. "I'll be sure to thank the pretty lady doc too. You guys make a good team. She your girlfriend?"

"Son," Mr. Schrader said, his voice rife with warning. "Don't mind him, Dr. Ross. That's all him and his friends think about these days when they're not surfing. Girls."

"I'll pass along gratitude to Dr. Kim," Holden said, dodging the uncomfortable questions and ignoring the squeeze of anxiety in his chest it caused. "Take care, all."

"*Mahalo*, Doc!" Tommy called again as Holden walked from the room to the nurses' station down the hall.

He should feel relieved to have another successful patient outcome under his belt, but now all he could think about was Leilani and their upcoming date on Friday.

Wait. Scratch that. Not a date.

He hadn't lied when he'd told her he didn't do that.

Life was too unpredictable for long-term commitments. The shooting had taught him that. Nothing was permanent, especially love. So now he chose short, sweet, no strings attached affairs. No deeper, messy, scary emotions involved, thanks. No connections beyond the physical. No chance to have his heart ripped out and shredded to pieces. Because that's what he wanted.

Isn't it?

Not that it mattered. He and Leilani Kim were work colleagues, nothing more. Best to keep his head down and focus on his work, then move on when this stint ended. That was the safest bet. And Holden was all about safety these days.

She'd show him around the city, then take him to the luau at the resort, as promised. That's all. Nothing more. And sure, he couldn't stop thinking about the feel of her beneath him on that stupid gym mat, the sweet jasmine and lemon scent of her hair, the warm brush of her skin against his and…

Oh God.

He was such an idiot. What the hell had he been thinking to bring up her invitation to the luau? He hadn't been thinking, that was the problem. Or more to the point, he'd been thinking with his libido and not his brain. Memories of her dressed in those formfitting leggings and tank top at the gym that day, how she might wrap those shapely legs of hers around him instead, and hold him close, kiss him, run his fingers through his hair. He shuddered.

No. No, no, no.

With more effort than should be necessary to concentrate, Holden finished electronically signing off on his notes on the Tommy Schrader case, then left instructions for his discharge for Leilani before handing it all over to the nurse waiting behind the desk.

"Dr. King asked to see you upstairs in her office when you have a moment, Dr. Ross," the nurse said.

"Thanks." Probably about that project she'd mentioned to him before. He took a deep breath, then headed for the elevators. The clock on the wall said it was nearly time for him to leave. Good. He'd see Helen, then head back to the ER to hand off his cases to the next physician on duty before going back to the hotel for some much-needed sleep.

Besides, talking to Helen should be a good distraction from his unwanted thoughts about Leilani. The elevator dinged and he stepped on board then pushed the button for the fifth floor, where the administrative offices were located.

He had to get his head on straight again before Friday. Hell, if he was really serious about keeping to himself, he'd cancel the whole day altogether. Given the surprised look on her face when she'd offered to show him around, she'd probably be glad to be rid of him as well. But then if he did cancel, she might take it the wrong way, and the last thing he wanted was to offend her. They still had to work together, after all.

You guys make a good team.

Tommy's words from earlier echoed through his head. The worst part was, they were true.

Working with Leilani on that case had felt seamless, effortless, *right.*

Which was just wrong, in Holden's estimation.

He didn't want partnerships anymore, professionally or personally. Getting too close to people only made you vulnerable and weak, especially when they could be taken from you so easily.

Ding!

The elevator doors swished open and Holden stepped

out into the lobby on the administrative floor. Thick carpet padded his footsteps as he headed over to the receptionist's desk in the middle of the plush leather-and-glass sitting area.

"Hi. Holden Ross to see Helen King, please," he said, feeling out of place and underdressed in his shift-old scrubs and sneakers.

"Dr. King's been expecting you, Dr. Ross." She pointed down a hallway to her left. "Last door on the right."

"Thanks." He gave the woman a polite smile, then headed for the office she'd indicated. The other times he'd met with Helen here in Hawaii, it had been outside the hospital, either at her home near Waikiki or at the fancy restaurant she'd taken him to on his first night in the city. Other than that, he'd never been up here, since regular old human resources was in another building entirely, half a block down from the medical center. He made his way to the end of the hall and stopped to admire the amazing view from the floor-to-ceiling glass wall beside the office before knocking on the dark wood door.

"Come in," Helen called from inside, and Holden entered the office.

For a moment, he took in the understated elegance of the place. It was Helen to a T, no-nonsense yet comfortable. "Wow, this is a big step up from Chicago, huh?"

Helen chuckled, her husky voice helping to soothe his earlier anxiety. "It doesn't suck. Please come in, Holden. Have a seat."

He did so, in a large wingback leather chair in front of her desk that probably cost more than his rent back home. As always, Helen's desk was spotless, with stacks of files neatly placed in bins and every pen just so. "The nurse downstairs said you wanted to see me?"

"I wanted to see how you're settling in," she said, sitting back in her black leather executive chair that dwarfed her petite frame. With her short white hair and sparkling blue eyes, she'd always reminded Holden of a certain British actress of a certain age, who took no crap from anyone. "We haven't talked in a few weeks. How are you liking things here at Ohana?"

"Fine." He did his best to relax but found it difficult. He and Helen had been friends long enough for him to suspect this wasn't just a social call. They could've gone to the pub for that. "The facilities are top-notch and the staff is great."

Better than great, his mind chimed in as he recalled Leilani.

Not that he'd mention his unwanted attraction to his coworker to Helen. The woman had been trying to get him married off since they'd worked together back in Chicago. If she even suspected a hint of chemistry between him and Leilani, she'd be all over it worse than the Spanish Inquisition.

"Glad to hear you like it." Helen steepled her fingers, then watched him over the top of them, her gaze narrowed, like M getting ready to assign her best secret agent a new kill. "But do you like it enough to consider staying?"

"What?" Holden tore his gaze away from the stunning views of the ocean in the distance and focused on Helen once more, his chest tightening. He frowned. "No. I'm locum tenens."

"I know," she said, sitting forward to rest her arms atop her desk. "But what if you weren't."

The low-grade anxiety constantly swirling in his chest rose higher, constricting his vocal cords. "But I am. You know I don't want to get tied down to anywhere. Not yet."

Maybe not ever again.

Helen blinked at him several times before exhaling slowly, her expression morphing from confident to concerned. "I'm worried about you, Holden. You've been on your own since the shooting, jetting off to a new place every few months, no connections, no home."

"I'm fine," he said, forcing the words. "Look, I thought you called me here to talk about that project you mentioned, not dissect my personal life."

"Are you fine though?" Her blue gaze narrowed, far too perceptive for his tastes. She sighed and stood, coming around the desk and leaning her hips back against it as she changed the subject. "Well, all that aside… Fine, let's discuss the project then."

Holden released his pent-up breath, his lungs aching for oxygen, and stared at the floor beneath his feet. Helen had saved his life after the shooting. Stitching up his wounds and staunching his blood loss until the orthopedic surgeons could work their magic on his leg and shoulder. Without her, there was a good chance he would've ended up six feet under, just like David.

An unexpected pang of grief stabbed his chest. Even a year later, he still missed his best friend like it was yesterday. The funeral. The awful days afterward, walking around like a zombie, no emotions, no light, no hope.

Still, he was here. He was coming back to life slowly, painfully, whether he wanted to or not. Like a limb that had fallen asleep, pins and needles stabbed him relentlessly as the emotions he'd suppressed for so long returned. Maybe that was why he felt so drawn to Leilani—her vibrant spirit, the sense that perhaps in some weird way she understood what he'd been through, how she made him feel things he'd thought he'd never feel again.

Plus, he owed Helen a debt he could never repay. That's why he was here in Hawaii. Why he was here now. She'd saved his life and his leg. The least he could do was hear her out. He cleared his throat, then asked, "What kind of project is it?"

"Twofold, actually." Helen clasped her hands in front of her. "First, our national accreditation is coming up for renewal next year and we need to make sure all of our security policies are up-to-date for the ER. I'd like you to help with that."

Holden swallowed hard and forced his tense shoulders to relax. "I can do that."

"Good." Helen glanced out the windows then back to him again. "Secondly, you know I'm looking for a new director of emergency medicine, yes?"

"Yes," he said. "But I'm here as a trauma surgeon."

"True. But you've got the experience and the temperament to head a department, Holden." She crossed her arms. "You were on track to run the ER back in Chicago, before the shooting."

He had been. That was true. But those ambitions had died along with David that day. He didn't want to be responsible for all those people, for all those lives. What if he failed again?

"I don't want that anymore. I'm happy with the temporary stint." His response sounded flat to his own ears and his heart pinched slightly despite knowing he couldn't even consider taking on a more permanent role. "Besides, Dr. Kim is doing a great job as temporary director. Why not offer it to her?"

"She's in the running, to be sure," Helen said before pushing away from the desk and walking over to the windows nearby. "But I like to keep my options open. And it's been nice having you here, Holden. I won't lie. We're friends. I know you. Trust you. Dr. Kim seems more than competent and her record at Ohana is outstanding, but every time I try to get to know her better, she shuts me down. I'm not sure I can work with someone I don't know and trust implicitly."

Holden had noticed Leilani deftly skirting his questions around her past too. Then again, he had no room to talk. He hadn't told her anything about what had happened to him either.

He exhaled slowly and raked a hand through his hair. He didn't like the idea of spying for Helen, no matter how much he owed her. Maybe he should cancel Friday, just so it wouldn't come back to bite him later, one way or another. Shut down any semblance of something more between him and Leilani before it ever really started. The fact he seemed more drawn to her each time they were together scared him more than anything, to be honest, and Holden was no coward. But damn if he wanted to open himself up to a world of hurt again, and some hidden part of him sensed that getting closer to Leilani would bring heartbreak for sure.

"I don't feel comfortable spying for you," he said bluntly. "Not on a colleague."

"No," Helen said, giving him a small smile. "I didn't imagine you would. Well, that's fine. Just keep an eye out during the project. If you see anything you think I should know about, let me know. Oh, and I haven't talked to Dr. Kim about it yet, so keep it under your hat, until I do. Okay?"

"Okay." Seemed an odd request, but an innocent one. "No problem. Anything else?"

"Nope. That's it." Helen walked back around her desk and took a seat. "I've got work to do, so get out of my office."

He chuckled and stood, his cane sinking into the thick carpet as he leaned his weight on it. "Let me know when it's safe to mention the project to Leilani. I'll be out until the weekend."

Helen gave him a quizzical look at his use of Dr. Kim's first name, and he kicked himself mentally. Then she winked and grinned as he hobbled toward the door.

"Enjoy your days off," she called after him.

"Thanks," he said, gritting his teeth against the soreness in his thigh. He needed to finish up his shift, then get back to the hotel, take a shower, rest, recharge, decide whether to cancel on Friday or spend the day with the one woman who'd somehow gotten under his skin despite all his wishes to the contrary.

"Oh, and Holden?" Helen called when he was halfway into the hall.

"Yeah?" He peeked his head back inside the office.

"Don't stay cooped up your whole time here in Hawaii," she said, as if reading his thoughts. "Get out and live a little. Trust me—you'll be glad you did."

Holden headed back down the hall and over the elevators, unable to shake the sense of fate weighing heavy on his shoulders. Too bad he didn't believe in destiny anymore. One random act of violence had changed all that forever.

Still, as he headed back down to the ER his old friend's words kept running through his head, forcing him to reconsider canceling his Friday plans with Leilani.

Get out and live a little. Trust me—you'll be glad you did...

CHAPTER FIVE

AT SEVEN FIFTY-EIGHT ON Friday morning, Leilani stood behind the reception desk at her parents' resort, feeding her parrot, U'i, and wondering if it was too late to fake a stomach bug to get out of her day with Holden.

"Who's a pretty bird?" U'i squawked, followed by a string of curses in three languages—Mandarin, Hawaiian and English.

Leilani snorted and fed him another hunk of fresh pineapple. She'd had him as a pet since right after the accident and loved him with all her heart, even though he acted like a brat and swore like a sailor sometimes. Considering he was sixteen and African grays typically lived as long as humans, U'i was definitely in his terrible teen years.

"More," he screeched when she wasn't fast enough with the next hunk of fruit. He took it in his black beak, then held on to a slice of orange with one foot while cocking his head at her and blinking his dark eyes. "Thanks, baby."

"You're welcome, baby," she said in return, scratching his feathered head with her finger and grinning. "Mama loves you."

"Mama loves you," U'i repeated, before devouring his treat.

"Hey," a deep male voice said from behind her, causing her heart to flip.

Leilani set aside the cup of fruit she'd snagged from the breakfast buffet in the dining room, then wiped her hands on the legs of her denim shorts before turning slowly to face Holden. *Too late to run now*, she supposed. She gave him a smile and prayed she didn't look as nervous as she felt. "Hey."

In truth, she'd spent the last twenty-four hours seriously questioning her sanity for offering to be Holden's tour guide today. Sure, she wanted to get to know him better, but that was a double-edged sword. Getting to know him better risked getting to like him better. And liking him even more than she did now was a definite no-no, considering she melted a little more inside each time she saw him.

Like now, when he was standing there, looking effortlessly gorgeous in a pair of navy board shorts and a yellow Hawaiian shirt that rivaled any of the loud numbers her dad wore. The open V of his collar beckoned her eyes to trail slowly down his tanned chest to his trim hips and strong, sexy, tanned calves. God. How was that even possible? Their schedules at the hospital were nuts. Who had time to soak up the sunshine? Apparently, Holden did, since he looked like he'd walked straight off a "hot hunks in paradise" poster.

He shuffled his feet and switched his cane from one side to the other, making her realize she'd been staring. Self-conscious now, she turned back to her pet and fed him another chunk of pineapple from the cup.

"Who's your friend?" Holden asked.

"This is U'i," she said, leaning in to kiss the bird's head.

"Huey?" Holden asked, stepping closer to look at the parrot, who was eyeballing him back.

"No. *U'i*," Leilani corrected him. "No *h*. It means *handsome* in Hawaiian."

"Ah." He reached up toward the bird, then hesitated. "Does he bite?"

"Only if he doesn't like you." She snorted at Holden's startled expression, then took pity on him, holding out the fruit cup toward him. "Here, feed him some of this. U'i's never met food he didn't like."

Sure enough, her traitorous pet snagged the hunk of melon from Holden's fingers, then gave him an infatuated coo that Leilani was lucky to hear even after a half hour of cuddles and tummy rubs. Seemed Holden's considerable charms worked on more than just her.

"African gray, right?" Holden asked, bravely stroking a finger over U'i's head.

"Correct." Leilani smiled despite herself. "You a bird fan?"

"A friend of mine back in med school had one. Smart as a whip and snarky too."

"Yep, that's my guy here." She gave her beloved pet one more kiss, then stepped away fast. Holden moved as well, causing his arm to brush hers, sending tingles of awareness through her already overtaxed nervous system. "So, are you, uh, ready to go?"

"Whenever you are," Holden said, stepping back and giving her a too-bright smile. "Doubled my pain meds, so lead onward."

For the second time since their conversation in the ER on Wednesday, the thought popped into her head that maybe he was as nervous about all this as she was. After all, he'd been stammering and shifting around as much as her, his frown still fresh in her mind. She'd assumed it was because he didn't really want to spend time with her, but now she wondered if it went deeper than that.

"Did you get Tommy Schrader released okay—the surfboard patient? He was doing much better the last time I checked. He told me *mahalo*."

"Yep. He was doing much better when I discharged him. Gave him your scripts too. I'm glad there wasn't any permanent damage to his voice box." She wiped her hands off again and tossed away the empty fruit cup before walking back around the desk and beckoning for Holden to follow her. Well, regardless of how he felt about things, they were both stuck together for the day now. Correction, day and evening, since they had the luau tonight after their day of sightseeing. Then they could go back to their separate lives. Leilani glanced at the clock on the wall again. Five after eight. Man, it was going to be a long day at this rate.

Okay. At least she had a full itinerary to keep them busy. First though, a few questions. She glanced at his cane, then back to his eyes. "How are you with walking?"

"Fine, I think," he said, adjusting his weight. "Like I said, I took my pain meds this morning and have another dose in my pocket in case I need it later. Actually, I think the exercise might do me good. My physical therapist back in Chicago is always on me to move more. Says it's the only way I'm going to get full function back and lose this someday." He waggled his cane in front of him. "I may need to take breaks every so often, but I'm looking forward to a day in the fresh air."

"Okay then. Great." She started toward the front entrance, slowing her usual brisk pace to make it easier on Holden. "I thought we could start at North Shore, since the beach there is a bit less crowded than Waikiki and you can get to Diamond Head easy enough on your own with it being so close to the hotel.

"We can maybe grab a quick breakfast at one of the

stands at North Shore too, then go see Honolulu's China-town markets, stop by the Iolani Palace downtown and visit the USS *Arizona* memorial, then end the day by hiking to Manoa Falls. It's short and mostly shaded, so it shouldn't be too tough for you. That should get you plenty hungry for the luau tonight when we get back to the hotel."

"Sounds great. Let's roll," he said, climbing into the hotel shuttle Leilani had commandeered just for their use today, then holding his cane between his knees. He seemed more relaxed now than she'd ever seen him, and Leilani had to admit she found him more attractive by the minute. "I'm all yours."

At his words, that darned awareness simmering in-side her flared bright as the sun again, and she said a si-lent prayer of thanks that she was sitting down, because she doubted her wobbly knees would've supported her. There was a part of her that wished more than anything that were true, that he was hers, and if that wasn't terri-fying, she didn't know what was.

She turned out of the hotel parking lot and wound her way through town before merging onto the H1 highway heading north, allowing the warmth from the sunshine and fresh air breezing in through the open windows to ease some of her tension away. His comment had been innocent enough and the fact that she instantly took it as more spoke to her own loneliness and neglected libido than anything else. Traffic thinned as they left the city behind. For his part, Holden seemed content to just stare out the window at the passing scenery, dark sunglasses hiding his eyes from her view.

Good thing too, since they were passing right by the spot where the accident had happened years ago. Man, she hadn't even thought about that when she'd been planning the itinerary for today, which only went to show how torn and twisted she'd been about this whole excursion. Now though, as they neared the junction of H1 and H2 and she veered off toward the right and the H2 highway, Leilani spotted a sign for the outlet mall close by and gripped the steering wheel tighter. They'd been going there that day, shopping for back-to-school clothes for her and her brother, when the accident happened. Her mouth dried and her chest ached as she held her breath and sped past the spot where they'd skidded off the road after impact, their station wagon tumbling over and over down into the ravine until finally landing on its roof, the wheels still spinning and groaning, the smell of gasoline and hissing steam from the radiator as pungent now as they'd been that long-ago day when Leilani had been trapped in the back seat, upside down, gravely injured, screaming for help while her loved ones died around her…

"Uh, are we in a huge hurry?" Holden said from the passenger seat, drawing her back to the present. "Speedometer says we're pushing eighty."

Crap.

She forced herself to take a breath and eased her death grip on the steering wheel. Throat parched, her words emerged as little more than a croak. "Sorry. Lead foot."

Holden watched her closely, his gaze hidden behind those dark glasses of his, but all the same, Leilani could feel his stare burning. Her cheek prickled from it and she focused on easing her foot off the accelerator to avoid the unsettling panic still thrumming through her bloodstream. It was fine. Things were all fine now. She was safe. They were safe.

"Everything okay?" Holden asked after a moment. "You look a little pale."

"No. It's fine." She took a few deep breaths as a couple of cars passed them. "Driving on the freeway bothers me, that's all."

His full lips turned down at the corners. "You should've said something earlier. If this is making you uncomfortable, we can go somewhere else. I can see the beach myself another time."

"No, it's fine." She kept her eyes straight ahead, afraid that if she looked at him, he'd see all the turmoil inside her. "Look. There's a sign for the Dole Plantation."

Holden looked toward his window then back to her. "Should we go there instead?"

"Nah." She shrugged, releasing some of the knots between her shoulder blades. "It's pretty and all, but not very exciting."

"Not very exciting isn't always a bad thing," he said, shifting to face front again.

The hint of sadness in his voice made her want to ask him more about his injuries, but after her flashbacks a minute ago, now didn't seem like the best time. Instead, she drove on toward the beach and, hopefully, something to keep them busy and away from dangerous topics. The rest of the forty-minute trip passed without incident, thankfully.

Sure enough, the beach was lovely. Fewer people and beautiful stretches of sand and surf for miles. They grabbed acai bowls in Haleiwa Town, then headed over to Ehukai Beach Park and the Banzai Pipeline to watch the surfers shred some waves.

They snagged some seats atop a wooden table in one of the picnic areas lining the sandy beach and had excellent views of the massive waves crashing toward the rocks just offshore.

"Man, that's impressive," Holden said around a bite of

granola, coconut and tangy acai berries. "Look at that. How big do the waves get here?"

"Up to twenty-five feet during the winter. We're at the tail end now, with it being March, but they can still get pretty big." She chuckled at a small boy running out into the surf. "Check him out. Can't be more than five and already fearless."

"Wow." Holden stared wide-eyed as the child held his own on the big waves right next to the adults. "That's amazing."

"Yeah. I remember being his age and coming here with my dad. I learned to swim not far from here at the Point." Sadness pushed closer around her heart before she shoved it away. "Those were good days."

"Really?" He blinked at her now, suitably impressed. "So, you can hang ten with these guys then?"

She laughed around another bite of food. "Back in the day, sure. It's been years since I surfed though, so probably not now. Though they say it's like riding a bike. You never really forget."

"Hmm." He finished his food, then tossed his trash in a nearby receptacle, scoring a perfect three-pointer. He swallowed some water from his bottle, the sleek muscles working in his throat entrancing her far more than they should. "Well, I certainly won't be doing much surfing these days with my leg."

He rubbed his right thigh again, tiny whitish scars bisecting his tanned skin. From a distance they weren't as visible, but this close she could see them all. The questions she'd been putting off rose once more, but before she could ask, he slid down off the table and toed off his walking shoes. "Think I'll take a gander down the beach, if you don't mind."

"No. Go for it." She watched him head off, then finished her breakfast before standing to throw her own trash away. It was a beautiful spring day, not too hot or too cold, the scent of salt and sand filling the air. Above her, seagulls cried and leaves of the nearby banyan trees rustled in the breeze. She'd used to love coming here as a kid, building sandcastles with her brother, or cuddling on her mom's lap beneath the blue sky. She wrapped her arms around herself and kicked off her sneakers, venturing down to the water's edge to dip her toes in the bracing Pacific waters.

Lost in thought, she didn't even hear Holden return until he was right next to her on the wet sand, his cane in one hand and his shoes dangling from the fingers of the other. His dark hair was tousled and the shadow of dark stubble on his chin made her want to run her tongue over it, then nuzzle her face into his neck. She swallowed hard and stared out at the horizon and the surfers balancing on the crests of the waves rolling in. "How was your walk?"

"Good. Needed to stretch my legs after the car ride." He took a deep breath in and glanced skyward. "Hard to imagine your dad out here though. Never thought of Joe Kim as a surfer."

"Oh, he's not," she said without thinking, then stopped herself. Too late.

Holden was looking at her again, reaching up to lower those sunglasses of his so his hazel eyes were visible over the tops of their rims. "I'm confused."

A few weeks ago, she would've walked away, shut down this conversation with him. But now, today, she felt tired. Tired of pushing him away, tired of keeping up her walls so high and strong, tired of running. Leilani sighed and shook her head. "The Kims aren't my real parents. They adopted me after my family was killed in a car accident twenty years ago."

"Oh," Holden said, his voice distant as he took that in. After a few moments, he seemed to collect himself and stepped closer to her to block the breeze. "I'm sorry. That must've been horrible."

"It's okay," she said out of habit. Years of distancing people took their toll. "I mean, it happened a long time ago, when I was fourteen. I've moved on." And she had, at least in most areas. Work. School. Anywhere that didn't require true intimacy. Speaking of intimacy, Holden's body heat penetrated the thin cotton of her pink tank top and made her crave all sorts of things that were best left alone. She moved away and headed back toward their car. "We should probably get going if we want to make our eleven-thirty ticket time at Pearl Harbor."

He lingered on the beach a moment before limping after her. "Right. Sure."

Three hours later, Holden sat on the hard bench seat in the Navy boat shuttle beside Leilani on their way to the USS *Arizona* Memorial, glad for a break to rest his sore leg. Not that he would've missed anything from their day. They'd already spent time at several of the other sites within the World War II Valor in the Pacific National Monument, including touring the USS *Bowfin* Submarine Park, the Pearl Harbor Aviation Museum, and the USS *Missouri* Battleship Memorial, as well as walking through the visitors center, the Road to War Museum, and the Aloha Court. Neither of them had said much since leaving the North Shore.

Holden had spent much of the time trying to wrap his head around what Leilani had shared with him. Being a teenager was hard enough without losing your entire family. He couldn't imagine what she must've gone through back then, the grief, the loss. That certainly explained the pain he saw flashing in her dark eyes sometimes though. Also explained why she'd known so much about that seat belt law in the ER that day.

He'd wanted to ask her more about what had happened, but then she'd not really seemed open to it on the ride to Pearl Harbor. Once they'd gotten inside the park there'd been films to watch and audio tours, and now Holden had no clue how to broach the subject with her again.

Of course, then there was the fact that coming here, to the site where so many had lost their lives in another act of violence brought all of his own pain rushing back to the forefront. December 7, 1941, was a long time ago, and he hadn't expected it to affect him as much as it did, but there'd already been several times when he'd nearly lost it.

The first time had occurred when they'd toured the Attack museum, which followed the events from Pearl Harbor through the end of World War II, and he'd seen the delicate origami crane by Sadako Sasaki, a young girl of only two when the bomb had been dropped on Hiroshima. Her goal had been to fold a thousand cranes during her time in the hospital for her injuries, which according to Japanese legend meant she'd then be granted a wish, but she'd only made it to six hundred and forty-four before her death at the age of twelve. Holden's chest still squeezed with sadness over her loss. Her family had donated the sculpture to the museum in the hopes of peace and reconciliation.

The second time had been during the film they'd watched before boarding the shuttle to tour the USS *Arizona* Memorial. Hearing the servicemen and women and the eyewitnesses to the event talk about their fallen comrades and the horrific things they'd seen that day had taken Holden right back to the shooting in Chicago—

the eerie quiet in the ER after the gunman had opened fire broken only by the squeak of the attacker's shoes on the tile floor, the metallic smell of the weapons firing, David's last desperate gasps for air as he'd bled out on the floor beside Holden, and the helpless feeling of knowing there was nothing he could do to stop it.

He forced himself to take a deep breath and focused out the open window on the gentle waves lapping the sides of the shuttle. The scent of sea and the light jasmine shampoo from Leilani's hair helped calm his racing pulse. This wasn't Chicago. They were safe here.

They docked a few minutes later and got out to traverse the new ramps that had been installed the previous year for visitors to the monument. The other passengers were quiet too, almost reverent at they stood before the iconic white stone structure. According the audio narration both he and Leilani were listening to through their headphones, it was built directly over the site of the sinking of the battleship *Arizona* in 1941 and to match the ship's length, to commemorate the lives lost that day.

Ahead of them in line was a group of six older men, dressed in hats and sashes from World War II. Some were in wheelchairs or walked with canes, like Holden. All of them were visibly shaken the moment they entered the memorial. Holden himself had goose bumps on his arms at the thought of the brave soldiers who'd perished that day with no warning, no chance to escape. He felt their panic, knew their fear, understood their need to protect others even at the cost of their own lives.

Lost in his thoughts, he barely noticed when the narration ended and Leilani put her hand on his arm. He leaned heavily on his cane, swallowing hard against the lump in his throat, and finally met her gaze. Her expression was both expectant and worried and he realized she must've asked him something. He removed his headphones and swiped a hand over his face. "I'm sorry?"

"I asked if you were all right," she whispered. "You look like you're going to pass out."

"I'm fine," he said, though he wasn't. Thankfully, a cool breeze was blowing in through the openings in the sides and ceiling of the stone monument, cooling him down a bit. At her dubious look, he gave her a wan smile. "Really. But could we just stand here a minute?"

"Sure." She moved them out of line and over to the railing, where the breeze was stronger, and the shade helped too. As the other patrons in their tour group made their way up toward the front of the memorial, where the names of all the people lost that day were etched into the stone, Leilani leaned her arms on the railing beside him and gazed out over the water. "Every time I come here it hits me. How fragile and precious life is. How quickly it can be taken from you." She shook her head and looked at the horizon. "Not that I should need the reminder."

"True." He watched the group of veterans approach the wall of names, most of them openly crying now, and he blinked away the sting in his own eyes. He never talked about the shooting with people he didn't know. It was still too raw. But for some reason, Leilani didn't feel like a stranger anymore. In fact, today he felt closer to her than he had anyone in a long, long time. He rubbed the ache in his right thigh and exhaled slowly before saying, "I shouldn't need the reminder either. Not after what happened in Chicago."

She looked sideways at him then, her tone quiet. "Is that where you were injured?"

He nodded, absently fiddling with the head of his cane. "There was an attack in the ER where I worked."

Leilani frowned and shifted to face him, the warmth of her arm brushing his. "Someone attacked you?"

Holden took a deep breath then dived in, afraid that if he stopped he wouldn't get it all out, and right now it felt like if he didn't get it all out at once, he'd choke. "A shooting. Gunman looking for opioids. Guy needed his fix. Came in, got past the security guards and opened fire when we refused to give him anything."

"Oh God. Holden, I'm so so—" she started, but he held up a hand.

"I tried to stop the guy. Well, me and my best friend, David. We tried to take him down before he could hurt anyone, but we failed. I failed." He swallowed hard and forced himself to continue. "Took a bullet to my right thigh. Shattered my femur but missed my femoral artery, luckily. David was applying a tourniquet to my leg to stop the bleeding when the gunman shot him point-blank in the back. He died instantly. The bullet that pierced his heart tore through my left shoulder as it exited his body. I lay there, bleeding beneath my best friend's body, until help arrived. Longest hour of my life. I thought I would die too. For a long time, I wished I had."

Silence fell between them for a long moment. Leilani reached over and took his hand, lacing her fingers through his before giving them a reassuring squeeze. "How long ago did it happen?"

"Almost a year." The group of veterans at the stone wall turned to make their way out of the memorial arm in arm, a brotherhood forged by grief and remembrance. Holden used his free hand to swipe at the dampness on his own cheeks, not caring now what people thought about him crying in public. Hell, almost every person in the place had tears in their eyes it was that moving.

He took another deep breath, then hazarded a glance over at Leilani. "I don't tell many people about that."

She nodded, staring at the lines of people going in and out. "I understand. I don't talk about the accident much either."

Her hand was still covering his, soft and strong and steady, just like the woman herself. He had the crazy urge to put his arm around her and pull her into his side, bury his nose in her sweet-smelling hair, hold her close and never let her go.

Whoops. No.

He wasn't staying here in Hawaii. He never stayed anywhere long these days. Leilani deserved a relationship that would last forever, not a fling with a broken man like him. She deserved better than he could give. So he kept to himself and pulled his hand away before he couldn't anymore. They still had the rest of the day to get through and the luau tonight. Best to keep things light and not mess it up by bringing his libido into the mix.

They got back in line and saw the carved names of the people who'd perished, then they rode back to the shore on the shuttle before exiting the park and making their way back to their vehicle. A strange sense of intimacy, a heightened connection, had formed between them after their mutual confessions about their past, but Holden refused to make it into anything more than it was. No matter that his heart yearned to explore the undeniable chemistry between them. Leilani was off-limits, same as before. They could be friends, good friends even, but not friends with benefits.

Nope.

Now, if he could just get his traitorous body on board with that plan, he'd be all set.

"So, where are we going next?" he asked, once they

were back in the car. He swallowed another pain pill, gritting his teeth against the lingering bitterness on his tongue, then forced a smile. They couldn't have a future together, but that didn't mean he couldn't savor the rest of the day.

"Figured we'd hit Honolulu Chinatown next, get some lunch, then head to the Iolani Place before hiking to Manoa Falls to round out the day." She grinned over at him before starting the engine and pulling out of their parking spot. "Sound good?"

"Sounds great," he said, ignoring the way his stomach somersaulted with need now every time he looked at her. He'd enjoy their time together, remember today and move on when it was over. No heartache, no emotions, no vulnerability. Because that's what he wanted.

Isn't it?

Except as they merged back onto the H1 highway toward Honolulu once more, the warmth in Holden's chest told him that quite possibly he'd already gotten far more attached to his lovely Hawaiian colleague than he'd ever intended, and the realization both thrilled and terrified him.

CHAPTER SIX

AFTER WANDERING AROUND the markets and arts district of Chinatown and enjoying a yummy late lunch of dim sum and noodles at the Maunakea Marketplace, they'd hit the Iolani Palace in downtown Honolulu before heading to a residential street just past Waakaua Street. Leilani parked near the curb and got out. It had been a while since she'd spent a day just enjoying all that her hometown of Honolulu had to offer, and she had Holden to thank.

She should also thank him for opening up to her about the shooting and for not pressing her about the car accident that had killed her family. In fact, she wanted to thank him for a lot of things, not the least of which was for helping her to relax and just breathe again.

Honestly, Leilani couldn't remember the last time she'd had such a fun, relaxing day.

No. Not relaxing. That wasn't the right word, given that her adrenaline spiked every time Holden brushed against her or leaned closer. More like exhilarating. She'd had an exhilarating day with him. Good thing the short hike to the falls would help to burn off some of her excess energy. Otherwise she just might tackle him and kiss him silly, which was unacceptable.

Leilani waited on the curb while Holden got out of the passenger side of the car, then hit the button on her key fob to lock the doors before they slowly started down the sidewalk toward the trailhead. He limped along beside her, looking better than he had back at the *Arizona* Memorial. When she first turned and saw him looking gray and desolate as a stormy sky, her immediate thought had been he was seasick. But then she'd seen the pain and panic in his eyes and feared an anxiety attack was on the way.

So she'd steered him over to the side of the space and heard his harrowing tale. Funny, but she'd always felt a bit isolated after the accident, as if she'd been the only person to experience such a violent and immediate loss. But hearing Holden speak about the attack in his ER made her realize that she wasn't as alone as she'd thought. Of course, she'd had twenty years to adjust to the past. For Holden it was still fresh, not even a year had passed.

Knowing what he'd been through made her want to reach out and hold him close, keep him safe from harm and soothe his wounded soul. Except she wasn't sure she could stop herself there, instead falling deeper into like or lust or whatever is was that sizzled between them.

She wasn't ready to go there, not now. Not with him. *Am I?*

No. It would be beyond stupid to get involved with the guy. He was only there temporarily, and even if he wasn't, he was her biggest rival for the job of her dreams—which she needed to remember to ask him about too. Amidst all the fun they'd had, she'd forgotten earlier, but now she needed to remember her true purpose for today. Find out more about him and why he was here, so she'd know better how to handle the promotion competition at work.

The fact that he looked adorable and smelled like sunshine was beside the point.

"It's only about a half mile ahead to the start of the

trail. Will you be okay?" she asked, giving him some side eye as they continued up the sidewalk.

"I'm good," he said, flashing her a quick crooked grin that did all sorts of naughty things inside her. "I took my other pain pill while we were in Chinatown, so I should be set for the next six hours at least."

"Great."

"Yeah."

They continued a while longer in companionable silence, dappled light through the palm fronds above creating patterns on the ground beneath their feet. The neighborhood was quiet and peaceful, just the occasional yap of a dog or the far-off rush of the ocean filling the air around them. The tang of freshly mowed grass tickled her nose and a pair of zebra doves waddled across the paths not far ahead of them.

"Did I ask you about Tommy Schrader?" Holden asked at last.

"Yeah, you did," she said, chuckling. "This morning back at the hotel."

"Right. Sorry." He looked away. "Thanks for today, by the way. All the places you've taken me to have been great."

"You're welcome." She pointed to the right and a sign for the trailhead. "There's so much more to see too. Besides Diamond Head, if you get the chance you should check out the snorkeling at Hanauma Bay. The zoo and aquarium in Waikiki are nice too. Oh, and Kualoa Ranch on the windward coast. It's beautiful, with a private nature reserve, working cattle ranch, as well as the most amazing zip line ever."

"Cool. I'd love to see it sometime." He closed his eyes and inhaled deep. "Maybe we can take another day trip together."

Her chest squeezed and she gulped. She'd like nothing better, so the answer was no.

When she didn't respond right away, he hurriedly said, "Or not. I'm sure I can find my way on my own. I didn't mean to—"

"No, no. It's fine." Liar. Leilani felt lots of things at the moment—excited, scared, nervous, aroused—but *fine* definitely wasn't one of them. Still, she'd gotten so used to blowing off people's concern over the years it was hard to shift gears now. "I mean, I appreciate the offer, but I'd have to check my schedule and things are a bit crazy right now at the hotel too, so my parents need my help sometimes in my off hours and…"

He gave her a curious look. "The Kims seem like good people. You were lucky to have them adopt you."

Glad for the change of subject, Leilani took the bait. "Yeah, they're awesome. They were friends of my parents, actually. It was easier for me to adjust to living with them than it might've been if they were strangers."

He nodded and continued beside her onto the wide, black, gravel-covered trail into the rain forest surrounding the waterfall. "Like I said before, I can't imagine how hard that must've been for you, losing your family. And at that age too. Being a teenager is hard enough as it is."

"True." The light was dimmer in here with the thick foliage and the temperature had dropped. Leilani shivered slightly and was surprised when Holden moved closer to share body heat. The scent of dirt and fresh growing things surrounded them, and the low hum of the waterfall ahead created a sense of privacy. She'd not gone into detail about the accident with Holden earlier at the beach, but with everything he'd shared with her about the shooting, she felt like, for the first time in a long time, she could open up with him too.

They crested a short hill and reached the falls. One hundred and fifty feet tall, the water cascaded down the granite walls behind it, shimmering with rainbows in the sun. She looked over at him, her pulse tripping a bit at his strong profile, his firm lips, so handsome, so kissable. He was almost as dazzling as the falls themselves. To distract herself she asked the most mundane thing she could think of. "Why'd you go into emergency medicine?"

Holden shrugged. "I always loved science as a kid and wanted to know how things worked, especially things inside the body. I'm a natural problem solver and detail oriented. But I'm also restless and a bit hyperactive, so I needed to choose a specialty that took that into consideration. Trauma surgery ticked all the boxes for me." He smiled, his teeth white and even in the slight shadows from the trees around them, and the barriers around her heart crumbled a bit more. "What about you?"

"Well," she said, moving her ponytail aside to reveal the scar on her neck. "See this?"

He leaned in closer, his warm breath tickling her skin. She suppressed another shiver, this one having nothing to do with the temperature and everything to do with the man beside her. "Wow. Is that from the accident?"

"It is." Leilani took a deep breath, then exhaled slowly before diving in. "We were on our way to the outlet mall, of all places. It was a sunny day and hot. The sky was blue and cloudless. Weird how I remember that, right?"

"Nah." Holden took her arm to pull her aside to let another couple pass them on the trail. "I remember all the details about the shooting. What people wore, what the room smelled like, how the floor felt sticky under my cheek. It's what trauma does to people's memories."

She nodded, then continued down the trail once the other people had passed. "Anyway, our car was an older model. When the other driver T-boned us, it sent us through the guardrail and down into a ravine. Car flipped over three times before landing on the roof, from what the police report says." She blinked hard against the tears that threatened to fall. "My brother and parents died instantly." They stopped under a natural canopy of tree trunks entwined over the trail, and Leilani rested back against their solid weight for support. "I was the only one left alive."

"Oh God." Holden stepped closer and took her hand this time, holding it close to his chest. The steady *thump-thump* of his heart beneath her palm helped ground her and kept her from getting lost in the past again. "I'm so sorry, Leilani. How in the world did you survive?"

"Sheer luck, I'm pretty sure." She gave a sad little laugh. "Both my legs were broken, but I was awake the whole time. I still have nightmares about it sometimes."

"I bet."

After another deep breath, she continued. "The scar on my neck is from a chunk of glass that lodged there. It nicked the artery but kept enough pressure until help arrived. Otherwise I would've died like the rest of my family. The only reason I'm here now is the paramedics and the ER staff who helped me that day. So that's why I went into emergency medicine. Because of their compassion and to pay my debt to them."

"Wow." He slowly slid his arm around her and pulled her into a hug. She didn't resist, too drained from telling her story and, well, it just felt too darned good being this close to him at last. He rested his chin on the top of her head and said again, "Wow."

The stroke of his fingers against her scalp felt so good it nearly hypnotized her.

"That's why you knew about the seat belt laws, isn't

it?" he asked after a moment, his voice ruffling the hair at her temple.

"Yeah," she said, pressing her cheek more firmly against his chest. "Seat belts and air bags would've made all the difference."

They stood there, wrapped in each other's arms and their own little world, until more people came down the trail and they had to step aside to allow them through. Once separated, neither seemed to know where to look or what to do with their hands.

For her part, it took all Leilani's willpower not to throw herself back into Holden's arms. But then, thankfully, her good old common sense kicked in, along with the warning bells in her head, telling her that no matter how tempting it might be to throw caution to the wind, she couldn't do that. Couldn't let him in because he'd either be leaving soon or possibly taking the job she wanted if he stayed. Both of which would only break her heart. And she'd had more than enough heartache for one lifetime.

Hoping for some time and space to get her head clear again, she started back down the trail toward the car, then waited for him to follow. "We should get back to the hotel so we can shower and change before tonight."

Holden stared at his reflection in the full-length mirror in his room early that evening and hoped he was dressed appropriately for a luau. Honestly, he had no idea what you wore to a party on the beach. Swim trunks, maybe, but that seemed a bit too relaxed.

He'd opted instead for a fresh Hawaiian shirt, this one in a pale turquoise color with small palm trees and desert islands on it and a clean pair of jeans. Flip-flops on his feet, per Leilani's advice, since it was the beach after all, and sand was everywhere.

His mind still churned through everything that had happened that day, all he'd seen, and the things he and Leilani had told each other. He still couldn't quite believe he'd confided in her about the shooting. He never really talked about it with anyone, outside of his therapist back in Chicago and occasionally with Helen. But telling Leilani about what had happened had felt different today. Scary, yes, but also strangely cathartic and right.

Maybe it was because of what she'd gone through with that awful car accident, but she'd never once made him feel judged or forced to go further with his story than he was willing. The fact that she'd also confided in him had made the exchange even more special. From working with her the past month, he knew she was almost as guarded as he was when it came to letting other people close, so for her to open up with him like that meant something.

Then, of course, there was that hug at the waterfall.

Couldn't deny that had been nice. Amazing, actually. And sure, it was ill-advised, given he had no business starting anything with Leilani. Holden never knew where he'd be from month to month, let alone year to year. Beginning a relationship only to move thousands of miles away wasn't fair to anyone.

Trouble was though, his heart seemed to have other yearnings where Leilani was concerned.

She was smart, sweet and made every nerve ending in his body stand at attention. But there was also a wealth of vulnerability lurking beneath her sleek, shiny exterior. Sort of like him. She'd been through things, dealt with pain most people never experienced, and yet she was still standing. That took guts. It also took a lot out of a person. Made them more resilient, yes, but at a cost. He absently rubbed the ache in his chest, then grabbed his cane.

Enough stewing over things that would never happen anyway.

He left his room and headed down to the lobby, where he was supposed to meet Leilani. Dinner was served at sunset, she'd said, but there were plenty of other things to see before then. It was going on seven now and the sun was just nearing the horizon. People milled about the lobby, most heading out toward the beach behind the hotel where the luau would take place. He'd chosen his outfit well, considering lots of other guys were wearing similar things. The ladies mainly had on casual dresses or skirts and a few had tropical flowers pinned in their hair. From somewhere outside the strains of ukulele music drifted through the air, and the general mood of the place was festive and fun.

Being taller than most people at six foot four did have its advantages, and over the tops of the people's heads, he spotted Leilani waiting for him against the wall near the exit to the beach. He started that way, only to find his path blocked by one of the hotel staff, a pretty Polynesian girl dressed in a traditional hula outfit.

"Aloha," she said, giving him a friendly, dimpled smile. She reached up and hung a lei made of black shiny shells around his neck, then kissed his cheek. *"Pōmakia'i."*

Blessings. He'd managed to pick up a few native words during his stay in Honolulu and he smiled down at the woman. Lord knew Holden and Leilani could use all the good fortune they could get.

"Pōmakia'I," he said in return.

He stepped around the woman and continued on toward the far wall, stopping short as he got his first full look at Leilani tonight.

Seeing her earlier today in shorts and a tank top or as she was usually dressed at work in scrubs was one thing. Seeing her tonight in a short, colorful sarong-style dress made of native tropical print purple and white fabric was, well... *Stunning.* Her sleek black hair was loose, streaming down her back like shimmering ink, and that strapless dress hugged her curves in all the right places, ending above her knee and revealing just enough of her tanned legs to give a guy all kinds of wicked fantasies.

She looked over and spotted him, then smiled, waving him over. He blinked hard, trying to clear his head of images of them hugging near the waterfall, of him pulling her closer, kissing her, holding her, unwinding that dress of hers and covering her naked body with his and driving her wild with passion until she was begging him for more...

Whoa, Nelly.

He ran a finger under his collar, wondering when the temperatures had gotten so warm. His pulse pounded and his blood thrummed with need, and man, oh, man—he was in serious trouble here.

"Holden," she called, "over here." The slight impatience edging her tone cut through his haze of lust, spurring him into action at last. He slowly limped through the people to where she stood near the open doorway. At least the spark of appreciation in her eyes as she took in his appearance made him feel a bit less awkward. She liked him too. That much was obvious. Too bad they couldn't explore it. If he'd had more time here, then maybe, just this once...

Helen's offer of the directorship position flashed back in his mind.

No. He couldn't take that job. Leilani wanted it. She'd be damned good at it too. Better than him, probably.

But if it gave me more time here in paradise...

"You look great," she said, her words a tad huskier than they'd been before. Or maybe that was just his imagination. Either way, the compliment headed straight southward through his body. "Like you belong here."

"Thanks," he managed, doing his best not to get lost in her eyes. "You look beautiful."

Pretty pink color suffused her cheeks before she looked away and gestured toward the outside. "Thanks. Shall we?"

He followed her out onto the cement patio, then down the stairs to the large grassy gardens spanning the distance between the hotel and the beach beyond. A line of palm trees designated the border between the two. Rows and rows of long tables and chairs had been set up for people to sit and eat, and along each side were buffet tables piled high with all sorts of food. Beyond those were other activities, like spear throwing and craft making. She led him through it all—the men weaving head wreaths out of coconut leaves, the women making leis, the young guys offering to paint temporary tattoos on the cute girls. All the hotel staff seemed to be participating, all dressed in native Hawaiian outfits—grass skirts for all with the women's being longer than the men's, elaborate neck pieces and headdresses, leis everywhere. It was walking into another world and Holden found himself completely enchanted.

"This is awesome," he said, accepting a leaf crown from one of the men weaving them. "I had no idea it would be so elaborate."

Leilani showed him a huge fire pit, where a whole pig was roasting beneath enormous banana leaves. The smell was so delicious, his stomach growled loudly. Lunch seemed way too far away at that point and he thought he could probably eat half that pig all by himself. "Don't worry," she said, as if reading his thoughts. "They've got more inside in the kitchen."

"Good, because I'm starving."

"Me too." She laughed, then took his arm, tugging him toward the front of the area, where a stage had been set up and currently a quartet of local musicians played a variety of Hawaiian music. That explained the ukuleles he'd heard earlier. Holden spotted Leilani's dad behind the stage and waved to him. Joe waved back. Leilani pulled Holden out of the way of a racing toddler, then kept her hand on his bare forearm, the heat of her searing his skin and bringing his earlier X-rated thoughts back to mind. They stopped near the best table in the bunch, front row, center stage. "This is where we're sitting for dinner and the show."

"Really?" He raised his brows. "Pays to know people in high places, huh?"

"It does." She winked, then pointed back to where the pig was roasting. Two burly staffers in native costumes had pulled away the banana leaves and were raising the whole roast pig up in the air with a loud grunt. The crowd applauded and Leilani leaned in close to whisper, "C'mon. Let's eat."

Didn't have to ask him twice. After loading up their plates with Kalua pig and barbecue chicken and *lomi* salmon and poi and fresh pineapple, they made their way back to the table just as Leilani's father took the stage as MC for the evening.

"Aloha! Welcome to the weekly luau at the Malu Huna Resort. Please help yourselves to the wonderful food and enjoy our entertainment this evening. Mahalo!"

The band started up again, joined by hula dancers, and Holden dug into his food with gusto. "This. Is. Amazing," he said around a bite of tangy, salty *lomi* salmon. The cold fish mixed with ripe tomatoes and onions was just the right foil for the sweeter pork and chicken. "Thanks for inviting me tonight. And thanks again for today."

"You're welcome." She smiled at him over the rim of her mai tai glass. "I love my hometown and am always glad to share it with others."

"It's great here. Seriously." He swallowed another bite of food, this time devouring a spoonful of poi. It was a bit like eating a mouthful of purple cream of wheat mixed with fruit. Not bad at all. Next he tried more pork and nearly fainted from the goodness. "Man, why does food never taste this amazing back on the mainland?"

Leilani snorted. "Probably because you didn't hike all over an island back in Chicago."

"True." He continued munching away as the band played on and more dancers joined them onstage. They were picking tourists from the crowd as well, but he kept his head down to avoid eye contact and not be chosen for humiliation. Finally, he'd had enough to eat and sat back, rubbing his full stomach and smiling lazily. "I don't think I've felt this full in forever."

"There's still haupia for dessert, don't forget." Leilani said, still eating. "Can't miss that."

"Nope." He sat back as a server cleared his empty dishes, then hobbled over to grab himself a plate of said haupia. It looked a bit like cheesecake without the crust, served on top of more banana leaves. He brought back two slices, one for himself and one for Leilani, then took a bite. It was good—creamy like cheesecake, but a burst from the coconut milk that was pure Hawaii. "Wow, this is really good too."

"Told you." Leilani finished her food at last, then pushed her plate aside and pulled her dessert over. "Speaking of Chicago, how exactly to you know Helen King?"

Holden almost choked on his bite of haupia but managed to swallow just in time. "She was a visiting surgeon at the hospital where I worked. We got to know each other there."

She saved my life.

He kept that last bit to himself, figuring he'd already told her more than enough about the shooting and there was no need to ruin the night by bringing it up again. "Why?"

"Just wondered." She shrugged, then watched the dancers for a bit. "I'm interested in the directorship position, you know."

Ah. So that's where this was headed. He wanted to tell her she had nothing to worry about, but then he couldn't really. Could he? Even if he didn't take the offer Helen had made him, there was the other issue of Helen not feeling like she knew Leilani well enough to trust her with that much authority yet. Maybe her temporary stint as director would become a full-time gig, maybe it wouldn't. Either way, Holden planned to be gone before then anyway. He tried to play it off with humor instead. "I kind of figured, since you're doing the job already and all."

"Has she offered you the job?" Leilani asked bluntly.

Yes.

"No," he lied. Helen had brought the subject up, but he'd turned it down. No need to bring that up either, right? Leilani watched him closely, her dark gaze seeming to see through to his very soul and for a moment he felt like a deer in headlights. Maybe he shouldn't have lied. If he told her the truth now though, that might be the end of all this, and he really didn't want it to be over. Not yet. He looked away, toward the stage, without really seeing it. "Why do you ask?"

"No reason," she said, the weight of her gaze resting on him a bit longer before moving away. "I just…" She sighed, then faced the stage as well, her tone turning resigned. "Listen, Holden. About what happened at the waterfall earlier. I don't want you to get the wrong idea. I like you. You're a good doctor, but I'm not looking for anything more, okay? We can be friends, but that's it." She took another bite of her haupia then pushed the rest aside. "And as friends, I'd appreciate a heads-up if you decide to pursue the directorship, all right?"

"All right." He was still trying to wrap his head around the swift change of subjects and how she'd sneaked in the bit about the waterfall into the mix, like he wouldn't notice that way. Of course, his analytical mind took it one step further, making him doubt the connecting and chemistry he'd felt between them earlier. He shouldn't care and yet, he did. In fact, her words stung far more than he wanted. Which was silly because he didn't want that either.

No strings, no relationships. That was his deal.

Isn't it?

Holden hung his head, more confused now than ever. Maybe it was the fact she'd beat him to the punch that bothered him. Usually he was the one stressing that there'd be nothing long-term. Yep, that had to be it.

He shoved aside the lingering pang of want inside him and brushed his hands off on his jeans, doing his best to play it all off as no big deal—when inside it felt like a very big deal indeed. "If I decide to go after the directorship, I promise I'll let you know. And don't worry about earlier. Look, we shared some personal things, hugged.

That was all," he said, trying to sound way more unaffected than he was. "No harm, no foul."

The band cleared the stage, replaced by a line of men with drums. Torches were lit around the area and the same big, burly guys who'd been weaving crowns and throwing spears earlier took the stage. A hush fell over the crowd as Leilani's father announced the fire dance. Much as Holden wanted to see it though, a strange restlessness had taken up inside him now and he needed to move, needed to get out of there and get some fresh air. Get his mind straight before he did something crazy like pull Leilani into his arms and prove to her that he didn't care about the job, to show her that their hug earlier really had meant something, no matter how much she denied it. Talk about fire. There was one raging inside him now that refused to be extinguished no matter how hard he tried.

Onstage, the male dancers stomped and grunted and beat their chests in a show of strength and dominance over the flames surrounding them. Holden pushed to his feet and grabbed his cane, feeling like he too was burning up from the emotions he'd tried so long to suppress after the shooting, but that Leilani had conjured back to life all too easily.

"I need to walk," he said to her before sidling away through the tables toward the beach beyond, one hand holding his cane and the other clenched at his side in frustration. "Be back in a bit."

CHAPTER SEVEN

LEILANI SAT AT the table for a few minutes, brain buzzing about what to do. He'd not really answered her question about the job, but she'd told him point-blank where she stood with that, so yeah. She'd put her cards on the table, careerwise. The next move there was up to him.

Emotionally though, there were still a lot of things she hadn't told him.

Things like if he'd have kissed her at the waterfall, she'd have let him. Would have allowed him a lot more than kisses too, if she were honest. An old, familiar lump of fear clogged her throat before she swallowed hard against it. Much as it terrified her to admit, she wanted Holden, plain and simple. If she were honest, she'd wanted him for a while now. That certainly explained the awareness sparking between them whenever he was around. She sipped her mai tai and tried to focus on the dancers onstage, but it was no use. All she could seem to think about now was him. About how well they'd worked together on the surfboard kid's case. About how adorable he'd looked that morning, awkward but adorable. About all the things he'd shared with her that day and how he'd made her feel less alone. About how he'd kept up with her, even though it had been hard with his leg. About how he'd not given up or given in.

He was kind and smart and more than competent as a surgeon. And truthfully, she'd always been a sucker for men with brains and brawn. Not to mention his dreamy hazel bedroom eyes.

Gah!

A waitress came by and replenished Leilani's drink, but she barely noticed now. All she could think about was the hug they'd shared earlier at the waterfall. The feel of him in her arms, the heat of his body warming her, the thud of his heart beneath her ear, steady, strong, solid.

The long-standing walls around her heart tumbled down even further.

Holden had lived through horrific events, just like her. He understood her in a way no other man ever had. And he didn't treat her differently because of what she'd been through either, whereas all the past men she'd been with had acted like she was made out of fragile china or something once they knew about the accident. Leilani wasn't breakable, well, not to that extent anyway.

She resisted the urge to rub the uncomfortable ache in her chest—yearning mixed with apprehension.

The trouble was Holden made her vulnerable in a whole new way. Part of her wanted to put as much distance as possible between them, let him go his way and stick to her own solitary path. But the other part of her longed to go after him, to find him on the beach and tell him that she didn't want forever, but she'd sure as hell take right now.

He made her want to take risks again. And that was perhaps the scariest thing of all.

Also, the most exhilarating. She couldn't remember the last time she'd felt so alive.

As the fire dancers reached a fevered pitch onstage, a volcano of feelings inside Leilani finally erupted as well, making her feel reckless and wild. She wasn't ready for a relationship with Holden, that was true. Relationships meant ties and connections and all sorts of other terrifying things that could rip out a person's heart and shatter it into a million pieces.

But a fling...

Well, flings were another beast entirely. If he agreed, a fling meant they could have their cake and eat it too. Given that Holden would most likely be moving on to another locum tenens position and the fact he'd flat out told her he wasn't interested in a relationship either, meant he might be game for an affair. He hadn't ruled that out at all.

She downed the rest of her mai tai in one gulp then stood. Desire vibrated through her like a tuning fork and adrenaline fizzed through her bloodstream. As the fire dancers' performance ended to thunderous applause and her dad took the mic again to introduce the Don Ho impersonator, Leilani weaved her way through the tables and headed for the beach in search of Holden.

Once she was past the light of the torches at the edge of gardens, it took her eyes a minute to adjust in the twilight. At first she didn't see him, then she spotted Holden near the shore, silhouetted by the full moon's light, his cane in one hand, his flip-flops in the other.

Heart racing in time with her steps, Leilani kicked off her own shoes, then rushed down toward the water, toward Holden, her mind still racing with discordant thoughts.

He wants you. He doesn't want you. It's all in your head. It's all in your heart.

Whatever the outcome, she had to try. Felt like she'd die if she didn't.

Leilani stopped a few feet behind Holden, hesitating before saying, "I lied."

For a moment he didn't turn, just stood there, staring out over the Pacific as the stars twinkled above. She lived and died in those few seconds. Then he turned to face her, his gaze dark in the shadows surrounding them. "About what?"

Feeling both brave and terrified at the same time, she stepped closer and forced herself to continue. She didn't do this, didn't run after men, didn't pursue her feelings. But tonight, with Holden, she couldn't stop herself. She wanted him and she'd have him, if he wanted her too. "I lied, earlier." She fumbled for her words. "I mean not about long-term things. I don't do those either. Not after the accident. But I do want you. I mean I want to be with you."

Damn. This was harder than she'd imagined. She took a deep breath and forced the rest out before she couldn't say it at all, grateful the darkness hid her flaming cheeks. "Do you want to have an affair with me?"

Yikes. Way to be blunt, girl.

Holden blinked at her a minute, unmoving, looking a bit stunned. She couldn't really blame him. Her statement had been about as romantic as a foot fungus. But then he moved closer, tossing his shoes aside along with his cane, to cup her cheeks in his hands. His expression was unreadable in the shadows, but the catch in his breath made her own heart trip.

Then he bent and brushed his lips over hers, feather-light, before capturing her mouth in a kiss that rocked her to her very soul. Forget romantic. This was mind-blowing, astounding, too much yet not enough. Would never be enough.

Oh man, I'm in trouble here.

He broke the kiss first, the crash of the waves against the shore mixing with their ragged breaths and the far-off crooning of the Don Ho singer belting out *Tiny Bubbles*. For the first time in a long time, Leilani felt more than just a sense of duty, more than pressure to succeed, more than the low-grade sadness of loss and grief.

She felt needed and wanted, and it made her head spin with joy.

Before she could think better of it, she slid her arms around Holden's neck and pulled him in for a deeper kiss.

Holden got lost in Leilani—her warmth, the taste of sweet pineapple and sinful promise on her tongue, her soft mewls of need as she pulled him closer, so close he wasn't sure where she ended and he began. His lower lip stung where the stitches pulled, but not enough to make him stop kissing her. He pulled her closer still, if that were possible.

Then the doubt demons in his brain crept forward once more. He shouldn't be doing this, shouldn't be holding her like this. He was broken and battered, inside and out, and didn't deserve a woman like her, a woman who was as sunny and vibrant as the island around her. A woman who'd overcome the darkness in her past to forge a bright new future for herself.

A future he wouldn't be around to share.

He summoned the last remnants of his willpower and pulled away—only a few inches, enough to rest his forehead against hers as they both fought to catch their breath. His hands were still cupping her cheeks, her silky hair tangled between his fingers, and her skin felt like hot velvet to his touch. But he had to let her go. It was the right thing to do.

He wasn't staying. He couldn't stay. He'd been running

so long—running from risk, from commitment, from the past—he didn't know how to stop. Leilani deserved so much more than he could give, even temporarily.

"I—" he started, only to be silenced by her fingers on his lips.

"An affair. That's all," she said, her voice hushed as the waves crashed nearby. "No strings, no pressure. I want you, Holden. For however long you'll be here."

The words made his pulse triple, sending a cascade of conflicting emotions through him—astonishment, excitement, want, sadness. That last one especially threw him for a loop. She was offering him exactly what he'd said he wanted. No strings attached. Just sex, fun, a fling. But for reasons he didn't want to examine too closely, the thought of a casual romp with Leilani made his chest pinch with loneliness.

She pulled back slightly, far enough to look up into his eyes, her own dark gaze as mysterious at the ocean beyond. "I know it's crazy. I just…" She hesitated, shaking her head. "I like you, Holden. And this chemistry between us is amazing. Be a shame not to explore that, right? Especially if we both know the score."

Right, his libido screamed in response, but he needed time to sort all this through to make sure he made the best decision. Because the last thing he wanted to do was screw things up between them. They still had to work together during his time here. If things went south between the sheets, it could have direct impact on their professional relationship, if they weren't careful.

And Holden was nothing if not careful these days.

The reminder was like a bucket of cold water over his head. He took a deep breath and tried again to speak, "Listen, I—"

Her dad called out from the garden area in the distance. "Lani? If you're out there, Mom and I could use some help in the kitchen."

With a sigh, she stepped back, letting her hands slide from around his neck and down his chest before letting him go completely. His nerve endings sizzled in their wake and his fingertips itched to pull her close once more, but instead Holden forced himself to turn away and pick up his cane and shoes.

"Be right there," Leilani called back, staring at him in the pale moonlight. The question in her gaze prickled his skin. "Just think about it, okay? When's your next shift at the hospital?"

"Sunday," he said, shaking the sand from his flip-flops to avoid looking at her. Because if he looked at her now, there was every chance he'd throw caution to the wind entirely and carry her back to his room to make love right then and there.

"Good. That gives us a couple days to think this through. I'm working then too." After a curt nod, she started back toward the hotel. "We'll talk again then."

Holden stayed where he was, watching her walk away and wondering when in the hell he'd lost complete control of his senses because damn if he didn't want to say yes to an affair.

CHAPTER EIGHT

LEILANI SAT IN her tiny office at the hospital two days later, working her way through a backlog of paperwork that had stacked up over the last week or so while she'd been too busy in the ER. Today was slower, so she'd decided to tackle some of it while she could.

Well, that and she needed a distraction for the constant replays of her kiss with Holden on the beach and her brazen invitation for them to have an affair.

You shouldn't have done that, the commonsense portion of her brain warned.

The thing was though, Leilani had spent her whole life up to this point doing what she *should* do. For once, she was ready to go with what she *wanted* to do. And what she wanted was Holden Ross.

Even if the whole idea of opening up with him like that pushed every crazy button inside her.

A one-night stand was one thing but having to get up the next morning and see that person at work was entirely another. Of course, there wasn't any specific rule against dating coworker's in Ohana policies. She'd checked. But there was still the possibility that things could go wrong. And the last thing she wanted was to mess up her good reputation here by getting chewed up and spit out by the rumor mill. At least that's the excuse she was going with.

Truth was she was scared and looking for an opportunity to back out of the whole thing. Perhaps that explained why she'd been avoiding him since Friday night. Making heated suggestions in the moonlight was one thing. Looking that person in the eye again in broad daylight was quite another. So she'd kept her head down and her nose to the grindstone since their kiss. Because of that, she hadn't really seen Holden much at all since Friday night.

They'd passed each other in the lobby of the hotel twice, her on her way in, him on his way out. Between the crowds and her parents' watchful gazes behind the front desk, neither of them had said more than a basic greeting. And today, they'd both been so busy working and had barely had two seconds to say hello, let alone get into anything deeper.

So yeah. Pins and needles didn't begin to describe what she felt, trying to figure out what to do. Thus, she purposely put herself in paperwork hell to keep her mind off things best forgotten. She rubbed her temple and concentrated again on the requisition form nurse Pam had filled out for the monthly supply order in the ER.

She'd just ticked off the charge for two crates of gloves when a knock sounded on her door. Without looking up, she called, "Come in."

"Dr. Kim," Helen King said, "do you have a moment?"

Leilani's heart stumbled. She swiveled fast on her chair to face the hospital administrator, wincing inwardly at the mess her office was in at the moment. She stood and quickly cleared away a pile of folders and binders off the chair against the wall, then swallowed hard, forcing a polite smile. "Yes, of course. Please, have a seat."

"Thank you." The older woman, looking crisp and professional as always, shut the door behind her and sat on the chair Leilani had just cleared for her. Her short white hair practically glowed beneath the overhead florescent lights and her blue gaze was unreadable, which only made the knot of anxiety inside Leilani tighten further. Beneath her right arm was tucked a large black binder.

"I wanted to speak to you about a project that needs done here in the ER," Dr. King said. "I'd like you and Dr. Ross to work on it together."

Right.

Leilani nodded. She'd forgotten about Holden mentioning that with everything else going on. "Absolutely. Whatever you need, Dr. King."

"Good." The older woman sat forward and crossed her legs, placing the thick binder on her lap. "As you know, we're preparing for our JCAHO recertification next year and part of that is reviewing all the security protocols in the emergency medicine department. Since you've been with us for nearly a decade and are interested in moving into the directorship role for the department in the future, this would be a great opportunity to show me your leadership skills."

"Absolutely."

"Great. I'll send you more information on what needs be done and the deadlines. I've asked Dr. Ross to assist you because he handled a similar project at a different facility, and I believe he'll be able to provide good insight on the project. I've already spoken with him about it and he's on board with assisting you in any way he can. I'll need the project completed by the end of next month." She handed the heavy binder to Leilani, who needed both hands to support its weight. "The current protocols are in there."

"Okay. Wonderful." Leilani set the thing aside on her desk, then stood when the hospital administrator did. "Is that all?"

"Yes. That's all for now." Dr. King walked to the door and stepped out, then leaned her head back in. "And thank you, Dr. Kim. I look forward to your completed results. It will go a long way toward helping me decide the best candidate for the directorship position."

Leilani stood there a moment longer after Dr. King had left, wrapping her head around her new assignment. One month wasn't a long time for a project of that size, especially when both she and Holden had other job duties to attend to as well. But if it meant impressing Dr. King and potentially winning her the directorship, Leilani would get it done.

Of course, that meant another mark in the "Don't sleep with Holden column," since the last thing she wanted was for a potential drama between the sheets to jeopardize their new project together. And Holden and Dr. King were good friends too. Couldn't forget that. If things with their fling went south, then that could impact her chances at the new job as well.

Ugh. Things were getting way too complicated way too fast.

As she sank back into her chair, her chest squeezed with disappointment.

Her whole body still thrummed each time she pictured them together on the beach, the feel of his hard muscles pressing against her soft curves, the taste of salt and coconut in his kisses, the low growl of need he'd given when she'd clung to him tighter...

Sizzling connections like that didn't come along very often. Plus, she liked spending time with him, talking to him, just being around him. Their day sightseeing together had been one of the best she'd had in a long, long time. But was exploring that worth losing the future she'd planned for herself?

Feeling more on edge than ever, she pushed to her feet and headed for the door. She needed to move, to think, to organize the jumbled thoughts in her head before she and Holden spoke again.

But she barely made it through the door before she collided with six foot four inches of solid temptation, wearing soft green scrubs and a sexy smile on his handsome face.

"Hey," he said, his voice a tad hesitant. "I was just coming to talk to you. I'm on break."

Hands off, her brain whispered, even as her ovaries danced a happy jig.

"Good. Because I need to talk to you too. Dr. King came to see me about the project."

She gestured him into her office, then closed the door behind him. Perhaps discussing work would keep her errant brain on track. Except as he passed her, the smell of soap from his skin and his citrusy shampoo drifted around her and her chest squeezed with yearning before she tamped it down. He took a seat in the chair vacated by Dr. King, then set his cane aside.

"Well, on the bright side, the work should go faster with two of us working on it, at least," he said.

"True." She leaned her hips back against the edge of her desk and crossed her arms over her lab coat and stethoscope. "I want to do a good job, since she said this will help her decide who gets the directorship position." Her gaze narrowed on him, trying to read past his usual stoic expression. "Are you sure you're not considering the job yourself? Tell me the truth, Holden."

A muscle ticked near his tense jaw and he frowned down at the floor. "I'm not planning on taking the job, no."

Good. One less thing to worry about.

Then he stood and stepped toward her and the desire she'd tried so hard to keep on low simmer since Friday rolled over into full boil again.

"Can we talk about something else now?" he asked, his rough, quiet tone sending molten warmth through her traitorous body. "Like Friday night."

Leilani squeezed her eyes shut and took a deep breath. "Yes."

When he didn't answer right away, she squinted one eye open to find him watching her with a narrowed gaze, his expression quizzical now, as if he was trying to figure her out. Finally, he took one more step closer and slid his arm around her waist, his hand resting on her lower back as she placed her palms on his chest. That same spark of attraction, of need, flared to life inside her, urging her to throw caution aside and live again, to take what she wanted from Holden and enjoy the moment because it would all be over too soon. She inhaled deep and hazarded a look up into his eyes, noting the same heat there, feeling the pound of his heart under her palms.

"If we're doing a project of this size, it would mean a lot of hours, a lot of time spent together," he said, his words barely more than a whisper. His hold on her tightened, causing her to bump into his chest. Her eyes fluttered shut as he bent and brushed his lips across hers before trailing his mouth down her cheek and jaw to nuzzle her neck and earlobe. "I haven't been able to think about anything but you since Friday."

She shivered with sensual delight, craving his touch more than her next breath, but that small part of her brain that was terrified of getting too close demanded she set boundaries up front. "Me neither," she panted. "But whatever happens, we can't let it interfere with work."

"Never," he vowed, his breath hot against her throat.

"I promise you this thing between us will stay between the sheets. I won't let it get out of hand."

"I won't either," she said, not knowing or caring if it was true or not. All she wanted right now was his mouth back on hers. That's when she noticed his stitches were gone. "You got them out?"

"I did. Removed them myself earlier today." He chuckled. "Good as new thanks to you, Doc."

He kissed her again then, deep and full of passion. When he finally pulled away, she felt bewitched and bewildered and all kinds of bothered. Holden straightened his scrub shirt, then gave her a sexy smile before grabbing his cane. "What time does your shift end?"

"Four," she managed to say past the tightness in her throat. "You?"

"Six." He headed for the door, then turned back to her with a wink. "Come to my room for dinner. Number 1402. Eight o'clock. Don't be late."

Holden stood before the doors leading out to his room's balcony later that evening, wondering exactly what had possessed him to be so bold earlier in Leilani's office. Maybe it was the fact he hadn't been able to stop thinking about her since their kiss on the beach. Maybe it was the fact that after that day they'd spent together and sharing their most traumatic moments in life, he felt the bond between them even more strongly than before.

Whatever it was, he was now on a collision course of his own making.

He turned slightly to look back over his shoulder at the small table set for two in the corner of his junior suite, set up by room service and complete with a white linen tablecloth and a bottle of champagne chilling in the ice bucket. The lights were lowered and the single candle at the center of the table flickered in the slight breeze drifting through the open doors, casting a soft glow around the room. The scent of surf and sea surrounded him, as did the occasional notes of music floating in from a party somewhere on the shore. All of it should've soothed him.

But Leilani was due to arrive any minute and Holden felt ready to jump out of his skin from a mix of nerves and excitement. Now he'd made the decision to pursue an affair with her, he was second-guessing himself. Was this the right choice? Yes, he wanted her more than he'd wanted any woman in a long, long time, perhaps ever. And yes, she'd already made it clear that this was only a temporary thing, that she didn't do forever. Usually he was the one saying those words, and honestly, he wasn't sure how he felt about that. His analytical brain said he should be relieved. Leilani had taken the guesswork out of it all, taken the burden off him by offering a no-strings-attached affair.

Instead though, he felt torn.

Which was stupid, because a guy like him who was too scarred both inside and out to settle down for long had no business wanting more than a few nights in paradise. He should be happy with what he got because it could all disappear in the blink of an eye anyway.

Then there was the fact they'd now be working on that project for Helen together. And while he'd agreed days ago to do it, even before Leilani knew about it, now he was feeling a bit off-kilter about it. The fact he should've thought it through better in the first place bugged him. Going over security measures in the ER would be triggering for him, regardless of whether they addressed a mass shooting scenario. But really, how could they not, since that type of violence was on the rise nationwide. Not to address it would be wrong.

But at the time of the meeting with Helen, he'd been eager to please and wanted to help in any way he could to repay her for saving his life back in Chicago. The fact she'd tried to pressure him about the directorship position didn't help either. Now he had firm proof from Leilani that she wanted the job, and he wouldn't go near it, even if Helen wanted otherwise. Leilani deserved the position. He scrubbed a hand over his face, then fiddled with the hem of his black T-shirt. No sense getting worked up about it now. He had bigger things to deal with at present.

Get out and live a little. Trust me—you'll be glad you did...

Helen's words echoed through his head again and made him wonder if perhaps his old friend had assigned them both to this security project as a way of bringing him and Leilani together.

He snorted and shook his head. Nah. He was just being paranoid now. Helen knew how squirrelly he was about commitment after the shooting, how he didn't want to stay in one place too long or form deep attachments. She wouldn't try to play matchmaker now to get him to stay in Hawaii.

Would she?

A knock sounded on his door while that thought was still stewing in his mind, making his heart nosedive to his knees. His pulse kicked into overdrive and his mouth dried from adrenaline, like he was some randy teen before the prom. No. Honestly, it didn't matter what Helen may or may not have intended. Both he and Leilani were consenting adults and they'd both made the choice to be here tonight. They were the engineers of their fates, at least in this room.

After a deep breath, he wiped his damp palms on the

legs of his jeans, then limped barefoot over to the door to answer, his trusty cane by his side.

Leilani stood in the hall, shuffling her feet and fiddling with her hair, looking as wary and wired as he felt. She'd worn jeans too, soft faded ones that hugged her curves and made his fingertips itch to unzip them. Her emerald green top highlighted her dark hair and eyes to perfection and contrasted with the pink flushing her cheeks. The V-neck of her shirt also gave him a tantalizing glimpse of her cleavage beneath and suddenly it seemed far too warm for comfort.

Holden resisted the urge to run a finger beneath the crewneck of his T-shirt and instead stepped back to allow her inside. "Hey. Come on in."

"Thanks." She gave him a tentative smile as she brushed past him, the graze of her arm against his sending a shower of sparks through his already-overtaxed nervous system and notching the want inside him higher. Leilani stopped at the end of the short entry hall and stared at the table set up in the corner. "Are we eating here?"

"Yeah," he said, limping up to stand behind her, close enough to catch a hint of her sweet jasmine scent. Her heat and fragrance lit him up like neon inside, and his body tightened against his wishes. To distract himself, he concentrated on dinner. "Uh, I thought after a busy day, it might be nice to just chill and relax. Is that okay?"

She exhaled slowly, then turned to face him with a smile as dazzling as the stars filling the cloudless night above. "It's perfect, actually. Thank you for thinking of it."

"My pleasure." Holden grinned back, imagining all the ways he'd like to pleasure her, with his mouth and hands and body. He cleared his throat and gestured toward the love seat against one wall. "Make yourself comfortable. There's champagne I can open if you want some."

"What are we having for dinner?" She walked over to the table and lifted one of the silver domes covering their plates, then the other before turning back to him. "Salads?"

"I figured it would be healthy and—"

And would keep for a while in case we didn't eat right away and ended up in bed first.

He didn't say that last part out loud, but then, it turned out he didn't have to, because next thing he knew, Leilani had kicked off her sandals and was heading back toward him, the heat in her eyes heading straight to his groin.

"Good. Because there's something else I'm hungry for right now..." She reached out and traced a finger down his cheek, his neck, his chest, lower still. "And it isn't food or booze."

Before he could rethink his actions, he let his cane fall to the floor and pulled her into his arms, kissing her again like he'd been wanting to since their encounter in her office earlier, since the night at the beach, since eternity. It started out as a light meeting of their lips, but soon morphed into something deeper and more intense. Leilani sighed and ran her hands up his pecs to his shoulders, then threaded her fingers through his hair, making him shiver as she pulled his body flush to hers. "How's your lip?"

"Never better." He whispered the words against the side of her neck, licking that special spot where throat met earlobe—the one that made her sigh and mewl with need. Holding her felt like the most natural thing in the world. Even when she slipped her hands beneath his T-shirt and tugged it off over his head, exposing the scar on his left shoulder from the shooting. Usually, he kept it hidden, a dark reminder of a dark day, but now with Leilani, he wanted her to see it all, every part of him, the good, the bad, the damaged and the whole. In fact, the only thing he was thinking about now was getting Leilani naked too, and into his bed—over him, under him, any way he could have her.

She leaned back slightly to meet his gaze. "Sure you don't want to eat now?"

"Oh, I want to eat all right," he growled, grinding his hips against hers and allowing her to feel the full extent of his arousal. "I plan to lick and taste every inch of you, sweetheart."

She snorted, then wriggled out of his arms to take off her shirt and toss it aside, revealing a pretty pink lace bra that served her breasts up to him like a sacred offering. He reached out a shaky hand to run the backs of his fingers across the tops of their soft curves.

Then Leilani undid the clasp, letting the straps fall down her arms before allowing the bra to fall to the floor, where she kicked it away with her toe.

Oh man.

His mouth watered in anticipation. Man, he couldn't wait to find out if she tasted as delectable as she looked, all soft and pink, with darker taut nipples.

Unable to resist feeling her skin against his any longer, Holden slipped one arm around her waist, tugging her close so her breasts grazed his bare chest.

Exquisite.

Then he went one step further, cupping one breast in the palm of his hand, his thumb teasing her nipple as he nuzzled the pulse point at the base of her neck, sliding his tongue along her collarbone. Her moan and answering shudder was nearly his undoing. He smiled, savoring the moment. "You like that?"

Her response emerged as more of a breathy sigh. "Yes."

"Good." Holden dropped to his knees, ignoring the protests from the muscles in his right thigh, and kissed her belly button, her stomach, the valley between her breasts, before taking one pretty pink nipple into his mouth.

"Holden," Leilani groaned, her nails scraping his scalp. "Please, don't stop."

"Never," he murmured, kissing his way over to her other nipple to lavish it with the same attention, his fingers tweaking it as he licked and nipped and sucked until she writhed against him, her head back and her expression pure bliss. Normally, he'd be unable to stay in such a position long, given his leg, but there was something about being with her that made his pain disappear.

The only thing that mattered now was this night, this moment, this woman.

Steering her by the hips, Holden managed to get them to the bed. His leg would protest the effort tomorrow, he was sure, but for now all he wanted was to get them both naked and to bury himself deep inside her. He'd stocked up on condoms in the nightstand, just in case.

Once Leilani's knees hit the edge of the mattress, she tipped back onto the bed, and he crawled atop the mattress over her. She ran her fingers up and down his spine, making him shudder again. It had been so long, too long, since anyone had touched him like this, since he'd allowed anyone close enough to try. And now that he had, he couldn't get enough.

Before he took his pleasure, however, he wanted to bring Leilani there first. Needed to see her come apart in his arms as he licked and kissed and suckled every square inch of her amazing body. To that end, he worked his way downward from her breasts, his fingers caressing her sides, her hips, before slipping between her parted thighs to cup the heat of her through her jeans.

"Holden," Leilani gasped, arching beneath him. "Please."

"Please what, sweetheart?" he whispered, nuzzling the sensitive skin above her waistband. "Tell me what you want."

"You. I want you," she panted, unzipping and pushing down her own jeans before kicking them off, leaving her in just panties. "Please. You're killing me."

He chuckled, ignoring the throb of his erection pressed against the mattress. He was determined to make all this last as long as possible. He parted her thighs even more and positioned himself between them, then slowly lowered her panties, inch by torturous inch, until she was completely exposed to him. The scent of her arousal nearly sent him over the edge again, but Holden forced himself to go slow.

After kissing his way up her inner thighs, he leaned forward and traced his tongue over her slick folds. Leilani bucked beneath him and would've thrown him off the bed if he hadn't been holding on so tight. Tenderly, reverently, he nuzzled her flesh, using his lips and tongue and fingers to bring her to the heights of ecstasy over and over again. When he inserted first one, then two fingers inside her, preparing her for him, she called out his name and he didn't think he'd ever heard a sweeter sound in his life.

"Holden! Holden, I…" Her breath caught and her body tightened around his finger as she climaxed in his arms. This was what he'd been imagining for days, weeks. Hearing her call out for him and knowing that he was responsible for that dreamy look on her gorgeous face.

Once her pleasure subsided, he kissed his way up her body, stopping to pay homage to her breasts again before leaning above her and smiling at the sated expression on her face. She gave him a sleepy grin, then pulled him down for another deep kiss. Her hand slid down his chest to the waistband of his jeans, then beneath to take his hard length in hand.

He could have orgasmed just from her touch, but he wanted more. Tonight, he wanted to be inside her. Tonight, he wanted everything with Leilani.

Summoning his last shreds of willpower, he captured her wrist, pulling her hand away from him and kissing her palm before letting her go. "If you touch me now, sweetheart, it'll all be over and I want this to last as long as possible."

"Me too," she said, touching his lips. "Make love to me, Holden."

No need for her to ask twice. He grabbed a small foil packet out of the nightstand drawer while kissing her again, then climbed off the bed to remove his jeans and boxer briefs, putting the condom on before returning to her side. Supporting his weight on his forearms, he leaned above her once more, positioning himself at her wet entrance, then hesitating. "You're sure about this?"

"Absolutely," she said, pulling him down for an open-mouthed kiss.

Holden entered her in one long thrust, holding still then to allow her body to adjust to his size. Leilani began to move beneath him, her hips rocking up into his and he withdrew nearly to his tip before thrusting into her once more. She was so hot and tight and wet, everything he'd imagined and so much more.

Pain jolted from his leg all too soon however, and he couldn't hide his wince.

She must have seen it because, before he knew what was happening, she rolled them, putting him flat on his back with her over him. He'd thought having her beneath him was hot. Having her above him like that though, with the moonlight streaming over her beautiful face as she rode them both to ecstasy drove his desire beyond anything he'd ever imagined. Soon they developed a rhythm that had them both teetering on the brink of orgasm again far too soon.

"Oh," Leilani cried. Her slick walls tightened around him, her nails scratched his pecs and her heels dug into the side of his hips, holding him so close, like she'd never let him go.

Then she cried out his name once more, her body squeezing his, milking him toward a climax that left Holden stunned, breathless and boneless and completely drained in the best possible way.

He might've blacked out from the incandescent pleasure, because the next time he blinked open his eyes, it was to find Leilani laying atop his chest, drawing tiny circles with her fingers through the smattering of hair on his pecs. He stroked his fingers through her silky hair and for those brief seconds, all seemed right with the world. In fact, Holden never wanted to move again.

Finally though, Leilani raised her head slightly to meet his gaze, her chin resting over his heart as she flashed him a weary smile. "That was incredible."

"It really was," he said, the remnants of his earlier excitement dissolving into warm sweetness and affection. Then his stomach rumbled, reminding him of the dinner they'd neglected. She giggled and he raised a brow at her. "How about a picnic in bed?"

She rolled off him before he could stop her and rushed across the hotel room naked to grab one of the giant Caesar salads topped with crab and lobster before rushing back to bed. They got situated against the headboard, under the covers, then she handed him a fork and napkin before digging into their feast first. "My favorite kind of picnic."

CHAPTER NINE

THE NEXT MORNING Leilani blinked her eyes open and squinted at the sunshine streaming in through the open doors to the balcony. It took her a minute to realize that she wasn't in her own room. The warm weight around her waist tightened and a nose pressed into the nape of her neck, close to the scar there.

Holden.

She yawned, then snuggled deeper into his embrace, not wanting to get up just yet, even though she was scheduled for another shift later that day. Her body ached in all the right ways and sleepy memories of the night before drifted back. Honestly, after their first round of lovemaking, she'd expected to have been worn out. But man, there was something about Holden that kept her engine revved on high. The guy definitely knew what he was doing between the sheets.

Not to mention his stamina. They'd ended up having sex twice more. Once in the bed and again in the bathtub, just before dawn. Afterward, they'd finally fallen asleep together, wrapped in each other arms.

Being with him had been amazing. Awesome. Enlightening.

She'd expected his past and injuries to maybe cause issues, but they'd found ways to make it work. In fact, some of the new positions they'd tried were better than she'd ever imagined. Plus, it was as if telling each other about their worst moments in life had opened them both up to just be present now and enjoy the moment. It was refreshing. It was energizing. It was addictive.

A girl could get used to that.

Except she really couldn't. Leilani sighed and slowly turned over to face a still-snoozing Holden. He would be gone soon, no matter how easy it might be to picture him now as a steady fixture in her life. Besides, she'd been the one to lay the ground rules between them at the start of all this. She couldn't be the one to change them now.

Could I?

She reached out and carefully ran her fingers along the strong line of his jaw, smiling at the feel of rough stubble against her skin. His long, dark lashes fanned over his high cheekbones and the usual tension around his full lips was gone. He looked so relaxed and peaceful in sleep she didn't want to wake him. Then she spotted the scar on his left shoulder and couldn't stop herself from touching that too. The thought that he might have died that day, been taken away before she'd ever had a chance to work with him, to know him, to…

Whoa, girl.

She stopped that last word before it fully formed, her chest constricting.

Nope. Not going there at all. No ties, no strings. That was their deal.

The happiness bubbling up inside her wasn't the *l* word. It was satisfaction.

Yeah. That was it. And sure, she liked Holden. Liked talking to him, liked working through cases with him. Liked the way he looked, the way he smiled, the way he smelled and tasted and…

"Hey." His rough, groggy voice wrapped around her like velvet, nudging her out of her head and back to the present. "What time is it?"

"Early," she said. From the angle of the early-morning sun streaming in, it couldn't have been much past six, she'd guessed. "You've got time before your shift. We both do."

"Good." He stretched, giving her a glorious view of his toned, tanned chest before propping himself up on one elbow to smile over at her, all lithe sinew and sexy male confidence. "How do you feel this morning?"

"Fine." The understatement of the century. Heat prickled her cheeks despite her wishes. "And you?"

"Leg's a bit sore after the workout last night, but otherwise, I'm excellent." He pulled her closer and she snuggled into his arms, tucking her head under his chin.

"We should try and get some more sleep while we can," she said against the pulse point at the base of his neck.

"Hmm." He kissed the top of her head and her whole body tingled, remembering how he'd felt moving against her last night, moving within her. The feel of his lips on hers, the taste of him on her tongue. If he hadn't mentioned his leg hurting, she might've climbed atop him again for round four and give him something nice to dream about.

As it was, she lay there until his soft snores filled the air, letting her mind race through what was becoming more undeniable to her by the second. Somewhere between the hospital and their day touring the island and their post-luau beach kiss, she'd gone way past *like* with this guy. In truth, she'd fallen head over heels for Holden.

Her muscles tensed and she took a few deep breaths to force herself to relax.

Love was a four-letter word where Leilani was concerned. Yes, she loved her adopted parents and U'i. But what she felt for Holden was different—deeper, bigger, stronger. And so much scarier.

She didn't want to love him. He'd be gone soon, and she'd be left to pick up the pieces, the same as she had after her family had died.

Unfortunately, it seemed her heart hadn't gotten that memo though, dammit.

She fell into a restless sleep, dreaming she was back on the highway heading for North Shore, then down in a ditch with Holden trapped and with her having no way to help him. She'd woken with a start, thankful to find him still asleep.

Leilani eased out of bed to shower before heading back to her room to have breakfast alone and get ready for her day. She'd hoped time and space would help her forget about her foolish thoughts of things with Holden being about anything more than mutual lust, but that pesky *l* word continued to dog her later as she started her shift at the hospital as well.

At least the ER was busy, so there was that.

"I haven't gone for a week and a half," the middle-aged black woman said, perched on the end of the table in trauma room three. "Tried mineral oil, bran cereal, even suppositories my family doc recommended. Nothing."

Leilani scrolled through the woman's file, frowning. "Well, I see here you're on a couple of different pain medications. Constipation is a common side effect with those. Are you drinking lots of water?"

"I'm trying," the woman said. "But my stomach's cramping and it hurts."

"Yes, it can cause a lot of pain. We can do an enema here today and see if that helps." She made a few notes on her tablet, then walked over to a drawer and pulled out a gown to hand to the woman. "Put that on and I'll be back in shortly to do an abdominal exam, Mrs. Nettles."

Leilani stepped back out into the hall and closed the door before walking over to the nurses' station. Pam was there, typing something into the computer behind the desk. She glanced up at Leilani, her gaze far too perceptive.

"Hey, Doc." Pam smiled. "You look awfully refreshed for a Monday. What'd you do over the weekend? Have a hot date or something?"

"What? No." Leilani frowned down at her tablet screen. "I'm probably going to need an enema for the patient in Room Three."

Pam snorted. "Way to change the subject. Dr. Ross seemed to have a bounce in his step too when I saw him a few minutes ago."

Leilani prayed her cheeks didn't look as hot as they felt. "Well, good for him. That has nothing to do with me."

"Uh-huh." Pam sounded entirely unconvinced. "Well, I think two people as great as you guys deserve happiness where you can find it."

"Thanks so much," Leilani said, her tone snarky. "But can we focus on patients, please?"

"Sure thing, Doc." Pam finished on the computer then came around the counter. "Heard you and Dr. Ross are going over the security protocols. That's good, since your loudmouth MVA patient showed up here again last night. We've all been a bit on edge since."

Her gaze flew to Pam's. "Mr. Chambers came back?"

"Yep," Pam said, gathering supplies for the enema patient onto a tray. "Claimed he still had pain and wanted more drugs."

"Did you call the police?" Leilani asked, concerned.

"No. One of the guards got him out of here." Pam snorted and shook her head. "But the guy was shouting the whole time about how we hadn't heard the last of him."

Damn. That wasn't good news. She had a bad feeling about that guy.

"If he shows up again, please text me right away, okay?" Leilani said, heading back toward room three with Pam by her side. "Let's finish examining Mrs. Nettles."

Hours later, Holden sat in Leilani's office, going over the safety polices for the ER. So far it hadn't been triggering at all, he was happy to say. In fact, it had all been about as exciting as watching paint dry. If it hadn't been for her nearness and the enchanting way she blushed each time their gazes caught, he probably would've dozed off a while ago. As it was, he couldn't stop thinking about their night together. Or the fact she'd been gone when he'd woken up again.

Usually, he would've been fine with that. Save them both the morning-after awkwardness. But being with Leilani last night had felt different. Seemed the more time he had with Leilani, the more he wanted. Which was not good.

He'd agreed to her terms. A fling, nothing more. He wouldn't go back on that promise now.

She didn't do relationships and he was the last guy in the world anyone should get involved with. There were too many shadows still lurking from his past, too many demons he still had to conquer from the shooting before he'd be good company long-term for anyone. Some days he wondered if he'd ever be victorious over them and get back to the man he was before the shooting. Not physically—since his physical therapist assured him his mobility would only improve with enough time and hard work—but emotionally. When he was with Leilani though, she made him feel like he could heal the darkness inside him, could open his heart and love again. Truthfully, after being with her, getting to know her better, he felt pretty invincible all around. But that was just the endorphins talking. He knew better than anyone what a lie that false sense of security was, that false high of connection that made you believe in rainbows and miracles and love…

Whoa, Nelly.

This wasn't love. They'd had one night together. Things didn't happen that fast.

Do they?

"Okay," she said, glancing over at him. "We've knocked out most of the updates, and I put this one off until the end, but it's probably the most important. I understand if you'd like me to handle this one on my own."

"The active shooter protocol." He raked his hand through his hair and shook his head, hoping to expel the sudden jolt of anxiety bolting through him. He'd been expecting this, and still it took his breath away. He pushed to his feet to pace. He could do this. It was important. It could save lives. "No. I can handle it. What's the current protocol?"

"It's pretty basic," she said, her expression concerned as she looked away from him and back to the black binder in front of her. "The last time this was revised was three years ago and the problem has only gotten worse since then. This only lists sheltering in place and calling the police."

"Both of those are good, but it's not enough." Holden

walked from one side of the ten-by-ten office to the other, then back again. His therapist back in Chicago had told him talking about what happened was good for him, better than keeping it all bottled up inside. Didn't mean it was easy though. Especially now, when he was still trying to process all his feelings from last night with Leilani. Still, this was a chance to create some good out of the tragedy he'd suffered. It's what David would've wanted. Perhaps he could find some closure too. Helen's suggestion that he help Leilani with the project made more sense taken in that light.

He took a deep breath, then began to talk his way through the problem while Leilani took notes. "We need to check out the Homeland Security website. They've got lots of good information and videos there to help us get the staff trained properly." He'd watched them all hundreds of times since the incident in Chicago, searching for reasons to explain why the shooting had happened and how to make sure it never happened again.

"Run, hide, fight are the three options basically. In the ER we've got both soft targets and crowded spaces to contend with." As he went over the whole "see something suspicious, say something" issue, Leilani gave him a worried look. He stopped his pacing and frowned. "What?"

"Nothing." She shook her head and scowled down at the paper again. "Pam mentioned that my patient from a few weeks ago, Greg Chambers, showed up here again last night asking for more pain meds."

"Did he make threats?" Holden asked, tension knotting between his shoulder blades.

"No." Leilani sighed. "Just lots of shouting and being generally disruptive. I told Pam to let me know immediately if he shows up again."

"Make sure to tell her to phone the cops too." He

clenched his fist around the head of his cane. "The shooter in Chicago was after drugs. All the staff need to be trained on how to handle those situations, so they don't escalate into something much worse. If we'd had the proper training back in Chicago, then…" His pulse stumbled at that and he leaned his hand against the wall for support. Dammit. The last thing he needed was a panic attack. Not now.

"Okay," Leilani said, getting up and guiding him back into his seat. She stayed close, crouching beside him, stroking his hair and murmuring comforting words near his ear to keep the anxiety at bay. Slowly, his breathing returned to normal and his vision cleared. The ache in his chest warmed, transforming from fear to affection to something deeper still…

No. No, no, no.

He didn't love Leilani. They'd only known each other a few weeks, hadn't spent more than a few days together, had only had one incredible night. None of that equaled a lifelong partnership. It was just the stress of this moment, wasn't it?

Except…

Holden took another deep inhale to calm his raging pulse and caught the sweet jasmine scent of her shampoo. Damn if his heart didn't tug a little bit further toward wanting forever with her.

"Hey," Leilani said, standing at last and moving back to her seat. "I think I can find enough information on the internet to handle this section of the protocol from here. How about I put it together and then you can go over it all later to make sure I didn't miss anything?"

He appreciated her concern, but needed to keep going, if for no other reason than if he didn't, he'd have nothing else to think about other than the fact he'd gone and done the last thing in the world he ever wanted to do—fall in love with Leilani Kim. And if that wasn't a disaster waiting to happen, he didn't know what was. He swallowed hard, then shook his head. "No. Let's keep going."

"Are you sure?" She cocked her head to the side, her ponytail swinging behind her.

"I'm sure."

They spent the next few hours watching videos online and reading PDF manuals, coming up with training programs and protocols for the staff. It would take a while to implement everything, but at least they knew what needed to be done and that was half the battle.

The knots that had formed between Holden's shoulder blades eased slightly and he sat back as a knock sounded on the door to Leilani's office.

Pam stuck her head inside. "Sorry to interrupt, guys, but the EMTs called. They've got a new case coming in. Toddler caught in the midst of a gang incident."

"Be right there," Holden said. "What's the ETA?"

"Five minutes out," Pam said before closing the door once more.

"I'll help," Leilani said. "I could use a break from all this stuff too."

They moved out into the bustling ER again, and Holden tugged on a fresh gown over his scrubs and grabbed his stethoscope from behind the nurses' station while Leilani did the same. They met up again near the ambulance bay doors to wait.

The knots inside Holden returned, but in his gut this time. Hurt kids were always the worst. Plus, there was also the unresolved, underlying tension of the situation with Leilani. He cared for her, far more than he should. Love made you vulnerable, and that led to heartache and pain in his experience.

An ambulance screeched to a halt outside and the EMTs rushed in with the new patient.

"Two-year-old girl, bullet fragments in left lower leg from a drive-by shooting," the paramedics said as they raced down the hallway toward the open trauma bay at the end. The little girl was wailing and squirming on the gurney.

"Please, help my daughter," the mother cried, holding on to her daughter's hand. "I tried to take cover, but it all happened so quick."

"She's in good hands, ma'am. I promise," Leilani said, glancing from the woman to Holden then back again. "Can you tell me your daughter's name?"

"Mari," the mother said. "Mari Hale."

Holden helped the EMTs transfer the child to the bed in the room, then moved in to take her vitals. "Pulse 125. BP 102 over 58. Respirations clear and normal." The little girl gave an angry wail and reached for her mom, who was fretting nearby as the cops arrived to take her statement. Holden placed a hand gently in the center of the little girl's chest and smiled down at her. "It's okay, sweetie. I promise we're going to take care of you."

Leilani moved in beside him to examine the wound to the little girl's leg. "One four-centimeter laceration to the left inner calf. On exam, her reflexes are normal and there doesn't appear to be any nerve damage or broken bones."

"Okay." Holden stepped back and slung his stethoscope around his neck once more as the nurses moved in to get an IV started. "Let's get X-rays of that left leg to be sure there's no internal damage and to visualize the foreign material lodged in there." He called over to the mother, who was speaking to the cops near the entrance to the trauma bay. "Ma'am, does your daughter have any allergies or underlying conditions we need to know about?"

The mother shook her head. "Will she be okay?"

"We'll do everything we can to make sure she is." Holden typed orders into his tablet for fluids and pain medications for the child, then waited while the techs wheeled the table out of the room and down the hall to the X-ray room. The mother went along, taking her daughter's hand again and singing to her to keep her calm.

Depending on how deeply the bullet fragments were embedded in the child's leg and where, would determine whether he could do a simple removal here in the ER of if she'd need more extensive surgery upstairs in the OR.

"You okay?" Leilani asked, her voice low.

"Yes," he said. Shooting cases always brought up painful memories, but he was a professional. He pushed past that to do his job and save lives. The fact that Leilani thought maybe he wasn't all right chafed. He turned away to talk to the cops instead. "What happened?"

"According to the mother, it was two rival gangs settling a dispute," one officer said.

"Gangs?" Holden scrunched his nose. "They have those in Hawaii?"

"Yep," the second officer said. "Not as bad as they were back in the nineties, but a few are still here. The mom and kid live in Halawa. Lots of the gang activity centered there these days."

Holden glanced sideways at Leilani for confirmation.

"The tourism board likes to keep it under wraps as much as possible, but unfortunately, it's true," she said. "The housing projects in Halawa are filled with low-income families looking for a way out. Gangs exploit that and use it to their advantage. And every once in a while there are turf wars."

"And this poor kid got caught up in one," the first officer said.

"Is the mother involved with the gangs?" Holden asked.

"No," the second officer said. "Just in the wrong place at the wrong time."

Holden knew all about that. "Did you catch the people who did this?"

"Not yet," the second officer said. "Neighbors generally don't want to get involved for fear of retaliation. The mother gave us descriptions of the men who opened fire though, so at least we've got that to go on."

"What about her and her daughter then?" Leilani asked, frowning. "Will they be safe when they go home?"

"Hard to say," the first officer said. "We'll add extra patrols for the next week or so, but that's about all we can do, since we're understaffed as it is at the moment."

Deep in thought, Holden exhaled slowly to calm the adrenaline thundering through his blood. The last thing he wanted to do was patch the kid up only to send her and her mother right back into a war zone.

The radiology techs wheeled the little girl back in a few minutes later. Both she and her mother were a bit calmer now, which was good. Holden pulled the films up on his tablet and assessed the situation. None of the fragments were too deeply embedded. He could remove them in the ER and send them on their way. Good for the little girl, bad for their situation at home.

Leilani peeked around his arm to see the images. "Thank goodness the damage is only superficial."

"Yes," he said quietly. "But I hate to discharge them until the guys who did this are caught."

"Then don't." She shrugged. "Say we need to keep her overnight for observation. I can make arrangements upstairs for a room with a foldout bed so the mom can stay with her."

"Are you sure?" He gazed down into her warm brown eyes and his heart swelled with emotion. The fact that they were on the same wavelength with the kid's case only reinforced the connection he felt for her elsewhere too. Which filled him with both happiness and trepidation.

Leilani nodded, and Holden turned back to the patient and her mother. "Right. I'll need to perform a minor surgery here in the ER to remove the bullet fragments still lodged in your daughter's leg, then we'll want to keep her at least overnight to make sure she doesn't develop any clots from the injury. Pam, can you get the procedure room set up for me?"

"Sure thing, Doc," Pam called, walking out into the hall.

"And I'll walk you through all the forms to sign and answer any questions you might have," Leilani said, guiding the mother toward the door. She glanced back once at Holden and gave him a small wink, then led the woman from the room.

Holden smiled down at the little girl. He couldn't do anything about the gangs out there, but he could keep her safe in the hospital, at least for tonight. Plus, helping his young patient and her mother gave him a break from stewing over the mess in his personal life. He took the little girl's hand and rested his arms on the bedside rail. "Don't worry, sweetie. We're going to take good care of you and your mom."

CHAPTER TEN

THE NEXT MORNING Holden was at the nurses' station, working through documentation on the charts from the patients he'd treated through the night. His mind wasn't fully on the task though, with part of it upstairs with little Mari Hale and her mother on the third floor. The two-year-old had come through the procedure to remove the bullet fragments from her leg nicely and there shouldn't be any lasting effects. He hoped that both the patient and her mother had gotten a good night's sleep in the peace and safety of the hospital.

Another part of his brain was still lingering on thoughts of Leilani. He'd missed sleeping with her last night, holding her close and kissing her awake so they could make love again. His body tightened at the memories of how amazing she'd felt in his arms, under him, around him, her soft cries filling his ears and the scent of her arousal driving his own passion to new heights.

But he shoved those thoughts aside. He was at work now. People needed him here. He needed to clear his head and get himself straightened out on this whole affair. No matter what his feelings were for Leilani, the thing between them was temporary because that's what she said she wanted. He refused to pressure her into anything she didn't want.

Period. Amen.

In fact, it was probably a good thing she'd been busy too since last night, dealing with her own cases and the security paperwork in her office, for them to have seen much of each other after dealing with the little girl. Images of her from their day on the town popped into his head. She'd been so happy, so relaxed and in her element as she'd showed him around the island. He honestly couldn't remember when he'd had a better day, or better company. It was almost enough to make him want to stick around Hawaii for a while…

"Hey, Doc," Pam called to him from her desk nearby. "Dr. King wants to see you again."

With a sigh, he finished the chart he was working on, then shut down his tablet and stood. Helen probably wanted to check in on their progress on the project. "Be right back then."

"Happy Monday, Doc," Pam said, chuckling as he headed for the elevators.

The ride to the fifth floor was fast, and the receptionist waved him into Helen's office even faster. She looked perfectly polished, as usual, which only made Holden feel more unkempt. He patted his hair to make sure it wasn't sticking up where it shouldn't, then took a seat, setting his cane aside and folding his hands atop his well-worn scrubs. "Good morning."

"Morning," Helen said from behind her desk, watching him over the rims of her reading glasses. She set aside the papers in her hands, then leaned forward, resting her weight on her forearms atop the desk. "So, Holden. Have you given any more thought to staying here in Honolulu?"

He had, yeah. But not for the reason Helen hoped, so he fibbed a bit. "Not really. I've been busy."

"Hmm. Working with Dr. Kim, I suspect," she said.

Well, it was due to Leilani, but not because of the project. "I've heard gossip that you two have been spending more time together."

He took a deep breath and stared at the beige carpet beneath his feet. Damn the rumor mill around this place. "I'm staying at the resort her parents own. We're bound to run into each other on occasion."

"Uh-huh." His old friend's tone suggested she didn't buy that for a minute. Helen sat back and crossed her arms, her gaze narrowing. "After everything you've been through, you deserve to be happy."

He hid his eye roll, barely. "Is this going to be some kind of pep talk? Because I really don't have time for it this morning. I need to get back to work."

"You know me better than that." Helen laughed. "I'm not a rainbows and sunshine kind of person."

Nah, she really wasn't. That's probably why they were such good friends. Helen told it like it was. A trait Holden appreciated even more after the shooting, when people treated him like he'd shatter at the slightest bump. Still, the last thing Holden wanted was relationship advice. "So, what is it you needed to see me about then?"

"I want you to think seriously about taking a permanent trauma surgeon position, Holden. That's what I want." When he didn't say anything, she continued. "Look, you turned down the directorship job, and I respect that. Having had a chance to go over Dr. Kim's credentials again, I think you're right. She is a better fit for the job. But that doesn't mean I can't use your skills elsewhere. You could stay in Honolulu, build a new life for yourself here. I can already see a change in you for the better since you arrived. You're more relaxed, less burdened by the past."

Holden took a deep breath and stared out the windows at the bright blue sky. Helen was right—he did feel better. Even his leg wasn't bothering him so much—well except for after his night with Leilani…

"Here," Helen said, handing him a job description. "At least look at what the job entails before you turn it down. I've added the salary I'm willing to pay in the corner there too, as an enticement."

Shaking off those forbidden thoughts, he focused on the paperwork. It was a good offer, with way more money than what he was making now, higher even than what he'd made back in Chicago. Plus, the benefits were great too. And it would allow him to put down roots again, if he wanted. Allow him to continue exploring this thing with Leilani too, if they both agreed.

But he wasn't quite ready to take the plunge yet. "Can I think about it for a few days?"

"Of course," Helen said, smiling. "Take as long as you need. I'm just glad you didn't flat out say no again. Now, get back to work. My next appointment should be here soon."

"Thanks." He hobbled to the door and opened it, stepping out into the hall before turning back. "I really do appreciate the offer and you're right. Staying in Honolulu would be nice."

He'd just closed the door and turned toward the elevators when he nearly collided with Leilani. He put his hand on her arm to steady her, then dropped it fast when he took in her stiff posture and remote expression. Not sure how to react, he fumbled his words. "Oh…uh…hi."

She blinked at him a moment before sidling around him, her tone quiet. "I have an appointment with Dr. King. Excuse me."

* * *

Leilani walked into Dr. King's office with her heart in her throat, Holden's words still ringing in her ears.

I really do appreciate the job offer and you're right. Staying in Honolulu would be nice...

Thoughts crashed through her brain at tsunami speed. When she'd first seen him in the hall, before he'd spotted her, she'd been happy, smiling, excited to be near him again. Then her brain processed his words to Dr. King. What job offer? The directorship? Did he want to stay in Honolulu? Did he want the same job she did? He'd said he didn't, but maybe he'd lied. Maybe he wanted to keep her off balance. Maybe he'd only slept with her as a distraction.

Wait. What?

No. Her heart didn't want to believe that, refused to believe that. But damn if those good old doubt demons from her past didn't resurface and refuse to be quiet. She ignored Holden's befuddled stare and fumbled her way past him and into Dr. King's office, closing the door behind her. She flexed her stiff fingers, more nervous now than her initial interview for the directorship position.

"Dr. Kim, please sit down." Dr. King gestured to a chair in front of her desk. "I wanted to ask you for an update on the security protocols for the ER."

Right. Okay. So, it wasn't about the job.

Why would it be, if she's already offered it to someone else? her mean mind supplied unhelpfully.

Leilani forced a smile she didn't feel and concentrated on explaining the pertinent details of the plans she and Holden had been working on downstairs earlier. "They're coming along well. We've worked through most of them already. The only one with substantial changes is the active shooter policy and I'm working on coming up with a substantial training protocol for the staff we can implement soon."

"Excellent," Dr. King said, fiddling with some paperwork on her desk, not looking at Leilani. "We'll need the details solidified by the end of the month to add to the rest of our recertification packet."

"I'll make sure it's completed." She swallowed hard, wondering if she should just come right out and ask about the directorship. Torn as she was about her feelings for Holden anyway, it would be better to know the truth up front so she could nurse her wounds in private. Her heart, her future, everything seemed to be on the line. If he'd lied, then she needed to know. Hurt stung her chest, but she shoved it aside. This was business. She had no right to be upset with Holden for taking the position out from under her. They were technically still rivals, after all. And the fact that she'd fallen for him anyway was entirely on her. Her heart pinched, but she pushed those feelings down deep. Personal feelings had no business in professional life. Honestly, if she'd been faced with the same choice, she would've made the same decision as Holden, wouldn't she?

Except no, she wouldn't have. Because she loved him, even though she shouldn't. It was so stupid. He'd never once said he wanted anything more than sex from her. She'd gone into their fling with her eyes wide-open and set the rules herself. No strings attached. The fact she wanted more now was her problem, not his.

Doing her best to stay pragmatic despite the monsoon of sadness inside her, Leilani cleared her throat and raised her chin. "Have you made a decision on the directorship position?"

"What?" Helen King looked up and seemed distracted. "Yes, I have, actually, Dr. Kim." Before she could say more, however, the phone on her desk jangled loudly, cutting her off. She held up a finger for Leilani to wait as she answered. "Yes, Dr. King speaking. What? Hang on." She covered the receiver and said to Leilani, "I'm sorry, I need to take this. Can we continue this later, Dr. Kim?" At Leilani's reluctant nod, Dr. King smiled. "Good. Have the receptionist pencil you in for another slot on your way out. Excuse me."

Right. Leilani left the office and headed back out to schedule her appointment then down to the ER, still stewing over things in her mind. She hadn't gotten the answers she needed from Dr. King, so it was time to be a big girl and confront Holden directly.

Determined, as soon as the doors opened and she stepped off into her department, Leilani made a beeline toward the nurses' station, her adrenaline pumping hotter with each step. "Where's Dr. Ross?"

Pam glanced up at her, her gaze a bit startled, and she took in Leilani's serious expression. "Exam room two. Stomach flu case. Everything okay, Doc?"

"Peachy," she said over her shoulder as she headed down the hall toward where Holden was working. She knocked on the door, then opened it to find him performing an abdominal exam on a middle-aged man. "Dr. Ross, can I speak with you a moment, please?"

"Uh, sure. Let me just finish with this patient first."

"I'll be waiting outside," she said, ignoring the curious look the nurse working with Holden gave her.

"It won't take long," he said.

Several minutes passed before he limped out of the room and followed Leilani down the hall to a quiet, deserted waiting area. "Is something wrong? Is it the little girl from last night?"

"No. The last time I checked in on her, Mari was fine."

Leilani crossed her arms, her toe tapping on the linoleum floor to burn off some excess energy. "Want to tell me about your meeting with Dr. King?"

His stoic expression grew more remote, telling her everything she needed to know. "Uh, no, Not really. Why?"

"Because it would have been nice to have a heads-up that you were taking the directorship job I wanted." Her anger piqued at his audacity, standing there looking shocked and innocent when he'd gone behind her back to swipe the job out from under her. She should've known better than to trust him. Letting people into your heart only caused you pain in the end. And yet Holden Ross had gotten past all her barriers. Dammit. She wasn't sure who she was more furious with—him or herself. "That's the offer you were thanking her for, wasn't it?"

"No." The confusion in his eyes quickly morphed to understanding. "Leilani, that's not what happened."

"So, she didn't offer you the directorship?"

"No, she did, but I turned it down."

She couldn't stop her derisive snort. "You turned it down? I don't believe you."

A small muscle ticked near his tight jaw. "Well, it's the truth. She asked me weeks ago about it and I told her I didn't want it. Told her I thought you should have it. She agreed."

"Excuse me?" she said, battling to keep her voice down to avoid feeding the rumor mills any further. "Then what offer were you thanking her for upstairs? And why would she ask for your opinion anyway?" Then a new thought occurred, as bad as the previous ones. "Wait a minute. Have you been spying on me for her?"

The more she thought about it, the more it made sense. All that time they'd spent together, the day touring the island, the cases they'd worked together, their night in each other's arms. All of it was a lie.

He cursed under his breath, crimson dotting his high cheekbones now. "No." He raked his hand through his hair again, something he did when he was stressed, she'd noticed. Well, she'd be stressed too if she'd been caught in a lie. "I mean, originally Helen did ask me about you because she said she knew so little about you, but all I told her was that you were more qualified for the directorship than me."

"Damn straight I am," she said, on a roll now, hurt driving her onward, completely ignoring the fact he'd all but said Leilani was getting the job. This was about far more than work now, as evidenced by the crushing ache in her heart. She'd loved him, dammit. Opened up to him. Trusted him. And look what it got her, more pain and sorrow, just like she'd feared. "So, I'm just supposed to believe you now, that everything that happened between us wasn't just some ploy to keep tabs on me for your friend?"

"Is that what you think? The kind of guy you think I am?" That knocked him back a step and pain flashed in his hazel eyes before being masked behind a flare of indignation. He turned away, swore again, then shook his head, his expression a blend of resignation and regret. "Well, I guess that works out just fine then, doesn't it? I'm glad to know the truth because that makes my decision a hell of a lot easier." He wasn't trying to keep his voice down now, and the other staff started noticing them at the end of the hall.

"You want to know about my meeting with Helen King? Fine. For your information, Leilani, the job I was referring to upstairs wasn't the directorship. It was a permanent trauma surgeon position. Not that it's any of your business. And if you don't believe me then there's nothing else I can say. I thought what we shared together the past few weeks, the connection between us, spoke for itself, but I guess I was wrong. I was so stupid to think this would work, to think there might be something more between us than a fling. You said you don't do relationships? Well, neither do I. Especially with a woman who's so afraid to let anyone in that she pushes everyone away."

"Me?" She stepped closer to him, her broken heart raging inside her. "You're the one who's always running. Always hiding from your past. Don't talk to me about trust when you flat out lied to me."

"I have never lied to you, Leilani," he said, the words bitten out. "I—"

Whatever he'd been about to say was silenced by what sounded like a firecracker going off near the front entrance to the ER. The loud bang was followed in short order by screaming and people running everywhere.

Leilani started down the hall toward the nurses' station. "What's happening?"

Holden grabbed her arm and hauled her back. "I don't know, but I do recognize that sound. It's gunfire."

CHAPTER ELEVEN

TIME SEEMED TO slow and speed up at the same time as Holden's mind raced and his blood froze. Shooting. Screams. Sinister flashbacks nearly drove him to his knees. Another ER, another gunman. David, bleeding out on the tile floor as Holden lay beside him, too injured himself to help.

Oh God. Not again. Please not again.

"Holden!" Leilani shouted, struggling to break his hold on her arm. "Let me go! We've got to help those people!"

He wasn't expecting the punch of her elbow to his stomach and he doubled over, releasing her as he struggled to catch his breath.

"Wait!" he called as she ran off toward the front entrance, toward danger. "Leilani!"

"Use the emergency phone to call the police," she shouted to him before disappearing around the corner.

Damn.

Blood pounded loud in his ears, making it hard to hear as he dialed 911. After relaying the info to the dispatcher, he hung up, then swallowed hard and hobbled toward the corner, his breathing labored from the anxiety squeezing his chest. If anything happened to Leilani, he'd never forgive himself. Regardless of what she thought of him now, he couldn't lose her, not like he'd lost David. He couldn't fail this time.

But what if you do...?

Teeth gritted, he pressed his back to the wall, the coolness shocking to his heated skin. He feared the shooter might be one of the gang members who'd shot the little girl upstairs, come to finish off the job. But as a male voice yelled, he realized it wasn't a gangbanger at all. He recognized that voice. Greg Chambers, the guy who'd punched him a few weeks back. The man Leilani had warned him about the day before in her office.

"Give me my opioids and no one gets hurt," the guy snarled. "Or don't and die."

Reality blurred again, between the ER in Chicago and now. The other shooter had wanted drugs too and he'd made the same threat. Made good on that threat too. Dammit. Holden cursed under his breath. The police were on their way, but what if they didn't make it in time? They hadn't been able to save David. No. It was up to him.

His analytical mind kicked in at last, slicing through the panic like a scalpel. Berating himself and "what if" thinking wouldn't help anyone now. Action. He needed to move, needed to find a way to take down Greg Chambers before he hurt anyone else.

Run. Hide. Fight.

Those were the words Homeland Security drilled into the heads of everyone who encountered an active shooter situation. Running was out, since the gunman was already here. Hiding would be good for those in the lobby, but not for Holden. He was the one person here who'd been through this before. He was outside the current hot zone and in the best position to surprise the attacker and possibly take him down and disarm him before the cops arrived.

More shots rang out, followed by screams and crying.

The unbearable tension inside Holden ratcheted higher as precious seconds ticked by.

Think, Holden. Think.

Eyes closed he rested his head back against the wall and thought through what he knew. Greg Chambers was an addict. He liked alcohol and drugs. Chances were good he'd be intoxicated now, since no sober person would attack an ER. If he was lucky, the guy's reflexes and reaction time would be affected by whatever substances were in his system. Holden could use that, if he could sneak up on the other man. He glanced down at his cane and winced. Hard to be stealthy with that thing. Which meant he needed to leave it behind.

Okay. Fine.

He set the cane aside, then took another deep breath, listening. Greg Chambers was still talking, but Holden was too far away to understand what he was saying. Then another voice, clear and bright, halted his heart midbeat. Leilani. As fast as his pulse stopped, it kicked back into overdrive again. If the bastard harmed one hair on her head…

Move. Now!

Holden hazarded a peek around the corner and spotted the shooter with his back toward the hallway. Saw Leilani near the nurses' station, hands up as she faced down the gunman while the people behind her cowered on the floor. She was so brave, so good, so beautiful and honest and true and he realized in that moment he'd do anything to keep her safe.

Even risk his own life.

After one more deep breath for courage, Holden inched his way toward the front entrance, doing his best to stay as silent as possible. His right leg protested with each step, but he pressed onward, knowing that if he didn't act now, it might be too late.

"Shut up, bitch!" Greg shouted, aiming his gun at Leilani again. "Sick of your talking. Give me my damned drugs before I blow your head off!"

"I can't do that, sir," she responded, her voice calm and level. Her dark gaze flicked over to Holden then back to the shooter, faster than a blink, but he felt that look like a lifeline. She'd seen him, knew he was coming to help. Leilani continued. "The police are on their way. Let these people go and put your gun down. You can't win here."

"Shut up!" Chambers yelled, his tone more frantic now as he looked around wildly. "I ain't going to jail again. I can't."

In the far distance, the wail of sirens cut through the eerie quiet in the ER. Holden spotted the two security guards near the automatic doors. One was down and bleeding. Holden couldn't see how badly. The other guard was kneeling beside him, trying to help his wounded comrade. Both guards' guns were at Chambers's feet, probably kicked there as the gunman had ordered.

"Give me the opioids and let me the hell out of here," Greg screamed again, waving his weapon around. "Do it, or I'll open fire. I swear I will. Ain't got nothing left to live for anyway."

He took aim at Leilani, at point-blank range.

"Bye, Lady Doc," Greg Chambers said. "You had your chance."

The snick of the trigger cocking echoed through Holden's head like a cannon blast. Adrenaline and desperation electrified his blood and he forgot about planning, forgot about strategy. Forgot about everything except saving the woman he loved.

Holden charged, wrapping his arm around Chambers's

neck from behind and jerking him backward along with his weapon, sending the bullets skyward. He wasn't sure what was louder, the bullets firing from the semiautomatic or the screams from the people crouched in the lobby. Florescent bulbs shattered and chunks of ceiling tile rained down.

The muscles in his right thigh shrieked from the strain, but Holden held on, knocking the gun from Greg Chambers's hands, then flipping the smaller man over his shoulder and tossing him flat on his back on the floor. Tires screeched outside the front entrance and sirens screamed inside as the Honolulu PD SWAT team raced inside and took control of the gunman.

"Get off me!" the guy screamed, fighting and wrestling to get free as the cops handcuffed him and hauled him to his feet, reading him his Miranda rights as they walked him out the door. "I ain't going to jail!"

The adrenaline and shock wore off, and Holden slumped back onto his butt on the floor, breathing fast as he started to crawl toward the injured security guard near the door.

"Doc, we need help over here!" Pam called from behind him. "She's been hit."

His chest constricted and his heart dropped to his toes.

Holden swiveled fast, his leg cramping with pain, to see Leilani slumped on the floor against the front of the reception desk, a blotch of crimson blooming on the left arm of her pristine white lab coat. She looked pale. Too pale.

No. Please God, no!

"Leilani," he said, reaching her. She frowned and mumbled something but didn't open her eyes. David had looked like that too, just before he'd lost consciousness. He'd never woken up again.

No. No, no, no. I won't fail this time. I can't fail this time. Please don't let me fail this time.

His hands shook as he carefully slipped her arm from the lab coat then pushed up the sleeve of her shirt. From the looks of it, the bullet had passed clean through. It had also passed perilously close to her brachial artery. Years of medical training drowned out his anxiety and emotional turmoil and spurred him into action once more. "Check her vitals. Order six units of blood on standby, in case she's hypotensive. We need an O2 Sat and X-rays to see the damage. Let's move, people."

While the residents dealt with the wounded guard and the other patients, Holden stuck by Leilani's side. He held her hand as they raced toward trauma bay one, refusing to let go, even as Helen King ran into the room and took over.

"Holden, tell me what we've got," she said as she did her own exam of Leilani's wounds. He recited back what he knew and what he'd ordered, all the while still clutching her too-cold fingers. When he was done, Helen came over and put her hands on his shoulders, shaking him slightly. "You're in shock, Dr. Ross. I've got her. Go and sit in the waiting room. You look like you're ready to pass out. You saved the lives of a lot of people today. You're a hero. Now go rest and talk to the cops."

Pam took Holden's arm and led him back toward the front entrance and helped him into a chair. He couldn't seem to stop shaking. "I can't lose her," he said to Pam. "I can't."

"She's in the best care possible, Doc. You know that." Pam shoved a cup of water into his hands before heading back toward the trauma bay. "I'll keep you posted on her condition."

A while later the cops took his statement, then left him

alone with his thoughts. Holden tipped his head back to stare at the bullet holes in the ceiling and swallowed hard against the lump in his throat.

You saved the lives of a lot of people today. You're a hero.

Helen's words looped in his head but rang hollow in his aching heart.

He didn't want to be a hero. He just wanted Leilani alive and well again.

Leilani blinked her eyes open slowly, squinting into the too-bright sunshine streaming in through the windows of her room at the hotel. Except…

She frowned. The windows were on the wrong side of the room. And where were the curtains? And what was that smell? Sharp, antiseptic. Not floor cleaner or bleach, but familiar, like…

Oh God!

Head fuzzy from pain meds, memories slowly began to resurface.

Gunshots, Holden tackling the shooter, shouting, screams, a sharp burst of pain then darkness…

She moaned and tried to sit up only to be held down by the IV, tubes and wires connecting her to the monitors beside her bed. Her left arm ached like hell and her mouth felt dry as cotton.

"Welcome back, Dr. Kim," a woman's voice said from nearby. Leilani blinked hard and turned her head on the pillow to see Dr. King at the counter across the room. "How are you feeling?"

"Like crap," she mumbled, trying to scoot up farther in her hospital bed and failing. The whole scenario brought back too many memories from after the car accident for her comfort. "What's going on? Where's Holden?"

"He's fine. Should be returning to your bedside shortly," Dr. King said, moving to check the monitors attached to the blood pressure cuff and the pulse ox on Leilani's finger. "I made him go home to sleep and shower. Otherwise he hasn't left your side since the surgery."

"Surgery?" The beginnings of a headache throbbed behind Leilani's temples as she tried to recall more about what had occurred in the ER. "I had surgery?" She glanced down at the bandages wrapping her left bicep. "Who operated?"

"Yours truly." Dr. King smiled, then adjusted the IV drip settings on the machine. "Holden was a bit too close to the situation to handle it. And he was exhausted after taking down that gunman."

That much Leilani did remember. Considering what he'd been through, his actions had taken a tremendous amount of courage. He'd been a hero, saving her and countless other people. She ached to hold him and thank him for all he'd done, to beg him to forgive her for accusing him of stealing her job. He hadn't stolen anything. Except her heart.

"Anyway, I had to make sure you healed up nicely. Can't have my new Director of Emergency Medicine less than healthy." Dr. King stood near the end of the bed as Leilani took that in. "If you still want the position, that is."

"I…" She swallowed hard. "Yes, I want it. But what about Holden?"

"What about him?" Holden said from the doorway. Limping in, he set his cane aside, then took a seat in the chair at her bedside. "You look better now. Not so pale."

"Her vitals are good," Dr. King said. "And her wound is healing nicely. I'm just going to pop out for a minute.

Dr. Kim, we can discuss your new position further once you're back to work."

An awkward silence descended once the door closed behind Dr. King, leaving Leilani and Holden alone in the room.

"So, I guess I should thank you," Leilani said at last.

"For what?" Holden frowned.

"For saving my life."

He gave a derisive snort. "I didn't save anything. In fact, I'm the reason you got shot in the first place. After all the research I did into active shooter situations, I should've known better than to tackle a man with a weapon."

"What?" Now it was her turn to scowl. "You're kidding, right? I don't remember everything that happened in the ER, but I do remember you taking that guy down. If anyone's at fault for me getting shot, it's Greg Chambers. You were a her—"

Holden help up a hand to stop her. "Please don't say hero. That's the last thing I am."

Leilani ignored the pain in her left arm this time and shoved higher in her bed to put them closer to eye level. "Well, whatever you want to call yourself, you saved a lot of lives down there and I'm grateful to you." She exhaled slowly and fiddled with the edge of the sheet with her right hand. "And I'm sorry."

"Sorry?" His expression turned confused. "What do you have to be sorry for?"

"For accusing you of stealing the directorship job. That was stupid of me. I should have believed you." She shook her head and gave a sad little chuckle. "I don't know why I didn't, except that I've been a mess emotionally since the luau and then that night we spent together and I took it out on you, and…" She shrugged, looking anywhere but at him. "I'm sorry."

"It's okay. I haven't exactly been thinking clearly myself since that night." He sighed and glanced toward the windows, giving her a view of his handsome profile. His hair was still damp from his shower and his navy blue polo shirt clung to his muscled torso like a second skin. Leilani bit her lip. He really was the most gorgeous man she'd ever seen, even with the dark circles under his eyes and the lines of tension around his mouth. She longed to trace her fingers down his cheek and kiss away his stress but didn't dare. Not until they hashed this out between them.

"Look, Leilani." His deep voice did way more than the meds to ease her aches and pains. "I know we agreed to just a fling, but the thing is, I don't think I can do that anymore."

"Oh." Her pulse stumbled and the monitor beeped loud. Apparently, she'd misread the situation entirely. Just because she'd fallen head over heels for the guy didn't mean he felt the same for her. She should have kept her barriers up, should have known better. "Don't worry about it," she said, doing her best to act like it wasn't a big deal and failing miserably as tears stung the back of her eyes. Leilani blinked hard to keep them at bay, but her vision clouded despite her wishes. "We can go back to just being colleagues. Probably better that way since we'll be working together permanently."

"Yeah," he said absently. Then his attention snapped to her and his scowl deepened. "No. That's not what I meant."

"You mean you're not taking the trauma surgeon job?" she asked, confused.

"No. I am. I just… I don't want to be your friend,

Leilani." Holden reached through the bedrail to take her hand, careful of her injuries. "What I mean to say is that I want to be way more than just your friend." He sighed and stared down at their entwined fingers. "I know I promised to just have a fling, no strings attached, but I can't do that anymore because I fell in love with you."

Stunned, she took a deep breath, her pulse accelerating once more. "Uh…"

"No. Let me finish, please." He exhaled slowly, his broad shoulders slumping. "You were right. I was running. I've been running since I left Chicago. Too afraid of getting hurt again to settle down anywhere. I never wanted to get that close to anyone again. Losing my best friend, David, nearly killed me, even more than the bullets did." He gave her fingers a gentle squeeze. "But then I met you. You were so full of life, so vibrant and smart and funny and kind. You were everything I didn't know I needed. You healed me, from the inside out. Showed me I could laugh again, love again. So no, I can't go back to just having a fling with you, Leilani Kim. Because I want more. So much more. If you'll have me."

She sniffled, her tears flowing freely now. "You're the one who healed me, Holden. I thought I'd gotten over the accident that took my family all those years ago, but I'd just walled myself off, thinking that not caring too deeply would keep me safe. All that did though was make me lonely. You opened my heart again." She laughed, then winced when the movement hurt her arm. "I love you too, Holden Ross."

"You do?" His sweet, hesitant smile made her breath catch.

"I do."

He leaned closer to brush his lips across hers, and she

let go of his hand to slip her fingers behind his neck to keep him close.

"I'm glad you're staying in Hawaii," she said at last, after he'd pulled back slightly.

"Me too." He nuzzled his nose against hers. "Does this mean we're officially dating?"

"I believe it does, Dr. Ross," Leilani said, winking. "The rumor mill will be all abuzz."

"Good, Dr. Kim." Holden kissed her again. "Give them something new to talk about."

CHAPTER TWELVE

One year later...

"WHAT DO WE have coming in?" Leilani asked, tugging on a fresh gown and heading toward the ambulance bay entrance.

Nurse Pam was waiting there for her, already geared up. "Per the EMTs, it was a rollover accident on the H1. Family of five. ETA two minutes."

Not exactly how she'd expected to spend the morning of her wedding day, but the ER had been short-staffed and as Director of Emergency Medicine, it was her duty to fill in when needed. Besides, it helped her stress levels to keep busy, since all the planning was done and all she had left to do was show up and marry the man of her dreams.

First though, it seemed like an ironic twist of fate that the last case she worked as a single woman was a rollover. Her biological family hadn't survived their similar accident, but today, she planned to do all she could to ensure history did not repeat itself.

Two ambulances screeched to a halt outside and soon the automatic doors whooshed open as five gurneys were wheeled in by three sets of paramedics. The trauma surgeon on call—not Holden, thank goodness—and a resident took the mother and son and the son's girlfriend. Leilani and another resident took the father and the daughter.

"You're in good hands, sir. Just lie still and let us do all the work, okay?" she said to the father as they raced for an open trauma bay. Then she focused on the EMT racing along on the other side of the gurney. "Rundown, please."

"Car rolled five times. Wife was driving," the EMT said.

"I just remember coming around the bend and that other car slammed into us. Then rolling and rolling."

"It was so scary," the daughter said as they transferred her to a bed adjacent to the one her father was on, her voice shaky with tears. "My first car accident. With the four people I love most."

Leilani's heart squeezed with sympathy. Twenty-one years ago, she'd experienced her first car accident too. Worst day of her life. Funny how life worked, because now—today—would be the best day ever. Once her shift was over, of course. She rolled her left shoulder to ease the ache in her bicep, then began taking the father's vitals while the resident working alongside her in the trauma bay did the same with the daughter.

"Do you remember what happened, sir?" Leilani asked the father.

"I remember my life flashing before my eyes," he said, his voice husky with emotion. "I remember glass flying and people screaming, then everything stopped. I'm just glad we're all still alive."

"Me too, sir," she said, swallowing against an unexpected lump of gratitude in her throat. "Me too."

"Patient is complaining of abdominal pain," the resident called over to Leilani. "I'd like to get an ultrasound to rule out internal injuries or bleeding."

"Do it," Leilani said before continuing her own exam on the father. "Where are you experiencing pain, sir?"

"My neck is killing me." He lifted his arm to point at his throat, then winced. "My chest hurts too. How are my wife and son? His girlfriend?"

"As far as I know, they're doing fine, but I'll be sure to check on that for you as soon as we get you set up here." She finished checking his vitals and rattled them off to Pam to enter into the computer, then carefully removed the plastic neck brace the EMTs had applied and examined the man's neck while a tech wheeled in an ultrasound machine for the daughter. "After you finish with that patient, I'll need a cardiac ultrasound over here too for the father, please. He's complaining of chest pain and has a history of high blood pressure and arteriosclerosis. Rule out any issues there, please. While we wait, let's see if CT can work him in for an emergency C-spine. I'm concerned about intracranial bleeding or neck fractures."

"Sure thing, Doc," Pam said, setting the tablet aside. "Keep an eye on your time too, Dr. Kim. Don't want to be late for your big day."

"I will. Thanks." She smiled at the nurse, then turned back to her patient. "Sir, we're going to get some tests done on you to make sure there are no underlying conditions going on I can't see on exam. Some films of your neck and head and also an ultrasound of your heart." She looked up as two techs came in to wheel her patient to radiology for his CT scan. "While you're doing that, I'll check in on the status of your family members, okay?"

"Okay." The father reached out and grasped Leilani's hand. "Thank you, Doctor."

"You're most welcome," she said, smiling.

The EMTs were still hanging out in the hall when she headed toward the other trauma bay to check on the mother and son and his girlfriend. One of the EMTs stopped her and showed her a picture he'd snapped at the accident scene of the mashed-up SUV lying on its side in a ditch. "The way that car looked, I'm surprised they all walked away. It's a miracle," the EMT said.

"It is." Leilani nodded, then headed for trauma bay two. "But miracles are what we specialize in around here."

She was living proof of that. She was also proof that you could not only survive the worst thing possible, you could thrive after it. Thanks to her wonderful adopted family, and Holden, who'd taught her how to love again. Her heart swelled with joy as she walked into the room where the son and his girlfriend were now sitting up and chatting while his mother gave her statement to a police officer. They appeared bruised and a bit rattled, but nothing too serious.

"I drive that route every day from our house," the mother said to the cop. "We were on our way home to watch a football game. That didn't work out so well." She sniffled. "When I saw that other car coming at us, I didn't know what to do. I didn't want him to hit us head-on, so I swerved to the left and my poor husband took the brunt." She looked up and spotted Leilani, her expression frantic. "Is he okay? Is my husband okay? I never wanted our day to end like this."

"He's fine, ma'am," she reassured the woman. "We're running a few tests to rule out any broken bones or bleeding internally."

The woman bit back a sob and reached over to take her son's hand. "Oh thank God. I'm so grateful we're all okay."

"Me too, ma'am. Me too." Leilani pulled the resident aside and got the scoop on the three patients in the room before they wheeled the father past the door of the room heading back to trauma bay one, and she excused herself to check in on her patient once more.

While Leilani went over the images, the ultrasound tech performed a cardiac ultrasound and Pam cleaned and bandaged up the lacerations on the man's hand. Of the five passengers in the car, the father seemed to be the one most badly hurt, but the CT had ruled out any fractures in his neck or bleeding in his head, which was great. The man would be sore for sure for a few days, but otherwise should make a full recovery, barring anything abnormal on the cardiac ultrasound.

"Everything looks fine, Doc," the tech said a few minutes later, wiping the gel off the patient's chest. "No abnormalities seen."

"Perfect." Leilani moved aside so they could wheel her portable machine back out of the room. "All right, sir. Looks like you're banged up a bit, but otherwise you'll be fine. I checked on the rest of your family as well, and they're all doing fine too. You all are very lucky."

The daughter, who'd been cleared to move about freely, jumped down and walked over to take her father's hand. Soon, the rest of the family entered to join them in the trauma bay.

"How are you, honey?" the mother asked her husband, kissing his cheek.

"My neck still hurts," he said, then held up his other hand. "And this got messed up a bit. But otherwise, I'm fine." He chuckled. "Remind me never to ride with you again though."

The mother promptly burst into tears and he pulled her down closer to kiss her again.

"I'm kidding," the father said. "You handled that situation better than I would have. I love you so much. It's fine. We're all fine, thanks to you."

Leilani checked the time, then backed out of the room while the family gathered around each other, hugging and laughing and saying prayers of thanks. Tears stung the backs of her eyes, as an unexpected feeling of completeness filled her soul. That's how it should have been for her family all those years ago. It hadn't been, but now at least she'd been able to give that gift of a future to another family. Circle of life indeed.

After finishing up the discharge paperwork for her patients, she checked the time, then discarded her gown and mask into a nearby biohazard bin.

Speaking of futures, it was time to get on with hers.

Holden stood on the beach in front of the Malu Huna Resort as a warm breeze blew and the waves lapped the shore behind him. Joe Kim stood beneath an arbor adorned with palm fronds, tropical flowers and white gauzy fabric that flowed in the wind, ready to marry off his adopted daughter. He'd gotten ordained just for the ceremony. Leilani's mother was passing out leis to the guests as they took their seats. Now all Holden needed was his bride.

He shifted his weight slightly, his bare toes sinking deeper into the sand. His leg hurt less and less these days, thanks to all the outdoor activities available in and around Honolulu. He loved hiking and swimming and had even tried his hand at surfing. The warmer temperatures helped too. And of course, having the woman he loved by his side while he did all those things was the biggest benefit of all. In fact, he'd left his cane inside the hotel today—as he was doing more and more often now.

He'd stop and get it though, before the reception, since there would be dancing involved later.

They'd decided on a casual, traditional Hawaiian wedding and he was not upset with it. His white linen pants and shirt were certainly more comfortable than some tuxedo monkey suit, that was for sure. Especially with the great weather. Blue skies, sunshine, a perfect day in paradise.

Hard to believe that a year ago he couldn't wait to get out of this place. Now he couldn't ever imagine calling anywhere else home ever again. He and Leilani had moved into her—now *their*—newly remodeled house three months prior, and things were pretty magical all around as they started their new life together. But even with the great beachfront abode, it wasn't the location so much as the people.

Once they'd told the Kims about their relationship, they had taken him in like a prodigal son. Family like that was something to appreciate and Holden didn't take one day of it for granted.

Same with Leilani. They'd both wanted to go slow, explore their relationship before diving into anything permanent too fast. Given their collective past, it was understandable. But now they were both ready to take the leap.

Holden glanced over and caught sight of his own parents sitting in the first row and flashed them a smile. They'd flown in from Chicago and were loving all Hawaii had to offer. Maybe someday they'd move down here too. He'd like that. As the guests' chairs filled in and the ukulele band they'd hired to play for the ceremony finished a sweet rendition of "Somewhere Over the Rainbow," a hush fell over the crowd. Holden looked up to see his bride at last at the end of the white satin runner covering the aisle of sand between the rows of bow-bedecked folding chairs.

He couldn't stop staring at her, his heart in his throat and his chest swelling with so much love he thought he might burst from the joy of it. She looked amazingly beautiful in a strapless white gown that was fitted on top, then flowed into a silken cloud around her legs, the breeze gently rustling the fabric. Like an angel. His angel, who'd been heaven-sent to teach him how to live and love again, who'd filled his life with so much purpose and meaning and emotion.

The band began "Here Comes the Bride" and the guests stood as Leilani slowly made her way toward Holden, her long dark hair loose beneath the woven crown of flowers on her head and her eyes sparkling with happiness.

She was everything he'd ever dreamed of and nothing he deserved, and his life was infinitely better because she was in it. He planned to tell her as much in his vows. They'd each written their own, but no matter what she said today, it would never mean as much to him as the moment she'd told him she loved him for the first time that day in her hospital room.

Music floated on the jasmine-scented breeze and Leilani reached his side at last.

Before the ceremony began, while the guests were settling into their seats again, Holden leaned closer and whispered for her ears only, "You look spectacular and I'm the luckiest man in the world. I love you, Leilani Kim."

Her smile brightened his entire universe as she beamed up at him. "I'm pretty lucky myself, Holden Ross. I love you too."

He leaned in to kiss her, but Leilani's father cleared

his throat. Chuckles erupted from the assembled guests. Holden winked down at his wife-to-be instead, unable to keep the silly, lovesick grin off his face. "Ready to do this thing, Doc?"

"So, so ready," she said, slipping her hand in his as they turned to face her father.

* * * * *

UNLOCKING THE
EX-ARMY DOC'S
HEART

JULIETTE HYLAND

MILLS & BOON

For my husband,
who always believed my stories
would land on readers' bookshelves.

CHAPTER ONE

Dr. Rafe Bradstone shivered as he stepped to the door of the small plane. Pulling his scarf across his mouth, he bounced from foot to foot as he grabbed his duffel bag. The wind blasted his face as he stepped onto the Tarmac, and goose bumps rose across his body. The heavy jacket he'd acquired at the last minute in LA seemed pathetically inadequate. How did the residents of the Arctic get warm?

Stepping into the airport waiting area, Rafe sighed as warm air slid around him.

"Excuse me." A woman with black curls pushed past him.

"Sorry, I didn't mean to stop in front of the door."

She didn't hear him as she raced toward a pair of happy kids. The kids hopped around her, each trying to outshout the other as their father hugged her. The love pooling between the small family was evident—these children never had to fight for their mother's attention.

Rafe's stomach tightened and he forced his eyes away from the lovely scene. It had been over a year since he'd found his mother, and two hundred and sixty-one days since she'd ordered him off her porch. Rafe wanted to believe the pain of her abandonment would fade, but his heart was still raw.

The woman with dark curls placed one child on her

hip and held the other's hand as she walked out of the airport. That was the way it was supposed to be: a mother loved her children, wanted to be with them. Glaring at his hands, Rafe wondered why *his* mother didn't react that way. What was wrong with him that his simple presence caused her pain rather than excitement?

His phone beeped. Burying the pain, he answered without looking at the caller ID. "Hello, Carrie."

His agent didn't waste words on a greeting. "Why are there social media posts of you in Alaska?"

Rafe started to roll his eyes but caught himself. Carrie was *supposed* to be interested in his professional life. It wasn't her fault this opportunity for him to serve in Blue Ash, Alaska, conflicted with his television duties, or that witnessing a family hugging their mom had put him in such a bad mood.

Keeping his tone level, he leaned against the wall. "Because I ran into a few fans of *The Dr. Dave Show*. They wanted a selfie, and I couldn't say no."

That wasn't true. He could have said no, but Rafe never wanted to. Whenever someone ran up to him, phone outstretched and excited, Rafe got to be a part of their life— to belong. It only lasted a moment, but he treasured each fan who wanted a memory with him. They never told him to go away.

Rafe had accepted the part-time host position on *Dr. Dave*, a medical talk show promoting healthy living techniques, hosted by a bevy of attractive practitioners, to help pay off his medical school debts. The legion of daytime television fans was just a great perk.

"You know that isn't what I mean." The sound of Carrie's nails clicking on her desk echoed down the phone.

Chuckling, Rafe ignored her tone. "I told you I was

volunteering at an outpost clinic in Northern Alaska for a few weeks."

"I assumed you were *joking.*" Her screech tore through the speaker. "You're Dave's favorite substitute host, and you're scheduled to be on during the live Thanksgiving special!"

"I know my schedule."

His stomach hollowed, and a sigh escaped his lips. Volunteering for the Thanksgiving and Christmas episodes was supposed to make him forget there wasn't a chair waiting for him at anyone's table, though it never worked.

"Rafe! Are you even listening to me? This is serious."

"You're pretty hard to ignore."

Taking a deep breath, he stared out the window, letting his eyes roam the frozen landscape. Trees coated with icicles hugged the side of the airport, dropping loose snow along the cars in the parking lot.

Rafe shivered; he didn't belong in Alaska. In his experience winter meant a windbreaker or a light sweater, not parkas and boots. He might need to wear all his socks just to keep warm.

But his cold feet were tomorrow's obstacle. Sliding down the wall, Rafe tried to get comfortable while he tackled his current problem. "I am a doctor first, Carrie. Besides, I owe Dr. Freson."

Jenn had covered for him during his disastrous visit with his mom. She had never asked why he suddenly needed an extra two weeks of vacation, or why he'd come back with no fun stories or pictures. He owed her, and the possibility that Dave might need him wasn't a good enough reason for Rafe to refuse to help a friend.

"Today is the thirtieth of September. I'll be gone four

weeks—six at the most. That puts me back in LA in plenty of time for Thanksgiving."

"Dave is looking to fill Dr. Bloom's spot at the end of the season, Rafe. That job should be yours. And rather than fighting for it you've disappeared."

Drumming his fingers on his knee, Rafe rolled his neck. He wanted that position. It wasn't the money or the fame. Rafe wanted Dave and the producers to choose him. For them to look at the other remarkable candidates and decide he was the best. Maybe that would quiet his mother's voice telling him he wasn't enough.

"There are other hosts; I need to do this."

Rafe frowned as Carrie sucked in a breath on the other end of the call.

"Rafe..." Carrie's voice shifted to the tone she used when letting her clients know they hadn't got a part. "Do you want me to issue a statement to the press? It isn't fair that the tabloids are accusing you of infidelity. Your reputation shouldn't be tarnished since Vanessa was the cheater."

He didn't want to discuss this topic either, but it was safer than worrying about Dave's penchant for firing hosts.

"Vanessa didn't cheat on me." The lie slid through Rafe's lips.

He'd met the movie star on the set of *Dr. Dave* six months ago. The paparazzi had loved getting pictures of the starlet and "her" doctor. She'd hidden her affair with another man—not that it had been hard to do. Their hectic schedules had resulted in more canceled plans than dates, but he'd assumed they were fine. She'd ended it over the phone while she giggled with her co-star and lover.

He hadn't thought they needed to issue a public state-ment announcing their breakup. Vanessa had insisted.

It had come as a nasty surprise when the tabloids had run a picture of him walking a patient to her car along with Vanessa's publicity statement saying that they had parted ways.

Seeing his name trending with "cheating" headlines had cut deeply. He'd bought every trashy magazine in the corner store by his apartment so he didn't have to see it. Rafe had always been faithful—*always*.

Vanessa could have corrected the assumption that he had cheated on her, accepted responsibility. He'd reached out to her a few times—unsuccessfully. If she hadn't corrected the story by now, she wasn't going to.

"My agent likes to remind me there's no such thing as bad press." Rafe blew onto his fingers.

Carrie clicked her tongue… "It does keep your name in the papers. Dave will like that."

Rafe pinched his nose. He wanted Dave to like his presence on set, his interview style, his high ratings—not his ability to land in the tabloids. Still, if that was what it took to land the gig, Rafe would accept the tabloid smear—even if he hated their falsehoods.

"I'll see you in a month."

Carrie's sighed. "A month is a long time in this town."

"And yet it's still only thirty days."

Static rose on the line, and Rafe shook his head. His agent wasn't great at goodbyes.

He smiled as a plump middle-aged woman rushed toward him. She danced on her toes while she waited for him to stand.

"Dr. Bradstone! It *is* you! I love *The Dr. Dave Show*. You should be on all the time. Your interviews are always the best. Better than Dave's! Can I get a picture with you?"

"Of course."

His soul felt a touch lighter as she slid her arm around his waist and his loneliness disappeared as she raised her cellphone. He owed this brief window of happiness to *The Dr. Dave Show*. Rafe was determined to get that fulltime host position and all the acceptance that came with it.

Patches of pink highlighted her cheeks as the woman stepped back. "Thank you." Pushing a strand of salt-and-pepper hair from her face, she scrunched her nose. "I'm Helen Henkle and this is my husband, Jack." She nodded toward a reed-thin man striding toward them. "We're your ride to Blue Ash."

Jack barely glanced at Rafe as he huffed, "You're going to need better shoes if you want to keep all of your appendages."

Variations on this theme had peppered Rafe's conversations since he'd crossed the Alaskan border yesterday. The tingle of cold in his toes made it seem more dire now that he was in the Arctic Circle.

Staring at his shoes, Rafe moved his digits. "We don't have much need for cold weather gear in Los Angeles."

"Well, up here it can mean the difference between ten toes or two. Don't want to explain to your grandchildren that you sacrificed a few toes rather than wear sensible boots."

Helen slapped her husband on the shoulder before offering Rafe a smile. "A man can get around on eight toes." Ignoring her husband's frown, Helen waved her hand toward Jack's feet. "It'll be a good way to ensure your children or grandchildren always wear their boots."

A flash of pain echoed across his belly as Rafe grabbed his bag and followed them onto the Tarmac. It didn't matter how many toes he kept, there were going to be no grandchildren to look at his feet. His family tree didn't have a great track record as parents, and Rafe didn't plan to extend that legacy.

Helen giggled as she slid into the seat next to him in Jack's tiny plane. "A real celebrity in Blue Ash. Well, if you don't count—" Helen coughed and smiled at her husband.

"Dr. A is expecting us. If you and the Playboy Doctor are ready, we'll get going."

Playboy Doctor... That tagline had been assigned to him because it sold magazines and received website clicks, not because it was true.

"That isn't a word I'd use to describe myself." The defense slid from Rafe's lips before he could stop it. He didn't owe these strangers, or anyone else, an explanation.

"Of course." The words were even, but the man's lip twitched before he let his eyes slide over Rafe.

Rafe shifted, hating the ball of tension pooling in his belly. He'd been weighed and found lacking. *Again...* It shouldn't matter. Rafe didn't know Jack or Helen. Still his tongue itched to defend himself, to make them understand that Rafe knew what playboys were and how much damage they could cause.

After all, he looked just like a particular one—though the tabloids didn't know that. To them it was a flashy headline. To Rafe it was a curse.

Rafe was his father's doppelganger. His mother had referred to him as his father's mini-me—though it hadn't been a term of endearment. Rafe's father had been an attractive professional dancer, and he'd been on the road constantly. His mother's stable job as an accounting assistant had kept a roof over their heads, but with each new trip away for his father, each new booking, each lonely night, she'd become more vindictive.

When his parents hadn't been arguing about his

father's many infidelities, they'd been yelling about Rafe. His mother would scream that she never got a break from being a mom—no fancy dancing getaways for her. His father would yell that he hadn't wanted a kid anyway.

Neither of them had paid any attention to the small child in the corner. Rafe might not have understood everything they were screaming about, but he'd always known that his father hadn't wanted him.

Why had he believed his mother had?

Rubbing his hands on his pants, Rafe tried to focus on the frozen scenery below. His father had died in a car accident with another woman a few days after his seventh birthday. A date neither of his parents had remembered, let alone celebrated. His mother had always constantly reminded Rafe of how he looked like the stupid cheater she'd married. She'd given up even trying to pretend she cared after that.

Infidelity had destroyed his family, and he would never repeat that mistake.

A few days before his eighth birthday, Social Services had taken custody of him. Rafe had bounced around the system until he'd aged out on his eighteenth birthday. He'd lived with many families but had never earned acceptance—never got to permanently *belong*. Now, when he was on set, he was the successful Dr. Rafe Bradstone, and for a little while that wound in his heart that had never closed bled a bit less.

Rafe was grateful no one attempted to make small talk on the short hop to Blue Ash. He needed to close off the pain twisting through him.

Rafe squinted as a small runway began to take shape ahead. "Are we going to land there?" The strip didn't look wide enough to handle the small Cessna.

Patting the plane's yoke, Jack grinned. "Don't worry, Doc. I've landed my baby in much worse conditions."

The broad smile spilling across Jack's craggy features did little to calm the nerves dancing in Rafe's belly. And as the wheels touched the ground they slid. Rafe's cry of alarm echoed through the tiny cockpit, but his fear was quickly replaced with embarrassment as Jack pulled the plane to a perfect stop.

"That runway has one patch of ice and you aimed for it. There was no need to demonstrate your skill on ice!" a husky voice yelled over the sound of the slowing propellers.

"Gotta toughen up the newbie. This region doesn't usually get stars whose faces are splashed across the tabloids." Jack tossed Rafe's bag to him as he turned to greet the young woman on the Tarmac.

"Tabloids are designed to make money, Jack, not to tell the truth."

The tiny welcome party was buried in an oversize parka, and her bright orange scarf hid everything but her stunning gray eyes. She met Rafe's gaze. The roar of the engine, the pilot's judgement, even the bite of the wind as it stole through his jacket—all vanished as her eyes searched his.

"I bet you're cold!" She motioned for him to follow her into what he assumed must be the clinic.

Heat marched up Rafe's neck. He hadn't even introduced himself—just stared at her. Matching her step, Rafe tried to think of a way to salvage this introduction.

"Welcome to Blue Ash."

Red hair tumbled from the hood of the parka as the woman hung her coat on a hook.

"Thanks."

Freckles danced across her nose, and Rafe sucked in

a breath. His fingers wanted to trace each one. It was a ridiculous notion. She was exquisite, but so were many of the women in and around LA.

Fire erupted across his skin as he tried to regain his composure. He was *not* going to make a fool of himself. Rafe flashed a bright smile as he hung up his own coat. He would swear he knew her, but it was a crazy thought. Rafe didn't know anyone in this state. His brain itched, urging him to find her name.

His heart sped up as his mind put the puzzle pieces together. He barely resisted the urge to slap himself. This Arctic goddess was a woman he and much of the world had once welcomed into their living rooms weekly.

"You're Charlotte Greene."

"I played the *character* Charlotte Greene." The phrase didn't sound bitter as it escaped her lips, just resigned— and exceedingly well rehearsed. "My *name* is Annie…"

"Right…"

Everyone knew who Annie was; she'd graced every teen magazine and even landed a cover for *Vogue* before she turned seventeen. He hadn't meant to refer to her as Charlotte Greene. It had just popped out.

"I didn't realize you were hiding in Alaska."

Regret pooled around him as her full lips turned down. He was saying all the wrong things.

Annie crossed her arms as she lifted her chin. "I'm not hiding."

Rafe raised a brow but didn't argue. Dr. Freson had told him the Blue Ash Clinic was growing, but it served a community of less than six hundred. It was an odd place for the famous Annie Masters to put down roots.

"Your mom—"

Annie flinched as she interrupted him. "Carrie and

I are not in regular contact. I cannot get you a meeting with her—and I doubt she represents television doctors."

Television doctors... Vanessa had made the same comment. Rafe might not win any awards for his work on *The Dr. Dave Show*, but the show helped people. He was more than a television doctor.

"I don't need an introduction."

Annie nodded, but Rafe doubted she believed him. She crossed her arms before offering him a tight smile.

But Rafe was not going to let the early stumble ruffle him. Smiling, he offered his hand. He always loved it when his fans talked to him about *Dr. Dave*. Annie probably didn't see many fans of *My Sister's House* in Blue Ash. Maybe if he flattered her work she'd relax a bit.

"I grew up watching *My Sister's House*. I've dreamed of meeting you since I was a kid."

Heat tore through him as she held his gaze again. Gold sparkled at the edge of her gray eyes as they traced his body. The camera had never caught that glimmer. *Annie Masters...* The intense connection Rafe had imagined on the runway bowled through him again.

"Nice to meet you, then, Dr. Bradstone."

Her cool tone rippled up his back. He was imagining their connection—just as he'd imagined a strong connection with Vanessa and his mother. He was not going to make that mistake again.

Sucking in a deep breath, Rafe straightened his shoulders. He didn't need to impress her. *He didn't...* He looked past her at the closed door to the back of the clinic.

Where was the doctor? He was supposed to be helping—not fumbling with words in front of a former starlet apparently now working as a receptionist in this remote Alaskan clinic.

Tipping his head toward the door, Rafe shrugged. "Is

Dr. A with a patient?" He hoped his use of the nickname Jack had used for the doctor might lighten the uncomfortable mood in the small reception area.

"It's Dr. Masters. Only my patients call me Dr. A."

Annie's sharp response slapped him.

"*Dr.* Annie Masters."

She raised her chin, daring him to ask how a child star had landed in this position—here.

His stomach lurched as his brain searched for words. "Dr. Freson failed to mention…"

Annie let out a soft chuckle, before shifting back on her heels. "Well, Jenn does have a wicked sense of humor."

"We need to get going." The awkwardness in Helen Henkle's statement carried across the room. She offered Rafe an uncertain smile as she continued. "If you need more supplies let us know, Annie. We probably only have a few more weeks of easy flights."

Rafe hadn't realized they'd followed them into the clinic. Rafe wondered if his star had faded a bit in Helen's eyes now she'd witnessed this interaction. Then her final words registered against his cluttered brain. "Wait—what do you mean only a few more weeks?"

"Winter sets in early. If you aren't out of here by the third week of November you might have to stay until mid-March, Dr. Bradstone."

Annie Masters leaned against the reception desk, the corner of her lip twisted in what he thought was a smile. Was she challenging him? He *couldn't* stay through the winter. He'd be in breach of contract if he missed the Thanksgiving and Christmas episodes of *Dr. Dave*.

"I have to be back in LA by the last week of November."

Annie—*Dr. Masters*—nodded. "You should be fine.

The worst of the winter is still weeks away." Her hand ran along the torn skin of her thumb before she shrugged. "If you're worried you don't have to stay. Jenn will be here before winter really sets in."

"And if she's not?"

Annie's shoulders tensed and her fingers trembled, but her face remained still. "I've handled four lone winters. It's—" Again Annie pulled at the skin along her thumb. "I'm used to being by myself."

Shifting on his feet, Rafe fiddled with the strap of his bag. "Lone?" Why did that worry him? Clearly she'd managed.

She shrugged, and Rafe's heart ached. Loneliness was apparently Annie's constant companion too. He'd learned to accept its presence after his mother's abandonment— why had a popular child star been forced to learn the same lesson?

Annie gestured toward the door leading to the back of the clinic. "*If* you're staying, your apartment is this way."

She turned and walked through a side door. She left it standing open, but didn't wait for him. This was a challenge—a test. She expected an LA television doctor to at least consider fleeing.

But Rafe was not going to be underestimated by Dr. Annie Masters. Hiking his bag up his shoulder, Rafe took off after her.

Annie hustled past exam rooms as she hurried toward the stairs leading to her apartment at the back of her clinic. She knew Rafe—*Dr. Bradstone*—would follow. The man was too cocky to flee—even if he wasn't cut out for the Arctic. His jacket and shoes wouldn't protect him. The clinic was on the edge of the Arctic Circle. By the end of next month it would be dangerous to be outside for more than a few minutes, even with proper winter gear. This life was not for everyone.

Still, when he'd landed she'd felt—

Annie bit her lip as she tried to understand why they'd stood on the runway staring at each other.

In that moment she'd felt warm, despite the chilly wind pushing against them. Her heart had sped up as if it was trying to escape her chest, though she doubted he'd noticed.

Rafe Bradstone was used to attention—lots of it. He was an excellent general practitioner—one of the best in LA. And his ties to the entertainment industry ensured anyone watching *The Dr. Dave Show* knew he was both skilled and gorgeous. He was constantly reaching out to his fans—and they seemed to be everywhere.

The clinic had fielded more appointment calls this week than it had for the last two months. Everyone wanted to see Dr. Bradstone. This was going to be her life for as long as Rafe was in residence. The man was a distraction—an exceptionally attractive distraction.

Why had Jenn sent Rafe as a temporary replacement? Annie had met her best friend on the first day of medical school. She'd been the only one to introduce herself and keep their conversation focused away from Annie's days on set. Her friend was passionate about medical access for all, and she'd promised Annie the best replacement doctor for her clinic.

Maybe she should have asked for the second-best.

Annie clenched her fists as the selfish thought slid through her. Her patients weren't as glamorous as the ones Dr. Bradstone usually treated, but they deserved the best. It wasn't their fault Rafe had used his medical knowledge, self-assurance and good looks as a path to celebrity.

Blue Ash had seen a population boom since Rickon Oil had announced it was opening a satellite location just outside of the town. The clinic needed two doctors to see to the expanding list of patients. Finding a doctor willing to spend the winter in near darkness, with temperatures south of negative twenty degrees, wasn't easy. Her last new hire had left her in the lurch, with winter quickly approaching. So when Jenn had offered to spend the winter with her in Blue Ash, Annie had quickly accepted.

Her friend had sworn that Rafe would help until the middle of November, and promised she'd be here by then. But what if Jenn decided she needed to stay in LA after she moved her father into his retirement home and Rafe left?

Swallowing the fear racing up her throat, Annie straightened her shoulders. She had overstated her confidence in spending the winter alone, but if she had to she would serve the community alone for another winter.

Passing the rows of silly photos and artwork her patients created, Annie resisted the urge to turn and gauge Rafe's reaction. His office in LA was probably professionally decorated, but she loved her homey clinic. It didn't matter what a celebrity doctor thought of her space—he was just a temporary Arctic resident.

When she'd first opened up, one of her young patients had painted a picture of Annie and her clinic. Annie was only recognizable by the crazy red curls on the stick figure's head, and the clinic was an amorphous blob, but little Nicole had been so proud when Annie had placed it on the wall. And over the last several years the clinic had become a miniature art and photography gallery.

Walking up the stairs and pausing at the apartment door, Annie took a deep breath before turning around. Rafe was several steps behind her. Tipping her head,

Annie pursed her lips. What was *wrong* with her? She'd dared him to leave. Not a good way to welcome the new doctor—even if he *was* an arrogant celebrity physician who'd called her Charlotte Greene.

That was a name that belonged to another lifetime, but Rafe wasn't the first to call her by name of the character she'd played from the age of seven to eighteen. Still, it hurt that the first name out of this stunning man's full, wind-chapped lips hadn't been Annie.

Even after all these years away from the spotlight, the role her mother had secured for her daughter still haunted her. Carrie had managed Annie's career right from her first commercial, and she'd had no plans to give up her position when her daughter had stepped into adulthood. So, in order to "help" Annie transition from child actress to adult superstar, Annie's mother had sold pictures of her daughter sunbathing topless.

The story that went with them hadn't talked about how Carrie had practically forced Annie onto the secluded "private" beach and criticized her tan lines until Annie had finally slipped off the bikini top. It had simply run with the headline *Child Star All Grown Up—New Roles Pouring in for Annie Masters.*

It had been the final straw. She'd known she had to do something—anything—to escape Carrie's control.

And at eighteen she'd marched away from her mother and from Hollywood—literally. She'd walked into an Army recruiting office during her mother's hair appointment and signed enlistment papers. The Army had been supposed to be Annie's escape—instead she'd found her purpose, first as an Army medic and then as a doctor.

But stepping away from Hollywood hadn't been easy. Annie had fought constantly to be taken seriously. She'd focused on proving herself in the field. Making friends had taken even longer. For a long time Annie hadn't been allowed to have any privacy without being called a snob, or worse. She'd hated it that everyone had expected the bubbly, personable Charlotte Greene. It had been almost as if she'd failed them by not meeting their expectations—particularly men. A lot of them had grown up watching her—fantasizing about her.

Except it hadn't been *Annie* any of them had wanted. In the decade since she'd left Charlotte Greene behind, only one man had seen past the character, and now he was gone too.

"I'm sorry. It was unfair to assume you weren't the doctor here." Rafe leaned against the wall, and ran his hand over his face. "And I apologize for calling you Charlotte Greene. I look forward to working with you, Dr. Masters."

His apology stole a bit of Annie's fire. And his reaction was normal—perhaps that was why it hurt so much. Maybe she still hoped to find someone who'd want Annie, not the character projected on a TV screen.

The role of Charlotte had given her financial independence, but how did you measure the cost of loneliness?

Wrapping her arms around herself, she nodded. Swallowing her pride, she offered a hand. "Want to start over?"

"Yes—but can you answer one question?"

"Ask away." She braced herself for some inane question about Hollywood, or the show she'd worked on. It wasn't his fault; it was what everyone wanted from her.

"Why am I still cold? I can feel the heat, but I swear my body refuses to accept it."

A pool of happiness opened inside her as his dark eyes held hers. Rafe wasn't going to press her for any

Hollywood details. It was a simple gesture, but she appreciated it.

"Southerners can be so weak." A small giggle escaped her lips. "It's because your feet are damp. The rest of your body is trying to compensate."

Resting his large hands on his hips, Rafe chuckled. "I don't think California really counts as the south."

The rich baritone of his chuckle filled the room, rushing through her body. Tingles raced down her spine and blood pounded through Annie's ears.

Trying to ignore the unexpected uptick in her heartbeat, Annie shrugged. "Anything south of the Alaskan border is the south."

How did anyone concentrate around this gorgeous man? Rafe was stunning! She hadn't found anyone so attractive since Blake.

Her fiancé had been gone for years, but she'd kept a few of his things. During her first two winters in Blue Ash, Annie had worn Blake's sweaters, and silly wool socks, not caring that they were four sizes too big for her. They were ridiculous items to keep, but donating them hadn't seemed like an option.

Last winter she'd pulled them out but hadn't worn any of them. Maybe it was time to finally clear out the drawers. Blake...

"Annie?"

Shaking herself free from the past, Annie took a step back. She needed to put a bit of distance between them. "Sorry, what did you say?"

Rafe moved closer, but he didn't crowd her. "I said, aren't you from California too?"

"Yes."

Sandalwood and lemon erupted across her senses. Of *course* Rafe would smell as good as he looked.

Annie gestured to her own feet. "And it took three winters before people stopped telling me all the different ways I was likely to lose my toes. Although I feel honor bound to warn you—"

"My shoes aren't made for winter. Several individuals have already informed me. So, in three winters I'll be a regular Alaskan—assuming I upgrade my footgear?" He laughed as he spun around her small kitchen.

"Your Arctic experience so far already has you thinking of becoming one of us?"

Annie pursed her lips, unwilling to admit to the leap of fire darting across her belly. It would be nice to pretend someone else would land in Blue Ash and see it the way she did—recognize it as home. But that was not going to be Dr. Bradstone. He wanted spotlights and a fan base— not long winters and nightless summers.

"Is there a place to set this down or am I sleeping in the kitchen?" Rafe let out an uncomfortable laugh. "I fear it's been a while since I slept on the floor, but I can manage."

Annie motioned for him to follow her to the guest room. "Do you enjoy camping?" She'd slept on the ground many times during her Army service and didn't particularly like it.

"No." Rafe's voice was strained as he laid his bag on the bed and began digging through it.

"Then why did you sleep on the floor? Was it a silly kids' game?" Annie had worked all through her childhood, but she was always fascinated to hear about the imaginary games other kids had played to occupy their time.

"Didn't always have a bed." Rafe's words were clipped.

Why hadn't he had a bed?

Rafe didn't elaborate as he grabbed another pair of socks.

Swallowing the questions stuck in her throat, Annie frowned at the thin socks in his hands. "You're in the Arctic, Dr. Bradstone. You *will* lose your toes if you wear those."

She turned to the closet. He might enjoy the trappings of celebrity, but she didn't want him to suffer under her roof.

"Here."

She tossed a pair of Blake's thick wool socks to Rafe. Rafe pulled them on and sighed—just like Blake used to. She had always joked that her fiancé loved putting on socks more than anything else.

Annie's heart clenched as Rafe slid his feet into the pair of boots she'd given him. Rafe wasn't Blake. He was attractive, and she didn't want him losing any toes on her watch. That was it.

"Do all Arctic residents maintain a supply of socks for us weak southerners?" Rafe smiled as he stood.

"No." The bell at the front of her apartment saved Annie from finding a reason for the socks. She didn't talk about Blake—ever.

"Dr. A? We need you."

A scream echoed up the hall as she raced for the front of the clinic, Rafe close behind her.

She saw Danny Mills' eyes dart quickly to the new-comer before shifting back to Annie. "I was moving some of the food drums for the animals and one fell. I didn't—"

"Who's hurt and where?" Annie interrupted as she looked behind him. She'd talk to Danny about the accident later—now she needed facts.

Danny's lower lip trembled. "Grandpa Mac. He tried

to catch the drum, but it landed on his leg. It's bleeding—bad. Jeremiah's bringing him in now."

Before Annie could say anything, Rafe rushed for the door—without his coat.

"Not a smart move…" Danny's whispered words held a faint hint of admiration as the door slammed shut.

Annie sighed. Rafe's decision was foolish. It was just the sort of showboating one might expect of a doctor on a television show. Still, she admired Rafe's dedication.

"Direct them into Room Three, Danny. I'm going to grab supplies."

Annie maintained only a small supply of blood. She knew Mac was O positive, but she quickly double-checked his chart. Any injury was going to slow him down heading into winter preparations. And the older man would refuse to take any days of vacation or rest. She mentally ran through a few arguments that might convince the hard worker to let his legion of children and grandkids do the heavy lifting for a week or so. Maybe Rafe could try his hand.

Another scream tore through the clinic, and Annie's fingers fumbled with the stitches she was laying out. Mac's pain tolerance was legendary. And people often overestimated the amount of blood their loved ones had lost. But what if Danny hadn't?

"Annie!"

Rafe's call sent shivers of fear down her spine as she grabbed the blood and ran from the room.

"What's…?" The word died on her lips as she stumbled into Room Three.

Mac's face was ashen. A jagged cut ran from his ankle to just below his knee, but the bone wasn't visible in the coating of blood. That was good.

"How much of this is dried blood?" Annie pushed past

Danny and Jeremiah, deposited the blood bag on a hook and moved to Rafe's side.

The wound needed to be cleaned, and it was going to require at least two dozen stitches. It was a simple fix, but with the amount of blood he'd lost…

Annie let those thoughts slide away as she looked to Rafe.

"Most of it—but there is still one bleeder up by the knee."

"What's that mean?" Danny's frightened voice swelled through the room.

"It means I need Dr. A's help to treat your grandfather." Rafe nodded to the teenager. "Can you and Jeremiah go get your grandmother?"

Danny's face lit up with relief and purpose as he pushed toward the door. "We'll be back real soon."

She shot a quick smile at Rafe. Mac's grandsons were too antsy to be allowed to stay, but Rafe had given them a job to complete rather than an order to vacate the room. It had been the right move, and Annie was grateful.

Turning her attention to Mac, Annie stepped up next to the bed. "We need to clean the wound, Mac, so Dr. Bradstone and I can get a better look. Then I think it's best if we move you into the operating theater. You're going to need a number of stitches and the light is better in there."

"You sure? Maybe just a Band-Aid?" Mac offered a soft smile as he grimaced.

"It's good you're still making jokes." Rafe winked at Mac before turning to Annie. "What would you like me to do? Clean or suture?"

Mac gripped Annie's hand. "Stay with me."

"Looks like you're suturing." Annie smiled at Mac before looking up to Rafe. "The sutures are laid out in the theater—it's the second to last door on the right."

Rafe nodded as he headed to the door. "I'll go get everything ready. I still can't believe I'm working with…" The words faded as Rafe disappeared through the door.

Unfortunately Annie's mind had no trouble supplying them. Everyone always wanted Charlotte Greene.

But Rafe was a temporary clinician—a man who wanted the fancy lights of Tinseltown. It didn't matter that he wished she was someone else.

It didn't.

CHAPTER TWO

ANNIE'S EYES WIDENED as she wheeled Mac into the small operating theater, but she didn't laugh at Rafe's attire.

Their patient didn't hold back, though. "Quite the outfit, Doc!"

He'd found a pair of floral scrubs in the scrub room. They fit his waist, but his calves were still visible. Unfortunately, none of Annie's scrub tops would get past his shoulders. His clean white T-shirt left little to the imagination.

Rafe pressed his lips together as Annie's eyes wandered over his outfit. He didn't look like a fancy television doctor *now*.

Her eyes finally darted to his and her lips twitched. Then, glancing at Mac, Annie headed for the door. "I delivered the local anesthetic three minutes ago. I should wash up again."

Her shoulders bounced with laughter as she bolted.

Mac's hands lay across his stomach, and his breath came in even pulses.

"I assume, since you laughed at my scrubs, that the numbing agent Dr. Masters has administered is working?"

"I can't feel the injury."

Mac nodded, but his eyes hovered over Rafe's feet.

And the older man's fingers twitched as he refused to meet Rafe's gaze. Was he trying to hide his pain?

"Mac, if you're not numb I need you to tell me. Stitching the wound is going to take some time, and I don't want to hurt you."

Mac's eyes finally met his. "I'm numb. I'm just embarrassed. When Dr. A. gave me those shots…" His cheeks flamed as he closed his eyes. "It burned like hell and I yelled at her."

Pain was a great equalizer.

Offering Mac a soft smile, Rafe tried to soothe his worry. "Lidocaine often burns. There's no shame in admitting to pain. I'm sure Dr. A didn't mind."

Rafe picked up the sutures and began working his way up Mac's leg.

"Of course not." Annie smiled as the door slid closed behind her. "I've had Army Rangers scream expletives that would turn your ears pink as I treated them. They used much more colorful terms than you did, Mac. I thought no less of them, and I think no less of you."

Annie nodded to Rafe as she took her place on the opposite side of the table.

"I think you'll need to stay tonight for observation," she told Mac.

Mac frowned. "Not that I'd mind spending the night with you, Doc, but my bed is more comfortable."

"Why, Mac! Are you flirting with me?" Annie pretended to flip her hair back as she looked at Rafe's sutures. "What would Molly think?"

"She'd tell me I could do no better than Dr. A but she'd shoot me if I tried."

"My heart flutters!" Annie laughed. "Tell me about your new great-grand-baby."

Annie smiled as she listened to Mac discuss the joys of

family life. The older man's family sounded chaotic, loud and perfect. Rafe's chest tightened as the happy stories floated around the room. He would have loved to belong to a family like Mac's. It sounded like there would be a large cadre of caretakers while Mac healed. Rafe hoped his family knew how lucky they were.

Taking a deep breath, Rafe let the world narrow to Mac's leg as he continued pulling the skin together. He'd already placed twenty stitches and had at least another twenty more to go. Mac's scar was going to be epic.

"Done." Rafe enjoyed the look of shock on Mac's face.

"Thought you were just getting started." The older man looked at the wound and paled.

Reacting fast, Annie put her hands under Mac's neck and gently lay him back on the table. "You lost a decent amount of blood and that wound is going to be tender for several weeks. We're going to get you back to your room and give you something to help you sleep."

Rafe frowned. Annie was an excellent doctor. She could practice anywhere. Why was she hiding in an outpost clinic in the frozen Arctic?

Mac's eyes bounced back to the wound before landing on the ceiling. He pursed his lips but managed a small whistle. "Going to be quite the scar."

"I did my best to minimize it, but the scar will be noticeable." He'd seen more than one patient tear up over a scar, though Rafe was surprised it bothered this hardened Alaskan. "Plastic surgery once it has healed might be an option—"

Mac waved his hand. "It's not my beautiful figure I'm worried about, Doc. It's my pride—I need to figure out a better story than being attacked by a food drum."

Rafe laughed. "Are there mountain lions in this area?" he asked.

Heat pooled along his neck as Annie and Mac looked at each other, clearly amused by the question.

"No mountain lions for a couple hundred miles, son." Mac's lips pulled to one side, but he didn't actually laugh.

Trying to salvage his own pride, Rafe asked, "What about bears?"

And at least neither of them dismissed that idea as they transferred Mac back to his room.

Mac's breathing slowed as the pain medication took effect.

"Where did you treat Army Rangers?" The question tumbled from Rafe's lips into the room as Mac's first snores started.

"In the Army." Annie gestured for him to follow her.

"I'm serious, Dr. Masters."

Annie shook her head. "I've been many things since I was Charlotte Greene. She's what people want to know about, but I served as a combat medic for four years before going to med school, Dr. Bradstone."

Rafe tried to picture the woman before him in fatigues. The image came much more easily than he'd anticipated.

"A combat medic?"

Awe spread through him. He had seen a lot of trauma during his emergency room rotations, and a few of those days were burned into his memory. He could only imagine Annie's experiences.

"I'd say you're a lot more than Charlotte Greene."

Annie offered a brief smile. "Thank you." She bit her lip. "You did a great job on Mac's leg."

It was a small compliment, but Rafe wasn't used to any. His heart burned for a moment at the simple words. And as he followed Annie down the hall he stared at the happy pictures on the wall.

"How does a famous television star end up as a combat medic?"

Stepping behind the room divider, Annie tossed him his clothes. "I'll wait here. Shout when you're decent."

He hadn't meant to ask the question, but Rafe yearned to know the answer.

Quickly stripping, he pulled his jeans and T-shirt back on. "Done."

He studied the petite beauty as she stepped from the divider. Annie's bright hair was pulled into a tight bun. Her scrubs hugged her hips just enough to hint at the spectacular curves beneath them. An uncomfortable need pulled at him.

"Seriously, Annie. How did you become an Army medic?"

Annie tilted her head and shrugged. "By enlisting in the Army. Come on, I'll show you where the laundry is— since my role as hostess does not include laundry duty."

Rafe wanted more information, but Annie's shoulders were pulled tight. Swallowing his inquiries, he playfully glared at the washing machine. "Wait… Dr. Freson assured me my laundry was covered in this gig!"

"Nope—that was a lie to make the Arctic more palatable. You're on your own in cleaning your tighty-whiteys." Annie shook her head, her eyes lighting up at the joke. Her shoulders relaxed, and a bit of the tension that had clung to them since he'd called her Charlotte evaporated.

Pressing a hand against his forehead, Rafe laughed, "I haven't worn those since I was a boy, Annie. As a matter of fact, I think the last ones I owned probably had Batman or Superman on them."

Annie tossed him a packet of detergent, her eyes widened as she pulled her hands to her hips. "You liked comics?"

Tossing the scrubs into the laundry, he cut his eyes to her. "Nope—I *loved* comics. Superheroes always help people."

Crossing her arms, Annie leaned against the dryer. "Is that why you became a doctor? To help people?"

Rafe shifted under her intense scrutiny. People loved asking doctors why they'd become doctors. Most said they'd been called to help people. Annie had walked away from Hollywood, served in combat and then gone to med school. Rafe was *certain* Annie was a doctor because she wanted to help people.

Rafe wished that was his story. He could lie, or avoid the question like he usually did, but he didn't want to. "No, although that would be a better story to tell. I—I was raised in foster care."

Rafe had passed through so many houses full of kids and adults. There hadn't time for him to be given the attention he'd wanted—needed. It might have been different if he'd stayed in his first home. His foster mother Emma had cared for him. But he'd lost her too. After his mother's abandonment, Emma's passing had been too much, and he'd shut everyone out.

"I spent most of my childhood angry at the world. Got kicked out of a lot of homes for being too much to handle. I needed love and attention to deal with the loss of my parents, but there was never enough to go around. One of my foster moms idolized doctors. Said they were the best."

Rafe pulled on the back of his neck. He didn't know why he'd started this story, but the words refused to slow.

"I told her one day that I was going to be a doctor. The best doctor ever. She laughed and told me I was more likely to end up serving time than being a productive member of society—let alone a doctor."

Annie sucked in a breath and her fists clenched. "That is a horrible thing to say to anyone—but to a child…"

She was angry on his behalf? When had anyone ever been angry about what had happened to him? Rafe's swallowed the lump pushing at the back of his throat. It had always been lonely, knowing no one truly cared about him. Annie acknowledging his pain was a salve he didn't know how to handle.

Rafe stared at the ceiling. "It was cruel, but she did me a favor. I studied every night, made it my goal to prove her wrong." Blowing out a breath, he let his gaze wander over the plain tiles. "She wasn't as impressed as I hoped when I got a scholarship."

Annie patted his arm and smiled. "Well, I think you're very impressive."

His chest heaved at the praise. She meant that—it wasn't a false platitude. Her hand disappeared from his arm and Rafe frowned. The faint scents of lavender and cleaning solution faded as she put distance between them. It had been a simple touch, but it had put a dent in the emptiness in his soul.

"Did you read a lot of comic books while you were on set?"

Gripping the edge of the dryer, Rafe clung to the cool metal to keep himself from reaching for her. Something about Annie called to a deep part of him, and he needed to remember that this was a temporary gig.

Annie's shoulders sagged and the mood in the room tilted. Wrapping her arms around herself, she seemed to shut down. "No." Her gray eyes slid to the window, a shadow of pain passing over her features before she took a deep breath. "I learned about comics in the Army. Blake loved—" Annie closed her eyes.

Rafe hadn't meant to ask something that clearly caused

her pain. He'd never served in the military, but Rafe had worked beside men and women who had. He'd seen a simple question touch a veteran in unexpected ways before. "Annie…"

She didn't look at him as she continued the story. "Blake would read them to the company as soon as his mom sent them—he made up silly voices for each of the characters. We used to laugh and joke about some of the more ridiculous plot lines, but we all loved it when those boxes arrived." Annie paused for a moment before adding, "Blake's mom still sent me boxes after—" She bit her lip before offering him a sad smile. "The good guy always wins in the comics. I wish life reflected that."

"Me too."

For a moment Rafe wondered what would happen if he put his arms around her. She needed comfort, but he barely knew her.

Before he could list all the reasons to keep his distance, Annie stepped toward the door. He knew it was the right move, but it stung.

Annie gripped the door handle. "You should get settled. I'll check on Mac after I see to the paperwork." Without waiting for a reply, she made her escape.

Glancing at the snow flurries outside the window, Rafe swallowed. Jenn needed to get here soon. He stared at the empty space Annie had occupied; the snow was the least of his concerns.

"Any particular reason you kept my identity secret from Dr. Bradstone?" Annie pulled her wavy hair into a tight ponytail as she talked to Jenn.

"I don't think of you as Charlotte Greene."

Annie rolled her eyes; Jenn didn't think of her as Charlotte Greene, but Rafe did. She hated it that it bothered her so much.

"Rafe called me last night," said Jenn.

Of course he had…

"To talk about meeting Charlotte Greene?" It wasn't Rafe's fault the most exciting thing about her was her past.

Dishes clacked on Jenn's end. "No. He called to complain about the cold and tell me how remarkable you are."

Remarkable? Her lip twitched. She liked it that he'd called her that—too much. She knew Rafe was a wonderful doctor. And after their awkward greeting he'd been surprisingly easy to talk to. And he was gorgeous. But she only needed his medical skills.

"Annie?" Jenn's voice was strained. "Are you still there?"

"Yep!"

That false peppy tone was her tell, and Jenn latched on. "What's wrong?"

Falling onto her mattress, Annie stared at the ceiling. "Nothing. Rafe's an excellent doctor and—"

Annie's throat seized. She didn't know the man, but she wanted to. And that was terrifying. His upbringing had been completely different than hers, but she recognized the scars of loneliness worn on his soul. She had several the same.

"He's attractive…" Jenn offered.

There was more to it as far as Annie was concerned, but those words were locked away. She was almost positive that Rafe had wanted to hug her yesterday. And, for the first time since Blake had died, she'd wanted to step into another man's arms. Wanted to feel the heat of another body, the comfort of knowing that for a moment she wasn't alone. The desire had terrified her, and she'd fled.

"He *is* gorgeous—which his legion of fans all know."

Annie strained her ears, listening for any sign that the stunning doctor was awake.

"There isn't anything else to talk about, Jenn." Ignoring Jenn's sigh, Annie pressed on. "I enjoyed talking to him yesterday, but he's only here a few weeks."

"Perfect for a fling, then."

Annie felt her chin hit her chest at Jenn's suggestion. "A *fling*?"

Jenn's laughter was contagious, and Annie placed a hand over her mouth to quiet her giggles.

"Why not? He's hot—you're hot." She giggled again before sobering. "I worry about you. You've been alone since…"

Jenn's pause tore through Annie's happy bubble. "Since Blake was killed."

Her former fiancé's name danced around the room. She never talked about Blake—except she'd talked about Blake's love of comics with Rafe yesterday. Rafe's eyes had lit up when she'd mentioned comics—just like Blake's had.

"Annie…"

"I need to see a patient."

"Give Rafe a chance, Annie. I bet he's very skilled with his hands!"

Annie glared at her phone before looking out the window. Rafe was standing outside without a coat—*again*.

She stood up. "I'm getting off the phone now, Dr. Freson."

Jenn was still chuckling as Annie disconnected.

Pulling on her coat, Annie ran through the clinic. Flinging open the front door, she almost fell into Rafe's arms. Despite his chilly embrace, her body sang.

Annie pulled him inside. "What are you *doing*?" She

made herself step back, hating the bloom of fire flicking across her skin.

Rafe shivered and blew into his hands before pushing a few buttons on his phone. "Trying to get a good picture of the mountains to load onto my social media. They are beautiful."

Social media?

Annie rolled her eyes. She'd been worried about him—raced like a madwoman to rescue him. But Rafe was risking frostbite to impress people he didn't know. It was ridiculous.

Annie wanted to shake him. Grabbing his cold fingers, she clasped them between her palms. "These are nearly frozen!"

She knew Rafe was capable of warming his own appendages, but she couldn't force herself to let go. He was too attractive, too smooth—too much for her. Annie wanted to yell at him for being foolish, and she also wanted to close the tiny distance between them.

That was dangerous. Getting close to the temporary Dr. Rafe Bradstone wasn't an option.

Rafe swallowed as Annie's soft hands viciously rubbed his aching fingers. He hadn't expected to be outside for so long, or for the cold to seep into his bones so quickly. Needles shot through his fingers as blood returned to the frozen digits. The sensation was uncomfortable, and it kept him from feeling Annie's touch.

He'd lain awake last night, thinking of her, replaying the conversation, wishing he'd hugged her. It was silly. He barely knew her. But that missed opportunity refused to leave his mind.

"I can feel them again." Rafe regretted the words instantly when Annie dropped his hands.

"This isn't the set for a television show, Rafe." Annie's cheeks were tinged with heat as she glared at him.

Television show? This had nothing to do with his role on *Dr. Dave.* He was so much more than a television doctor. Rafe wanted her to understand that—needed her to see him as more than a pretty face on a talk show.

His phone dinged as fans started interacting with his post, destroying his planned denial. "I know that, Annie." Rafe shook his head as he stepped closer.

"*Do* you?" Annie glared at his pocket, where his phone continued to buzz. "Then put on a coat and a good pair of boots if you insist on posting Arctic pictures. Unless you're trying to demonstrate what frostbite looks like?" She turned on her heel.

He should let her go, but he didn't want to start the day off on the wrong foot. "Annie?" Rafe moved quickly, halting her retreat.

She raised an eyebrow as his phone buzzed with more notifications. Those pings usually brought him a bit of joy. Knowing that others enjoyed his thoughts and pictures made him feel wanted—briefly. Under Annie's gaze it felt shallow. He shifted as the uncomfortable feeling rolled through him.

Reaching in his pocket, Rafe silenced his phone. "Thank you for checking on me. I will not venture outside again without a coat. Promise."

Annie nodded before offering a small smile. The upturn of her full lips sent a thrill racing down his spine. She was perfection—and not for him. This was a temporary assignment, and this morning had certainly proved that he didn't belong in the Arctic.

Except that for a moment, when she'd been in his arms, he'd wanted to. That terrified him.

Annie's skin tingled as she raced for the back of the clinic. She'd only meant to warm up his fingers for a minute, but if Rafe hadn't told her that he could feel his fingers again she'd have kept holding him.

She was just lonely. Lust wasn't love.

Her heart clenched as she leaned against the door to her office. *Love.* She'd had a chance at love, and it had been terribly short-lived.

The few dates she'd been on in the last several years had been unqualified disasters. The men she met were only interested in her past. After the last catastrophe had resulted in her date attempting to sell photos of them to a tabloid, Annie had retreated from the dating pool. Romance had never crossed her mind.

Until Rafe.

Her heart pounded as his name reverberated around his brain. It was nothing. She'd been worried about a colleague—that was why she'd rushed to his side this morning.

And yesterday?

Swallowing, Annie tried to rationalize her need to talk to Rafe then. It had seemed natural, because Rafe's love of comics had reminded her of the man she'd lost. That was all…

Blake.

Annie never discussed her fiancé. Even Jenn knew not to ask about the lanky man who'd played such an important role in getting her to Alaska.

Blake had been the only person in her boot camp to see past Annie's Hollywood image. The Army, even with its demanding routines and shouting sergeants, had been her first taste of freedom. Making friends hadn't been easy—everyone had seen her as soft or, worse, thought she'd joined to get publicity—but Blake had given Annie the idea of adding an additional thirty pounds to her rucksack for the company's ten-mile run. That stunt hadn't earned her many new friends, but the whispers had turned into a quiet respect.

She and Blake had become as inseparable as the Army would allow. She'd cried when he'd been assigned to the Cavalry, rather than medic training with her. And most of their relationship had occurred in the brief R & R weeks they'd carved out.

Blake had proposed in Germany, on the night before he'd headed back to Iraq. She'd worn his ring for less than a week before being called into her commander's office…

The smell of mint aftershave interrupted her thoughts as Rafe leaned over her shoulder to grab a patient's file.

"You okay?" Tilting his head, he narrowed his eyes as they focused on her posture.

"Fine."

Rafe's eyes widened at Annie's clipped response, but he didn't push. Leaning against the wall he wiggled his fingers. "I really am sorry I gave you a scare this morning."

"Sorry I scolded you. They're your fingers and toes." Annie laughed.

How did Rafe manage to put her at ease and make her so uncomfortable all at once?

"Mac's wife just got here. I told her he could go home and come back at the end of next week so we can remove the stitches. He made a cheeky comment about his plans for when he gets home."

Her fingers brushed his as he passed her the clipboard

with Mac's recent vitals. Her heart jumped as she forced her eyes not to linger in the chocolate depths of his.

"Mac's going to be a real terror. Luckily Molly is up to the task of keeping him in line."

Rafe let out a low laugh. "They sound like they're something."

"Been in love for more than half their lives." Annie knew her wistful tone carried down the hall before she pushed away from the wall.

"Dr. Masters is a romantic?" Rafe tapped her shoulder with the chart as he followed her into the office.

"You think so?" She had been—once. Annie tapped a pen against the chart as she studied Rafe. "Are you?"

Rafe looked up from Mac's chart, crinkles darting at the corner of his eyes. "Am I what?"

"Are you a romantic?" Annie swallowed, and her gray eyes refused to meet his.

"No. Love doesn't last, so why bother with romance?"

"That is a sad statement."

Rafe's chest felt tight as Annie frowned. He should have made a pithy comment about roses and boxes of chocolates. That would have been the safe conversation topic—not his actual thoughts on whatever people meant when they said love.

For some reason Rafe seemed incapable of keeping his distance from Annie. That was dangerous. Rafe was leaving, and she didn't approve of "television doctors."

When Annie had fallen into his arms that morning, he'd wanted to hold her. Had wanted to kiss away the tiny line that appeared between her eyebrows when she frowned. His mind spun. Annie was smart, talented and gorgeous, but that didn't have to mean anything. Even if they had chemistry, it would only result in disaster.

"The emotion we call 'love' is just the brain releasing norepinephrine and dopamine. The scientific studies on brain chemistry are fascinating, but most people don't spend their free time reading scientific journals." Rafe shrugged.

Annie's fingers twitched and an emotion he couldn't read spread across her face. "No. What you're describing is lust and attraction. Love is so much more."

The certainty in her voice shot through him. What made her so certain?

"Then what is love?" Rafe leaned against her desk, his eyes hovering over her. This wasn't a conversation they should be having so early in the morning—or at all—but he was intrigued. What made Annie so sure about love that her eyes glistened?

"Love is *life*. Smiling, fighting, tension, joy…" Annie pursed her lips. "And pain."

Rafe understood pain, but before he could agree Annie continued.

"It's the promise that you're never really alone. The realization that even when you're so angry with each other, life would be empty without your partner. It's knowing that if you're separated by oceans, there's still someone who is on your side. A person who will fight *for* you and *with* you. Someone who will always choose you. It's everything."

Annie had evidently loved someone deeply—Blake?—and yet she was alone. Rafe clenched his fists. She'd given so much of herself to someone and they'd left her. He was a little jealous that she could argue that love existed after the man she'd cared for had clearly chosen some other life.

Rafe's heart pounded in his chest. He wanted her definition to be true. "That is a beautiful sentiment."

"But you don't believe it?" Annie's eyes searched his, but he didn't know what she was looking for.

"I want it to be true…" Rafe's words faded. He wanted to believe someone could choose him over everything else. But if even his mother hadn't chosen him, why would anyone else?

Rafe smiled as his insides twisted. "We are having a very deep conversation before 10:00 a.m., Dr. Masters."

A soft chuckle left her lips and Annie pulled at the stack of patient files in front of her. "We have a full schedule today. I think most of the women in town are hoping you'll give them a well-check."

"Annie—"

The front doorbell chimed and Annie headed for the door without looking back. "I'll take Mrs. Anderson. You get Mrs. Hillard."

Glancing at his phone, Rafe stared at the reaction to his snow post. He waited for the bubble of happiness it usually brought, but the rising count of "likes" felt fake. Rafe glared at his phone for a moment before shutting it off.

"Your blood pressure is elevated, Mrs. Hillard."

"Really?" Touching his arm, Mrs. Hillard leaned in close. "So, what are you doing to help with the Fall Carnival?"

He pulled away and stared at the grin on his patient's face. They needed to focus on her blood pressure not some carnival.

Offering a pat on her wrinkled hand, Rafe tried his "firm but friendly" tone. "Is there a history of high blood pressure in your family?"

Green eyes sparkled at him through thick glasses.

"Don't know. Now, the carnival—what would you like to do?"

"Do…?" Rubbing his face, Rafe reached for some patience. Leaning against his desk, Rafe smiled at his elderly patient. "I don't know anything about the carnival, but I'm happy to discuss it after we talk about your blood pressure. Elevated blood pressure puts you at an increased risk for heart attack, heart failure, organ failure and stroke. It's serious."

Mrs. Hillard smiled at him. "I'm not worried about those things."

Crossing his arms, Rafe tried to keep the frustration out of his voice. "Mrs. Hillard. This is serious."

"I'll be eighty next summer."

"And you're exceptionally healthy otherwise." Rafe sighed, wondering how to make her understand.

Mrs. Hillard's eyes shimmered for a moment. "My Thomas has been gone for two years, Dr. Bradstone. He was my everything. Now I'm just kicking it—as my great-grandson says—until I meet my maker."

Rafe didn't have any words to follow that declaration. He couldn't tell her he understood.

Pursing his lips, he tried another tack. "What is the Fall Carnival?"

Mrs. Hillard's tongue pushed against the small gap between her front teeth as she smiled. "The whole community takes part. There are games, food—and the dance competition."

"Dance competition?"

"It started a few years ago." Her finger tapped her chin before she shrugged. "I don't remember why, but people perform routines in costume. The winner gets a silly trophy. It's great fun, and all the money raised goes to the library. It's my favorite time of year."

This was clearly important to her. Rafe raised an eyebrow and took a shot. "If I agree to do anything you want at the carnival, will you follow a diet and exercise plan for a few weeks? If that doesn't lower your blood pressure, will you consider taking medication? I'm sure your husband doesn't want you joining him before a few more Fall Carnivals."

Mrs. Hillard studied him. "I might be willing to make that deal. Do you dance?"

"Only a little."

That wasn't exactly true, but Rafe didn't feel like explaining. His agent Carrie had insisted he take lessons. She'd claimed it would help him land a role on a reality dancing competition. And he was a natural, according to his dance instructor—just like his father.

That was the comparison he'd feared—and hated. Before his death, Rafe's mother had always cooed about how much he looked like his father. He was an exact replica. But it was that resemblance that had turned her love into neglect and finally to hatred. If he looked like his father, danced like his father, how long into a relationship before he managed to destroy any woman who cared for him?

"Fantastic. Another couple dancing will bring in more money. Your job is to be Dr. A's partner for the dance." Mrs. Hillard clapped her hands and her eyes darted to the door.

"Dance with Annie?"

Rafe's tongue felt dry even as Mrs. Hillard's eyes glittered. He wanted to pull Annie into his arms, spin her around the floor and explore the heat that struck him each time their hands brushed. Wanted it too much...

"What if I make the cotton candy?"

"I have the Jones boys making cotton candy." Mrs. Hillard reached for her coat. "It's for charity. The other groups have been dancing together for years—the families really get into it."

"I'll talk to Dr. Masters."

Rafe was surprised as those words tumbled forward. He'd meant to say no—explain that he might not even be in town. What if he asked Annie and she said no? What if she said yes?

"I'll mark you down. Just remind Dr. A that the library needs a new children's section." Mrs. Hillard grabbed the notes Rafe had made about diet and exercise as she headed for the door. "Nice to meet you, Dr. Bradstone."

"Schedule your follow-up for six weeks from today!" Rafe called as the spry woman raced down the hall. "And follow the instructions on those papers!"

"A deal is a deal!" Mrs. Hillard laughed as she disappeared.

Annie's chuckle hit his back.

Spinning, he crossed his arms. "Was that a test, Dr. A?"

Annie pulled her chin to her chest. Her eyes sparkled. "No…"

"You're covering your mouth, hoping I won't notice the smirk! You *did* give me a difficult patient."

Lowering her hand, Annie shrugged. "It wasn't a test—not really. I've been attempting to get Nancy Hillard to take her blood pressure seriously for the last year. Guess I was hoping your charms would work."

"You think I have charms?"

Rafe had meant it as a joke, but he studied Annie as she stared at him. He wanted her to say yes; he wanted her to be intrigued by him too. That was a ridiculous desire, but he couldn't quiet it.

Pursing her lips, Annie held his gaze. "I think you know you're charming. Did my plan work?"

Cocking his head, Rafe smiled. "I made her a deal. She's promised to try a diet and exercise program and consider medication if it doesn't work."

"Wonderful!"

Annie's smile warmed his insides. Rafe wanted to bask in it, but he took a deep breath. "And in return we're partners for the Fall Carnival dance. She drives a hard bargain."

Annie's eyes widened, and her tongue darted around her lips as she stared at him. "I can't be your partner for the Monster Mash."

Rafe refused to acknowledge the pain that statement caused. It didn't matter that she didn't want to dance with him—it *didn't*.

He raised an eyebrow. "Monster Mash?"

"What else would you call a charity dance during Halloween? The whole town cheers the contestants. It's a lovely spectacle."

He watched as Annie crossed her arms. She was being oddly defensive of a dance she didn't want to participate in.

"She said to remind you the library needs a new children's section." Leaning closer, Rafe tried to ignore Annie's soft scent. "Don't make me use my charms."

Annie opened her mouth and then closed it. She offered him a tight smile. "Sorry, Rafe. I can't dance with you."

"It's for a good cause," Rafe pressed.

He knew he should drop it, but he wanted her to say yes.

Choose me...

"I guess it *is* for a good cause..." Annie looked at him, her teeth dug deep into her lip.

"If you keep biting like that, it's going to start bleeding."

Rafe ran his thumb over her lip, pulling it from her teeth before dropping his hand. His ears burned as he stared at her. His tongue stuck to the roof of his mouth as he tried to determine if he should apologize or make a flirty statement. Neither action felt right.

Annie's fingers brushed over her lips before she offered him a soft smile. "The library does need a new children's section."

Her hip swept against his as she slid her chart into the file holder behind him.

"I haven't danced in years, but it's nice you want to participate. Let Mrs. Hillard know that I'm too stubborn. She won't have any issue finding another partner for you. I bet several of your fans would love to spend the evening dancing with Dr. Bradstone. She could even auction it off, raise more—"

"I don't want to be auctioned off!"

Rafe hadn't meant to interrupt. Hadn't meant to be so defensive, but he didn't want a fan. He wanted Annie. Heat pulsed through him as the scent of lavender touched him. Swallowing, he slid Mrs. Hillard's file into place and picked up the next patient's—anything to keep his fingers from reaching for Annie again.

"Sorry, Rafe."

Stepping away from her, Rafe raised his chin. It was a silly Fall Carnival dance; he'd been turned down for so many other things it didn't matter.

Nodding, Rafe shrugged as he looked over the next patient's file. "I'll probably be back in LA by then anyway. It was a dumb idea."

Annie's lips slid open, but Rafe didn't stay to hear her excuse. His Alaskan residency had a termination date; he just needed to find a way to put distance between him and Annie until then. It would be easier if they weren't working and living together—easier if he actually wanted to put distance between them—but he was not going to make a fool of himself with another starlet—not even Annie.

CHAPTER THREE

AN ALARM RACED through Rafe's dreams. Rubbing his eyes, he tried to orient himself. Where was that pinging noise coming from?

Stepping into the hallway, Rafe followed the noise to Annie's room. A flashing red light caught his eye. The pinging was coming from an alarm next to her empty bed. What was going on?

"Annie?"

Rafe started toward the kitchen. The door leading down to the clinic stood wide open. *An emergency.* Rafe's heart pounded as he raced down the stairs.

"He jumped from the bed." A frantic sob echoed from the first examination room. "I put the boys in bunk beds when they moved into my apartment. I didn't think—"

"Deep breaths, Maggie. It's a small fracture on the ulna."

Annie's calm voice floated toward Rafe as he stepped into the room. An X-ray of a tiny arm hung on the wall. Clearly he'd missed most of the action.

Why hadn't she woken him? Their professional relationship was excellent. He might have retreated from all personal interaction over the last two days, but this was why he was here—to help.

She'd asked him to dinner last night and he'd made an

excuse about needing to work. When he'd drifted into the kitchen an hour later Annie had been gone. It was probably for the best. Since Annie had declined the dancing invitation there had been no more deep conversations about comics or love.

He missed them.

"Jonah just needs a cast," said Annie.

The young woman, Maggie, barely glanced at Rafe as he stepped up next to Annie. A boy who couldn't be more than five lay whimpering on the table.

"I want the top bunk."

"It's mine." A sullen boy who might be around eight yawned from the corner. "Could have just left me at home, Maggie."

"You're seven, Chris. I'm not leaving you home alone."

"Mom always did."

"Not now, Chris." Maggie sighed.

"You're not Dr. Henkle." Jonah's voice was weak with exhaustion and pain as he stared at Rafe.

"Nope. I'm Dr. Bradstone, and I'm going to help Dr. A get you feeling better."

Jonah's eyes shifted between him, and Annie.

"Now comes the important question." Annie winked at Jonah. "What color cast do you want, little man?"

His eyes widened, but he didn't hesitate. "Blue."

Annie yawned as she reached for the stockinette and padding. She was clearly exhausted.

"Why don't I do the cast?" said Rafe.

Shocks traveled up his arms as his fingers brushed hers. He held her eyes for a moment before focusing on Jonah's gaze.

"I had a blue cast when I was about your brother's age. I got it falling off a friend's bike."

Jonah didn't say anything, but Annie mouthed *thank*

you as she leaned against the wall. She and Maggie made small talk while Rafe plastered Jonah's arm. When it was finally set, Annie carried Jonah to Maggie's car while Rafe grabbed his sleeping brother.

"Sorry it's so late, Dr. A." Maggie sighed as she buckled Jonah in. "I keep second-guessing myself. Everything seems so hard…" Maggie ruffled Chris' hair before opening her car door.

"You're doing great." Annie offered her a quick hug, then waved the small trio off before trudging back to the clinic.

Annie yawned as she locked the door. "Sorry—I forgot to turn the alarm off when I hit the bottom of the steps."

"It's fine, Annie." Rafe smiled and yawned too but made no move to head back to his room. "I'm here to help. You should have gotten me."

Despite her exhaustion, Annie had no desire to go back to bed. Rafe hadn't immediately retreated. If the wall he'd placed between them was down, Annie didn't want to rush away.

He'd barely said two words to her since she'd declined his dance offer. She'd expected him to jump at the opportunity to auction off his time at the dance, to bask in the worship of the television doctor, but she'd misread him. She'd spent her whole childhood being misread by fans and critics. She'd hurt Rafe with her assumptions, and she hated the distance he'd put between them.

She missed their easy conversations, the few fun moments they'd shared. She wanted to fix it, but Rafe no longer seemed interested in dinner conversation or breakfast banter. And she wanted to dance with him. That worried her—but not finding a way to bridge the gap between them worried her more.

The stubble along Rafe's strong jaw gave him a rugged look. How did anyone look at him and not imagine kissing him? Annie rubbed her eyes. She was exhausted and letting her brain wander to places it shouldn't.

"Do you answer many 2:00 a.m. calls?"

Rafe's eyes were hooded, but there was a spark of concern behind them. Or maybe she just wanted there to be.

"Some. The nearest hospital is almost three hours away. If it's something I can fix…"

"Where's their mom? Maggie barely seems old enough to care for two young boys." Rafe's voice was tight, and his eyes stared past her.

Annie nodded. "Their mother has substance abuse issues and is serving time. Maggie is twenty and just got custody of her brothers."

Rafe let out a low whistle. "Lucky boys. The system isn't any place to grow up." Rafe shuddered, and Annie put her hand on his. Rafe stared at it for a moment but didn't pull away.

"They are lucky, but Maggie still fears she'll turn out like her mom."

Rafe shook his head. "I understand. I can't imagine wanting to pass on *my* family genetics to the next generation. My parents' genes were all bad."

"No, they weren't!"

How could he think that? He'd spent the last hour being kind to a tired, hurt child while casting his arm. He'd answered every one of Jonah's questions. He'd been the perfect doctor. And her heart had sung as she'd watched him.

Rafe raised an eyebrow. "You didn't know them."

"But I know *you*."

Or I want to.

Annie's breath caught as Rafe's chocolate eyes held hers. It was too late for this conversation, but she saw the hurt bubbling under the surface. He didn't see himself clearly, and he should. Rafe was amazing.

"Their genes are in you, and you turned into an intelligent, caring man. You literally help people for a living, Rafe."

Annie bounced on her feet as he stared at her. He was so close, but still he didn't say anything.

"My mother wasn't great at the parenting thing either—doesn't mean I don't want kids someday," she said.

Annie wanted to push those words back in. Exhaustion was loosening her tongue—or maybe it was just Rafe's effect on her.

Swallowing, she pointed to the clock. Maybe tomorrow she'd find a way to broach the topic of the dance. "We should try to catch a few hours of sleep."

Annie's heart pounded. She liked being close to him. But she was too tired to try to work out those feelings.

"Who is Dr. Henkle? Is he related to the pilot and his wife who flew me out?"

Rafe hadn't meant to ask any questions, but despite the late hour he wasn't ready to say good-night.

"Dr. Henkle is their son and my business partner." Annie paused outside her door.

Her eyes shone, but the dark circles under them worried him. She was so used to doing everything on her own she hadn't even thought to get him tonight. This "partner" couldn't be much help.

"Partner?" Rafe's mind twisted around the word. Was

this the man Annie had thought of when she was explaining love? "Where is he, then?"

A shadow crossed over Annie's eyes before she shrugged. "Liam travels a lot. He serves the remote communities."

"But Blue Ash is a remote community." Surely her partner should be alleviating some of her burden?

"No, it isn't. Not exactly anyway. The roads here can be used for most of the winter. Planes can reach us... There are villages farther north that only see a doctor when Liam arrives."

"Why not hire another physician?"

Annie didn't answer, but her fists clenched.

It was too late to argue, but Rafe couldn't stop the flow of words. Annie must handle after-hours calls far more frequently than she wanted to admit—Rafe was almost sure of it.

"If it's a monetary issue, you could probably use your fame—"

"Are you *kidding* me?"

"No, I just— I only..."

The words died on his lips as fire shot from her gray eyes. She was lonely and tired, even if she wouldn't admit it.

Her eyes still glittered as she stepped toward him. "Why do you think Jenn is coming? Liam and I have hired two doctors over the last three years. Neither was willing to stay past October. As you've pointed out, we're remote by most people's standards."

"I'm sorry." He flinched as she turned her face away from him. "I worry about you." The words were out and he couldn't take them back—didn't want to. "You deserve a break. Who helps you?"

"A break?" Annie's features softened. "Like dancing at the carnival?"

All the oxygen seemed to have evaporated from the small hallway. How had she flipped this conversation? It didn't matter.

Rafe leaned against the door and smiled. "I was thinking more of a vacation, but dancing is good for stress relief."

Annie's cheeks flamed as she met his gaze and looked away. "I heard there was a physician who needed a partner."

"It *is* for a good cause." Rafe smiled.

"True." Annie laughed. "I'm sorry I misread your offer. I figured you'd prefer a fan to a washed-up actress."

"You aren't a washed-up actress, Annie." Rafe pushed a tight curl behind her ear. "You're an intelligent, caring woman."

He winked as he repeated the compliment she'd given him. He wanted to kiss her, to close the tiny distance between them, but he was afraid she'd back away if he moved.

Annie smiled. "If you don't mind a rusty dancer I would like to be your partner—*dance* partner."

Rafe's breath hitched as she offered him a quick hug. Her curls trailed along his chin, but the contact was too short.

"I promise not to step on your toes. Thanks for your help tonight. It's nice not to do everything alone."

Then she was gone.

Rafe was just drifting back to sleep when he realized Annie had avoided his question.

No one helped Annie.

Rafe's heart twisted. She was alone, and she needed more than a temporary doctor could provide. He'd make certain that she understood he was available for all after-hours calls. At least that way he'd relieve a bit of her burden for a few weeks—and he was looking forward to her stepping on his toes…

Rafe slammed the screen on his laptop and winced as the noise reverberated around the kitchen. Carrie had sent three emails today. She'd tried to schedule two video interviews for him and she wasn't taking his refusal well. It didn't help that she'd seen he'd lost a few dozen subscribers on his social media profile. He'd been gaining followers for the last several months—he wasn't now.

Rafe's stomach tossed at his agent's pointed questions regarding his lack of new social media posts. He usually posted a few times a day, but after Annie had chastised him for chasing followers in the cold he hadn't posted again. He'd started several, but hadn't published any.

In the week he'd spent with Annie time had flown. His social media profile hadn't seemed important. His need for "likes" faded when Annie was near. He'd taken to counting the number of times he made her laugh or smile instead. The joy those moments brought lasted longer than the pings on his phone.

He wasn't going to be around Annie forever, though. He had a life in LA, and a career—a plan to make his place on *Dr. Dave* permanent. Carrie's reminder now that Dave was monitoring his social media accounts stung.

"Everything okay?" Annie's fingers brushed his as she passed him a cookie.

"Sure." It wasn't really a lie, but his stomach flipped as Annie raised her eyebrow.

Rafe bit into the cookie, making sure to keep his eyes focused on the plate. Since her late-night declaration about him being an amazing man, he'd had a hard time meeting her gaze. He wanted it to be true—wanted to be worthy of someone as magnificent as Annie.

The cookie stuck against his throat as he thought about Carrie's emails. He still hadn't told Annie about his agent being her mom. He wasn't hiding it—not really.

Nibbling on her own cookie, Annie interrupted his tense thoughts. "My friend Holly makes the best baked goods. For two years, she made cookies and cakes out of her small kitchen. A few weeks ago, she opened a bakery in town. I still haven't managed to sneak over there, but Holly delivers!"

Annie handed him another, and gold shimmered in her eyes as she laid her hand over his. "What's wrong?"

Her nails were painted a light pink, but the skin around her thumb was still red and raw. What had she done?

Rafe rubbed his finger along her palm, before forcing himself to pull away. He wanted to touch her more than he'd ever wanted to touch another woman. He had assumed the need would pass, but it had only grown.

Since fixing Jonah's arm they'd worked together every day, before retiring to Annie's apartment. When they'd done the dishes last night, Annie's hip had bumped his several times. Rafe had studied his ceiling well past midnight as he'd weighed up whether she was interested in touching him too.

Annie leaned over the table and tapped his nose, "Earth to Rafe?"

Laughing, he squinted at her. "Sorry, I was just plotting how to get you onto a dance floor."

He'd tried to schedule their first practice a few times, but she'd always managed to duck the appointment. He wanted to dance with her, hold her in his arms—maybe then his need to touch her would disappear.

Annie's blush spread across her cheeks and neck.

"We don't need much practice—no changing the subject. What's wrong?"

"Nothing." Rafe bit his tongue as he rushed the word out. Pain ripped across his mouth. "Hell!"

Annie chuckled as she leaned back in her chair. "See—there are consequences for lying."

Rafe stuck out his injured tongue. "Fine—you're right."

"I know I am. What's going on? I'm a pretty good listener."

"My agent's getting a lot of requests for me to do interviews. She's angry I'm not responding." *His agent*—he'd failed to use Carrie's name again.

Annie's brows knitted together as she picked at her thumb. "You're avoiding your agent?"

Avoiding. That descriptor didn't seem quite right, but as he sat with Annie the tiny pull he'd felt to answer Carrie disappeared. LA seemed so insignificant when he was sitting in Annie's homey kitchen.

He frowned as Annie whittled at the skin by her nail, then reached for her hand. Desire flooded him as her fingers wrapped around his. "You're going to make yourself bleed," he said.

"Probably." She frowned at the broken skin. "Sorry—it's my nervous habit."

"Do I make you nervous?"

She made *him* nervous. More with each passing day. Annie Masters made him think about topics he wanted to bury. His parents, his character, his desire to know what she tasted like, if her body would flush with pleasure…

"Yes."

Before Rafe could process that answer, Annie rushed on.

"Are you going to do the interviews?"

"No." It was an easy answer.

Squeezing his hand, Annie lifted her chin. "Why?"

"Because I'm here."

The interviews would help his chances at landing a permanent spot on *Dr. Dave*, but what if people realized he was here with Annie? Dave would chase *that* story. Rafe wasn't willing to share his precious time with her. Besides, she'd worked hard to get away from Hollywood. He was not going to bring it to her doorstep.

Annie squeezed his hand again before she pulled away. "Are you hiding here?"

Looking at his hand, Rafe frowned. He wanted to reach for her again. Panic shot through him as her eyes held his.

"Why would I hide?" he asked.

She raised both her eyebrows. "Vanessa Hutchinson?"

"I didn't realize you read the gossip magazines."

Rafe tapped his fingers against the table, hating the defensive tone in his voice. Was that why she'd initially said no to dancing with him?

"The clinic has a subscription to a few. And I…" Annie's voice faded as she looked at him. "I *may* have read a few articles before you arrived." She bit her lip as her eyes floated over his. "I'm sorry, Rafe. I know they're trash. I know that you didn't cheat on Vanessa."

"How do you know?"

Rafe leaned forward. Dave and a few of his colleagues had all snickered about how he'd messed up a perfect thing. People who should have known his character had believed him capable of hurting someone he cared about.

"I guess…"

Why did she know it?

Annie stared at Rafe. He wasn't a cheater; she didn't know why she was so certain, but she was.

"I think you're too good of a person to do something so dishonorable. Am I right?" Annie held her breath.

"I didn't cheat on her." Rafe let out a breath and a bit of tension leaked from his shoulders. "Vanessa isn't interested in correcting the press and I don't want to answer questions."

"I'm sorry she didn't correct the story. Hollywood's lights can be blinding."

Rafe laughed. "At least you don't have to worry about their glare here. This is the perfect place to get away from it all."

Annie's belly twisted. Rafe was right—this was the perfect place to hide from the nagging cameras and questions. But that wasn't what she was doing.

It wasn't.

She took another bite of cookie, focusing on the explosion of orange and sugar until it almost drove the niggle of worry from her mind.

Eventually Annie stood and dumped the last of the cold tea down the sink. When she turned Rafe was behind her. Heat poured from his chest as he held her gaze.

"Thank you for seeing the best in me."

Rafe's soft words brushed against her skin, and Annie wrapped her hands around his waist without thinking. His muscular arms captured hers and she stared at him. His lips were so close…

Rafe made her feel things she'd thought lost when she'd buried Blake. When he talked to her he was interested in her present more than her past. When she was around him the specter of Charlotte Greene disappeared.

If she didn't move now she would kiss him.

He let her go, and Annie's soul cried as she put some distance between them. *Coward.* Her brain screamed for her to run back into his arms, but the moment was gone.

"Want to help me at the community center tonight?" Annie placed a hand over her hot cheek.

"Of course. Are we going to practice our dancing?"

"Nope!" Annie smiled. If she stepped into his arms again it would be impossible to ignore the connection between them. What if she risked it and lost everything? "We'll be painting—so change into something you don't mind getting dirty."

"All right." Rafe paused before he left the kitchen. "Annie...?"

She raised an eyebrow. "I promise it's really not too messy. Are you having second thoughts about joining me?"

"Never."

Her heart leapt at the admission even as he leaned against the door. His coffee-colored eyes held hers.

"We're going to dance tonight too."

"Is the snow bad tonight?" Rafe ran his hands along his knees as he stared out the window.

"No." Annie frowned.

A light dusting of snow covered the road, but the lazy flakes floating down were hardly worth mentioning.

"Then why are your knuckles turning white?"

The car slid slightly as Annie released her death grip.

"Sorry!"

Her cry echoed in the truck's cab as Rafe's hands flew to the dashboard.

A chill shot down Annie's back and she reached to turn the heat up. Rafe's fingers brushed hers and electricity shot up her arm. The memory of their hug burned through her. If life had a rewind button Annie would replay that scene. Kiss Rafe and hope it would be enough.

It wouldn't be...

Rafe's phone buzzed and he laughed as he checked the message. "I know social media is a necessity these days, but a fan has just asked me to help chaperone their kid's dance. Does anyone expect someone they don't know to say yes to that?"

Annie shook her head, but what was she supposed to say? She didn't think social media *was* necessary. It was a good reminder that Rafe belonged to a different world. She'd tasted that Hollywood dream and its bitterness still stung her.

Leaning her head against the seat-back, Annie forced her fingers to hold the wheel normally. The emotions raging through her warred with her need for self-protection. It should be easy to stay away from Rafe. Except everything about the man besides his connection to Tinseltown called to her.

She relaxed around Rafe, laughed with him, was just Annie with him. Rafe fit into the clinic and into her life perfectly. It was wonderful and terrifying. Attraction, longing, need—those were things Annie had set aside.

Until Rafe...

Parking the truck, Annie shifted in her seat.

She froze as Rafe's eyes held hers.

Rafe's finger pushed a stray curl behind her ear, scorching her cheek. Annie stared at his lips. He was going to kiss her. *Finally!* Would he kiss with wild abandon or soft, delicate brushes?

"Annie...?" Rafe leaned back, zipped his coat and wrapped his scarf around his neck. "Are we waiting for someone?"

Her tongue refused to move. She'd completely misread his intentions. Had she misread the situation in the kitchen? Maybe she was just lonely and looking for a connection that wasn't there. Her lip trembled, and she hated the hurt blooming in her belly.

Pulling on the reserves she'd developed on set as a child, Annie straightened her shoulders. She would pretend everything was fine. Besides—it was. Tonight was about painting and dancing—nothing more.

"Nope. It's just us tonight." The bright tone was the standard voice she'd used as Charlotte Greene. It wasn't real, but it put people at ease.

"You sound weird…" Rafe's eyes wandered across her face.

Sucking in a breath, Annie opened the truck's door. "I'm fine. You won't need the scarf."

"You were very serious about my need for correct winter attire. I'm not going to disappoint you again." Rafe chuckled—but it wasn't his deep, cheerful laugh.

Did he know she'd wanted a kiss? Was he embarrassed for her?

It didn't matter—mustn't matter.

Annie marched to the community center door, grateful she could blame her warm cheeks on the frozen wind.

Annie was staying a few paces ahead of him, her step quickening whenever he got beside her.

He'd thought she'd kiss him earlier, but she'd just offered a hug. It wasn't enough. Then he'd hesitated a moment too long in the car, and now that moment was gone too.

That bright, cheerful voice was Annie's "Charlotte tone." He'd labeled it that after watching her deal with a patient who'd wanted to discuss the finer points of the show's final season with her. She slipped into it whenever she was putting distance between herself and others. It had been directed at him when they'd first met, but he hadn't realized what it meant. Now—it stung.

Pictures covered the entrance hall. The residents of Blue Ash captured with deep smiles as they watched plays, ate barbecue and danced at the community center. The changing fashions marked years of fun.

An image of Annie dressed in a knee-length black dress, green stockings and a pointed hat caught his attention. "You make a very cute witch."

Laughing, Annie began pulling the covers off ghosts, witches and candy corn. "Thank you. I've used that costume for all four Fall Carnivals I've been to. I heard a rumor that there's a bet on when I'll finally retire it."

Rafe studied the happy families. He knew several of the people in these pictures already. "Think they'll put up one of us when we win the dance competition?"

It would be nice knowing that part of him remained in Blue Ash after he went back to LA.

"About the dance competition—" Annie started.

"Nope." Rafe interrupted. "We are practicing tonight. You and I are going to hold that silly stuffed bear trophy high and have our picture taken."

Blue Ash was incredible. Each and every one of his patients had invited him to the Fall Carnival. Life here was slower than LA, but the hours skipped by with a comfortableness he didn't remember feeling before. If it wasn't for his place on *Dr. Dave* this town could feel like home.

Home...

The word echoed in his brain and he froze. That word had never held much meaning for Rafe. It was just a word for a thing he'd never seemed to have and didn't need. Except now, standing next to Annie, staring at a wall full of fun, Rafe had a hard time convincing himself he didn't want it.

Annie's hip bumped his as she handed him a brush. "Do you want the ghost or the witch?"

He pursed his lips. "The ghost?"

Annie grinned at him before passing a large can of white paint. "And after you splash all that white on you get to tackle the candy cutouts."

"That was a trap!" Looking over his shoulder, Rafe shuddered playfully at the stacks of colored cutouts in desperate need of a fresh coat of paint. All contained at least three different colors and multiple patterns. "Maybe I'll take the witch…"

Hugging her paint can, Annie picked up the witch. "Oh, no. First choice is final!"

Laughing, he popped the top off the white paint. "I could argue you were deceitful, Doctor."

"Prove it, Doctor!" She winked.

His phone dinged and Rafe set it to silent.

"More DMs?" Annie crossed her legs as she painted the witch's dress.

He stared at her for a moment. "Whatever it is, it's not as important as spending tonight hiding away with Annie Masters."

Fire bristled in her gray eyes. "I am *not* hiding."

A popular and rich young actress left Tinseltown, joined the Army and then disappeared from public life to run an Arctic medical clinic. Even if she didn't have any interest in being in front of the camera, Annie was an excellent doctor—she could work anywhere. She might not want to call it hiding, but it certainly looked like it.

"Sorry, Annie. I guess it's just hard to think of anyone walking away from Hollywood. So many people want the glitz and the glamour."

The fact that Annie avoided all of it was fascinating.

He loved stepping on stage, interacting with fans—being well-respected and important.

"You enjoy acting?"

"*The Dr. Dave Show* isn't really acting—but, yes, I enjoy it. I get to be part of people's lives." Rafe coughed. "A therapist would probably argue I'm trying to fill the hole in my soul."

"*Are* you?"

Annie leaned her head against her knees. Her gray eyes studied him, but Rafe didn't see any judgement in her expression. Maybe that was why talking to her seemed so natural. He'd always kept a part of himself from the women he dated. No one needed to know how broken he was. But Rafe wanted to tell Annie *almost* everything.

"Maybe. My mom—" Rafe coughed again.

He'd almost told Annie about his mother's abandonment—about the pain it had caused him, his desperate need to make someone—anyone—see him.

"Well, there was never enough attention to go around when I was growing up. Maybe that's why I enjoy interacting with the fans so much. They see Dr. Bradstone, a successful doctor, sitting on Dave's stage offering medical advice—not a lonely kid with no place to call home."

Annie's gray eyes bored through his soul.

"Plus, I do love standing in those lights."

Annie offered him a shy smile. "It's not bad to want those lights, Rafe." Annie bit her lip. "The image your fans see is the real you. You *are* a successful, talented, kind doctor. If they can see it, maybe you should too."

Rafe wanted to pick her up and squeeze her tight. Find the words to tell her how much that statement meant—how much all her words meant. Part of him had been knitted together that night she'd told him he was more than his parents' horrid genetics. A few others had said it, but Annie made him want to believe it.

"How about some music?"

Before he could answer Annie hustled over to a small closet. Speakers crackled on, followed by the musical tones of a song from *Les Misérables*.

"Show tunes? Dr. Annie Masters likes show tunes?"

"Of course. They tell a story."

"A sad one," Rafe joked as he moved to paint the ghost's eyes.

"Not all of them." Annie stuck her tongue out as she returned her focus to the witch.

For an hour, show tunes danced across the speakers, and Rafe tried to keep his focus on the decorations before him rather than the beauty next to him. It would have been easier if he hadn't caught her staring at him— several times.

After finishing his third candy corn, Rafe stood and marched over to the speaker system. He wanted to dance with Annie and they needed to practice, but that was secondary. Rafe wanted to hold her, and he was tired of trying to pretend the need would disappear.

"Time to dance."

As the lyrics hummed around the room Annie frowned. The Fall Carnival wasn't a real dance competition. Most people just did silly dances they'd seen on the internet or let their kids make up something fun.

"Rafe, the dance is—"

His arm slid around her waist and Annie's tongue refused to utter the truth. She wanted to stay in his arms. Let him hold her.

"So how rusty *are* you?"

"A little. But…" Annie pinched her eyes shut. "I was

a child actor. My mother started me in ballet and tap as soon as I turned three. She made sure I had a diverse résumé."

Her mother had never cared if Annie actually liked the activities. Dancing, singing, violin, horseback riding were all just accomplishments that directors might like.

Annie had loved dancing, but it was families and partners who danced at the carnival. Annie didn't have either. Her stomach twisted as Rafe pulled her closer. If she wanted to, she could lean her head against his chest.

Instead she licked her lips and looked up. "I've never had a partner for the Monster Mash."

Smiling, Rafe held her gaze as he began to move them around the room. "Well, you do now, and we are going to win that ridiculous stuffed bear trophy."

Rafe's footsteps were confident as he spun her. Her heart pounded as she rolled back into his firm grasp. "Where did you learn to dance?"

"My father was a professional dancer. He taught me several things when I was little. I've taken a few classes. It was fun, but I've never had a full-time partner. No one has ever matched my steps like you do."

Sparks shot through Annie as a swing song started. "I *love* swing dancing."

Rafe's eyes lit up, and her heart pounded in her ears. Why had she put this off? The world disappeared when she was in Rafe's arms. The arguments she'd made about keeping her distance evaporated as she matched his steps.

A slow song started, and Rafe pulled Annie to his chest. Her cheeks were pink, and he felt all his barriers tumble down as she placed her head on his shoulder.

Dancing with Annie was the definition of perfection,

and Rafe suspected he would never get tired of holding her.

"That trophy is as good as ours," he said.

Ours...

The word hung off Rafe's lips and he couldn't take it back. Not that it mattered; Rafe didn't want to. He'd never experienced an "ours" moment. Everything was either Rafe's or someone else's—easy to separate when relationships soured.

He desperately wanted to share that silly trophy with Annie. For a precious moment in time Rafe would belong to something so much bigger than his fans. He'd make sure the photo made it on Blue Ash's wall of memories.

Annie's forehead nuzzled against his neck as she whispered, "I think we may need more practice."

Her breath on his neck set fireworks off across Rafe's skin. He'd dance with her any time of day, in any circumstance.

"You just have to step into my arms..."

Rafe pushed a curl that had escaped from her tight ponytail away from her cheek. For a moment he feared she'd step away, but instead her full lips moved toward his.

The front door slammed shut and Annie jumped out of Rafe's arms.

"Sorry, Annie." Helen Henkle's eyes shifted between the pair of them and the unfinished decorations.

Jack said nothing as he carried a load of boxes to the other side of the room, but his eyes held Rafe's.

"It's fine." Annie looked at her feet as she walked toward the paintbrushes. "We were just practicing. Rafe is a natural. That trophy might spend a year in the clinic."

Helen smiled as she stared at Rafe. "Is that so?"

Rafe shrugged. His arms ached without Annie, and he crossed them to keep from pulling her back to him and finishing what they both clearly wanted. "It's going to look great on the reception desk."

Thoughts kept worming their way through Annie's mind as she stared at the northern lights dancing through her skylight. Normally the peaceful sight provided her with a meditative place to sink into dreams.

Annie buried her head in her pillow. She'd almost kissed Rafe. Three times there'd been an opportunity, and she still didn't know how he kissed.

It was a dangerous thought, with no answer.

Annie enjoyed Rafe's company, but he was tied to a life in front of the camera. He loved the stage. Any person who was with Rafe would have to be part of that world. It had taken her years to carve out her own paradise away from the camera.

But Rafe was leaving. She didn't have to be part of his world if this was temporary.

The argument beat against her. She didn't want "temporary."

Sighing, she slid her feet into her panda slippers and tiptoed to the kitchen. The pint of chocolate ice cream calling to her from the refrigerator might not help her sleep, but it would make the time more enjoyable as it passed…

Freezing, Annie stared at Rafe as he lifted a spoonful of ice cream to his lips.

"Are you craving ice cream at midnight too?"

Grabbing a spoon, Annie tried to ignore the pull of need as she joined Rafe at the table. "I hope you saved some?"

Crimson stains traced his neck as he turned the empty carton toward her. "Sorry, Annie…"

"Not even a spoonful left?" Annie shook her head.

"Annie—wait," Rafe grabbed her hand, spinning her toward him. "I'm so sorry."

"It's not a huge crime, but it does mean we need more ice cream."

Annie offered him a weak smile. Ice cream wasn't what she really wanted. She thought about stepping into his arms. If they danced around the kitchen would he kiss her?

"I'll get more."

Rafe headed out of the kitchen before she could work up the courage to tell him ice cream wasn't what she craved.

"Do you know even where the ice cream is?" Had she ever told him where the clinic fridge was? Her mind was mushy with exhaustion and longing as she followed him.

"I'm sure I can find a gas station."

Annie's heart thudded as she followed him to his bedroom. "Rafe, that's a sweet offer—especially as the closest open convenience store is more than thirty miles away." She grabbed his shoes. "Luckily, I have three pints of cookie dough ice cream, two more chocolate and a rainbow sherbet I bought for reasons I cannot remember in the clinic freezer. There must have been at best six bites of ice cream left in that pint you pilfered."

"It was closer to four…" Rafe laid his keys on the dresser and she saw his eyes wander to his bed.

Why had she followed him in here? The soft scent of sandalwood and his shampoo clawed at her senses. Her eyes kept hovering above the rumpled bed sheets.

She hugged his shoes to keep herself from stepping into his arms as she backed out of his room.

"I'll grab you another pint too."

Pain shot through her arm as she bumped it against the wall. A small cry escaped her lips, but she kept moving.

"Annie?"

She spun. "Yes?"

"If you'll hand me my shoes I'll come with you."

Desire spun across his dark eyes, but he didn't reach for her. His eyes traveled over her. It shouldn't matter, but she pulled at the sleeve of her long blue nightshirt. It wasn't an enticing outfit, but her insides burned as he studied her.

She tossed him his shoes. "Don't you trust me to bring back your goodies?"

"How do I know there aren't more flavors you don't wish to share?"

Throwing a hand across her forehead, Annie pretended to faint. "You wound me! However, the raspberry chocolate is for special occasions, and you are to leave it alone."

Rafe's lips brushed the top of her head as he threw an arm over her shoulder. It was a friendly gesture—safe and so unsatisfying.

"So there *are* secret flavors!"

Energy danced along Annie's spine as Rafe's laughter pulsed through her. "Only the one."

At the freezer, she grabbed a pint of cookie dough and stood aside so Rafe could make his selection.

Grabbing another chocolate, Rafe snapped a quick picture with his phone.

"What are you doing?" Annie stared as he swiped a few buttons.

Rafe shrugged as he dropped the phone back in his pocket. "I haven't updated my social media much since I arrived. My large follower count is one of the leverage points my agent is using to get me a permanent position on *Dr. Dave*."

His agent—the words threw a damper on her desire.

Rafe didn't belong here. He belonged to the lights and the crowds.

Back in the kitchen, her ice cream sat unopened on the table. "Have you lost many followers while you've been here?" she asked.

Guilt strode across her belly as Rafe dropped his spoon. He flinched as his phone squawked. He'd wanted the "likes," so why was he embarrassed now? Annie considered apologizing, but the words stuck on her tongue.

Rafe's foot tapped against the table and he didn't meet her gaze. "My fans are used to hearing from me a few times a day. Social media is a tricky world of algorithms and…" His voice died away.

"I'll take that non-answer as a yes." Annie blew out a breath as she pulled the lid off her ice cream. Life was so much more than a fake online presence and fans who loved you Monday and hated you Tuesday.

"Fame isn't real, Rafe. I know it can seem like it, with the intoxication of being recognized…" She stuffed the spoon into her mouth to stop the lecture. He *wanted* the fan interaction. It wasn't bad; it just wasn't the life Annie needed.

"It feels good, though. For a little while I get to belong. Without *Dr. Dave* I won't get that." Rafe laid his hand on the table, but his fingers didn't reach for hers.

Annie stared at his hand for a moment, weighing her words. It was fine to want the attention, but Rafe was looking for more than his fans could provide. "What your fans want from you isn't real belonging. They want a fantasy."

"What do *you* want?" Rafe's tongue darted across the chocolate ice cream dripping down his spoon.

You.

That declaration stayed buried as she grabbed another

bite of ice cream. Finally, she continued. "I just want to be Annie. And that's not enough for many of the fans who grew up wishing to meet Charlotte Greene."

"You already have that." Rafe's fingers traced the edge of the table, so close to hers but still not touching.

"I have it in Blue Ash—not anywhere else."

Annie blew out a breath. Her chest hurt as she replayed that statement. She *wasn't* hiding in Blue Ash. Annie wanted to believe that, but—

Rafe's phone continued to ding. Apparently his late-night ice cream post was popular. He ignored it, but the outside world invaded their private haven with each buzz.

I want you. The real Rafe. The swing dancer who has a midnight sweet tooth and gets cold easily. Not the persona that makes an algorithm happy.

Annie swallowed the words as she spun her pint of ice cream toward him and grabbed his. "My turn for the chocolate."

A smile pulled at Rafe's lips. Lifting his spoon, he laughed. "I don't want cookie dough. *En garde*, Annie."

Giggling, she defended the chocolate from the swipes of his spoon as he dove for the carton. *This* was belonging. Laughing over ice cream, late at night, with no audience. How could she make him understand?

Finally she pushed it to the middle of the table. "Guess I can share."

The bottom of the carton appeared too quickly, and Annie waved away Rafe's offer to let her have the final bite. Looking at the clock, she reluctantly pushed away from the table.

If she didn't leave now...

"Thanks for keeping me company. We have a full schedule tomorrow. I think we both need some sleep."

Annie's fingers brushed his as they reached for the

empty ice cream containers at the same time. Lightning flashed between them, and suddenly Annie didn't care about the buzz of the phone, or anything else. She just wanted—needed—to know how he kissed.

"Rafe…"

Ignoring the tension racing through her belly, she leaned forward. He tasted of chocolate, heat and summer. Her heart gasped at the tender way his mouth shifted under hers, accepting her exploration.

If she took his hand, he'd come with her to bed…

The thought excited her before panic rushed into its place.

Stepping away, she stared at him. "I—"

Rafe placed a finger against her lips. "Don't apologize. Please."

Pursing her lips, she grabbed the containers, holding them before her like an empty sugar wall between her and temptation.

"I wasn't going to apologize."

Annie held her breath, wishing she had the courage to ask him to follow her and hating the uncertainty that kept the words buried.

Rafe soft lips brushed her cheek. "I'll see you tomorrow."

His words held a promise and an escape.

CHAPTER FOUR

JUST AS HIS fingers touched the blue cotton of Annie's nightshirt Rafe's alarm sounded. Wiping the sweat from his forehead, Rafe glared at his phone as he turned the alarm off. All of his dreams had involved Annie.

His body hadn't operated on so little sleep since his residency. Rolling his head, Rafe grimaced as his shoulders revolted. If the scattered bed sheets had been because Annie had spent the night in his bed Rafe wouldn't have minded the exhaustion.

The light press of her kiss had nearly driven him over the edge. Her fingers twisting along his shoulder had ignited the longing Rafe had been trying to ignore. He'd wanted to lift the light cotton separating them and kiss the line of freckles that disappeared under the nightshirt's scooped neckline. If Annie hadn't stepped away he'd have gladly stayed awake for several more hours, getting to know every inch of her.

Desire tugged at his groin and Rafe sucked in a breath. Annie had kissed him and walked away. He wanted her, but he was concerned about the connection vibrating between them. Annie was a romantic. She believed in love and the long-term. Rafe should keep his distance, but he didn't want to.

He needed to find another way to occupy his thoughts.

The smell of coffee wafted through his door. Caffeine called to him as he grabbed a sweater and headed for the kitchen.

Annie yawned as she turned to greet him. Grabbing the coffee pot, Annie tipped it toward him. "I made it extra-strong. Figured we needed it after—" heat traveled up her cheeks "—after our late night."

Lightning scattered across his body when Annie's fingers brushed his. She was just passing him a coffee mug, but Rafe hoped she meant more with that small touch. His mouth watered as his eyes wandered Annie's full lips.

Those lips shook slightly, before she gestured to the cabinet. "Do you want cereal or oatmeal?"

I want you.

Rafe cleared his throat. "A donut sounds good, but I'll settle for oatmeal." It was a dumb joke, and Rafe felt heat travel up his neck.

"Donut?"

Rafe wanted to believe Annie's brain was foggy with desire too, but his non-sequitur was surely to blame for her confusion.

Rafe winked, trying to recover from the flub. "Guess I'm just craving something sweet this morning."

Pink traveled up Annie's neck as she headed to the table. She was adorable. He wanted to kiss her. But Rafe leaned against the counter instead. "What's your favorite donut?"

It was a silly question, but he needed the answer. He wanted to know everything about Annie.

Annie hesitated. Was he really asking her about *donuts* after last night's kiss? Annie had wanted to jump into his arms this morning. Instead she'd forced herself to pour coffee and act normal. But if he was talking about pastries, then Rafe must want this morning to be like any other. That was good—but it stung.

"Are favorite donuts too personal?" Rafe teased.

"No…"

Annie ran a finger along her coffee mug. She didn't typically share details of her life. She'd spent her childhood and teen years being interviewed. When people probed it usually set off alarms in her mind. But Rafe always seemed genuinely interested in just *her*.

"I've never had a donut."

Rafe pushed his large hands through his dark hair and stared at her. What would those hands feel like running across her skin? Annie's stomach tightened with longing. A night with Rafe would be memorable, but he didn't believe in romance or love, and Annie didn't do flings. But she wanted Rafe—desperately.

Rafe's knee brushed hers as he slid into a chair. "How have you made it to adulthood and not had a double chocolate donut?"

His toffee eyes pressed against her soul.

He really wanted to know her history with pastries.

If she moved her pinky finger she'd brush his thumb.

She was in trouble…

Rafe's mouth watered, but it wasn't the oatmeal on his spoon he craved.

"Seriously, Annie, how have you managed to avoid donuts all this time? Every TV set I've ever been on has a sweet table. It sets my eight-year-old self and my doctor self at odds every time."

A shadow passed over her eyes as she lifted her coffee mug to her lips. "I wasn't allowed to eat anything that hadn't been approved by my mother. Charlotte had to look the same each season; it didn't matter that I was growing and changing."

Rafe's jaw clenched. "How could your mom—?"

Annie flinched and Rafe bit his lip. That was a stupid question. He *knew* her mother. Carrie was responsible for his entertainment career. She was driven, but "caring" and "maternal" were not adjectives anyone would ascribe to the woman. Living with her, being unable to fire her, must have been a nightmare.

Rafe opened his mouth to say so and then clenched it shut. He hadn't told Annie that Carrie was his agent. Their introduction had gone so haywire he hadn't wanted to inflame it even more. Now the omission hung between them like a knife.

"Sorry…" Rafe's voice trailed off. He was unsure if he was apologizing for Carrie's mistakes or his own.

"You don't need to apologize." Annie squeezed his hand.

He rubbed her thumb, grateful when she didn't pull away.

"Now you know my history with pastries, are there any other secrets you want to hear?" Annie winked, but her voice wavered slightly.

"All of them. I enjoy learning about you."

"Well, I had an 'interesting' childhood…" Annie's peppy voice raced across the kitchen.

Rafe gripped her hand tighter. "You're so much more than Charlotte Greene, Annie."

Her eyes sparkled but her lips turned down. How could she not see how amazing she was?

"You, Dr. Annie Masters, are fascinating." His heart lighted as she smiled at him. "And before I leave you are going to try a double chocolate donut." Rafe ran his finger along the soft skin of her wrist before forcing himself to release her.

"We're in the Arctic, Rafe."

"Really? I thought the snow was a hologram."

The sound of Annie's giggles sent a thrill through him.

"I'll still bet there's a donut shop here!"

"And what if I hate double chocolate donuts?" she teased, laughing harder as he threw a hand over his heart.

"Then we will just have to find a donut that calls to you. I firmly believe everyone has one that when they see it, they just have to taste it."

"Really?" Annie's eyes narrowed. "You are giving a lot of power to donuts."

Rafe's knee moved against hers as he leaned toward her. The soft scent of mint and lavender clung to her hair. Her lips were so close. He pressed his tongue to the roof of his mouth, willing the dry texture away.

"Whenever I moved to a new foster home I always found the closet donut shop. Double chocolate donuts were my dad's favorite, and on my worst days that donut always made me feel better. Donuts have a ton of power, and I refuse to believe otherwise."

Annie wrapped her fingers around his and Rafe closed his eyes. If she closed the distance between them Rafe would kiss her, run his hands through her hair… Sucking in a breath, Rafe tried to release the tension in his chest. He knew what it was like to kiss her now, and one taste hadn't been enough. Rafe suspected it would never be enough.

"I think I'd like to eat donuts with you," Annie said.

"Now I'm *definitely* going to find a donut shop."

Annie raised her coffee mug and her cheeks burned bright. "Well, let me know when you do."

* * *

Heat stormed across Annie's skin as she headed for the clinic. A conversation about donuts and she'd wanted to invite Rafe to spend the night with her. The invitation had been on the tip of her tongue.

She'd never thrown such an invitation to a partner before. She was reserved, cautious—an overthinker. She'd waited months to finally confess her attraction to Blake and lost precious time in the process.

Grabbing a stack of files from her desk, Annie toyed with the Band-Aid on her finger. Nerves warred with desire for control of her stomach. There were always going to be reasons to say no, but Annie didn't want to anymore. Tonight she was going to step into Rafe's arms and enjoy the limited amount of time they had.

A light tap against her door forced Annie's attention away from Rafe. "Dr. A?"

"Yes, Miranda?" Annie smiled at her receptionist as she stepped into the hall.

"Ms. Werth is in Room Three and she's cranky."

Tara Werth was always cranky. She'd moved to Alaska with the oil company's first wave of employees and dated every eligible man in town before declaring Blue Ash to be devoid of culture and acceptable bachelors. Her gripes were well rehearsed and well-known. She must be extra moody for Miranda even to notice.

"Thanks for the heads-up."

She took a quick look at Tara's chart before stepping into the exam room. There wasn't anything written down under "complaints." Bracing herself, Annie stepped into the room—and dropped the chart.

"Ms. Werth? Do you need my help to close your exam gown?"

The woman's shapely derriere clenched as she turned and glared at Annie. "I thought Dr. Bradstone was going to check my mole." She crossed her arms. "I specifically told Miranda I wanted to see Dr. Bradstone."

Bending to pick up the chart, Annie barely caught back a reprimand. Tara's plan was ridiculous—the sort of scene one might watch playing out in a cheesy made-for-TV movie. Dating patients was unethical anyway. Rafe would have looked at what Annie suspected was a nonexistent mole and sent the woman on her way.

This was the price of Rafe's rising star. Dealing with excitable fans willing to act out in order to get the attention of their object of fascination. This wasn't belonging—it was fans taking, expecting him to give whatever they demanded.

Offering what she hoped was a pleasant smile, Annie walked over. "Which mole would you like me to take a look at?"

"I don't want *you* to look at any of them. You're not *him*." Spittle formed at the corners of Tara's lips as she vibrated with anger.

Annie sat on the small stool in the room and waited for Tara's fury to subside. She'd seen this behavior before—the need to get to someone you admired and fantasized about. Though that had been people trying to get to *her*.

Taking a deep breath, Annie started again. "Tara—"

"I want to see the *famous* doctor!"

Patients' demands were often unmanageable, but this was ridiculous. Annie would look at Tara's mole and then make sure Tara was not released from the room until Rafe was with a patient. She might not be able to protect Rafe from the rabid fans in LA, but in Blue Ash she could ensure he wasn't accosted at work.

"Tara, I'm happy to examine your skin, but I will not interrupt the flow of my clinic. Now, where is this mole?"

Tara stuck her lip out, but Annie didn't waver. Finally, Tara frowned before pulling her gown up over her hip. A quarter-sized mole jutted out just below her waist.

"Obviously it's nothing," she huffed, and marched over to her clothes.

"Wait." Annie stepped closer. "I need to see that again."

"Why? It's just a dumb little mole." Tara's lip shook and a tear raced across her cheek.

"Do you have any history of skin cancer in your family?" Patting Tara's hand, Annie led her back to the exam table.

Tara's shoulders trembled as she nodded. The range of emotions patients displayed when they were scared was infinite.

"My mom had skin cancer. I've spent a lot of time in tanning beds… It's grown. I should have come in, but…"

She'd come because of Rafe. His star power had overridden Tara's fear. "Then it's a good thing you did."

Her waiting room had been packed since Rafe's arrival, but if they caught even a handful of diagnoses for patients who wouldn't have walked through her door otherwise, then Annie was grateful for his Tinseltown ties.

"I'm going to remove the mole and send a sample to the lab."

"It's *cancer*?" Tara's voice ricocheted around the room.

The word terrified everyone, but Annie needed Tara to stay calm. "It might be a basal cell carcinoma. It's a very treatable form of skin cancer. If necessary, we can use a cream to kill any other cells. I'll call with the results as soon as we have them."

Tara wiped a tear from her cheek. "Can Dr. Bradstone call me instead?"

"No." Rafe was a doctor—not public property. "Since I'm treating you, and I'm your physician of record, I'll make the call. You can feel free to contact the clinic with any questions."

Annie stepped out of the exam room and glared at the giggles echoing from the room where Rafe was seeing a patient. Pain shot along her jaw, and she forced her teeth to unclench. It wasn't Rafe's fault people were booking appointments just to meet him.

She was jealous. Her muscles tightened as the emotion ripped through her. If she wanted to explore her connection with Rafe, this was one of the prices to be paid. Did it matter that so many people vied for his attention?

Annie waited for fear or uncertainty to tumble through her, but it was excitement and longing that materialized.

It didn't matter that Rafe was extremely popular with his fans. It didn't matter that he was returning to LA or that he liked his fame. Annie needed to know what would happen if she stepped into his well-defined arms and followed through on the desire bubbling in each of them.

"Enjoying the snowstorm?"

Annie's soft scent released a little of the tension in his shoulders. "Didn't realize we were having a snowstorm," he said.

"It won't be too bad, but for the next two weeks our patient load will be pretty light. I've got snowmobiles in the garage if there's an emergency."

"Two weeks…" Rafe croaked. Winter was closer than he wanted to admit.

"These early snows always melt faster than the weathermen predict." Her lips folded as her eyes met his. "Don't worry—Jack can still fly you out if necessary."

He hated that her first thought was his escape plan. Rafe didn't want Annie worrying about what the snow meant for *him*. He was worried about *her* winter plans. He knew Jenn was still trying to get her father situated in his retirement home.

Rafe stared at the snow piling up in the parking lot. "What if Jenn can't get here?"

The question hovered between them. Rafe wished he could pull it back. He wanted to joke about donuts or discuss musicals—not remind them both that his time in Blue Ash had an expiration date.

Annie shrugged. "Then I winter it alone—again."

Again. He hated that word. "What about Dr. Henkle? He should be here to help out."

"Liam is busy." Annie's smile faltered.

His brain flipped at her statement. "So are *you*, Annie. Doing everything yourself isn't sustainable."

Annie looked at the ceiling. "Liam can't be here full-time. He just can't."

Had they been lovers? Was that why her partner was keeping his distance? Jealousy pooled through him, and he pushed it away. Everyone had a past.

"I can't stay through the winter."

"I'm not asking you to!" She threw her hands in the air.

The pain rolling through Rafe surprised him. He should be *glad* she wasn't demanding more than he could give—that he didn't have to disappoint her. Except he wanted to be able to make Annie promises.

"I'm sorry. I shouldn't probe about your clinic staffing. You've run this place through four winters."

Alone.

"I appreciate the concern. I really do." Annie's eyes darted to the falling snow. "This wasn't how tonight was supposed to start."

Annie's sigh punched at him. He'd wanted tonight to start differently too. "I'm worried about you. You shouldn't be alone."

Rafe stepped forward, praying she wouldn't retreat.

"What about you?" Annie stepped closer. "Despite all those fans you're alone."

Rafe ran a finger along her chin. "I don't feel alone when I'm with you."

"I'm glad." Annie stepped into his arms.

Everything shifted as he closed the distance between their lips. Annie had kissed Rafe last night; now he kissed her.

Her soft lips opened and Rafe thought his senses would explode. Running his fingers along her back, Rafe lost himself in the subtle sighs echoing from Annie. Blood pounded in his ears. He wanted nothing more than to race upstairs, but he'd arranged a surprise for her.

"I have something for you."

Rafe had asked one of his patients where to get donuts. The sweet woman had recommended he call Annie's baker friend, Holly. She'd personally delivered her favorite dozen during her lunch break.

Small lines danced at the corner of her lips as Annie smiled. "You do?" Her eyes sparked with anticipation as she placed a light kiss against Rafe's jaw. "Why don't we look at it upstairs?"

"I'll grab it from the back and meet you there."

Rafe's heart raced as Annie smiled at him.

Holding the donuts, he climbed the stairs to the apartment two at a time. Tonight held so much promise.

Rafe hesitated in the kitchen. "Annie?"

"I'm in my room. Come on—the show is about to start."

Rafe held his breath as he stepped across the threshold of Annie's private sanctuary. This was not a place she invited people, and Rafe was humbled that she wanted him here.

The room was huge—larger than any of the studio apartments he'd lived in since moving to LA. A large blanket was lain across the floor, and Rafe's heart felt like it wanted to explode as he gazed at the massive skylight. His body tensed with longing as he moved his eyes away from her iron post bed with its homey pink-and-gray quilt.

Rafe set the donuts on the bright purple chest decorated with sunflowers at the end of her bed. "This is unique," Rafe said, as he slid the top off the box.

"Unique?" Annie laughed as she crossed her legs. "I made it. Everyone needs a winter hobby. Mine is repurposing furniture—usually in bright colors! I can smell sweetness from here; did you buy dessert for the show?"

Rafe turned his head, looking for a television. "You want to watch a movie?"

"No! In about ten minutes the northern lights are going to dance across that skylight."

Rafe smiled as he placed one of the donuts on the plate Holly had kindly included. "I promised you a double chocolate donut."

A slow smile spread across Annie's face as she stared at the gooey pile. "You bought me donuts?"

"Yep. For future reference, your friend Holly doesn't just make cookies and cakes. Something you might learn, if you spent a bit more time away from the clinic."

Rafe hurried on, not wanting to start another spat, "Holly was very impressed I was wooing you with donuts."

Annie's hands hovered over the box. "Wooing me with donuts? You *are* a romantic."

Leaning across the blanket, Rafe pressed his lips to the soft dimple in her cheek. He liked that Annie thought he was a romantic, but it wasn't true. He didn't want to give her expectations.

"It's just donuts, Annie. Romance is grand gestures and sweeping statements." He was only offering a donut.

Staring at the donut, Annie laughed. "You're wrong. Romance is the little things." Tearing the donut, Annie handed him half. "You, Dr. Rafe Bradstone, are a romantic."

Rafe raised an eyebrow but didn't argue. He suspected anyone Annie let get close would want to do things for her. It was impossible not to fall under her spell.

"To donuts on a blanket, under the northern lights, with great company."

As she bit into the donut Annie's eyes lit up. "Oh, that is *good*." Annie leaned her head against his chest and sighed. "Thank you, Rafe."

"Anytime."

Running his fingers along her shoulder, Rafe smiled. He'd waited all day for this quiet moment with Annie. This moment—her sitting in his arms eating a donut—was one Rafe suspected he'd spend the rest of his life replaying. Leaning closer, he inhaled the soft scent of chocolate and lavender cascading off her. If there was a better place to be than the Arctic with Dr. Annie Masters, he wasn't sure he wanted to find it.

"Rafe…"

His name on her lips sent need racing through him. Swallowing, Rafe let his eyes linger on her soft mouth for only a moment before meeting her gaze.

"Yes?"

"Kiss me."

The simple request nearly undid him.

The sky lit up as his lips met hers. Blues and greens burst through the skylight as Annie ran her hands along the base of his neck.

"Rafe…"

She tasted of chocolate, sugar and simply Annie. His name on her lips sent waves of need cascading through him. Rafe pulled her into his lap, let his hands stroke the back of her neck before he moved to undo the tight bun she always wore.

Annie pulled back, doubt crossing her eyes. Rafe sucked in a ragged breath. He wanted her, but if she had any doubts…

"Annie, if you want to watch the lights—"

Her hands trembled as she reached for the rubber band. "My curls are crazy. My hairdresser used to spend two hours straightening them when I played Charlotte." Tight curls sprang from their confines, cascading past her shoulders. "Everyone expects—"

He captured her statement with his mouth. Rafe didn't care about Charlotte. Didn't want that name lingering between them.

"You're gorgeous, *Annie*."

Tonight, there was only Rafe and Annie. Her fictional character was a cardboard illustration compared to the woman before him.

Annie smiled, but he could see that Charlotte's ghost clung to her.

Pulling her hand across his stomach, Rafe kissed her cheek and waited until her eyes met his. "It's *you* I want touching me. The woman who helped me with Mac's leg and joked about superhero undies, who told me I needed new shoes if I didn't want to lose my toes, who decorated that bright purple-and-yellow chest and who I watched devour her first donut. It's *you*, Annie."

Annie placed her hands on either side of Rafe's face and urged him to kiss her. Demanded it. And he was more than willing to oblige.

Gripping her butt, Rafe fell into the kiss. Dipping his head, he traced her neck with his tongue before turning his attention to the buttons of her shirt. He kissed each inch of skin that appeared as he pushed her shirt to the floor. He skimmed the line of freckles dotting the tops of her breasts.

"You are amazing, Annie…"

As Rafe turned his attention to her full round breasts, Annie felt the room start to shake.

Worry transited her veins, but the small earth tremors that were a monthly occurrence here didn't really bother her.

Rafe—she could fall for him. A part of her already had…

Annie's thoughts were jumbled as Rafe's soft lips captured hers.

Her pictures clacked against the wall and the building creaked as the room swayed. Was the earth celebrating this union or warning her?

Annie threw off the random thought as Rafe's heat melted through her. And as they melded together Annie's worries floated away. She wanted him—even if it was only for tonight.

Annie wrapped her arms around Rafe's shoulders as the earth shook. His fingers gripped her hips.

"Was that an earthquake?"

Annie grinned. "Don't you live in California?"

"Yes—but, in case you haven't noticed the snow and extreme cold, this isn't California."

Fire exploded across her skin as Rafe's lips trailed along the top of her breasts.

No, it wasn't California.

Running her fingers along the zipper of his jeans, Annie felt her stomach flutter when his breath hitched. "There was a tremor the day you arrived too. Were you so taken with finding me you didn't notice?"

Rafe nipped her shoulder. "I was, and still am, *very* taken with you."

His fingers slid down her back. He unhooked her bra and sat up. His dark eyes swept across her body, but he didn't touch her. Panic traced up Annie's spine as he stared at her. Was she not what he'd expected...wanted?

"You are perfect."

Her lips trembled at the simple statement. She wasn't sure it was true, but she appreciated the words.

"Glad you like freckles."

Rafe's brows furrowed, and then he gripped her buttocks, lifting them both as he stood.

"Rafe!"

Gentle fingers laid her across the bed. "I like everything about you, Annie." Rafe's head dipped as he licked the top of her chest. His fingers swept along the top of her jeans. "You are exquisite."

He grazed the delicate skin along her belly while he unzipped her jeans. Then, kneeling beside the bed, he pulled her to the edge.

Annie sat up and reached for him, but Rafe shook his head. "I've spent far too many minutes wondering what you taste like, and now I plan to find out."

"Rafe..." Her breath caught as his teeth nipped the soft skin of her thighs.

Rising, his lips captured her moans. "We have all night, and I plan to savor you."

Feather kisses sent tiny shocks across her skin, but it wasn't enough. Her body burned, pulsed with desire. "Please…"

Hovering over her stomach, Rafe chuckled as Annie pressed her hips against him. "Demanding? I like that."

She wasn't normally demanding, but Rafe had unleashed an unexpected delightful wantonness in her. Cool air caressed her butt as Rafe removed her lacy panties. She quivered as he nuzzled her, his mouth teasing her, driving her closer to the edge. When his tongue dipped into her Annie wrapped her legs around him.

"Sweet, succulent and perfect."

Pleasure rocketed through her as Rafe drove her over the edge. It still wasn't enough.

Annie's hands ruffled his hair. "I need you, Rafe. *All* of you—please!"

Rafe quickly deposited his clothes on the floor. He'd never seen a sexier sight than Annie's closed eyes when she finally surrendered. She was perfect…and his—at least for tonight.

"I need you…"

Her breathy words broke him. Quickly sheathing himself, Rafe pulled her to the edge of the bed and drove home. She met his thrusts, demanding more, but he refused to hurry.

Gripping her hips, he forced their pace to slow. "I'm not rushing this."

Rafe held Annie's gaze as he thrust. Her eyes were dilated, and her ankles dug into his tight buttocks as Rafe bent his head to capture a rose-colored nipple between his lips.

Her fingers dug into his shoulders. "Rafe…"

Annie's body convulsed around him, but he refused to adjust his pace. If he lived to be a hundred Rafe doubted there would be a better sound than his name as Annie climaxed.

Her lips caressed his shoulder and a growl of desire echoed through him. Finally, he gave in to his own need. Annie's hips met his as he drove into her, and waves of heat and need pulsated through him as she crested over pleasure's edge a final time. And then reason turned to oblivion as Annie clung to him. At last, Rafe let himself join her.

Annie sucked in a deep breath. "That was—"

He loved the pink blush traveling up her cheeks as she stared at him.

When she didn't elaborate Rafe pressed. "Yes?"

Annie laughed. "I have no words."

He chuckled at her quiet statement but didn't argue. Tonight had been simply perfection.

CHAPTER FIVE

ANNIE'S FINGERS TRACED Rafe's shoulder blade before she placed a light kiss against his back. Careful not to wake him, she rolled over. Her eyes wandered across the ceiling as she tried to convince herself she'd be okay when he left. Last night had been amazing, but that didn't have to mean anything. They had a connection, an attraction, something they each wanted to explore.

Annie was lying to herself—and it wasn't even a good lie. She cared for Rafe—and not in a temporary "say goodbye in a few weeks" fling way.

She hadn't felt this way since Blake, and she hadn't gotten the chance to spend forever with Blake. Was she willing to risk her heart with Rafe?

She'd already risked it—except in the morning light everything might change.

There hadn't been many men in her life. The two she'd gotten close to since Blake's death had ended the relationship soon after they'd slept with her. Everyone went to bed with Charlotte Greene and woke next to crazy-haired, freckled Annie Masters.

She didn't want to believe it would happen with Rafe, but as his soft snores hit her back she slipped from the bed. It was a cowardly retreat, but she couldn't bear to see his face if that shift happened.

Pulling on some torn jeans and a flannel shirt, she walked into her living room. Taking the picture of Blake and Liam off the shelf, she ran her fingers across Blake's soft smile. She'd always love him. It felt wrong that she hadn't told Rafe that part of her heart was already gone. Would he still want her if he knew she'd always love another?

"Who's that?" Rafe's deep voice rolled through her as he slipped his arms around her. He pressed a kiss to her shoulder.

"That's Liam and his brother, Blake." Annie looked up at him and kissed his cheek.

"Blake? Your friend from the Army."

Friend. That title was inaccurate and her stomach twisted. She hadn't meant to downplay their relationship.

Her mouth was dry, but she managed to force out, "Liam is Blake's brother, and Helen and Jack are his parents."

Rafe tightened his fingers along her shoulder. "You came to Alaska after he died?"

She set the photo down before turning in Rafe's arms. If he didn't understand it would be better for her to find out now. Annie hated digging into this part of her past but keeping this information from Rafe was wrong. She loved Blake and she wasn't going to hide that.

"This was Blake and Liam's land—their home. They thought it would make an excellent clinic. They were worried about the lack of medical personnel in this region of the Arctic."

"Blake joined the Army and planned to head to med school after serving his tour. I promised to help him get the clinic off the ground."

The Army had brought them together, and then it had ripped them apart.

"You loved him."

Rafe kissed the top of her forehead, but there was an emotion hovering in his eyes that she couldn't place.

"Yes. Blake made me believe I was more than Charlotte Greene."

So do you.

She sucked in a breath. Blake's loss had devastated her, but time had healed most of the wound.

"Blake was my best friend and my fiancé. He died in combat the week after he proposed."

"Fiancé?"

Rafe's voice was strained, but he didn't let go of her. She leaned her head against his shoulder. Blake was her past, but if she wanted a future with Rafe—even a temporary one—he deserved to know this.

"I should have told you."

Looking up, she met Rafe's gaze, willing him to say something.

"Is this why you left our bed?" he asked. His finger trembled as it ran along her cheek.

Our bed...

The words sent a shiver of delight down her legs. She wanted an "ours" with Rafe. She was in trouble—serious trouble.

"Did you run from me this morning?"

She couldn't force the words out, so she nodded, hating the flash of pain falling across his face.

Rafe's heart shattered as he looked at Annie's freckles. "If you don't want to continue our relationship, I understand," he said, but his words died as he ran a hand through his hair.

He stared at the smiling man in the picture on the shelf. He couldn't live up to him. He had become a doctor for all the wrong reasons. He chased the spotlight while Blake had served his country—sacrificed everything. He was the hero Annie described when she talked about love.

Annie wrapped her arms around his neck. "I—I want to wake in your arms tomorrow. I just needed you to know about Blake. I know this is temporary, but it felt wrong that I hadn't told you."

Temporary—he hated that word. But it was good that she wasn't counting on him. He wasn't Blake...wasn't forever.

"I'm glad you told me. He was a lucky man."

His phone rang. The interruption brought his life in LA to the forefront. Rafe pulled it out of his pocket and silenced it.

"Do you need to get that?" Annie asked.

"I can call my agent back anytime."

Annie frowned and stepped away. Just the word was enough to make her pull away from him. But Rafe knew her thoughts on Hollywood—it shouldn't sting.

"You didn't look—"

"She's the only one who calls me, Annie."

The sad statement ripped from him. No one called him.

Annie pulled his phone out of his pocket and slapped it into his hand. "Put my number in."

"What?"

Annie rolled her eyes and tapped his phone. "Put my number in. Your agent isn't going to be the only one calling you, Rafe. Not anymore." She kissed the tip of his nose before heading to the kitchen. "Call her back while I make coffee."

Rafe stared at the photo of Blake and Liam for several more minutes. Annie had come to Alaska to fulfill a promise to her fiancé. She wasn't hiding in this remote location. She was serving it in the place of a local man, a man she'd loved who'd never come home.

Rocking on his heels, Rafe tried to determine the emotions swirling through him. Annie still loved Blake and she always would. That didn't bother Rafe, but what if he wasn't worthy of her? If he opened his heart to her, would she accept all the baggage he carried? Annie deserved the best. Rafe knew that wasn't him, but he didn't want to walk away.

His phone rang again, and Rafe glared at the reminder of his other life. The glow of the cameras and the excitement he felt on stage were amazing. He wanted to believe there was a way to have both. But—

The phone buzzed again and he finally answered. "Carrie—"

Before he could get more out, his agent launched into a well-rehearsed script, "Rafe, we have a problem. Dave is demanding each of the hosts being considered for promotion to full-time host give him an interview. I've already worked out the details. We'll get a crew up there—a remote wilderness location is an interesting topic…much more intriguing than what Dr. Milo and Dr. Dean have planned. I already spoke with Dave, and he loves the idea. The job is as good as yours!"

"Wait."

Chills cascaded through him. Annie had walked away from Hollywood. He wasn't bringing those lights here.

"When does the interview have to be done?"

Carrie's silence dragged and Rafe smiled.

"Your silence speaks volumes."

He would postpone it—at least until he got back to LA. His ratings were significantly higher than the other potential hires; he didn't need the remote wilderness.

Bile raked across his tongue as he stared at Blake's image. He couldn't ask Annie to give up Blake's dream for Hollywood's shallowness. But he'd spent the last several years working toward a permanent position on *Dr. Dave.* If he gave it up he'd have nothing when Annie realized he wasn't enough for her. If he gambled on chemistry and lost...

Swallowing the lump at the back of his throat, Rafe vowed he'd make the most of their temporary time.

"Rafe! If you want this job then you'll do this interview now—before the others do. The other doctors are basing their shoots in LA. You'll be the only one with the sexy Arctic wilderness. It's what Dave wants."

He flinched as Carrie's sharp rebuke echoed in his ear. Staring at the ceiling, he tried to slow the creep of unease worming through his belly. "Sexy Arctic wilderness..." That wasn't what Annie's clinic was.

"Rafe, you've spent the last two years proving yourself to Dave," Carrie hissed. "He's going to offer you the permanent position. I'm certain of it." His agent paused for a moment, and her voice was softer when she offered, "Don't throw it away."

Sinking into the couch, Rafe ran his hands through his hair. This was more than Annie's clinic and her home—it was her mission. He couldn't ask her to give up her privacy so that he got a promotion.

"The clinic I'm at isn't really interested in publicity."

Carrie hesitated for a moment, and he heard her breathing hitched on the line before her falsetto cracked over the phone. "Dave wants an in-depth look at Arctic wilderness medicine and lots of snow. If you sell it to Annie as advancing remote medicine and the need for rural practitioners she'll do it."

Rafe though he might be ill. This morning was too full of revelations. "You know I'm in Blue Ash."

"The two social media posts you've done have location tags in Blue Ash." Carrie's sharp statement cut across the line.

"After you ran away to Tennessee for four weeks last year, it seemed prudent to keep track of you."

"I didn't run away."

Rafe pulled at a loose thread on his jeans. He'd chased a dream in Tennessee, and it had gone up in smoke. He wasn't going to lose his chance at the promotion now.

Looking out the window, he stared at the snowflakes pouring down. "*If* I ask Annie to participate—and I am not promising—Dave needs to understand this is a state-of-the-art clinic. We can talk about remote medicine and doctor shortages, but I won't downplay the amazing work she's done here."

"How *is* my daughter?"

Rafe buried his head in his hands. Carrie's quiet question held so many others as Rafe tried to force air into his lungs. He'd never told Annie about his agent being her mom. His other life hadn't seemed to matter much. But he knew it was more than that. He hadn't trusted her to accept it. Now he didn't know how to tell her without driving her away.

Blowing out a breath, he stumbled over his words. "Would Annie want me to answer that?"

"No." His agent's voice—Annie's mother's voice—cracked as she sucked in a rough breath. "Maybe you should have taken another vacation to Tennessee instead of heading to the Arctic. Dave really wants the northern story now."

Carrie didn't know about what had happened in Tennessee, but her statement tore through him. "Well, I'm not in Tennessee!"

Rafe slammed the phone to the floor, not caring that he hadn't said goodbye.

"What's in Tennessee?" Annie looked concerned as she stood in the doorway.

How much had she heard?

"Nothing is in Tennessee!"

A frown tripped across her face. *He'd* done that, and he hated it. But it wasn't a lie—nothing *was* in Tennessee…at least not for him.

Why hadn't he told her about Carrie? Rafe wanted to flay his earlier self. That single omission threatened everything now.

He tried to force words out, but his tongue refused to move. "I…uh… I…need to see to a few things in my room." That wasn't what he'd meant to say.

"Of course." Annie's voice was barely audible.

She didn't stop him as he pushed past her. Not that he blamed her. Annie had shared an important part of her past with him this morning and he'd walked away. If he wanted another reason to see how he didn't measure up to her former love, there it was.

Boxes were scattered across the reception area when Rafe finally found his way downstairs. A smiling ghoul hovered over the reception desk and a cauldron full of sugar-free candy had materialized by the door. His clinic in LA didn't bother with Halloween decorations; it was the same sterile beige walls and flowerpot pictures no matter the season.

Annie was hanging pumpkin string lights along the outer edges of the room. The tight pull of her shoulders made his heart ache. He'd hurt her. There was so much he needed to say.

"Annie, I'm sorry. I shouldn't have snapped at you."

"We all have things we don't want to talk about."

Holding up the strand of lights, he swallowed. This wasn't a tale he'd ever divulged. "Maybe but—" He coughed as she stepped off the step ladder.

"You don't owe me an explanation."

"I do." *For so many things.* Gesturing to a box, he tried to work up his courage. "What can I help with?"

"Those cobwebs need hanging on the windows." She pointed to the white pile of fluff on the floor beside her. "And there are pretend spiders in one of those boxes to add to them."

Twisting a cobweb through his fingers, Rafe stared at the spiders. "You told me about Blake, to give me the option of walking away. But you aren't the only one with baggage that changes things."

"Vanessa?" Annie tilted her head. "Rafe, I don't care about those tabloid headlines."

"Vanessa is an ex. We all have those. I meant my parents. The reason I need the attention you abhor."

Rafe sucked in a breath and then began.

"My mom was in Tennessee…" Tears coated his eyes and he clenched his fists. He was *not* going to shed any tears over that woman. "Actually, she still is in Tennessee. I think." He wrapped the cobweb around a nail on the window seal.

"She's still alive?"

The pumpkin lanterns trembled in Annie's hands as she stared at him. What would she think of him after he told her his own mother hadn't believed him worthy of love?

Rafe watched a few snowflakes melt against the window before he nodded. "Yeah. My dad died in a car accident when I was seven." He pushed a few spiders into the web before turning around. "Mom supported him while he chased his dreams of being a dancer. He cheated on her. Despite his cheating, she never left him. I remember her screaming at him how much she loved him, begging him to stay. She turned hard as glass when she found out he'd died in a car with her best friend. They'd been having an affair for months, apparently."

"Wow."

"Yeah—it's the stuff of TV movies." Rafe didn't try to stop the bitter laugh tumbling from his lips. "I look just like my dad. I act like him too—my walk and the way I talk. He used to call me his mini me."

He'd taken the burden of all the rage his mother hadn't been able to use on his father. All his small misdemeanors had resulted in long lectures on how he'd eventually be a liar and a womanizer.

"After he died she couldn't look at me. I used to scream at her, but she looked right past me."

Annie pulled the web from his hands. "She put you in foster care?"

He closed his eyes, hating the tear sliding down his cheek. "After he passed she stopped taking care of me. When Social Services were called in she didn't even fight for me."

Annie's arms were wrapped around his waist, and he drew strength from her heat.

"Despite that, I always thought it was a mistake. That she'd looked for me, but the authorities wouldn't tell her where I was. I had quite the fantasy life—most kids in the system do. Easier to pretend our parents miss us. I guess some do, but not mine."

Rafe inhaled the soft scent of Annie's hair. Would she

still hold him like this when he told her about his connection to her mom?

Burying that fear, he continued, "I made the mistake of tracking her down via social media last year. I should have reached out on the internet, but in my head I thought our reunion would be better if I just showed up. That's how the movies play out. Everyone gets their happy ending, right?"

"Fiction is often nicer than the real world." Annie squeezed him before kissing his cheek.

Laying his head on top of hers, Rafe watched the snow fall as he went on. "I honestly assumed she'd be happy to see me."

Rafe's chest clenched as he reached the end of his story. His mother didn't want him. Thought he was unworthy. How could anyone see worth in him if his parent couldn't?

"She *should* have been happy to see you. Proud of the man you've become." Annie placed a light kiss along his cheek as she laid her hand against his heart. "It's her failing if she wasn't—not yours."

The tension in Rafe's shoulders relaxed as he wrapped his arms around Annie. She'd seen the good in him. A burden lifted off his heart as he stared into Annie's welcoming gaze. The rest of the story tumbled forth, but the bitterness coating it had dissipated.

"I'd played our reunion out in my head so many times." He had bounced outside her door, excited for what he had known was going to be an amazing day. "Instead, she ordered me off her porch, hissing that her new family didn't know I existed."

Rafe laid his head against Annie's curls. Opening up to her seemed so easy.

"Seems I look even more like my dad now. Before

slamming the door in my face, she told me I was better off alone. That all the men in my family were users and incapable of love."

"That was a bitter hateful thing for her to say, and it was a lie." Annie's lips met his, their softness molding against them. "You are *not* responsible for your parents' faults."

"I know your mom." His words squeaked out.

"I think *everyone* knows my mom." Annie's smile was brittle as she squeezed him.

"Annie—"

She laid a finger over Rafe's lips. "Please. I don't want to talk about my mother. I'm too busy convincing a very handsome doctor that he is so much more than the awful words flung at him."

Annie's fingers pressed against his chin, and she laid her head against his chest.

"Don't let your mother's venom poison your future."

Hope pushed against Rafe's heart. Maybe someone *could* love him. He'd convinced himself he didn't need love—that the emotion didn't exist. What if he was wrong?

Holding Annie, Rafe felt his heart overriding his mind's objections. Maybe Annie—

His phone buzzed and the tiny bubble popped. Again Rafe had failed to tell Annie her mother was his agent. His brain screamed that he was a coward.

But he wanted to believe Annie. Wanted to think that there was a place for him on her shelf and in her life. But Rafe knew he wasn't worth keeping. His mother, Vanessa, countless foster families... No one had ever wanted to keep him. Eventually Annie wouldn't want him around either.

They'd already discussed Blake and his mother this

morning. He'd find a better time to tell her about Carrie. But that interview was not happening in Blue Ash. It would happen in LA if he couldn't find another "exotic" location for Dave. Rafe was *not* bringing cameras to Annie's clinic. No promotion was worth destroying her serene home.

CHAPTER SIX

RAFE SMILED AT Annie as she dropped one patient's record off and grabbed another. The past few days had been blissful. He'd briefly worried that working together would be awkward after they'd begun dating, but it actually made the day so much better.

They started the day with breakfast, went over patient's records, and Annie often shared little notes to make his patient interactions easier. At lunch they grabbed a quick sandwich in the main office, usually while finishing up morning patient notations, and then they met up for dinner.

The schedule already felt familiar—and perfect.

Now he had one final patient, and then he could spend the rest of his evening laughing, talking and making love to Annie before starting the wonderful cycle over again tomorrow.

Stepping into the exam room, Rafe held out his hand. "Good afternoon, I'm Dr. Bradstone."

"Amelia Clarke." The woman's cheeks flushed as she gripped Rafe's hand. "I can't believe I get to meet a famous person!" She squealed, and then immediately started coughing.

Rafe nodded. He'd run into several exuberant fans since his arrival in Blue Ash. They saw Annie regularly too, but no one seemed to react to her the same way. "Well, why don't you let me check that cough?"

Amelia waved a hand. "It's nothing. I came because my ear hurts."

Rafe frowned. Her cough sounded painful, but she'd turned her head and was pointing at her ear. He'd start with her complaint, but he was going to listen to her chest too.

Her eardrum was inflamed and pulsing. "Your right ear is infected," he told her. "Now I want to listen to your lungs."

"I'm just not as young as I was, Dr. Bradstone. I've had this cough for a few weeks. It will go away. Really."

She started to hop off the table but Rafe put his hand up. "Humor me." He held up the stethoscope and smiled.

Amelia sighed but acquiesced.

Her lungs were raspy. Rafe suspected she had walking pneumonia. The ear infection might be related, but it was more likely her body was trying to fight the pneumonia and hadn't been able to battle the dual infection.

Rafe pulled up a chair and folded his arms. "Mrs. Clarke—"

"Please call me Amelia."

"Amelia." Rafe smiled—everyone in Blue Ash insisted on first names. He liked that; it made him feel closer to Annie's patients. "I think you may have walking pneumonia. I need to schedule a chest X-ray to confirm. The clinic is closing now, but come in first thing tomorrow. Until then, I'm going to start you on some antibiotics for the ear infection."

Amelia frowned as she held his gaze. "Well, at least I'll get to tell my canasta group that a real celebrity checked me out twice."

Rafe laughed. "You've been checked by Dr. A before.

Even though she hasn't acted in years, she's still more famous than me."

"Yes, but Dr. A is *family*. Family doesn't count for famous." She chuckled before coughing again.

"Family?" Rafe asked. He'd thought Carrie was the only relation Annie had.

Amelia smiled, but it didn't quite reach her eyes as she patted his knee. "I taught her fiancé Blake in high school. He was such a smart boy. I never had children of my own, so I adopted all my students. Blake loved Annie, so that makes her family too. I didn't see them together, but she turned his dream into a beautiful legacy so they must have been wonderful."

Rafe's chest was heavy as he wrote out the order for an X-ray. Emotions raced through him and he had a hard time catching his breath.

"That is lovely." He knew his voice sounded stilted, but Amelia didn't seem to notice.

"I tried setting Annie up with my nephew when she moved to town. They went on two dates, but I think that was just to humor me. Colin said she was polite, but clearly not interested. Some people only love once."

Rafe swallowed as he stood. *Love.* That emotion didn't have a place in his world. So why did the thought that Annie might be incapable of loving someone else tear through him?

Amelia grabbed the paper from his hand. "Look at me…gibbering on." She shook his hand and headed for the door.

Rafe didn't follow. Looking around the room, Rafe sighed. This clinic, and the work Annie was doing here, was impressive. It was a testament to her love for Blake, ensuring his legacy.

What was Rafe's legacy? The uncomfortable question rolled through him.

If he died today, people would have only YouTube videos and social media posts. Nothing that matched the scale of a clinic providing medicine to an underserved community.

"There you are." Annie pecked his cheek as she stepped up beside him. "Amelia has scheduled her X-ray for tomorrow before we officially open, so our shift is starting early." She bumped his hip. "Earth to Rafe?"

He placed a kiss against her forehead. "Sorry, I guess my mind is wandering."

Heat ripped up his arms as Annie wrapped her fingers through his.

"Where was it wandering?"

"Nowhere important." Rafe squeezed her tightly.

"Rafe?" A line appeared across Annie's forehead. "What's wrong?"

Brushing his lips against hers, Rafe smiled. "Nothing, sweetheart. Promise. I just got lost in thought at the end of a long day." Tapping her nose, Rafe winked. "We've been seeing patients for over ten hours. How do you keep up this schedule?"

Annie laughed, but the worry line didn't move. "You get used to it." Pulling him toward the door, Annie squeezed his hand. "Let's order in."

"Sounds good."

Rafe wrapped his arm around Annie's waist. He had to leave in a few weeks—it didn't matter that Blake had been her one true love or that Rafe's legacy was a daytime talk show. *It didn't*.

The pillow was cold against Annie's hand when she reached for Rafe. Sitting up, she rubbed at her eyes and glared at the clock on her phone. It was a few minutes before five—where was he?

She shivered as her feet hit the cool floor. Grabbing her robe, she padded to the kitchen. It was empty.

Frowning, she headed for the guest room. Rafe hadn't used it in two weeks. If he'd left their bed for—

Her stomach clenched as she pushed the door open. She was not going to worry. *She wasn't.*

Panic rippled down Annie's back as she stared at the empty room.

"Rafe?" The name echoed in the hallway, but no answer floated back.

Racing for the clinic door, Annie tried to calm her hammering heart. Rafe wouldn't leave without telling her. She was overreacting.

But she couldn't seem to catch her breath.

The clinic was quiet, but a light in her office showed under the door. Taking a deep breath, Annie wanted to slap herself. Rafe was fine and her overreaction was ridiculous.

Swallowing, Annie considered going back up to their room. *Their* room? When had her sanctuary become theirs?

The moment she'd invited him to spend the night.

Her heart squeezed as that truth hit her and she walked toward her office. Whatever time they had left, she wanted to spend it with him.

Rafe was staring at the computer and furiously writing notes. His full lips were pursed as he read something on the screen.

Leaning against the door, Annie drank in his image. Need coated her nerves as she stared at his mussed hair and the stubble coating his chin. He was perfect.

His lips parted as he finally raised his eyes and saw her in the doorway. "Annie?"

"Nope. I'm a sleepy snow nymph who's come searching for her partner." She laughed as she dropped a light kiss against his lips. "If you're so tired that you don't recognize me in the doorway, maybe you shouldn't sneak from our bed so early in the morning."

She yelped as he pulled her into his lap.

"Rafe…" Annie moaned as the rough stubble along his chin rubbed against the sensitive skin at the base of her neck.

His hands locked around her waist. "Sorry, Annie. Stephen Donovan is having some issues. Dave wants an interview that Stephen doesn't think is a good idea. He's sent me the research—asked me to take a look and give my opinion to Dave."

"Isn't Dr. Donovan a full-time host? Why wouldn't Dave listen to him?" Annie shifted in Rafe's lap so she had a better view of the computer screen.

Rafe's fingers tapped a few keys and he pulled up an academic study. "They got into an argument a few seasons ago—before I came on board. Every so often I get a request from one of the other doctors to talk Dave out of a crazy segment. He usually listens to me—not sure why."

Rafe highlighted a few things on the screen. "Stephen sent me a panicked text a little before three. I didn't mean to wake up so early. Apparently, Dave wants to cover hot yoga and its benefits for cystic fibrosis."

"What?" Annie turned her focus from Rafe's sexy features to the screen. "Is there any scientific support for this?"

"From the research I found—minimal. It could also cause harm if the studio isn't clean. I shot off a few emails this morning to Dave and the producers, suggesting it was a poor topic. Hopefully they'll listen." Rafe's fingers slipped up her spine.

"I never realized you did so much for the show."

She'd assumed it was just an avenue for attention—a chance to stand onstage. That was what Rafe had said. But clearly it was so much more. It mattered to him.

"It's not a giant legacy, but it's the most important thing to *me*."

"Legacy?" Annie's voice was tight as her brain focused on his final statement. The show was the most important thing to Rafe?

What else would it be?

Rafe's lips trailed light kisses down her neck. "Weird word to assign to a daytime talk show, I know."

Rafe chuckled, but the tone of it was off. There was something he wasn't telling her.

"People listen to Dave," she said. "They believe the things he tells them because he has a show and wears a white lab coat. If you're keeping phony science off the air, you're helping keep the viewers safe. That is a noble thing, Rafe."

"Maybe."

But his eyes narrowed as they held hers. He didn't believe her.

"Rafe—"

Before she could argue more, he captured her lips.

CHAPTER SEVEN

STRONG ARMS WRAPPED around Annie's waist and a light snore echoed in her ear as the first hint of sun poured through her skylight. Turning, she drank in Rafe's features, softened in sleep. Annie pressed her lips to his. Heat pooled on her skin as his hand skimmed along the top of her butt.

"I didn't mean to wake you…" Annie kissed his chin.

"Hmm…" Rafe's lips found her neck as his fingers traced her inner thigh. "I think you did."

He rubbed his chin along her clavicle, the bristles raking her delicate skin. Annie let her fingers trail his hard length as her body quivered.

"If stubble is such a turn-on, I may need to grow a beard."

Kissing the top of his head, Annie inhaled the soft scent of his shampoo. "I wouldn't mind that."

She sighed as his mouth found her nipple. This had been their routine for the last two weeks. It was perfect—and that was the problem.

Annie ran her hands down Rafe's back, trying to push the bubble of fear away. These last few weeks were ingrained in her soul. A piece of her was attached to Rafe, and she didn't know what that meant. She'd always love

Blake, but he'd gone where she couldn't follow. And Rafe was heading back to LA.

She wanted to believe they could find a way to move forward—Rafe was only going to be a few plane trips away—but they never talked about the future. Instead, they were cramming a lifetime into just weeks. They fell asleep in each other's arms, woke together, made love and pretended the passing days didn't mean anything.

She lifted her thigh over his. "Rafe…" His name sounded like a prayer as he slipped inside her.

Rafe rocked them. There was no rush for orgasm, just the need to be as one. She thought her heart might explode.

"I think I could spend an eternity touching you and still never trace each of your freckles."

Rafe's lips tripped along her nose before capturing her inevitable rebuttal. How did he make the flaws she saw seem gorgeous?

Pressure built within her and soon the deliberate strokes he maintained were not enough. Rolling, Annie straddled him. His grin mesmerized her as she drove her hips into his. She needed to claim him, leave the kind of mark on his soul that she knew was on hers.

Rafe's hands gripped her thighs, but he didn't attempt to slow her quickening pace. Lifting, he pulled himself into a seated position, growling with pleasure as her ankles locked behind his back.

"Rafe…" Annie twisted her fingers through his hair as she forced their lips together.

His tongue met each of her demanding strokes as she slammed against him. Holding his gaze, she rode him, accepting, demanding all the pleasure he could give. Panting against his shoulder, she crested with him.

Goose bumps rose along her scorched nerves as Rafe's

fingers wandered over her back. Tears pressed against her eyes, but she refused to let them fall. She was not going to spend a minute of her time mourning the future. The present was too precious.

Rafe was going to keep seeing Annie. He wasn't sure how, but he knew he'd find a way to make it work.

The world intruded on his thoughts as his cell buzzed. Sighing, Rafe picked it up, barely resisting the urge to throw it.

Conference call with Dave and me Tuesday at noon— not negotiable.

His stomach clenched as he stared at Carrie's order. His fingers hovered along the buttons.

He still didn't have another interview location to pitch to Dave, and Annie's clinic was amazing. The story of a doctor who managed a thriving miniature ER at the edge of the Arctic Circle would entice anyone. The clinic was remote, exotic and had a gorgeous proprietor who had served her country before turning her sights on an underserved community. Surely it was a story that deserved to be told.

The problem was Charlotte Greene. That was the story Dave and everyone else would want.

His hands shook a little as he typed out the simple word, Fine.

And if Rafe didn't have a better idea by Tuesday… Well, his ratings were still better than the other contenders. That had to count for something.

Show tunes echoed down the hall as he made his way to the kitchen. When Annie came to LA he was taking her to a musical. The thought of Annie in his apartment, visiting his home, made Rafe's heart sing. He would show her his life—find a way to make her part of it.

Annie's voice carried the melody and her wet hair bounced on her back as she swayed.

"Did you ever want to do musical theater?" Rafe slipped his hands around her waist, loving the sigh that escaped her lips.

Pulling the last of the bacon from the pan, Annie turned the oven off before pressing her lips to his. "No. Why?"

Rafe wanted to rub away the tight lines on her forehead. "You're an actress and you love show tunes."

"I'm not an actress anymore." Annie pulled away from him and grabbed a few plates. "I'll get these ready; you pour the coffee."

"Annie…" Her shoulders were tight, but Rafe pressed ahead. If she wasn't running from the past, visiting LA would be easier for her. "Why do you want to pretend Charlotte Greene didn't exist?"

Annie rounded on him. "Excuse me?"

The hairs on his arm stood up, but he didn't back down. "I only asked about musical theater because you love show tunes."

"I am more than Charlotte." Her hands trembled as she backed away from him.

Rafe tried to ignore the shivers running down his back. "Of course you're more than Charlotte. I asked a simple question about show tunes. You can't wipe Charlotte from your slate any more than I can wipe my mother's abandonment or my foster families from mine. She is part of you."

Stepping into her arms, Rafe sighed as she let him pick up her left hand. Annie followed his steps and her breath slowed as she fell into the rhythm of the dance.

It would be better to drop the topic. Let romance spin them around the room. These were the simple moments he craved. It was easy to be romantic with Annie. He wanted to make her smile so he followed the quickest path to see her ruby lips tip up.

"When you come to LA, I bet I can find a theater where they're performing one of these shows."

Rafe managed to keep his face blank as Annie's heel landed on his toes.

"Oh."

She tried to pull back, but Rafe held her tight. He'd meant to *ask* her to come to LA—not make it sound like she'd already agreed.

"I can't come to LA, Rafe. I mean I know it's only a few flights—two if I leave on a Wednesday…"

She'd thought about it and decided against it.

Rafe closed his eyes as pain ripped up his back.

Annie stepped away and he didn't attempt to hold her. "Annie—"

She held up her hand before sliding into her chair. "The clinic needs me."

Heat tore up his neck. She *had* to come to LA—not permanently, but because the city was important to him. His successes were there, and he needed her to see it through his eyes—not Charlotte's. Was this really only about the clinic?

Pushing past his fear of rejection, Rafe tried to make his case. "You're allowed to have a life, Annie. To visit your—"

The word *boyfriend* caught on his tongue. They hadn't discussed their relationship and he hated the label. He didn't want to be Annie's boyfriend—he wanted something more.

Refusing to acknowledge the deep need pulling at him, Rafe pressed on. "I can visit Alaska, but there are times I need to be in LA."

Her gray eyes refused to meet his as she traced an ancient groove in the table. "I haven't left the clinic since I founded it. Liam helps out when he's in town. And I'll try to hire another doctor after winter. But if I'm not here…"

He understood the need to protect your patients. Rafe didn't have the same connection to his as Annie to hers, but he still wanted the best for them. But… "You need to take a vacation, Annie, even if it's not to LA." His voice caught. "It would be good for your patients too, if you had a break."

Her left eye twitched as she glared at him. "I don't need a break."

"You're a true general practitioner, Annie. In an era when most GPs are forced to choose family medicine. You deliver babies, stitch wounds, set bones—do all the general illness things. But this small town is growing. The oil company will be bringing at least a few hundred more people here in the next few years."

Reaching for her hand, Rafe ran a finger along her palm. He needed to touch Annie, calm the racing in his mind that screamed he could lose her.

He refused to worry about that now.

Rubbing Annie's cheek, Rafe kissed the tips of her fingers. "If you don't rest occasionally you're going to fail your patients. Maybe not tomorrow, or next month, but at some point this clinic is going to be overwhelmed with an illness or a mass casualty event, and if you're burned out…" Rafe hated making her unhappy, but she needed to hear this.

Her lip twitched, but she didn't meet his gaze. "Mass

casualty?" Annie ran a finger over her lip. "I don't think I need to worry too much about gun violence here."

"I wasn't speaking of gun violence—although it's a sad truth that I don't think you can scoff that away, sweetheart." Placing his palms on the table, Rafe laid out his concerns. "There have been two earth tremors while I've been here. Alaska is part of the Ring of Fire. What happens if a major quake hits this area? What happens if there's an avalanche and you have more than two people buried? Or a mudslide in the summer? Or a flood?"

Her hands shook as she laid her coffee mug on the table and shifted in her chair. "Enough."

She was preparing for battle. Part of him hated forcing the issue, but he didn't back down.

"Annie, you're taking a huge risk by working all the time and not taking care of yourself."

"I take time for myself."

"When? After-hours the clinic phone rings in your bedroom; the front doorbell echoes through your whole apartment; you have an alarm by your pillow for all emergencies. You don't even want to consider a vacation or spend the weekend away."

With me.

"You act like I'm the first physician tied to my work." Her cheeks trembled as she drummed her fingers against the table. "*Your* free time is spent shooting a medical television show and courting fans. That is hardly the life I want."

Rafe sucked in a breath as he stepped back. His heart tore at her sharp tone. He knew she didn't like the show, but she'd helped him with a few research projects since she'd found him looking into hot yoga weeks ago. He had thought she respected what he did. Respected his part in the show.

* * *

Annie reached for him and cursed herself as he pulled away. What was *wrong* with her? Rafe was talking about the future. She wanted to talk about what happened next. Why was she picking a fight?

LA, though...

"Rafe—I'm sorry."

Rafe nodded, but the gleam in his eye was gone.

"You're right, Annie. My life is wrapped around my California clinic and *Dr. Dave*, but I have other things in my life too. I can still volunteer at an Alaskan clinic and take the occasional vacation. You're hiding here."

He laid the accusation at her feet.

"I'm not." Annie's fingers shook as he raised an eyebrow. Why was he pushing this?

Gripping his coffee mug, Rafe nodded. "Great. I'll buy you a ticket for LA this afternoon. We can order it for six months from now—that way you'll have all winter to hire a new doctor and get ready to come see LA."

She raised an eyebrow and her bitter laugh shot across the table. "I've seen it, Rafe."

They were the wrong words—again. This morning had gone completely wrong.

"You haven't seen it with *me*, Annie. I want to take you to the places I love, not the TV studios." Rafe pushed his hands through his hair. "Places like the Thai restaurant where I order so often they know my Tuesday, Friday and Sunday orders. The park where I spend Saturdays taking yoga, parkour or any other random free class that's offered. I want to introduce you to my neighbor Martha. She was a pin-up girl, and she loves to tell stories about her glamour days while serving old store-bought biscuits."

Rafe laughed.

"Fair warning: they taste like cardboard—but she loves them. I wash down two with the horrid green tea she's so fond of. I know there are bad memories for you there, but we could make some new ones too."

Annie wanted to do all those things too, but she hadn't been in LA since she was eighteen. She couldn't go back—she just couldn't.

Stepping into his arms, Annie held him tightly. "Rafe, I can't leave. The clinic—"

Lifting her head, she captured his mouth. He didn't pull away, but the kiss felt off. She wanted to scream. She couldn't lose him—she *couldn't*.

As she broke the kiss Rafe stepped back. "It's fine, Annie. I understand. This place matters too much." He ran a finger along her chin. "I get it. It was just a thought." He brushed his lips against her cheek. "Now I need to grab something before our patients get here."

Annie knew she should follow him—but she couldn't get her feet to move.

She'd spent the morning trying to find a way to keep him. If he lived anywhere else... The selfish thought slapped Annie.

He was right—she *was* hiding.

Blake's picture hovered in the corner of Rafe's eye as he stormed past the living room. Halting, he stared at it. Annie had moved to the Arctic for Blake, but she wouldn't visit LA for *him*.

Pressing his hands to his forehead, Rafe wanted to rip the horrid thought from his brain.

He was trying to make her choose between Blue Ash and LA. She'd always choose Blue Ash. She *should* choose Blue Ash.

Staring at the shelf, Rafe sighed. Had he really expected Annie to view his life, his show, as being as important as her clinic?

Except it mattered to him.

Rafe swallowed the bile rising in his throat. He wanted her to choose him, but they'd known each other for only a month. He didn't need to rush this; he could wait and hope.

Annie tapped her foot as she waited for Rafe's last patient to finish up. He'd managed to avoid her all day. He'd nodded to her once in passing this afternoon, but otherwise Rafe had always seemed to be occupied when she had a few spare minutes.

She'd hurt him and she wanted—needed—to fix it. She wasn't ready to cross the border to LA, but Rafe was right. She deserved a vacation.

"Rafe."

He smiled at her before he said a quick goodbye to Mr. Hamilton.

Annie waved at Mr. Hamilton before pulling Rafe back into the exam room.

"I'm sorry."

Bouncing from foot to foot, Annie pulled at the torn skin along her thumb.

"I know LA is important to you. And I—" Annie wrapped her arms around her waist. She wanted to promise to come, but the words stuck in her throat.

It was just a city.

Rafe kissed the top her head. "I'm sorry too. I shouldn't have pushed so hard."

"Maybe—"

"Dr. A! Dr. Bradstone!" Miranda's call echoed down the hall.

"We're fine, sweetheart—promise."

Rafe gripped her hand as they headed for the door, and Annie wanted to believe him—but how long would he wait for her to overcome her fears?

"Lily Banister fell off her bike." Miranda was out of breath as she rushed toward them. "Her mom has a towel pressed against her face, but she says you can see her chin bone."

Annie sighed. "Okay."

Before she could warn Rafe that Lily was trying when she felt well and a hellion when she was ill, he was rounding the corner. He was already examining Lily's chin by the time she caught up.

"You're going to need stitches." Rafe winked at the child as she glared up at him.

"I don't want stitches. Dinosaurs don't have stitches."

Rafe raised his eyebrows. "Are you sure? I think I've seen dinosaurs with stitches."

Lily's eyes widened as she tried to determine if Rafe was being serious. Pursing her lips, she squinted—before letting out a giant roar.

Before Lily's mother Tina and Annie could react, Rafe smiled and laughed. "That was an excellent dinosaur roar. You still need stitches, though."

Rafe reached for Lily's hand and Annie's mouth fell open as the child gripped his hand and followed him to the suture room.

In five short years Annie had stitched Lily's cheek, and her arm, and splinted two broken fingers. The young girl insisted she could do all the bicycle tricks her brothers could. Usually she was right. Unfortunately when she was wrong the damage was epic.

Lily hopped on the table when Rafe asked her to, then turned her attention to Annie. "Are you passing out lollipops or good candy at the carnival tonight?"

Tina cringed as her youngest child's bold question tumbled forth. "She doesn't mean that."

"Tommy says they're bad." Lily pouted as her mom glared at her.

Tina rolled her eyes as she sat down next to her daughter.

Annie covered her mouth. If she laughed, Lily would continue to tell the room what her brother thought.

Rafe grinned at Annie before turning his attention to their small patient. "I need to give you a shot before I can stitch you."

Lily glared at the needle. "I don't like shots."

"Me either," Rafe commiserated. "How about we do a dinosaur roar after the shot—to make the pain go away?"

Lily crossed her arms, but she nodded.

Annie laughed when Rafe and Lily roared. Rafe was an excellent doctor, and great with children. He'd make a brilliant father.

Annie's brain shifted as that thought rolled around her skull. Since Blake had passed, Annie had walled off the desire to be a parent. Rafe had broken down more walls than she'd realized. Of course, if she didn't ever leave Blue Ash, she'd never find out if that dream was possible.

Annie sat at the head of the table and put her hands on either side of Lily's head. "You can show all your friends your stitches at the carnival tonight. I bet they'll look great with your costume."

Lily stuck her lip out. "I'm going as a *fairy*. I wanted to be a man-eating dinosaur."

Rafe slid beside Lily. "I think a fairy is an excellent costume. I'm going to start now, so I need you to stay still."

"Can I get a sticker?"

Annie bit her lip. Lily might be calmer for Rafe than

she was with her, but she was still laser-focused on the sticker drawer.

"Stay still and I will let you pick three stickers."

Lily's eyes widened and she gripped the side of the table.

Three stickers? Annie doubted anything would make the child move now.

Rafe talked about dinosaurs, fairies and his superhero costume as he pulled the wound on Lily's chin closed. Lily soaked up each of his words, never budging.

His easy tone sent an aching need through Annie. She didn't want to go to LA, but if Rafe was there…

"All done."

Rafe's happy tone broke through Annie's mental ramblings.

"What's *your* costume?" Lily stuck her tongue through the empty space for her front tooth as she peered into the sticker drawer.

Annie knew Lily didn't really care, but she popped down beside the little girl. She'd been treating Lily since she was three months old.

"Dr. A is going as a candy witch," Tina replied, before Annie had a chance to offer an answer.

"Actually, I was thinking of changing my costume this year."

Tina's mouth fell open before she covered it with her hand. "That's great, Dr. A."

She glanced at Rafe; his eyebrow was raised, but he didn't comment. She'd bought the costume as a surprise for him, but what would he think now?

Annie swallowed the bulge in her throat.

Lily pulled the back of her heart sticker off and stuck it to her nose. "Can fairies eat people?"

Rafe crouched so he could meet Lily's gaze. "I don't think so. Want to do one more roar?"

The room echoed with Rafe and Lily's dinosaur noises and Annie thought her heart might burst. He was a natural with children.

She opened the exam room door. "I need to see to a few things in the office. Dr. Bradstone will walk you to the front."

Lily ignored her, but her mother turned and waved. "I can't wait to see the new costume."

"New costume?" a deep voice boomed across the hallway. "Are you feeling okay, Annie?"

The air in the hall was hot as Annie tried to breathe normally. *Why* had she admitted to having a new costume? She'd ordered it on a whim two weeks ago. She'd tried it on once and put it back in the bag. She'd meant to return it but hadn't been able to. It was new, and different, and she had kept it because Rafe would love it.

Now she just had to have the courage to wear it.

Annie folded her arms. "I *might* have something different. I think I need to get some new candy too."

Liam Henkle's head snapped back. "Did someone finally tell you those sugar-free suckers are gross?"

Rolling her eyes, Annie glared at her partner. "You know, this is information *you* could have passed along."

Crossing his arms, Liam looked at his feet. "You were ridiculously proud of those things—I didn't want to hurt your feelings."

Liam's dark hair was longer than Blake's, but the motion reminded her of his brother. Blake wouldn't have told her the candies were bad either. He'd have dutifully eaten a few to spare her feelings.

Would Rafe have eaten them? No. He'd have said they were terrible and suggested another option. Even if she didn't want to hear it. That was what he'd done this morning—pointed out what she needed to hear—and she'd let him walk away. Let him think he wasn't enough to pull her to LA.

The carnival didn't matter right now. Rafe wanted her to visit his home, and she wanted to try.

Liam was here, so they needed to discuss options for the clinic to make that happen. Fear and excitement warred within her belly, but Annie motioned for Liam to follow her. She was *not* running away from Rafe.

"I need to talk to you," she said.

Liam closed the office door. "Is this about the handsome replacement doctor you're dating?"

"Nothing is a secret in this town," Annie muttered as she closed the office door. "No, this is not about Rafe. Well, not directly."

"Is it supposed to be a secret?"

"No." Annie's fingers ran along her thumb as she stared at the man who looked so much like his brother it had hurt to see him right after Blake's death. Those feelings were softer now. "I don't want to hurt you...or your parents."

"Annie." Liam wrapped strong arms around her. "Blake would have wanted you to be happy. *We* want you to be happy."

Happiness burst like a dam inside her. "I'm glad—because I think we need to put more focus into finding a reliable partner. I want—I want someone we trust in case we both aren't here."

Liam raised a brow as he blew out a breath. "Thinking of heading south?"

Annie shrugged. "I haven't had a vacation for a while."

"Planning a trip to California?" Liam slid into the chair across from the room's lone desk.

"Maybe…"

Annie's knees shook as she tapped her foot. She wanted to see Rafe's home, meet his neighbor and see his life. See if their connection could manage more than a few blissful weeks.

She pulled out a notepad. "I haven't left since we opened—but it's more than that. The town's population is expanding. With the new oil pipeline opening, I expect it to nearly double in the next five years. As it is, the clinic runs six days a week. If we position ourselves right, we could support three full-time physicians and a physician's assistant."

"You don't have to sell it to me, Annie. I've actually been thinking that it's time for me to spend more time in Blue Ash. I should be around more."

"Really?"

Annie leaned forward. Liam had graduated from med school a few years before her, but he'd never stayed at the clinic for more than six weeks. It reminded him too much of Blake. Time didn't heal wounds, but it made the pain less raw.

Liam shrugged. "I think it's time I pulled a little more weight here—but there are still a few remote locations I need to visit every few months. I planned to discuss it with you after the carnival tonight." His hand pushed through his hair. "Think Dr. Bradstone might be interested in the Arctic life?"

Annie shook her head. Rafe's life was in LA. The TV show was important to Rafe. He'd earned that promotion on *Dr. Dave*, and she wanted him to succeed.

"Rafe doesn't really like the cold. Besides, his show is based in California."

"We could still offer…"

"He's under contract with *The Dr. Dave Show.* You don't just walk away from that—and this isn't about Rafe."

She cared for Rafe.

The word *love* floated between her eyes and Annie sighed.

She *loved* Rafe. That was why she was so terrified of what the future held. Losing Blake had nearly destroyed her—if it didn't work out with Rafe how would she cope?

Blood pounded in her ears. *Love* meant encouraging Rafe's dreams, even if they were based in a city she loathed.

Liam raised an eyebrow. "We don't have to rush into this. I'll stay through the winter…let you have a bit of downtime." Liam winked. "Take a vacation that might or might not be in California."

"Annie—" Rafe stepped through the office door and stopped. "Sorry. I didn't realize you had company." Holding out his hand, Rafe smiled. "I'm Rafe Bradstone."

Liam stood and gripped Rafe's hand. "Liam Henkle— Annie's partner."

Folds appeared along Rafe's forehead. "Nice to meet you."

"You too. I managed to make it back for the Fall Carnival. It's my parents' favorite time of the year."

"And then you'll head out again?"

Annie saw Rafe's lip twitch as he stared at her partner. His posture was tight.

"Liam's actually planning to spend the winter in Blue Ash," said Annie, and skirted around the desk.

Rafe nodded, but he still didn't meet her gaze. Her heart tore as he kept his distance.

"I'm going to make sure the waiting room is clean."

She was halfway down the hall before she realized the office door was closed. What were they doing?

* * *

"Are you really planning to stay through the winter?"

Rafe crossed his arms. Annie had made it clear that Liam never remained in Blue Ash for long. It had infuriated Rafe. Liam *had* to know how much she needed help.

"Yes."

Rafe swallowed. If Liam stayed, a major part of Annie's reason for insisting she had to remain in Blue Ash faded.

He pushed the hope from his mind. She didn't want to be in LA and he was not going to force it. He'd take whatever Annie offered him, for however long she offered it. It just hurt that she didn't want *all* of him.

"Annie deserves a vacation," Liam stated, his eyes holding Rafe's.

"I suggested the same thing this morning. She wasn't happy to hear it."

Liam shrugged. "I think she might be coming around to the idea."

Rafe wanted to ask why Liam thought that, but Liam pressed on.

"Annie's very protective of this place."

"Yes, she feels like she owes it to Blake."

Rafe bit his tongue. His chest burned. He knew Annie's connection to Alaska was stronger than his to LA.

"My brother will always hold a special place in her heart."

"As he should," Rafe agreed.

Annie's love for her former fiancé was part of her. He'd never want to strip that away.

"That doesn't mean it should be used to bind her here."

Liam's eyes widened and his lips split apart. "Wow…" Pulling a hand across his neck, Liam met Rafe's gaze. "That accusation cuts a little close."

Good.

Rafe swallowed the word as he leaned back on his heels. Closing his eyes, he sucked in a deep breath. His argument about the clinic's staffing wasn't any different if Liam took Annie's place. The people of Blue Ash still needed a fully staffed facility. And Annie wouldn't be able to relax if Liam was here alone.

Rafe tried to keep his frustration at bay.

"Annie deserves a full-time partner," he said, and his fingers vibrated as he stared at Liam. He'd left Annie, counted on her to tend to his brother's dream. "I know you've been serving the remote communities, but this clinic shouldn't be staffed by only one doctor—whether it's you or Annie. We've seen patients from eight until six most days since I've been here. That doesn't include the after-hours emergencies that have come in too."

A crease crossed Liam's forehead. "How long have you been here?"

"Four weeks tomorrow."

"You care about this clinic?" Liam circled the desk and picked up a notepad.

"Of course—this clinic cares for the whole community. But if you have an outbreak, one doctor is not going to be enough. Two might not be either, but it's at least a start."

"When I was little, a flu outbreak killed over twenty people here," said Liam. "We didn't have a doctor in the community then. It's why Blake was so intent on coming back here as a physician."

That kind of thing could happen again. Rafe kept that fear buried.

"From everything Annie has told me, he sounds like an amazing person. She's made sure his dream has come true, but you need to help her now."

Liam smiled. "I see why she likes you."

Tapping the pad with his pen, Liam jotted a quick note.

"I mentioned our need for a reliable partner the last three times I've been here, but I didn't push. It was the first thing Annie talked about when I arrived today. I'm not sure what you said, but it worked. Can you do me one more favor?"

"Sure."

Annie had mentioned hiring another physician to Liam? Rafe's heart leapt.

"When she visits you, take her picture by her star on the Hollywood Walk of Fame. I've told her it would look great in the clinic."

Fury rolled through him. If he ever managed to get Annie to his home, the last place he was dragging her was to the Walk of Fame.

Leaning across the desk, Rafe growled, "I'm *not* doing that. She isn't interested in that star, or in anything it stands for."

Liam's cheeks puckered as he smiled. "You're a good man."

"That was a test?"

"Yep." Liam winked. "I don't even know if she *has* a star, but I do know she would never want a picture with it. You aren't the only one interested in protecting her."

Before Rafe could find an answer, Annie opened the door. "We need to get ready for the carnival," she told them. Her eyes flicked from Rafe to Liam. "Everything okay?"

"Yep. I can't wait to see your new costume."

Liam laughed as he ducked past Annie.

CHAPTER EIGHT

"ARE YOU EVER going to exit the bathroom?"

Despite the tight faux leather suit, goose bumps erupted across Annie's skin. "Just one more minute."

This wasn't a trip to LA, but she hoped Rafe liked it. Drawing a dark line across her eyelids, Annie took a deep breath. It was now or never.

"I'm coming out. Close your eyes." Annie giggled as Rafe's sigh echoed through the door. "Sorry. That was overly dramatic."

"I've been waiting for this reveal for the better part of five hours," Rafe said, his eyes pinched closed.

"So much drama! It's only been an hour and a half. I just need to put my utility belt on and then the costume is complete."

"Utility belt? I'm intrigued."

Annie took a deep breath. Her cheeks were *not* going to be beet-red when Rafe opened his eyes.

Snapping the belt into place, Annie let her eyes wander over Rafe's impressive body. He didn't need any help filling out the impressive red, white and blue superhero outfit. He looked like he'd stepped directly out of a comic book.

Rafe folded his arms. "I'm counting to five, Annie, and then I am opening my eyes."

"Go ahead."

She stood up straight and waited. It had taken her over an hour, but she'd managed to straighten her red curls and to cover her freckles with more foundation than she'd worn in fifteen years. If she was dressed in a cotton sun dress with a big bow she'd look just like Charlotte Greene. Instead she was squeezed into a form-fitting costume to match Rafe's.

Annie's arms twitched as Rafe's gaze wandered across her. She was *not* going to fold them across her belly. Did she look enough like a kick-ass spy?

"For goodness' sakes, say something."

"You got a costume to match mine." His Adam's apple bobbed as he stepped toward her. "Not to mention you're dressed in skin-tight leather—"

"*Faux* leather," Annie countered.

"Faux leather…" Rafe muttered as his lips skimmed the base of her neck. "I think my brain forgot how to make words for a second there. You are the sexiest woman I've ever seen."

She loved making him speechless, but worry crept across her belly. "It's a bit different from my candy witch costume…"

Rafe's fingers tripped along her waist and he leaned into her hair. "You look amazing, Annie—but if you would feel more comfortable going in your candy witch outfit, go change."

He kissed her cheek before heading to her closet. The black dress looked shapeless as he draped it across his arms.

"Tonight is supposed to be fun. If you're my partner it doesn't matter whether I'm with the sexiest spy or the wickedly hot candy witch."

Rafe laid the dress on her bed and grabbed her bent

witch's hat. It had spent a year stuffed under her sweaters and looked terrible.

Rafe really meant it. He didn't care if she wore the outfit that matched his or went with the safe choice. Her worry popped. Rafe was smiling and the uncertainty she'd felt since this morning vanished. She looked amazing, and she wasn't going to let fear drive her tonight.

Grabbing her water gun, Annie smirked as she placed it in the utility belt. "I think I make a pretty convincing superhero!"

His lips captured hers. The world exploded as his fingers traveled across her back.

Home.

It was a ridiculous word to attach to a kiss.

But as Annie melted against him she sighed. Rafe *was* home. She didn't know what that meant for the future, but she knew she couldn't give him up just because their lives were geographically separated.

Annie's head was leaning against his shoulder. Standing in the crowd around the dance floor, they looked like half a dozen other couples. Maybe this was what love looked like? Rafe sighed. Maybe it really was things like dancing in matching costumes to win a silly trophy that made life rotate from good to amazing.

Rafe didn't know how he was going to keep his LA life separate from Blue Ash, but he was going to find a way. Any woman who was willing to dress as a superhero to match him was worth the world. He'd fly back as often as he could, and maybe they could meet in Seattle every few weeks. Some time with Annie would be better than none.

As a couple and their two children bent and pulled at imaginary cords he cheered with the rest of Blue Ash.

The family's rendition of the lawn mower dance was followed by the children bouncing on the floor in an excellent version of the worm, while their parents twisted their hips.

Tapping his own hip against Annie's, Rafe laughed. "I think our swing dance is going to be out of place."

Annie's cheeks burned as she moved her head on his shoulder. "I'm sorry. I meant to tell you a dozen times that our practices weren't necessary. Most of the community probably started practicing only a few days ago—or this morning. I just wanted the excuse to step into your arms."

Rafe didn't know it was possible to be this happy. He pressed his lips against her forehead. "You can step into my arms anytime, my love."

The endearment had slipped out and Rafe tightened his hug, trying to gather his own thoughts. All of them screamed the same thing. He loved Annie; this wasn't a passing chemical high.

The Fall Carnival wasn't the place for a huge declaration, though. She might not think romance needed giant gestures, but he was going to find a special way to tell Annie he loved her.

Shifting topics, to keep from blurting his feelings out in front of the entire community, he nodded to the dancers. "How do we vote?"

Annie studied him, but didn't mention his use of the word *love*. "There are big jars on the back wall. A dollar gets you ten candy corns; five dollars gets you seventy-five. Jar with the most candy corn wins."

"Candy corn?" Rafe glared at the jars. "Why are they using good candy?"

Annie's hand pressed against his chest as she laughed. "Oh, that's *funny*." Her eyes sparkled with the orange lights hanging around the room.

"You don't like candy corn?"

Annie's lips fell open. "It's colored wax. You really like it?"

Rafe shrugged, staring at the jars as they filled up with tiny triangles. "My foster mother Emma used to give us some after dinner. She would have loved everything about this dance." His throat tightened as he remembered Emma's yellow house.

Annie pushed a bit of hair behind his ear. "Tell me about her."

Placing his hands around her waist, Rafe smiled as Emma's tightly wrapped gray bun floated in his memory.

"She swore that bright colors lifted the spirit. I was an angry preteen—I still believed my mother wanted me, and I hated everyone for keeping us apart. I made fun of everything and was generally a horrid brat. I told Emma her bright green-and-pink rooms were ridiculous. I said I preferred black. Made some awful joke about it being the color of my soul."

His cheeks flamed at the memory of his angsty response.

"When I got home from school the next day she'd painted my room black."

He laughed as Emma's cheeky smile floated in his memory. She would have loved Annie too.

He kissed the top of Annie's head as she wrapped her arms around his waist. "She'd used white-and-yellow paint to make star patterns. She told me stars shone brightest in the dark, and she believed I was a star. She swore that one day I'd light up the night." He chuckled. "Maybe that's why I love the spotlight so much."

Annie squeezed his hand. "How long did you live with her?"

"Six months. She had a stroke." Rafe's voice faltered. "Before she passed, she told me to remember I was a star."

"So there was someone who believed in you and she sounds amazing."

Annie pulled him away from the dance floor. She handed over a five, popped a few candy corns in her mouth and then tossed Rafe the bag.

"Thought you didn't like them?" Rafe said, and sighed as the treat melted in his mouth.

"I don't have the same history with them as you do." Annie kissed his cheek. "But they're not as terrible as I remember."

"A ringing endorsement."

Rafe laughed as he dumped a few more in his mouth. Emma had believed in him—trusted that one day he'd shine. But her words had been lost in his mother's warnings that he'd end up a liar and a user like his father. Now, with Annie by his side, it was easy to believe Emma's words and recognize his mother's remarks for what they were—lies.

"I'll buy you some more after we tear up the dance floor."

He grabbed her hand as she pecked his cheek, "Why have you never participated in the dance before? You're an excellent dancer and this whole town either moonwalks to eighties music or flosses to pop."

Wrinkles crossed her forehead as she stared at him.

Charlotte, he thought.

"You didn't want them comparing you to your character?"

She nodded before leaning toward him. "I don't care what anyone thinks when you hold me, though."

Rafe captured her lips, pulling her tight against him. Her hands wrapped around his neck and he lost himself in pleasure. Annie Masters, this wonderful, compassionate, breathtakingly beautiful woman, had chosen him.

"If the doctors can tear themselves apart for their dance…" A few cheers went up around them as the master of ceremonies held out a hand.

Annie smiled as the shouts echoed around them. She was basking in the attention—because she was with *him*. When he ranked his happiest moments he knew they'd all contain Annie, but this would always vie for position as one of the top nights.

Rafe clasped her hand in his and pulled her into the center of the stage. "Let's show them how it's done!"

Her giggle was drowned out as their peppy swing tune echoed through the speakers. The crowd disappeared as Annie's hips twisted away from him. It was just him, Annie and the music. She glowed each time she landed in his arms.

Rafe gripped her hands as they did the rock horse.

Love. The word hung about them as he matched each of her steps.

He didn't fear telling Annie that he loved her—didn't doubt that she'd want him too. For once, someone was going to choose *him*. He wasn't sure what that meant for his life in LA, but Rafe didn't care. He needed Annie more than anything else.

Annie's chest hit his as they bounced together to the rhythm. A whistle echoed through the crowd as he picked her up, swinging her legs to the left and then the right. Laughter rippled around the room as Annie wagged her finger and danced away from him, her hair tumbling across his shoulders. Finally, she rushed toward him, and Rafe caught her as she swung around his hips.

The community center erupted as the song ended and they bowed.

"Well, folks, that is going to be hard to beat! Voting will remain open for the next hour." The master of ceremonies knocked his hand against the mike, and when that failed to grab the crowd's attention he placed it next to the speaker to create feedback.

Annie pressed her head against Rafe's neck as the squeal blasted through the center.

"Dr. A and Dr. Bradstone's performance was amazing—but there are still three more groups to go!"

Rafe pulled Annie to the side of the dance floor and took his phone from his pocket. Kissing Annie's cheek, Rafe snapped a picture.

"What are you doing?"

"Capturing our moment of triumph!"

"Don't celebrate yet. Someone else might get the trophy."

Rafe flipped the phone toward her. "I don't care about the trophy, Annie."

He didn't. All that mattered was how much Annie had enjoyed the dance. They'd moved together as one, and it had felt magical.

"We danced together, in front of everyone, and you loved every minute. This picture cements *that* triumph!"

Rafe's heart exploded as his lips captured hers. The community center, the congratulations, the trophy, the world—all of it vanished as Annie pressed into him.

"We are *great* together."

Annie ran her fingers across the picture Rafe had taken before she melted into his kiss. She'd loved every second of their dance. And Rafe was right—it didn't matter if the whole town watched or no one at all. She wanted to dance with Rafe forever.

Cameras were flashing everywhere as Annie and Rafe made their way through the crowd.

"Dr. Bradstone!" A young woman bounced in front of them. "Can we get a picture together?"

Rafe smiled and then frowned. "I don't think now…"

"Go on!" Annie patted his chest. "I'll go stuff our jar with more candy corn."

A tingle crossed her spine as Rafe kissed her cheek. "Save some for me."

Women were lining up, each one wanting their thirty seconds with the handsome TV doctor. Arms were wrapped around Rafe's waist, and he smiled for all of them. Rafe loved the attention.

Annie waited for the jealousy she'd experienced weeks ago to form, but it was just excitement that was rocketing through her. Rafe might have pictures taken with his fans, but it was *her* he wanted.

"That's a great costume." Danny, Mac's grandson, beamed as he stepped up next to her.

"Thank you. How is your grandfather doing?"

"He's good. Around here somewhere—though Grandma made him promise to take it easy." Danny was dressed in the same costume as Rafe, though his costume was padded to fill out the muscles. He rubbed at his neck before leaning toward her. "Can I get a picture with you?"

"Why?" Annie bit her lip as the teen stepped back. "Sorry, Danny. I guess I'm just not used to people wanting pictures with me."

That was a lie; she'd spent years pretending to smile for her fans. Rafe made it look easy, but it had drained her. Cameras and first-generation smartphones had captured Annie at dinner, working out, or just walking on the street. Flashes of light still sent ripples of unease across her skin.

"I don't look as great as Dr. Bradstone, but a picture with you in that costume would make me look more *real*."

Annie squinted at him. Danny's cheeks were bright red. "You want a picture because of my costume?"

Danny's bushy brows twisted as he frowned. "Uh, yeah, Dr. A. Why else would I want your picture?"

Placing her hands on her hips, Annie laughed. "I have no idea." She tilted her head. "Let's do this."

Grabbing his plastic shield, Danny handed his phone to a friend before kneeling in front of her. He waited for a moment, before sighing. "Dr. A?"

Annie looked down at him. Why wasn't his friend taking the picture?

He cleared his throat. "Can you strike a pose?"

This really *was* about her costume.

"My apologies, Danny!" Annie pulled her water gun out and held it against her chest as she glared at the camera.

Danny hopped up, looked at the phone and beamed. "Perfect!" He showed it to a few friends and then disappeared into the costumed crowd.

Danny's happiness was infectious. Was this how Rafe felt when his fans swooned over their photos with him?

"For someone who claims she isn't a good dancer, you looked like a professional out there." Holly threw her arm around Annie's waist.

"I might have fudged a little, but Rafe is an excellent partner."

Annie glanced over at him. He was posing with a fan who was wearing a giant inflatable T. rex costume. The image was ridiculous—and perfect.

"I bet he's excellent at other things too." Holly giggled as they made their way to the dessert area.

Holly's baked treats were the real stars of the carnival. People talked about them for months and begged for their favorites to make the annual spread. There were orange pastries that turned your teeth red when you bit into them, ghoul sugar cookies and chocolate-raspberry spider webs.

Grabbing a cookie decorated to look like a witch's finger, Annie winked at her friend. "He's quite skilled in *all* areas."

Her cheeks heated and she pursed her lips. Annie rarely discussed personal topics; she was always worried that people, even friends, would sell the information. Now, though, it seemed like another thing she'd let Charlotte steal from her.

Holly rearranged a few trays. "Good. It would be a shame if he was so attractive but poor between the sheets." Holly's dark skin gleamed in the lights as she winked.

"That is quite the innuendo for Minnie Mouse to make." Annie pointed at Holly's ears as her cheeks burned once more.

Suddenly Rafe's strong arms slid around Annie's waist as he nodded to Holly. She felt secure in his embrace. Any part of the future seemed possible when Rafe's heart beat next to hers.

Annie grinned as she handed him a bag of candy corn. "I got these for you."

"For voting or eating?"

"Your choice." Annie laughed as Holly glared at the bag.

"There is a perfectly good dessert table here, Rafe." Holly pointed to her creations. "And now I need to put out the goody bags. Annie, can you help me grab them from the supply room?"

Rafe popped a few candy corns in his mouth and smiled at Holly. "Why are they in the supply room?"

"If I put them in the kitchen they'll disappear. I only make enough for each kid to have one goody bag. No one looks in the supply room."

"That's because it's a disaster zone." Annie chuckled as she poured a few candy corns in her hand and handed them to Rafe. "Once we fetch them you should help pass them out, Rafe."

Rafe dropped a candy in his mouth. "Why me?"

A child dressed as superhero walked past and high-fived Rafe without breaking his stride.

"Because you are a natural with children," said Annie, and pointed at the retreating child.

Rafe's eyes flickered. "No. I'm not." His voice was strained.

A bead of fire licked up Annie's back. She laid a hand against his cheek. "You calmed Lily this afternoon, and every child in this room has spoken to you tonight. You aren't broken, Rafe Bradstone. And I'm going to make you believe that, no matter how long it takes."

"Annie…" An emotion danced behind Rafe's eyes that she couldn't read.

Laying a finger on his lips, she kissed his jaw. "I have to get the goody bags. Then we'll pass them out together."

"Okay," Rafe muttered, but she knew his focus was somewhere else.

Annie squeezed his hand and ran to catch up with Holly. She tried to ignore the pinch of worry creeping along the base of her neck as she helped Holly get the heavy supply room door open. A box in front of the light switch tumbled over, and Annie let out a cry as the edge caught her arm.

"Are you okay?" Holly flipped the light on and grabbed Annie's arm.

A small stream of blood trickled across her wrist, but it was the slice in her costume that angered her. Superheroes were *never* destroyed by boxes.

"You okay?"

"Yes, I suppose," Annie grumbled, before sighing. The blood was already clotting, and a bit of black thread would fix the rest. "Wow, this place is a mess. After the carnival we need to see about cleaning it out."

Holly chuckled as she stepped over a box of Christmas decorations and the head of an Easter bunny. "I think we say that after every event, and yet…" She held her arms out and sighed.

Bending, Annie grabbed the box that had attacked her. At least she could find it a new location. Kicking at another box, Annie forced her way to the back of the long room.

"This is just ridiculous."

Then the room started to sway, and the box dropped from Annie's fingers. She let out a cry as the piled-up boxes started shifting around her. Screams echoed from the community center as the earth tremor's shakes became more violent.

"Annie!"

The panic in Holly's voice sent a bolt of terror down Annie's spine. She'd lived in this region for years and the tremors had never lasted this long. The stack of boxes beside her tumbled to the ground.

"I'm fine. Stay where you are."

"Annie—" Holly's words were lost as the roof creaked. A wooden pallet became dislodged from the wall and pain shot through Annie's head. Her knees cracked as they connected with the floor. She didn't have time to raise her hands before the world darkened.

CHAPTER NINE

ANNIE... RAFE'S BRAIN screamed as he pushed toward the crying people at the front of the community center. He needed Annie. But duty came first. Besides, she was probably racing toward the same scene.

Rafe looked at the sea of heads, desperately searching for her bright red hair.

The small boy who'd high-fived him earlier cradled his arm on the raised stage. A cut ran from his elbow to the middle of his arm. It looked painful, but it wasn't very wide or deep.

Squatting beside him, with a woman dressed as a fighter pilot, Rafe touched the boy's arm. "Can I have a look at that?"

The child sniffed a few times before holding out his arm.

Rafe grabbed an unopened bottle of water and washed off the blood.

The boy pulled away, and Rafe offered him a smile. "What's your name?"

"Mitchel."

"Well, Mitchel..." Rafe tapped his knee, forcing his mind to focus on the kid. "I know you're scared, but I need to check your arm."

The cut wasn't too bad, and he didn't think the little guy needed any stitches.

"You're obviously a superhero, Mitchel, because this will be fine in a few days."

Mitchel's face lit up.

Maybe Annie was right. Rafe had never considered children before, but the idea didn't make him want to flee. That couldn't happen if he was in LA and she was in Blue Ash. Could he give up *Dr. Dave*?

Yes—for Annie he could do anything.

Rafe stood and let his eyes wander across the room. His stomach clenched as he failed to locate her. The room contained most of the population of Blue Ash, but he should still be able to find her. Where *was* she?

Liam rushed to his side. "Mr. McHenry sprained his ankle when he fell after his wife grabbed him, and I think Margery Stevens needs a butterfly bandage for the cut above her eye. Other than that..." Liam ruffled Mitchel's hair. "We seem to have come through unscathed."

"Have you seen Annie?" Rafe's stomach lurched as more minutes passed without her.

"No." Liam sat back on his heels and frowned, his eyes wandering over the room. "But she was a combat medic. Maybe she's treating someone I didn't see." Rafe's eyes drifted over each of the costumed inhabitants. Annie's spy costume and Holly's Minnie Mouse costume had stood out all night. Their absence hung in the community center.

A husky Mickey Mouse skidded to a stop in front of them. Holly's husband.

"Liam..." Doug's cheeks were pale and his eyes refused to stay still. "Have you seen Holly? I can't find her."

Rafe's stomach plunged. "Annie and Holly were going to the supply closet. Maybe—"

Liam's face blanched. He and Doug took off and Rafe's feet pounded behind them. It was only a supply closet. Why were they so worried?

Doug pushed at the door, but it refused to move. "Holly!" Holly's husband pounded against the door, tears streaming down his face. "Liam, I can't get it to move!"

"Let me try." Liam patted Doug's arm.

Several spectators had gathered around, trying to see what was happening. Rafe stepped up to the door, throwing his shoulder into it too. The door finally gave way under the pressure. A Christmas tree scraped across Rafe's arm as it tumbled out of the messy room.

"Dad!" Liam grabbed Jack Henkle by the collar. "Annie and Holly are somewhere in here. We need your help in carefully clearing the boxes and I need Mom to run to the clinic. We need Annie's portable med kit." He offered Rafe a tight smile. "We'll need it for the butterfly Band-Aids at least."

The words provided Rafe with no comfort. Annie and Holly were under this debris and they were quiet.

She had to be fine.

He had so many things that needed to be said.

Sucking in a deep breath, Rafe slid the first box to the side of the door and stepped over three more.

"Annie! Holly!"

Blood pounded in his ears. The shelves on both walls had come loose. He shifted a few more boxes and started passing them to Liam and Doug.

"Holly!" Doug's broken voice poured out behind Rafe.

"Doug!" Holly's voice was pinched as it came from the back of the room. "I'm behind the shelf on the left side—where we store the Easter crafts."

Doug's elbow shot into Rafe's stomach as he climbed over boxes toward his wife.

"Annie!" Rafe called, praying she'd answer him.

"She's on the other side, Rafe. She—"

The tremble in Holly's voice tore through him.

Annie was fine; she had to be fine. He needed her. Life without Annie wasn't an option.

"She hasn't answered me..."

Liam darted toward Holly as Rafe headed to the other wall.

"Annie!"

The silence was deafening.

"Annie, *please*—"

Rafe's voice broke as he forced his feet to move carefully. The room was a landmine of fallen boxes and chintzy decorations. Annie could be under any of them.

"Annie, sweetheart, please make some noise."

Tears streamed down his face, but he didn't waste time pushing them away. He'd only just found her; he couldn't lose her.

"Annie, *say* something."

Let her be okay. His brain screamed the prayer even as he called out.

"Annie!"

The world without Annie—

Rafe pushed the fear away.

"Annie!"

"Rafe..."

The hushed word was so low Rafe thought he'd imagined it. "Annie—where are you?"

His heart screamed as a box shifted a few feet ahead of him.

"Annie!"

An old wooden pallet lay next to her; her blood was spilled across the top of it.

Rafe dumped a few more boxes. He didn't care where

anything landed, provided it was away from her. Pushing at a box marked "Parade Supplies," Rafe stepped over some tinsel and a tipped-up popcorn machine.

He fell to his knees beside her. He'd never wanted to pull her into his arms more, but that wasn't an option. Relying on all his med school training, Rafe tried to examine Annie as if she were any other patient. He couldn't risk hurting her because he was unfocused.

Blood drizzled from a cut above her eye. Her bangs were matted, but the wound was already clotting.

"What hurts?"

"My head…" Her words were slurred. "I need to sit up."

"No," Rafe commanded. He'd seen this before. After a head injury people were confused, and often tried to stand up and move. It was a defense mechanism—the body's attempt to flee the threat. Unfortunately, it could injure a patient further.

"My head hurts." Annie pushed at his shoulder, scowling.

"Sweetheart, I need you to stay still. You have a concussion, and I need to see if there's any other damage before we move you." Rafe placed a light kiss against the uninjured side of her head before he moved down her body.

"My head hurts!" Annie repeated her complaint, tapping on the pallet. "This fell on me. My brain feels fuzzy."

"I know, sweetheart, but I need to examine you."

Rafe's chest seized as he pressed his finger to the bruise forming on her cheek. The best thing he could do was see to her injuries, but the initial rush of adrenaline had leaked from his body.

He took a deep breath, letting his eyes scan Annie.

He frowned and his fingers trembled, but he carefully kneaded the soft skin around her ribs.

She let out a low giggle and groaned. "Don't tickle me!"

Her flailing hand landed on his cheek and pain erupted across his face. His tongue revolted as a coppery taste coated his mouth. At least her ribs weren't broken.

"Sorry… My body feels heavy." Annie's eyes fluttered.

"I'm fine, but I need you to stay awake, Annie." Rafe tapped her nose, ignoring the glare she sent him.

"I'm tired and my stomach hurts." She sighed. "My brain is fuzzy…"

His stomach knotted as she repeated the "fuzzy brain" comment. Concussions were the result of brain swelling. The more confusion she exhibited, the longer she'd take to recover. At least Liam was here, because the clinic was going to be operating without Dr. A for at least a week.

Sitting back on his heels, Rafe knocked a cotton candy machine over and glared at the pink-and-blue dust covering Annie's legs. What *hadn't* they stored in this room? Rotating her ankles, he gently pressed his fingers across the skin there. She whimpered when he moved her knees, but her pants were too tight for him to do a full exam.

Liam dropped down beside him with Annie's med kit. "What's the damage?"

"She has a concussion that's causing nausea, bruised knees…maybe a cracked cheekbone." Rafe ran a hand through his hair. She was hurt, but she was going to be fine. Rafe kept repeating that to himself, trying to force the final tinge of fear away.

Liam stood, pushing a bit more of the debris away from Annie. At least now there was a clear aisle to walk her out.

"Doug's going to bring Holly to the clinic too. Her wrist may be broken."

Sliding his arms around her waist, Rafe gently lifted Annie in his arms.

"I want to go home." Annie leaned her head against Rafe's shoulder.

"Liam?" Rafe nodded toward the door. "Any chance you can get them to cut the lights and tell everyone to let us pass without any fuss?"

"No." Tears slipped down Annie's cheeks as her eyes shifted from Rafe to Liam. "I'm not a diva."

Pressing his lips to her head, Rafe ran his finger along an unbruised section of her chin. "This isn't about being a diva, Annie. We need to take care of you."

Rafe turned, but Liam had already disappeared through the door.

"I could walk…"

Annie squeezed at his shoulder as he carefully walked the narrow path Liam had charted for them. He was not going to ask her to loosen her grip. With her concussion, she was not steady enough to navigate the supply room.

"Let me carry you," he said. "It makes me feel better." It wasn't a lie. Rafe needed her in his arms. His heart needed the reassurance that she was going to be okay.

"I don't like this…" Annie muttered as he maneuvered them through the supply room.

"I know, sweetheart. If you *did* like the feel of a bruised brain I'd be worried."

The room was dark and somber as they made their way to the door.

"I can't believe they stopped the carnival for me."

"Everyone loves you."

Love—the word hung on the edge of his lips. If he'd had any doubts about the emotion, tonight's disaster had cemented his feelings. He loved Annie. She gave him life and breath. And as soon as her head was better he was going to tell her. He didn't know how, but it was going to be a moment she'd always remember.

"We forgot our coats. My mother always got me the prettiest coats…"

"I'm sure someone has noticed me carrying you into the snow without them. I bet they're delivered before we even get the truck started."

Annie's concussion must be muddling her mind if she was bringing up a happy memory tied to Carrie. *Carrie.* How could Rafe tell Annie he loved her when he still hadn't told her about her mother—or that Dave wanted to interview her?

His heart clenched—he couldn't.

"Rafe, my side is going to have a permanent imprint of your fingers."

Swallowing the lump in his throat, Rafe forced himself to relax. "Sorry." He stood her carefully by the truck as he juggled the keys in his hand.

"I can buckle myself," she said, when she got in. But the blood rushed from her face as she turned to grab the buckle. Biting her lip, she gripped the seat belt and jammed it into the clasp. "See."

His nose twitched, but Rafe didn't argue.

"Rafe! Annie!" Helen Henkle rushed toward the car.

"See—coats." Rafe turned to accept the heavy bundles from Helen before draping both coats across Annie's lap.

"Jack will drop the trophy off tomorrow." Helen gripped Rafe's shoulders. "Take care of her."

"Of course."

Before he stepped from her grasp, Helen kissed his cheek. "You're a good man."

"Thank you."

Helen didn't know those simple words held power, and Rafe swallowed the knot in his throat.

Turning, Helen fussed over Annie while Rafe got the truck started. She tried to shut the door softly, but the heavy door's clang still made Annie flinch.

"We won the trophy," he told her.

Annie gripped his hand. "I bet it's the sympathy vote."

"Maybe." Rafe's lips brushed her fingers as heat started to pour from the truck's vents. "Now, I am going to drive slowly. Try to keep your head as still as possible."

"This is *not* how I planned to spend the night." Annie ran her fingers across her cheek, pressing them against her temple, and then yawned.

Keeping his eyes on the dark road, Rafe chuckled. "I think most of the night went well."

"Sure…" Annie sighed. "I'm tired…" Her voice was groggy and her eyes fluttered shut.

"What *were* your plans?" Rafe raised his voice.

His heart hammered as he let his eyes drift from the road to Annie for a moment. He wanted to shout that he loved her or whisper it softly. Instead, he ran a finger along her uninjured cheek. He understood his need to touch her, to prove to his mind she was safe, but his heart refused to stop pounding.

Rafe tried to focus on keeping her awake. "How *did* you plan to spend the night, sweetheart?"

"I love when you call me sweetheart." Annie laid her hand on his leg. "I just love *you*."

The air in the truck's cab evaporated. Did she mean that or was it the concussion?

"Annie—"

The truck quivered as the right-hand wheel popped into a large pothole. Annie cried out and Rafe cursed. He'd hurt her. Her brain was bruised and he'd lost focus.

His lip trembled and he gripped her knee. "I'm sorry, Annie. We're almost home." Rafe stroked her leg, trying to calm the shake in his fingers. "I'll take care of you. I promise."

Her fingers covered her eyes. "I know you will. I trust you."

Trust. That word was like a slap in the face. He was hiding too many things. But he could fix that. He *had* to.

CHAPTER TEN

ANNIE STARED AT RAFE, trying to pretend his glassy expression and quietness this morning were symptoms of exhaustion. Over the last three days he'd only left her side to treat a handful of patients. Still, something wasn't right. Her brain fog was finally clearing, but worry pressed against her heart.

If Rafe was awake, his head was buried in his small journal and furiously writing notes. The journal had sat by the bed for weeks. Rafe always jotted down a short note in it before sleep, but it hadn't left his nightstand since he'd done that research on hot yoga.

Now it was his constant companion.

She'd asked about it twice and he'd said he was making a list. She hadn't had the nerve to ask what kind. Was he preparing to leave and trying to put distance between them? Was it because she hadn't agreed to go to LA?

"Damn it." Rafe's brows crossed as he seemed to slash items off today's list.

"I'm worried about you," she said. *And terrified you want to leave me.*

Annie left that fear unstated as she poured more coffee into her mug before taking the seat next to him.

Rafe's lips were warm as they pressed against her

nose. "I'm the one who should be doing all the worrying. How's your head?"

"Sore—and my cheek is an ugly purple. At least it matches my knees."

Annie tried to catch his mouth, but her lips met his cheek instead. His avoidance of her kisses sent alarm bells ringing across her mind. *What was going on?*

"Bruises always look worse a few days after the injury. I bet the edges will be lighter tomorrow." Rafe scribbled another note before ripping the page from his notebook.

"Want me to throw that away?"

Rafe stuffed the page into his pocket. "No need. I might decide I need it later. I've done that a few times. I have several torn pages hiding in this journal." He caught his lip between his teeth as he tapped his pen on the table.

It was a reasonable statement. Annie had a hard time throwing away any notes she took too. But that knowledge did nothing to quiet the fear that he was hiding something from her.

"I didn't know you wrote in your journal so often."

Rafe's brows crossed as he looked up. "I don't. Not usually. However, when I'm trying to solve problems it helps me to make lists."

Problems?

She pulled his free hand into her lap. "What are you working on? Maybe I can help."

"Nothing." His fingers rubbed her palm, but his eyes met hers for less than a second before turning back to the journal.

Annie sighed. Why wouldn't he look at her? Was it her bruises? She'd never considered herself vain, but this morning she'd cried as she pulled her hair into a loose topknot. Purple stains traveled across her high cheekbones, meeting in a jagged cut at her temple.

She didn't look like a pretty actress right now. Was that why Rafe couldn't look at her for more than a few seconds?

Drumming her fingernails against her coffee mug, Annie tried to push the worry away. Rafe wasn't a shallow man, and the bruises would fade. Of course his kisses would be more reserved because she was suffering from a concussion. These suspicions didn't serve either of them.

Still, she couldn't shake the uncertainty clawing across her spine.

There were other reasons he might be pulling away.

Was he upset that she'd told him she loved him? *Had* she told him? Her memories were cloudy apparitions, shrouded in pain. She was almost certain her feelings had slipped out through her fog of confusion.

She remembered Rafe calling her his love before their dance, but a term of endearment wasn't a declaration. Annie had combed her muddled memories, but she was certain he hadn't said he loved her. She knew her brain, even bruised, would have retained *that* memory.

Fear had seemed to be her constant companion since the carnival. She wanted to talk about their future, offer to go to LA for a few days, but Rafe was too concerned with whatever was in that journal.

Annie didn't know how to go back to the happy bubble they'd lived in before her injury. Her heart pounded as tears filled her eyes. She didn't want to spend the rest of his time here pretending she was okay with this shift.

"Did I do something wrong?"

The words had escaped. There was no way for Annie to draw them back, and she didn't want to. She needed an answer—even if it ripped her heart in two.

"What?" Rafe's mouth hung open as he stared at her.

Dipping her head, Annie shrugged. "You've been…"

Annie hesitated, not wanting to accuse him of anything. "Distant. You're always taking notes and…" The last of her courage evaporated. "Maybe I'm just being nosy, and it's certainly not my place…"

The rambling words echoed in her head. At least she could blame the concussion for her circular thoughts.

Offering a soft chuckle, Annie started to stand, but Rafe grabbed her hand.

"You haven't done anything wrong." His eyes wandered across her bruised features and his fingers squeezed hers. "I just…"

She held her breath as he paused. Why couldn't she push away the fear that he was hiding something?

"I have a meeting with Dave and my agent at noon. I keep trying to find the answer to a question they have, and my mind refuses to give it." Rafe let out a bitter laugh. "I swear my brain is stuck on repeat."

"No fair—that's *my* excuse." Annie kissed his lips. Her aches disappeared as Rafe deepened the kiss and pulled her into his lap.

"If you weren't black and blue…" Rafe leaned back in the chair. His smile was wide, but it didn't quite reach his eyes.

"What's their question?" Annie leaned her head against his chest. She always overthought things—maybe this question really was all that was weighing on Rafe's mind. "My TV show experience is dated, but I remember the nerves."

Meeting with producers and directors had always left her stomach in knots. And sharing her home with her agent had meant any notes she'd been given had been drilled into her at the dinner table, before bed and first thing every morning. Just the memories sent a shudder through her.

"Dave wants me to do an interview. Actually, I *have* to do the interview."

Annie frowned. "You talked him out of the hot yoga topic. I'm sure you can talk him out of this."

Rafe kissed her forehead. "I've tried. He seems set on this one. He even responded to my last email by forwarding a copy of my contract. If I don't provide something I'll be in breach, and the penalty is steep. It will wipe out all my savings, plus some."

His breath hitched and his arms tightened on her waist.

"I need something to wow him—something he can't say no to."

Annie's heart pounded and she closed her eyes to keep the tears at bay. If this interview went well his contract wouldn't matter. They'd negotiate a new one with his promotion. Rafe hadn't said those words, but she knew how Hollywood worked. He might not like Dave's interview topic, but the show was his dream. It was what mattered to him most.

"What's the topic?"

Rafe's eyes were hooded, and Annie felt the pinch of fear again.

"Rafe?"

Rubbing his hand along his neck, Rafe looked at her. "He wants me to do something that doesn't have any real medical focus. But I've never done gimmicks. I don't want to start now."

Annie had dealt with the fallout of Dr. Dave's fad diets and vitamin gimmicks in several of her patients. It was good that Rafe was telling Dave no. So why did it feel like there was more to the story?

Rolling her head slowly, Annie forced the uncertainties away. Rafe hadn't given her any reason to doubt him. This was just her fear about the future transferring itself to everything else. After his meeting was over she and Rafe were going to talk—and she was not going to chicken out.

She focused on the thing weighing against his mind. "We don't have much time. Let's get brainstorming. What other ideas do you have?"

This was important to Rafe, so it had to matter to her. Their relationship could weather the long distance and his fame—she had to believe that.

Rafe's arms fell from her sides. "You don't mind helping me with my *Dr. Dave* material?"

Sitting back, Annie pulled on all her acting skills. She needed to look happy for him. "You want that promotion, Rafe. And it should be yours."

"I didn't mention the promotion." Rafe's arms trembled as they wrapped around her again. "And you don't watch *The Dr. Dave Show*. So why do you think it should be mine?"

"You've talked about that promotion since you arrived. It's not hard to read between the lines—even with a bruised brain. You want them to choose you…to recognize what you bring to the table."

Rafe bit his lip. "It's always nice to be chosen."

For a moment Annie didn't think they were talking about the show. But she swallowed and forced that hope aside.

Tapping his cheek, Annie kissed his nose. "I don't watch the show, but I'm biased as hell about the wonderful Dr. Bradstone."

Annie loved the smile beaming on Rafe's features. Hopping off his lap, she sucked in a breath as the world tilted around her.

Rafe caught her before she could topple over. "You still need to move slow, sweetheart."

"I love that you call me that…" The words slipped into the quiet kitchen.

Rafe kissed the top of her head before helping her back to the chair. "Well, I *like* calling you sweetheart."

She'd never had a nickname. Most people assumed her real name was Anne, but her mother had chosen Annie because she'd thought it sounded like a good stage name. Annie rubbed her finger on the rough skin of her thumb. Even as a child, her mother saw her as a potential subject to turn famous.

When *she* had children, she'd make sure they had cute nicknames for Rafe to whisper in their ears.

Chills warred with warmth as Annie stared at Rafe. And as the image of him chasing dark-haired children soaked through her she sighed. He'd be an excellent father. But that life couldn't exist if they were thousands of miles apart.

Could she leave the clinic?

That question had seemed impossible even a week ago. There were plenty of practices in LA, but Blue Ash had meant everything to Blake. It meant so much to her too. But if she wanted a life with Rafe she had to find a way to live in the same state as him. If he needed the spotlight, she would find a way to stand beside him.

"Come on—tell me your ideas." Annie gripped his hands. Relationships were partnerships; she could do this—for *him*.

Rafe clicked his tongue and picked up his journal. "How about we brainstorm while snuggling on the couch? You can help me weed out all the awful ideas."

"I bet you have at least one winning idea in there."

He was so talented; she knew Rafe was destined to sit in one of the permanent chairs on Dave's set.

Annie ran her hands along the wall of the hall. She

knew where each dip and hole of the clinic's log cabin walls was—but this hadn't always been home. Home was where the people you loved were. It was with Rafe.

"I don't know why you keep trying to add more topics. Discussing the lack of medical support in rural and low-income communities is the best."

Annie crossed off all the other topics they'd hashed out over the last hour.

She was right—but Rafe didn't want her to think he was looking to interview *her*. Rafe knew how much she hated the spotlight. She'd been exploited by her mother and the Hollywood machine. He didn't want to perpetuate that for his own gain—wouldn't perpetuate it.

"Annie..." Rafe's tongue stuck to the roof of his mouth. "If I do this, what should I highlight?"

Her eyes narrowed. Did she think he was using her? Nothing could be further from the truth. Rafe had spent every day trying to find another topic for Dave. He'd scoured his contract, but Dave was within his rights to demand a specific topic.

However, if Annie didn't agree to the interview Dave couldn't force *her* to participate. But Rafe hadn't asked her. Annie was kind, compassionate and supportive. She might agree to it to help him get the promotion. Except that the promotion didn't matter much when she was beside him.

Rafe had to find another avenue without risking her.

"I remember seeing an infographic from the American Medical Association a few months ago. I think the greatest shortages are in Mississippi and Idaho. It isn't just locations, though..." Annie pushed a curl behind her ear.

Rafe ran his fingers along the top of her thigh. It was one of the few places where she wasn't bruised. His need to touch her had only increased since her accident. He'd woken from the same nightmare every night since the carnival. He kept running down crowded aisles in a storage room, but he could never reach Annie.

He couldn't risk losing her—nothing was worth that.

After this meeting he'd wrap the final threads of his life together. Then he was going to tell her everything. Buy a huge box of donuts and declare his love. He'd planned his gesture over the last three days. It was going to be perfect.

Rafe forced himself to focus. "What do you mean, it isn't just locations?"

Annie started to shake her head, but caught herself. Her concussion was healing faster than he'd expected, but he knew she was still frustrated with the limited range of motion her brain allowed.

"If the AMA's predictions are correct, we're going to be desperately low on general practitioners, psychiatrists and OBGYNs in the next two decades."

"Hmm… I might have the perfect interviewee for that." His phone buzzed and his stomach rumbled. "But I need to grab a sandwich and place a quick call before the meeting."

"No." Annie kissed his cheek. "I'll make lunch. You head into the bedroom and make that call." She glared at his phone. "Maybe after this meeting your phone will stop buzzing all the time!"

Rafe laughed. "That was *your* phone, sweetheart."

Joining his chuckles, Annie checked her phone. His stomach lurched as she frowned. Was something wrong?

"Annie?"

"Jenn's dad has to have emergency heart surgery. Guess it's a good thing Liam is planning to hang around this winter."

His replacement wasn't coming, and Liam would need to spend at least a few more weeks in the remote communities before coming back.

"Annie—"

She patted his knee as she interrupted him. "It's fine, Rafe. This was always a possibility." She forced a smile as Rafe's phone dinged. "That is your life calling. Go make your call and do your interview. You've earned that promotion."

"Annie—"

Her eyes were downcast. She'd asked him if everything was all right this morning. Was she doubting him?

His lungs refused to accept any air. He hadn't said he loved her—hadn't convinced her she was what mattered, not the promotion. She didn't yet realize he'd choose her—always. They'd spent the morning planning his interview with Dave. Now his replacement wasn't coming and there wasn't time—

Rafe's phone buzzed again.

Why didn't life have a pause button? There was so much to say.

I love you.

"We need to talk."

"There isn't time." She kissed his cheek. "I'm rooting for you."

Annie disappeared into the kitchen. He should go after her—his soul cried out for him to follow.

The ding of his phone forced his hand. But as soon as this meeting was over Rafe was turning off his phone and he was going to tell Annie how much he loved her. They'd find a way to make this winter work.

Soon…

CHAPTER ELEVEN

IT WAS TEMPTING to drop a few pieces of ham on a piece of bread and rush a sandwich in to Rafe before his meeting started. Part of her brain still screamed that she should do it, but she refused to give in to the cowardly desire. If Annie planned to be a part of Rafe's life she'd meet Dave and his agent soon anyway.

Pushing her fears away, Annie turned the griddle on. Rafe was right: she was more than Charlotte Greene. It was time to step out of the past—particularly if she planned to spend some time in LA.

Her phone buzzed.

Annie tried to ignore the sadness pushing against her. It wasn't Jenn's fault. Annie would just have to push her vacation to springtime. At least with Liam in town the winter wouldn't be too lonely. Except without Rafe—

Annie pushed that thought aside. She was not going to beg him to stay.

Taking a deep breath, Annie swallowed the dread tingling in the back of her throat. She loved Rafe. She wanted to believe he loved her too. But he'd never said it. He was worried about his contract. She understood that panic. Studios were ruthless. She was just overthinking this.

Again her phone interrupted her mental wanderings.

She tried to understand the words on the screen. Helen never texted her—she claimed it was too difficult for her to see the tiny letters on her phone.

Annie's fingers trembled.

I am so sorry. Let me know if you want Jack to fly him to Anchorage this afternoon.

Helen's message was followed by a link to an online tabloid.

"No!"

The phone tumbled from her fingers—its case shattered as it connected with the kitchen tile. Tears floated in her eyes, but she refused to let them fall. Bending, Annie retrieved the phone. She was tempted to let the story remain unread, but maybe it was false. Tabloids made their money off half-truths, paid informants and lies.

Sucking on her lip, Annie followed the link.

Playboy Doctor Uses Child Star to Secure Promotion

The picture Rafe had snapped after they'd stepped off the dance floor headed the article.

Only he had that image. Only he could have given it to the press.

He'd lied to her…made her believe—what?

Rafe had never said he loved her. He'd said they needed to talk.

God, she was a fool.

When Dr. Rafe Bradstone departed for Alaska a few weeks ago his fans assumed it was an escape— a few weeks away to rehab his playboy image. But

apparently the Playboy Doctor wasn't just volun-
teering his medical expertise. Instead he was seek-
ing a desperate starlet, hiding in the wilderness.

CelebNews Weekly *has learned that Dr. Rafe*
Bradstone has secured the permanent co-host spot
on The Dr. Dave Show. *How? By scoring an ex-*
clusive interview with child star Annie Masters.

Ms. Masters currently works at a clinic in Blue
Ash, Alaska. The clinic had not responded to our
message left on its answering service by the time
of reporting.

Dr. Bradstone's agent, Ms. Carrie Forester, re-
fused to comment, citing a formal press release to
be issued later. Ms. Forester also refused to com-
ment on Annie Masters. Ms. Forester is, of course,
Annie Masters' mother, and was her longtime man-
ager during her daughter's successful decade-long
career on My Sister's House.

Has Annie Masters spent all her wealth? Is that
why she's working in an outpost clinic in Alaska?

CelebNews Weekly *will update this story as*
more details are unearthed.

Bile coated her tongue, and she had to take several
deep breaths to settle the nausea rolling through her
stomach. The writer hadn't even bothered to research
the clinic. The deed was publicly available—as was her
medical license. Even her Army enlistment would be easy
to find—several magazines had run short pieces about
it. It would have been easy to discover she wasn't a desperate or destitute starlet—but that didn't bring website
clicks and ad revenue.

Dr. Annie Masters had been reduced to a "child star"

and "desperate starlet." She was so much more, but no one had ever seemed to see it.

Rafe had almost made her believe, but that was a lie too. Her transformation from child star to doctor at an outpost clinic was the perfect leverage for his interview— Annie had even given him a picture for the cover.

Now this morning's snuggles were tainted. Rafe had needed a reason to interview *her*. An interview about the need for healthcare professionals in remote areas— how could she have been so blind? He'd even managed to make it seem like it was her idea. Of course he knew "the perfect interviewee"—she'd been sitting next to him.

Her fingers trembled as she finished reading the story. It was all about *Dr. Dave*. Rafe had told her it was the most important thing. Annie had hoped she'd take that spot eventually, but now—

She closed her eyes as pain rolled through her.

If he'd asked, she'd have immediately agreed.

Her chest was tight and black dots floated before her eyes. Why had he had to make her believe he wanted her? Cared for her?

Annie's lungs refused to fill and she sat down on the floor. She couldn't risk reinjuring her head.

Carrie was his agent. *Her mother.* Carrie had managed Annie's childhood and, given the chance, would still be directing her life. Everyone saw Annie as Charlotte Greene because Carrie hadn't allowed Annie to be anything else.

But Army enlistment contracts were binding. Carrie had screamed, but she'd been forced to let Annie go. She hadn't spoken to her daughter since.

Carrie.

Annie leaned her head against the cabinet. Rafe had

talked about his agent since his arrival. How had she failed to notice that he'd never used her name?

Her phone buzzed. Holly's name flashed, along with the link and an offer for Doug to haul Rafe out of the clinic.

This was going to be her life for at least the next several days. Answering polite, probing questions about Rafe's lies. She couldn't stay here—couldn't watch the pleasant smiles as people asked how she was, listed Rafe's faults and told her she was better off without him.

Laying her phone aside, she closed her eyes—what was she going to do?

Six new messages popped in and she put her fist in her mouth to keep from screaming. The last thing Annie needed was for Rafe to come running to her aid.

"Annie?" Liam stepped into the kitchen.

"Don't ask any questions about him, please."

She bit the words out, pressing her palm into her forehead. Her head was screaming, her heart was crying, and her bruised brain didn't know how to handle any of it.

"I need you to ask your dad to fly Rafe out tonight. Can you handle it here alone for a week or so? Even if my concussion was healed…" Annie sucked in a breath "…I just can't stand the looks."

"Of course." Liam's keys landed in her lap. "Why don't you stay at my cabin? It's fully stocked. I can use your guest room here."

"Thank you." Her lips trembled, but she held herself together.

"Where is he?" asked Liam.

"In a meeting with my mom and Dave. Bet he's letting them know how he got me to agree to participate in his stupid interview."

She leaned her head against her knees. She should have realized what he was doing.

"You've agreed?"

Pursing her lips, Annie stared down the hall to where Rafe was probably promising her help right now. "No—not really."

"I'll handle that, then." Liam stepped beside her.

Annie sucked air between her teeth as she stood up and pulled Rafe's half-burned grilled cheese from the skillet. His lunch was still edible, but it wouldn't taste good. Did it make her a horrible person that she was happy about that?

"Please don't…" Annie shut her eyes, praying the tears would stay buried. "Please don't be cruel to him. He—He—"

"If you're about to tell me he doesn't deserve it, I will lose it," said Liam.

Annie swallowed the lump pressing against her throat. She loved Rafe—it hurt that she'd misread his actions, but she didn't hate him. Couldn't hate him.

"Rafe is driven and talented. I told him I was rooting for him to get this promotion. I wasn't lying. I hate the way he did it, and that he didn't tell me, but he needs the show. It makes him feel whole."

She'd thought she soothed some of the wounds on his soul… But she couldn't let her mind wander that path.

"He doesn't deserve you."

Annie didn't have any more words. She wanted to get out of the clinic before Rafe's meeting ended, but she refused to play the coward. Her chest seized; she couldn't make a bigger fool of herself…

Annie nodded to Liam as he went to call Jack and then tell Rafe and his companions that their clinic was not available for *The Dr. Dave Show.*

Her phone buzzed, and she turned it off without checking the message.

Walking downstairs to the clinic, Annie played the voicemails on the clinic's line—twenty-nine calls from different tabloids, and even a few news outlets. Charlotte Greene's image had taken over her refuge, and Rafe had invited them in.

Annie let the dreams Rafe had awakened die with each press of the delete button.

Pacing next to Annie's bed, Rafe stared at the number on his phone. Annie was right: this interview *should* be about the need for doctors in underserved areas. And she was a great reference, but she wasn't the only physician serving in the trenches. Rafe's college roommate, Dr. Demarcus Martin, ran a free clinic in one of the poorest counties in Mississippi.

Demarcus didn't approve of Rafe's participation on *The Dr. Dave Show*, but he might be interested in this topic.

"If you're going to call, stop talking to yourself and push the button," he told himself aloud.

Demarcus was unlikely to answer, but he could leave a message. Pushing his hand through his hair, he closed his eyes and listened to the rings.

"Rafe!" Demarcus's warm tone echoed in Annie's room.

"I want to catch up, but I—I don't have a lot of time..." Rafe stuttered.

"This is related to your show?"

"It is," Rafe muttered as he pulled up his notes. "But how you manage to make *show* sound like a curse word is beyond me."

Demarcus huffed. "Doctors should be serving the community—not strutting like peacocks on the small screen."

Rafe flinched at the harsh words. "Ouch!"

Demarcus sighed. "That is mostly directed at Dave. I'm not interested in flying out for an audition."

"This isn't an audition. It's an interview. Just listen..." Rafe outlined his plan, watching the minutes tick away. "We aren't educating enough physicians to cover the needs of our remote and low-income population."

"I've seen the AMA's predictions," Demarcus growled. "I don't see what that has to do with my clinic."

Tapping his foot, Rafe made sure the camera and microphone were off on his laptop. Dave never called in on time, but if today was an exception Rafe didn't want him overhearing his next statement until Demarcus was on board.

"Your community is dreadfully underserved. This interview would let us talk about your community's current requirements and highlight the need for reform in med school costs, healthcare expenses, and the uneven access to medical care across the country."

The phone was quiet for a few seconds, and Rafe checked twice to make sure the call hadn't been dropped.

"Not sure that makes great television...but it's a piece I can get behind. Sure—count me in."

Rafe punched the air. "*Yes!* You are *not* going to regret this."

Rafe let out the breath he hadn't known he'd been holding. His contract was up at the end of the year. He'd do a quick trip to Mississippi next week, interview Demarcus, then fly to California, film the Thanksgiving and Christmas shows and then put his life in LA behind him. This piece would be his final legacy in Hollywood.

Dave wouldn't like him withdrawing his name from

the promotion pool, but Rafe didn't care. He might have kept a few secrets, but he was free to tell them all to Annie now. He might never be as perfect as Blake, but he was going to spend the rest of his life making Annie happy. Helping her fulfill her dreams here.

"Rafe?"

The quiet quality of Demarcus's voice sent a shiver across Rafe's spine.

"I am not sure how you managed to get Dr. Annie Masters to agree to this too, but one day I want to hear that whole story."

"What?" How did Demarcus know about Annie?

His computer screen started to ring.

"I'll call you with the details in a few days. Thanks, Demarcus."

He knew Dave wanted an interview at the Arctic clinic, but he would make him understand that Demarcus's clinic provided a better example. People expected the Arctic to be sparsely populated, but Demarcus served nearly a thousand patients on a shoestring budget. And it was happening in a town that looked more like everyday America.

Rafe slid into the chair, barely managing to click off his phone before Carrie appeared in the center of the screen.

"Congratulations, Rafe!"

Blood rushed through his ears as Carrie raised her water bottle to him. Why was she congratulating him?

"I take it you haven't seen the *CelebNews* site?" She grinned.

"No, why? Did you leak something to the press?" Raising an eyebrow, he tried to calm the worry pressing against his chest.

"Not me…"

Her gray eyes almost matched her daughter's, but they didn't contain Annie's warmth. Rafe wasn't sure he believed her, but a three-way conference call was not the right time to have an argument with his agent.

His belly rumbled and he looked at the door. What was Annie fixing for lunch?

"Rafe!" Dave's cheery tone echoed around Annie's bedroom. "Is that a *bed* in the background? I expected to see the clinic." Dave folded his arms as he sat back in his chair.

"I'm in the apartment above the clinic. The doctor I'm helping was injured this weekend, so the clinic is only open for emergencies through Thursday. Luckily we haven't had any of those, but if the bell rings I'll need to step away."

Rafe made a show of pulling up his notes. This was a pitch meeting—not a sightseeing tour of Annie's clinic.

"Well, the duvet makes a nice touch." Dave didn't manage to hide his sneer quickly enough.

Rafe wanted to immediately jump to Annie's defense, but he had no plans to bring her into this talk.

Carrie had other ideas. "How *is* Dr. Masters?"

"She's fine."

Carrie nodded at the perfunctory statement, but didn't push for more information. How could she have raised such a caring woman?

Annie was right—genes didn't matter much. His mother had walked away from him, abandoned him, but he was never going to leave Annie. If she was willing to keep him Rafe would make sure she and—if they were lucky—their children always knew how much they were loved.

"Good." Dave leaned into the screen. "Rafe, the interview team will be there next Wednesday."

"Wait." Rafe slapped the desk, feeling it wobbled with the pressure. "I plan to do this interview at a clinic in Ransburg, Mississippi. Dr. Demarcus Martin is prepared to talk about the same issues we would discuss here."

Dave took a large sip of green smoothie. His voice was diplomatic, but unyielding, when he started his argument.

"Mississippi isn't exotic like the Arctic. I'm not bending on this. This is a television show—we don't want people getting bored. Boredom leads to low ratings and cancellations." Dave looked at his nails and frowned. "I've leaked that you're the new co-host, but we can retract that." His eyes narrowed.

New co-host? Rafe's mind swam. He'd focus on that after Dave agreed to let him do the interview at Demarcus's clinic.

"This is an important segment, Dave. We have a responsibility to use our platform."

"We have a responsibility to our network producers. They are the ones who pay our salaries."

Rafe rubbed at his face. "Then make the producers understand. You're a *doctor*!"

His stomach plummeted when Dave shrugged. "Rafe, you understand the math here. Your suggestions always steer the show to higher-rated stories or away from things that might result in lawsuits. You're a brilliant tactician."

Dave didn't care about the message they provided—only the ratings and the ad revenue that message produced. Rafe followed the ratings, but for him the stories, and helping their viewers, came first. Except Dave hadn't seen that. He'd seen a man determined to sit in the spotlight—driven by attention. A man like him.

How could he have been so blind?

Drawing in a deep breath, Rafe tried once more. Even if he never sat on Dave's TV set again, this was a message he needed to get out. And Demarcus was the perfect spokesman. "I really think if you could see Demarcus's clinic you'd understand. The work he's doing is remarkable—"

Dave clicked his tongue as he interrupted. "Is this Dr. Martin a former child actor who disappeared from public life? Is he running a clinic on the edge of the world? Did he serve as an Army medic?"

The air rushed from Rafe's lungs as he tried to make sense of Dave's words. How did he know about Annie?

"I—"

"Charlotte Greene is the story I want—not her clinic."

"Her name is *Dr.* Annie Masters," Rafe growled.

Dave's eyes widened, but he didn't say anything.

"How did you know about her?"

Rafe's eyes cut to Carrie, but she shook her head. His stomach turned and the eggs he'd fixed for him and Annie this morning threatened to reappear.

"How?"

"Everyone knows about Annie. The clinic's phone is ringing off the hook."

Liam Henkle's cool voice cut through the bedroom as he leaned against the doorjamb.

"Congrats on the promotion."

Liam tipped his head toward Rafe before he marched to the desk.

"My apologies for interrupting. *Dr.* Masters has asked me to speak on behalf of *our* clinic. We are not going to permit you to do any interviews here."

Dave sputtered, but Rafe didn't care. His entire body was frozen. How had Dave learned about Annie and why was the clinic phone ringing so much?

"I'll call you back."

Rafe closed the laptop without waiting for Carrie or Dave to say anything.

"Annie!"

Ignoring Liam, Rafe tore through the apartment. A burned grilled cheese sandwich sat on a plate in the kitchen. Grabbing his coat, he rushed for the clinic.

"This is Richard Dixon from *Gossip Weekly*. We are attempting to reach Annie Masters. My phone number is—"

The voicemail message was cut off and another started in its place.

"This is Josephine Warren from *All Celeb News*—"

Annie's gray eyes met his as she hit the delete button. "Congratulations on your promotion."

Rafe felt as if his soul had been ripped from his body. "How…?"

He didn't realize he'd spoken the word aloud until Annie spun the clinic's laptop around.

Playboy Doctor Uses Child Star to Secure Promotion

The picture he'd taken of them at the carnival was splashed above the headline. It had come from his social media account. Rafe must have uploaded it without thinking. Annie was just Annie to him—didn't she know how much she meant to him?

The answer crushed him.

No.

He'd kept those words locked away. Instead he'd delivered the media to her door. All his plans to keep her safe looked like manipulation. His motivation was different from his father's, but the result was the same—he'd hurt the woman he loved.

"You should have asked before you had it splashed across the front page of *CelebNews*."

Annie had a green duffel bag sitting next to her feet.

"This isn't what it looks like." Rafe shook his head. "Annie, sweetheart…" Blood pounded in his ears—what was he supposed to do? "I didn't mean—"

The phone rang and Annie's jaw clenched, but she picked it up.

"Blue Ash Medical Clinic. No comment."

She slammed the phone down.

"Didn't mean to make it so I have to leave my own home? Didn't mean for me to find out about the interview? Or didn't mean to hide the fact my mother is your agent?"

Annie caught back a sob as she picked up the bag.

"Didn't mean to make me believe you cared about me? That I was more than Charlotte Greene to you?"

"I *do* care. God, Annie—you are so much more than Charlotte Greene. Why can't you see that?"

A bitter laugh left Annie's lips as she glared at him. "It's what everyone expects me to be. No matter what I do, everyone I love wants Charlotte. My mother needed Charlotte to advance her career, and you—"

Another choked sob echoed from Annie's chest as she rubbed the back of her hand across her nose.

"I even made it easy for you. You can't tell what my Halloween costume is in that picture, but I'm a dead ringer for an older Charlotte Greene."

Annie pointed to the computer, but Rafe refused to look away from her. She loved him, and he'd delivered a nightmare to her haven.

"This isn't what it looks like," Rafe repeated as he pulled at his hair.

"So you *weren't* given a promotion in exchange for

getting me to tell Dr. Dave's audience how I went from being Charlotte Greene to Dr. Annie Masters? The worst part is, if you'd asked I would have agreed to it. I would have said yes to help you. I am *such* a fool."

How had he managed to destroy this so completely? It didn't matter that Rafe had been trying to protect Annie. He'd left so many things out—and lies of omission were still lies.

His body shook. "You are not a fool. You are amazing, beautiful—"

"And the key to extending your time in the spotlight." Glaring at the screen, she shuddered. "Is this enough attention for you?"

Rafe flinched as she leveled that barb at him. How had this day turned into such a nightmare? But before she threw him away he needed her to know one thing.

Gripping her hand, Rafe pressed his journal into her fingers. "This wasn't about Charlotte—it's never been about Charlotte for me. Please read that. I want you to see yourself the way I do. See the intelligent, caring, beautiful creature that you are. I want you to look in the mirror and see Annie."

Annie stared at the journal, but she didn't drop it.

"I took that photo because I was happy to be with you."

I love you. The words stuck in his throat. His mother had thrown those words into arguments, trying to make his father stay. Rafe wasn't going to use them that way.

Annie hesitated for a moment and his heart sped up. Then the phone rang. Annie slipped past him as Rafe picked it up.

"No comment!"

A single tear slid down her cheek. "You promised not to use me." She bit her lip as the phone rang again. "I trusted you, and you shone your spotlight *here*. Now I have to leave the place I carved out for myself—the place where I was supposed to be just Dr. A."

He *had* used her. Not to get the promotion, but to put the pieces of his heart back together. He'd used her to find the meaning of love.

"Please don't walk away."

"There's nothing here for me. Goodbye, Dr. Bradstone."

I'm here... Choose me... Believe me...

He wanted to scream, to beg her to stay, but the words stuck in his throat as she headed out the door. Instead Rafe stepped aside. His father had destroyed his mother with his infidelities, and Rafe's need for the spotlight had taken the thing Annie loved most from her—her clinic.

"I love you..." Rafe whispered as the clinic door slammed shut.

CHAPTER TWELVE

"I'll help you pack."

Liam's gruff comment hit Rafe's back as he watched Annie get into her truck.

"No."

The word surprised Rafe as it slipped from his lips. It felt right, though. His father had run away from his marriage. His mother had run from her parental duties. Rafe was ending that cycle.

Folding his arms, Rafe turned around. Annie needed a break from the clinic—from him—but Jenn wasn't on her way. The clinic needed two physicians. This was Annie's sanctuary, and Rafe would take care of it until she came home.

And if she sent him on his way when she returned—

His heart clenched. If Annie asked him to leave, he would go—but not until he'd told her how much he loved her. She deserved to know that someone loved *Annie*—not Charlotte Greene or her past.

Liam raised an eyebrow as the engine of Jack's plane roared to life outside. "I could make you go."

Rafe cocked his head. "Maybe—but I'm banking on you giving me a chance."

"Why should I?" Liam scoffed.

Pulling at the collar of his shirt, Rafe looked at the

ceiling. "I don't have a good reason. But I love Annie. I believe she loves me too. I can't prove that to her if I run now."

Running a hand through his hair, Liam shrugged. "She might kill me for not forcing you to get on that plane."

"She might." Rafe nodded.

He doubted it. Annie was too kind and generous to stay mad at Liam. Rafe wasn't sure how long it would take him to earn back her trust, but he was ready to wait.

"Let me try to make this right."

The shrill ring of the phone interrupted him. "Blue Ash Clinic." Rafe rolled his eyes as another reporter launched into her spiel. "No comment."

Reporters were clogging the line. What if there was an emergency—?

"How many in the town know your cell number?"

Liam's head rocked back. "Why?"

"We need a line for people to call if there's an emergency."

He waited for Liam to argue, but he shook his head as he lifted his phone.

"Mom? Activate the town call chain. If anyone wants to reach the clinic they need to call my cell or—" Liam snapped his fingers and motioned for Rafe to write his own mobile number down, then read it to Helen. "That's Rafe's cell."

Liam was quiet for several minutes. Rafe didn't want to know what Helen thought of him.

Finally, Liam interrupted his mother. "Well, I need a physician here until Annie is healed and he's staying."

Rafe smiled. It wasn't a ringing endorsement, but it was a start.

Liam turned to him. "All right—why don't you walk me through the clinic's records for the past few weeks?

Assuming Annie doesn't flay me for letting you stay, I'm going to need to know what's going on with our patients."

Our. The subtle inclusion warmed Rafe's heart. This was home—now he just had to convince Annie that her attention was all he needed to feel whole.

The cold water of the shower beat across her back, but Annie couldn't find the strength to turn the faucets off. Laying her head against the wall, she let her tears fall. What did it matter if goose bumps rose along her skin or if her cheeks were blotchy from the cold and her tears? If she could slide down the drain with the water she'd gladly disappear.

When her tear ducts had finally emptied, Annie wrapped a warm towel around herself and sat on the floor. Her body was heavy.

If she left Liam's cabin now would Rafe still be at the clinic? Did it matter if he was?

She choked out another sob. Why would Rafe stay? *For me?*

Except it wasn't Annie he wanted—not really.

She wanted to bang the questions out of her head but aggravating her concussion wouldn't help anyone.

Sighing, she looked up. Drops of water clung to the popcorn ceiling. "I should have gotten out when the water slipped from cool to freezing," she said aloud. Pressing her palms to her eyelids, she sighed as the pressure relieved a bit of her headache. "And now I'm talking to myself—about water!"

Swallowing, she closed her eyes. More tears leaked down her cheeks. Why had Rafe needed her interview for the promotion? He was the best doctor on the show, he drew the most viewers—it would have been his without her.

Annie wanted to believe that he hadn't used her. If *CelebNews* had plastered any other picture on that page…

She put her fist to her mouth, but it didn't stop her sobs from echoing against the bathroom tile.

Forcing herself to stand, she secured the towel around herself and stared at the fogged mirror. Raising a hand, she swiped at it until her face stared back at her. Her eyes were puffy, and her face was still bruised, but Rafe's words hung around her heart.

When she looked in the mirror what did she see?

A mess.

She covered her lips as hysterical laughter escaped her mouth. She was a soggy, pathetic, freckled mess. She was pretty sure any dictionary could use a picture of her rather than words and people would instantly understand what *pathetic* meant.

"I see me."

The phrase echoed in the small bathroom as Annie tried to make herself believe it.

"I see *me*."

A tear ran down her cheek. It was Charlotte Greene staring back at her, and Annie stamped her foot and let out a scream.

"Go away!"

Her image mocked her.

"I'm Dr. Annie Masters."

How long was she going to let her past haunt her?

"I'm Dr. Annie Masters!"

Shaking her head, Annie turned her back on the mirror. Arguing with herself wasn't going to change anything.

She tried to rub some heat into her body as she pulled on a sweater and headed into the kitchen. Rafe's journal sat on the counter. She'd meant to hand it back to him.

Ignoring the black leather, Annie grabbed a mug and made a cup of tea. *She was not going to read Rafe's journal.*

Opening a drawer, Annie threw the journal into it. Slamming the drawer shut gave her a moment of satisfaction before her stomach dropped.

Rafe was gone—or would be soon.

Her head ached, her heart wept and Annie didn't know what to do.

Downing two headache tablets, Annie walked to the living room. Falling into the couch, she stared at the picture of Blake on Liam's mantel. He was wearing his Army fatigues and smiling.

Annie wrapped her hands around the mug, willing the heat from the tea to touch her soul. She'd given her life to make Blake's dream come true.

Would she have founded a clinic in LA if he'd asked? No.

The question and her mind's immediate answer tore through her. She'd made Blake's dream come true because she loved him, but Blue Ash had given her the privacy she craved. It had let her hide.

Blake had called her brave once. Told her she could do anything. What would he think of her now?

Annie closed her eyes. She'd been so lost when he'd died. She had lived for the clinic—hadn't let anything else touch her heart—until Rafe had wandered through her door.

Blake would be so proud of the clinic—but he wouldn't approve of her hiding here. He'd be furious that she wasn't taking vacations. Livid that she had used his dream as a reason to avoid going back to LA.

Annie's mind raced.

What if Rafe hadn't used her? What if he wanted all of her? Past, present and future?

Rubbing the pulled skin along her thumb, Annie stared at the light snow drifting across the edge of Liam's picture window.

She couldn't lose someone again.

Annie shook as she sobbed. Her heart was already broken. She'd lost Rafe. She'd walked away from him.

She pulled her knees up to her chest.

When Blake had died, she hadn't been able to follow him—but she could go after Rafe.

She stood and walked back to the kitchen. Her palms itched as she pulled Rafe's journal from the drawer.

What did he want her to see?

Only one way to find out.

Annie stared at the binding on the journal. What if she opened it and found out it was Charlotte he needed?

Her brain screamed as her heart burst.

Charlotte. She was *not* going to let Charlotte Greene stop her from finding out what Rafe wanted her to know. Her character was a part of her, but it was a small part. She refused to live in her shadow anymore—no matter what was in Rafe's journal.

Running her fingers along the journal's binding, she inhaled and broke open the cover. The first page was ripped out, and the next three pages were grocery lists and workout schedules. Frowning, she riffled through the following pages. A torn page slipped to the ground. It had been crumpled and then smoothed out.

Her heart broke as she looked at the lines.

Goals:
Get into med school
Secure residency position

Complete residence
Move out of studio apartment
Visit all fifty states
~~Get permanent position on Dr. Dave~~
~~Find Mom~~
~~Meet Mom~~
Tell Annie you love her
Buy shoes that work for the Arctic
Move to Alaska

Her heart wanted to sing, but Annie wasn't going to celebrate yet. This page had been ripped out. What if there was another list that had all the ways he could use Annie's old fame to advance his position?

Flipping through the well-used journal, Annie held her breath. Rafe might have ripped those pages out before handing her the journal, but Annie doubted it. He wanted to let her see what he'd been thinking. Let her know his hopes and dreams.

A list of the interview ideas they'd worked on that morning appeared. She'd been so happy as she'd sat beside Rafe. Ink stained through the next page, and she couldn't make out some of the words. Whatever this list was, Rafe had clearly worked hard on it.

Ways to tell Annie I love her:
Just say it
Dinner
Roses
Dinner with roses
Donuts!

Tears showered her cheeks. He'd been hiding surprises and she had told him to leave. Accused him of using her when she knew how much that accusation would cripple him.

But it didn't matter what these pages said if Rafe was gone.

Rafe loved her.

There had to be an explanation for the *CelebNews* story, and only Rafe could give her that answer.

Annie sucked in a breath. Liam was in town and would run the clinic for a few days without her. Her fingers hovered over Rafe's list. She needed to pick up a few things and pack. If Rafe was in LA, then that was where she needed to be too.

Annie yawned as she made her way up the clinic's steps. In order to avoid the questioning eyes of the people of Blue Ash and aggravating her concussion, Annie had begged Holly to run a few errands for her. Holly hadn't agreed until Annie had told her about Rafe's lists. However, she'd needed to wait until the bakery closed. Then a car accident on the highway had derailed her friend's quick return.

But now Annie had everything she needed to head to California, and she'd promised Holly a nice souvenir for all her trouble.

Lugging her bags up the stairs, Annie's heart clenched at the thought of sleeping without Rafe. She'd grown accustomed to his warm weight beside her, his light breath on her neck…

If all her flights were on time she'd be in his arms the day after tomorrow. *Too long…*

Dropping the bags in the kitchen, Annie stumbled through to the living room. She didn't want to risk waking Liam. He'd have questions, and she was too exhausted to address any of them.

Her toe landed against something hard, and Annie let out a screech as she tumbled forward. Strong arms grabbed her before she hit the floor.

"Annie?" Rafe's voice was groggy with sleep as his hands ran over her. *"Annie?"*

He blinked as she flipped on the light. "What are you doing on the floor?" *What was he doing still in Blue Ash?*

That question stayed buried as she ran her fingers over his arms. He was here—he was still here.

"Sleeping."

Rafe smiled at her. This wasn't the frantic desire of his subconscious. Annie was here. *She was here.*

"Why are you sleeping on the floor?"

Her cheeks flushed as she stared at him.

"Wasn't sure you wanted me in our bed."

Rafe rubbed his hands across his face as he drank her in. Reaching a finger out, he pushed a loose curl away from her cheek, grateful that she didn't pull away.

"What are you still doing here, Rafe? Your show—"

"Doesn't matter," he interrupted. "This clinic needs more than one physician. I couldn't leave it—couldn't leave *you*."

"I am so sorry, Rafe. I'm glad you didn't leave. I should have chosen you—not run." Annie hiccupped as she pressed her lips to his cheek. Her shoulders shook as she laid her head against him. "Can you forgive me?"

Rafe wrapped his arms around her. She was here. Annie—*his Annie*—was home with him.

"Forgive you? I'm the one that kept major secrets and took a picture that landed on the front page of a tabloid."

Her lips stole the apology tumbling from his. The world shifted and nothing else mattered as she melted against him. Annie was here; she was choosing him.

Time slowed as her fingers pulled against his neck, demanding he deepen the kiss.

"I love you." Rafe pulled her into his lap. "I just need you to know that before anything else. I should have said it after the carnival, but I was hiding so many things."

He brushed his lips against her cheek. "I didn't tell you about the interview because I thought you'd agree to help. You're too sweet, and I didn't want to take advantage of your good nature. Figured if you didn't know I could tell Dave you hadn't agreed. I should have just told you everything."

Annie placed her arms around his waist. "You were trying to protect me."

Rafe pressed his head against hers. "I feared you'd hate me if you thought I was trying to find a way to use an interview with you to get the promotion. My dad used my mom for so many things, and I—" Rafe pressed his lips together. "I never want you to feel I used you."

"I was so afraid of my past that you didn't feel you could be honest with me." Annie laid her head against his shoulder. "I'm so much more than my character, but Charlotte is a part of me. I can't keep running from her. You made me see that."

She was grinning. He'd never seen her smile when the name Charlotte crossed her lips. He thought his world might explode.

Inhaling, Rafe pushed away his fear. "I love you."

He just needed to repeat those words.

"I love you. So, what if we put the past behind us and focus on the future?"

He didn't care about the late hour as Annie's smile radiated through him.

"I'm still under contract through the end of the year. I need to do that final interview and the Thanksgiving and Christmas shows. I don't know if I can be here this winter."

Annie laid a finger across his lips. "I want you here this winter, Rafe Bradstone, but I don't want you to give up all of the spotlight."

"Annie—" He gripped her fingers.

She ignored his attempt to interrupt. "What if the Christmas and Thanksgiving episodes were pre-recorded and shot at our clinic?"

Our—he loved that word. But...

"Dave likes the Thanksgiving show to be live. I'm not sure he'll go for it."

"Even if I'm the other host?"

Annie let out a whoop as Rafe picked her up.

"You'd co-host so I could stay here for the winter?" Rafe's heart felt as if it would burst as she held onto him.

Annie nodded. "If you're by my side I can step in front of any camera."

"I love you." Rafe smiled. "We'll do the shows and then we can tell Hollywood so long."

"No." Annie laid her hand on his chin. "I think we should do a few shows a year—in the summer, when it's easy for me to get replacements for us here."

"Us?" Rafe's fingers shook as he traced her jaw. "You'd come to LA with me."

"I'll go anywhere with you." Her fingers were soft as they ran along his unshaved cheek. "I'll bet Dr. Dave is willing to settle for a part-time Dr. Bradstone. But I'm not—so we spend most of the year in our clinic and a month in LA. We're a package deal now."

"I love you," Rafe said again. No other words seemed adequate.

Grabbing his hand, Annie led him to the kitchen. Her cheeks were flushed and her breath tightened as she stepped away. Opening a bag, she tossed him his journal before grabbing a pen.

"I think there's an item you need to check off."

Running his hand along the spine, Rafe smiled again. "Actually, I think there are a few items I can mark off."

"True." Annie giggled as she handed him a bag. "But this one is very important."

Rafe raised an eyebrow. "What's this?"

"Only one way to find out." Annie crossed her arms. "Open it!"

His breath caught as he stared into the bag. Slowly, he lifted out a heavy navy-blue boot. "You got me—" His voice cracked.

Knocking her hip against his, Annie lifted the other. "These are rated to minus forty degrees Fahrenheit. Can't have Dr. Bradstone losing any toes! Welcome home, Rafe."

Home. The precious word rumbled through his soul.

"Thank you." Rafe kissed the top of her head. "These are perfect. However, if it's negative forty outside, I have every intention of curling up next to you beside a warm fire—not stomping around in the snow."

"I think we can arrange that." Annie smiled.

"Marry me?"

The words slipped into the quiet kitchen. He should have planned it out. Given her a fancy dinner, flowers or donuts—something. But Rafe couldn't wait.

"Yes!" Annie leapt into his arms.

Annie had chosen *him*—all of him.

Dr. Rafe Bradstone was finally home.

EPILOGUE

"Is Daddy going to be done soon?"

Lilah pulled at Annie's dress and raised her arms. Lifting her daughter was getting more difficult these days.

Annie looked at the program set, where Rafe was confidently talking to a surgeon about a new hand reconstruction technique. Most of the segment would be cut—if not all of it. It was interesting to doctors, and some researchers, but the average daytime television viewer would have tuned to a new show within the first three minutes.

"If he can stop geeking out with Dr. Jameson, he'll be done soon."

Lilah frowned. Then the three-year-old laid her head against Annie's shoulder before letting out a squeal. "The baby kicked me again!"

Setting her daughter down, Annie caught Rafe's eye. He smiled when he saw her motion for him to move on. If he didn't want a screaming toddler to interrupt Dr. Dave's taping, it was time to go.

Annie had appeared in a few episodes but returning to show business held no appeal for her. Rafe still loved it, though. Usually Lilah and Annie stayed far away from the set, but they were supposed to head to the airport as soon as this was over. She had every intention of being back in Blue Ash by tomorrow afternoon—if her husband would wrap up his showboating.

Rafe rushed over as soon as the segment ended. "Is everything okay?"

Placing a kiss on his lips, Annie smiled. "Yep, but your daughter is ready to go." Leaning up, she nipped the bottom of his ear, enjoying the way he shuddered and pulled her close. "And your wife is too."

"In a rush to get back to the snow?" Rafe laughed as he lifted Lilah.

"The baby kicked me!" Their daughter's bottom lip stuck out as she repeated her complaint to her father.

Annie covered her mouth and looked away. If Lilah saw her giggle, she'd pout the whole way to the airport.

"He does that to me too," Rafe murmured as he led his small family out of the studio.

"Really?"

"Yes—when your mother snuggles up next to me, your brother kicks quite hard. But so did you."

Rafe winked at Annie as he buckled their daughter into the car. He laid a kiss on Lilah's head before sliding into the driver's seat.

"Dave wants to know if you'll let him do a spring segment at the clinic. He wants a follow-up about its growth over the last four years."

Annie leaned over, capturing her husband's mouth. "I have all winter to decide. Do you have your boots?"

Rafe grabbed the boots she'd gotten him all those years ago and smiled. "Always."

Annie sighed as his lips met hers. "I love you. Let's go home."

* * * * *

COMING SOON!

We really hope you enjoyed reading this book.
If you're looking for more romance, be sure to
head to the shops when new books are
available on

Thursday 28th
May

MILLS & BOON

Coming next month

FROM HAWAII TO FOREVER
Julia Danvers

It had been like this for the past few days. He was able to focus just fine during the emergency jobs. Just like always, when Jack was in the middle of an emergency, he was at his peak performance. There was something about getting caught up completely in the moment to focus on a medical emergency that allowed him to re-center himself, no matter what kind of emotional turmoil he might be going through.

But during the quieter times, when his mind had time to wander...it wandered straight back to Kat.

And specifically to that kiss with Kat. He was completely mortified by his lack of professionalism. He'd been struggling to maintain a detached, clinical demeanor, and he'd utterly failed. Kat had been vulnerable and afraid, and he'd taken advantage of her vulnerability. He couldn't have felt worse.

But couldn't keep his mind from returning to the way his hand had fit perfectly around her hip. The softness of her skin. The way her hair tickled his face when he buried his nose in it, and inhaled the faint tropical scent that wafted from her.

To make matters even worse, not only had he failed to hold himself to a professional standard...he'd liked kissing Kat. He'd felt... desire.

The plain fact was, he wanted more of Kat. Try as he might to deny it, he knew, deep down, that he wasn't going to stop thinking about her. His body burned to finish what they'd started.

But would Kat even want to talk to him, after he'd let himself get so carried away? They'd known each other for a little over a month, and yet this was already the second time he'd been unprofessional with her in a medical setting.

And yet, during their kiss, he'd felt her hands clutching at him, sensed her body pressing against his. In the heat of that moment, she had wanted him, too.

He had tried to give Kat plenty of space since the quarantine had ended. He didn't want her to feel that he expected any more of her than she wanted to give. If she were interested in him, then she could make the next move.

He wouldn't blame Kat if she never wanted to see him again.

Which was why he was completely surprised when he turned around with his supply box and saw her standing in front of him.

"Sorry," she said. "Didn't mean to startle you."

She walked up to Jack and took the supply box from him, setting it onto the floor. "Well, this takes me back," she said. "It's been a couple weeks since we were in such close quarters together."

Was she angry at him?

Her face bore the same resolute look, with the same determined set of her lips that he'd noticed while in quarantine. Whatever she wanted to talk to him about, he realized that there was no avoiding it. Not when she looked like that.

"I've been thinking," she said. "We're both adults. We've gotten to know each other quickly, in a pretty short amount of time, due to circumstances beyond our control. But no matter how unusual those circumstances may have been, they don't change the fact that we're in this situation now."

"And…what exactly is our situation?"

She took a deep breath. "I've been thinking a lot about that moment in quarantine."

He waited, without breathing. He thought his heart might have stopped.

She went on. "You know the moment I mean. When we…kissed." Her eyes flickered straight to his, and he knew his heart hadn't stopped after all. It was pounding jackhammer-hard.

"I don't know about you," she said, "But I've had a hard time not thinking about it. The kiss, I mean. And I know that you said you don't believe in relationships. Well, neither do I. But in a way, that makes us kind of ideal for one another, right now."

He wondered where this was going. "How so?" he said.

"Well," she continued, looking nervous but determined to carry her point through, "anything involving emotions would probably be a terrible idea, for both of us. But then I started thinking that not every relationship has to involve emotions. Some relationships have a more…physical… basis."

He was suddenly very aware that without the supply box in his arms, there was nothing between the two of them. He would barely have to reach to slip an arm around her waist. Her nose was inches from his. It was very hard to think clearly, with her standing so close.

"Emotions are complicated," he agreed, his voice growing husky. "Are you suggesting that we try letting things get more…physical…between us?"

Continue reading
FROM HAWAII TO FOREVER
Julia Danvers

Available next month
www.millsandboon.co.uk